# THE SECRET SONG OF SHELBY REY

# THE SECRET SONG OF SHELBY REY

A NOVEL

RAYNE LACKO

SPARKPRESS

Copyright © 2025 Rayne Lacko

All rights reserved. No part of this publication may be reproduced, distributed, or transmitted in any form or by any means, including photocopying, recording, digital scanning, or other electronic or mechanical methods, without the prior written permission of the publisher, except in the case of brief quotations embodied in critical reviews and certain other noncommercial uses permitted by copyright law. For permission requests, please address SparkPress.

Published by SparkPress, a BookSparks imprint,
A division of SparkPoint Studio, LLC
Phoenix, Arizona, USA, 85007
www.gosparkpress.com

Published 2025
Printed in the United States of America

Print ISBN: 978-1-68463-312-8
E-ISBN: 978-1-68463-313-5
Library of Congress Control Number: 2025901874

Interior design and typeset by Katherine Lloyd, The DESK

All company and/or product names may be trade names, logos, trademarks, and/or registered trademarks and are the property of their respective owners.

This is a work of fiction. Names, characters, places, and incidents either are the product of the author's imagination or are used fictitiously. Any resemblance to actual persons, living or dead, is entirely coincidental. The author is in no way affiliated with any brands, songs, musicians, or artists mentioned in this book.

NO AI TRAINING: Without in any way limiting the author's [and publisher's] exclusive rights under copyright, any use of this publication to "train" generative artificial intelligence (AI) technologies to generate text is expressly prohibited. The author reserves all rights to license uses of this work for generative AI training and development of machine learning language models.

*For Joseph*

## CHAPTER ONE
## 2010

### SHELBY

The last semester of high school, I kept a list called "Things I Won't Miss After Graduation" in the back of my chemistry binder. The instigator of the list was the periodic table. It seemed impossible that so much magic should be boiled down, parsed, categorized, and then fenced together in cubes. What is dug from the ground or fallen from stars, what is reactive, noble, or admittedly unknown after millennia, can and should be revered as nothing short of divine. But is there anything less reverential than the periodic table's rigid and linear bureaucracy? The elements' names are downsized to a couple of letters, boxed, and shelved. Their powers are pushed into a corner. Their inscrutability is scrutinized and junked together with dubiously related elements that, to me, are far more different than they are the same.

Goodbye, periodic table. Elements, you deserve better.

I'll never shed a tear for Ms. Allen's tenth-grade geometry class either, or any math class before or after. Math's morals are better than mine. I'm all gray area. Math is right or wrong, yes or no. In Ms. Allen's class, I was "wrong," I was "no," I was a glitch in a formula that would never result in the correct answer.

Ms. Allen believed math was accessible to everyone because it didn't change. She said you could rely on it. I don't think I could ever trust something that never changes. If this is all life is, it isn't enough. I've got nothing if nothing changes.

By the end of January in sophomore year, it became clear to Ms. Allen that geometry and I were not meeting at a right angle. She held me back after class to evangelize about quadrilaterals and parabolas. I didn't mind, because I wasn't in any hurry to get home.

It was just the two of us in her classroom. Ms. Allen had me sit at Romy Rivera's desk at the front, as if Romy's superior math genes might somehow seep through my jeans by osmosis. They didn't.

I could see the fading pulse of Ms. Allen's patience in the flattening line of her lips. She steadied herself as, squeezing my shoulder, she attempted to explain a theorem for the third time. I don't know if the squeeze was meant to cheer me on or to bolster her, but that's when I heard it: the music inside her, streaming from the palm of her hand into my shoulder.

What I should've done is pulled away, but I didn't. What I shouldn't have done was stare, but I couldn't help it. I wondered how music got in her veins and how I could hear it through her touch.

The music coming from Ms. Allen's hand wasn't any song I recognized, but at the same time it was familiar. It seemed like a song I might have heard at a middle school dance (when I still went to things like that, before Dad up and offed himself and everyone at school stopped talking to me, because what do you say to a girl whose dad ups and offs himself?). Or maybe I heard it at the club where Mom works and blocked it out along with everything else in that place: the dingy carpet, the sticky walls that grab the dust of dead skin cells hovering in the fog-machined air.

I heard her. The entirety of Ms. Allen. The song inside her was adrenaline-spiked hip-hop; the lyrics mentioned, among other things, a misdemeanor and jail time for possession.

I was angry that she'd made me feel even weirder and less competent than I had already, angry that I was unable to grasp what came so easily to Romy Rivera. So, before I could stop myself, I blurted out the lyrics to the beat of her music.

I've never been much of a singer, and certainly I'm no rapper. I was as caught off guard as Ms. Allen when I couldn't keep my fool mouth shut. The lyrics came like hornets, and I spoke them as though swatting the hornets away, wondering why she was telling me in the first place.

Ms. Allen came undone.

Well, first she turned to stone. Then she came all undone, her eyes darkening to black holes.

She wanted to know how I found out. Not even the principal or the school district knew she had faked her background check. She screamed at me, threatened me, and, finally, begged me to tell her how I knew. I told her I didn't know. She didn't believe me. I told her I hadn't wanted to hear the song in the first place, but she refused to believe she was the one who'd made me listen to it.

She gave me an A in geometry but treated me like a mental case wrapped in a tripwire for the rest of the year.

I don't blame her. She was scared and confused. I know it because I was afraid too. And messed up about it, because after that day, the music didn't stop. I started hearing it everywhere, in anyone who touched me. I wasn't sure what was harder, busting out another person's innermost secrets in song or trying to maintain a no-touch zone around my body at all times. I started sitting farther toward the back of my classrooms, closest to the door.

I wanted to be the last to arrive and the first one out. Survival meant keeping my distance.

I'd somehow merited entry to another realm of hearing, but it was making me crazy. As in, locked-up psych-ward crazy.

Then it occurred to me that if the music was the problem, maybe it could also be the solution.

I fished around the apartment for Dad's old headphones and radio. The headphones clearly weren't the best even when they were new, but I liked that they were big. They served as an effective shield even when the radio's batteries were dead. With my ears covered, other people gave up talking to me. When I turned the volume up, the music canceled their mutters about me in the hallways at school. Best of all, I could control what I heard. With music playing in my ears around the clock, there wasn't much room for my classmates' startlingly revealing songs when they bumped into me in the cafeteria while waiting for nuggets and mashed potatoes, or for the songs of strangers when they copped a feel on a city bus.

Sometimes this whole music thing feels like a curse. But it's funny; now that I've been living with it for a while, I've started to worry that it might disappear as unexpectedly as it arrived. The hornet sensation went away after I got used to the lyrics coming. Once that happened, I stopped feeling attacked and started to feel curious.

Turns out some people have pretty decent music.

I figure it's no coincidence that all I have left of Dad is his old AM/FM radio. I think he meant for me to have it. One night, after he'd put back a few too many, he told me he had originally bought it for my grandma, who passed before I was born.

"She really got into pop and electronic music back in the early '80s," he said, a faraway admiration warming his drawn face. "She just wanted to dance."

The radio exhumed a glimmer of the boy he used to be, holding him afloat for a while. He wasn't sleeping around that time, and I had no notion he was thinking about ending his life.

Like a stupid kid, I told him he should have gotten an MP3 player so he could load Grandma's favorite songs onto it. He shook his head, cradling the radio in his palm like it might contain a genie granting wishes.

"You got to tune in to the pulse of the moment. Give yourself over to whatever the radio might play. It's a chance encounter, Shelby. That's what she used to say."

Dad's radio still holds a memory of what was, the best of something that will never be again. It's my lineage, the root of my father and my father's mother before him. I always wonder what my life would have looked like if he were still around or if Grandma hadn't died, if I had someone to count on. Mom barely speaks to me even though we live in the same apartment. When I hear other people's music, I catch a glimpse of what it's like to have a family, a place to belong, a reason, and a history.

All I have is music. Not a playlist of my own design, only the "chance encounters" Dad told me about.

I haven't met anyone else who can do it, get an earful of everything that makes up a person just by touching them. It's a one-sided conversation, a blind confessional, listening to a stranger who can't hear me. And lonely.

A couple of months ago, I was busy counting the days until graduation. With high school behind me, I thought, I'd finally be free. But I spent so much time wishing away the homework assignments and homeroom roll calls that I forgot to figure out what I would do once it was over. Now here I am with graduation behind me, and I only have a couple more weeks to use the free bus pass they give kids who couldn't get to class otherwise. I didn't have any other options. Even if she'd wanted to drive me, Mom couldn't have. She failed the written part of the test three times before deciding the DMV had it out for her and she wasn't going to give it the privilege of making her feel bad.

I like the bus the same way I like an elevator. There's space to breathe when I'm suspended in time, always leaving one place and heading to another.

The 8:23 a.m. westbound bus going under the freeway and into Laguna Beach is a long ride. Seven or eight full loops of the route should fill the time until Mom leaves for her night shift and I can have the apartment to myself. I head to the back row and dump my backpack on the seat next to me to block anyone from sitting there.

I put my headphones on and watch the morning traffic negotiate the fast lane. Drivers inch along, balancing coffee cups, answering cell phones, and painting lashes black. How do they put the whole thing together—the job, the car, the home they came from and will return to in the evening? Mom says I can't stay at the apartment any longer. I guess I'd understand if it was because I freaked her out or something, but that's not it. She just doesn't want me around, plain and simple. *You're old enough to live on your own*, she says. If being "old enough" was enough, I'd have a job. A place to live. A seat to fill, where someone calls my name and checks to see if I'm present, like school. The irony bites at me.

When I was little, I thought I'd enlist in the army like Daddy. We always had a decent place to live and food to eat. The problem was we moved a lot. Dad would get stationed across the country, or a county social worker would get wind of my bruises, the kind a kid gets when her parents are falling-down drunk or when one finds out the other is getting a little side action, and we'd pick up and leave.

I wish Dad were still around. He'd point me in the right direction.

The bus lumbers on through traffic, occasionally lurching to a stop. New passengers shuffle on: an immigrant mother pushing a baby stroller loaded with groceries, surrounded by two silent children not yet old enough for school and an older lady in a maid's uniform who's clutching a lunch box. The women are careful not to meet each other's gaze, yet they both scowl at me.

Next on, a guy with a twelve-pack of beer in a grocery bag who looks me up and down with hopeful eyes. I hate that all I have to wear are Mom's clothes. Between the silver tunic and the heels, too big and too high, my fellow passengers probably think I'm either hooking or on my way to dance at Mom's club.

The manager at Mom's club tells me no one will ever pay me as much as I could make dancing. This smells like a lie to me. It seems it's Mom who pays to dance, maybe not in cold, hard cash but in something cold and hard. That will never be me.

I should have filled the back of that binder with what it means to be free.

I close my eyes, rolling the tuner on my radio back and forth, dusting the last few specks off a station that plays music without words by people with extraordinary names like Tchaikovsky and Haydn. Their music fills me with a savory kind of sadness, sometimes more than I can bear, like when I think about what happened to Dad. I once heard about *saudade*, a Portuguese word that means finding comfort in longing for someone or something that is gone. I always remember that word because to me it sounds like "so daddy."

Tuning the radio, I search for chance encounters with my favorite songs. I don't listen to people talking, talking, talking about stuff that happened to someone somewhere, the weather, or a war between two countries that ultimately want the same thing. I already know the story they'll tell because I hear it in the music. Songs are all about those things, even when the lyrics aren't. The rise and fall of the tempo and the melody tell all the talkers' stories of troubles, triumphs, of people hurt or lost or reunited. There's nothing the talkers can say that the music hasn't already told me. Music is my only friend.

As the bus edges closer to the coast, I people-watch for a half-dozen stops. There is a change in the mood of the passengers as we get closer to the beach. The listless stares at the scuffed, black-matted floor become far-off glances out the window into the salted marine air. Conversations shift to plans for the weekend; excitement grows. There is buoyant hope for the possibility of fun.

I'm killing time. Tomorrow, more will die. Weekend plans would be nice, but I'm in the market for a life of my own. I wish someone would tell me what to do, because I'm stuck. All I have is music, and what am I supposed to do with that? I don't play any instruments, and I've never been much of a singer.

I wouldn't sing at all if I could help it.

The trouble is that everyone has a song, and if someone gets too close, if we connect, I can't help but hear it roaring inside them. It's like a shadow gasping for sunlight. I give the shadow a voice so it can breathe. The way I see it, my singing is mercy. Not pity, I don't do pity. Mercy.

But most people don't know their own song. That is, they don't know it until I voice it back to them. Then, they can't help but hear the truth of it. And what do they do? Shove it right back into darkness, and shove me down while they're at it.

I'm learning to keep my mouth shut. But it isn't easy.

After the incident with Ms. Allen at school, I made the mistake of telling Mom what had happened. She ratted me out to a social worker, who ratted her out to a psychiatrist, who gave me pills I didn't want. The only thing worse than hearing music inside everyone who touches me is hearing music inside everyone while getting kicked around by side effects from meds. I was dizzy, and then drowsy, and then dizzy again. My eyes blurred and my heart raced. I got a rash around my belly button. I had weird periods.

"The drugs make me feel sick," I told the doctor, and that was true. But the side effects weren't what bothered me most. What bugged me was that agreeing to take them felt like agreeing with his judgment about me: that I was hopeless, a lost cause.

I'm not interested in giving up my hope.

A couple squeezes up the steps of the bus, hip crushed against hip in the narrow entrance. The only open seats are next to me. I turn my gaze away as they approach, their whispers toppling over one another as they exchange ideas for how best to spend a day by the water. I can almost feel the warmth of their regard for one another.

I steal a glance at them, wondering how they found each other—how anybody ever finds anybody—when I realize I've been holding my breath, longing for a connection of my own, a hand to hold mine that won't let go.

I cross my arms and tuck my hands under my elbows. It won't happen now, I guess.

I always hoped I might find someone and that we'd do what my parents couldn't: love each other and no one else. Mom said it was only fair that she had some company when Dad was on tour of duty, but somehow it was always my fault when he got home and found out. When they were happy, they didn't need much to be happy: a six-pack of Bud Light, *South Park* on the TV, their knuckles brushing when they reached for a can at the same time.

"You mind?" the woman asks, standing over me. I pull my backpack into my lap and she plops down, her thigh wedged tightly against mine. Through her bare leg, I can hear her, the song she holds inside, the rhythm of her selfish assumption: "If no one finds out, no one gets hurt."

They're cheaters, I can tell. Escapees from marriages no longer joined at the hip.

I press my headphones closer against my ears and turn up the volume to drown her out. I look out the window and stare at the asphalt scudding below. I need to keep moving forward. When I get some money, I'm moving away. *Old enough to live on your own,* Mom says.

    I keep trying to edge my bare leg away from hers, but every bump in the road pushes her more fully against me. We're jammed together at the shoulder, elbow, thigh, and knee. My radio and earphones can't drown her out, even at full volume. All I hear is her desire, the wicked thrill of risk, the danger of being caught, and a gaping difference in their age I didn't notice when I first looked at them. She's carrying guilt, too, but even that is some kind of freakish turn-on for her. Whatever she's doing with that man, she doesn't care who she's hurting.

    I don't want to know any of this about her.

    The slow-moving bus feels stagnant. All this close contact is itchy, and it hurts. When I try to pull my legs closer to me, I get mad at myself. Why am I worried about the people attached to this couple—people who aren't even here, people I'll never meet? It's because I get it. I have an idea how they will feel when they find out about these two. And they will find out. The truth is the only sure thing.

    I keep my radio playing at full blast, but her lyrics seep through my skin, enter my blood, and catch in my throat. I have to spit them out. If I don't, I might suffocate or something, I don't know. Looking away, I cover my mouth with one hand and let it out, trying to keep my voice down as I do. The little kids flanking the stroller turn and stare at me.

    I swear I've been good at keeping my singing under control lately, but this woman has me pinned, and I can't get away.

    The music in my headphones argues with the song oozing from her. I jumble her lyrics and have to start over, singing where I left off. My skin is hot, and I can't move any farther away. The woman's guilt dukes it out with her desire in the chorus and I trip up, stuttering. I don't want to sing any of it, but slamming my lips shut tight only makes me choke, and I have to start over once again.

It crosses my mind to leap out the window into oncoming traffic, but the window doesn't open that far.

I try to make sense of her music, to sing it correctly at least once through so I can finally get it out of me.

A sudden sting sears my scalp where a few caught strands of my hair are yanked from my head. My music rips away in one motion, pulling at me as it goes like a bandage left too long over a wound. I gasp and cover my ears where my father's headphones should be.

The woman is holding my headphones and radio in her fist, strands of my hair poking out between her fingers. The older man with her leaps to his feet, yelling at me to shut up, flailing his arms like I'm an uncaged, rabid animal ready to bite.

I'm scared he might hit me or something, but I can't take my eyes off my radio. I have to get it back. Now.

I lunge at the woman, grabbing for it. The man dives between us, pushing me away to protect her. I fall to the floor and my backpack thunks down next to me.

"Keep your hands off her," he yells at me.

I get up quickly, ready to fight. I need my radio. I don't want to touch her. I don't want either of them to touch me. But she's still got my radio in her grip.

"Thief!" I yell, scanning the faces of the other bus riders for help. "She stole my music!"

No one moves to help me. Lazy and unbothered, they do nothing. They just sit there looking at me like I'm as crazy as one of those drug-addled doomsday preachers standing on a street corner screaming about the end of days.

The driver pulls the bus to a stop, and everyone groans when he calls for police assistance.

"I got a mental chick on my bus," I hear the bus driver say over his walkie-talkie. "Disturbing the peace. Probably under the influence."

## CHAPTER TWO
### 2010

A stout guy with a nearly indiscernible neck leans over the high counter to chat up Dr. Gibson's receptionist. One thing about LA, every damn front desk girl could pass for a model. It's a freak phenomenon I binged on when I first moved here.

Lots of girls offer "you-get-what-you-pay-for" hookups, fun and done. Good genes will get you so far, but as aphrodisiacs go, cash and publicity incite an inelegant madness. I get it, every conquest is a stepping stone. But there's always another guy, richer and more famous than me. They say no one walks in LA. Truth is, no one settles in LA. I'm glad I figured that out fast and hooked up with Ashtynn Kingston.

The waiting room's carved-wood door swings open, and the guy at the counter swirls his stocky body away from the receptionist. I glance up and am surprised to see Dr. Gibson stroll through carrying a cardboard tray with four coffee cups. He was Ash's doctor when she OD'd. It was only eighteen months ago, but I barely remember him. I feel like I'm looking at a distant uncle or second cousin I met once at a family reunion.

It's one thing to make me sweat it out in his waiting room, but showing up late? Who's the rock star here, bud?

"Coffee boy this morning, eh, Roland?" the stocky guy teases him.

I begin to reach for my phone to text Berger about Gibson rolling in late, then freeze. My manager dumping me in the lap of some shrink who doesn't give a crap looks a lot like step one in a not-so-covert plan to finish me.

Dr. Gibson grabs my frozen hand and shakes it. "Good morning, Mr. Wyatt. Nice to see you again. I look forward to working with you."

I shake his hand and size him up, searching for sincerity behind his veneered smile.

Gibson turns and nods toward the stocky guy and the receptionist. "Zac Wyatt, I'd like to introduce you to Dr. Elliott Rachman and our assistant, Carly."

That burly dude is Elliott Rachman? The so-called "counselebrity"? I've always wondered why Ash didn't choose him as her therapist. Now I get why she picked Gibson instead. He's a PR-friendly pretty boy.

"Take my word for it, Roland's all about serving his flock," Elliott says with a wink. "Be glad it's only coffee. He might offer to wash your feet next."

I appreciate Rachman taking a few jabs at the man who's got my balls and my future at the mercy of his professional opinion.

"It's an Americano," Gibson says, handing me a coffee. Rachman grabs one of the other cups from the tray, takes a sip, and winces.

"That was Carly's chai tea," Gibson chides him, and points to a different cup. "This is your mocha."

Rachman spits the tea back into the cup and hands it to Carly like that's not a completely sketchy thing to do before grabbing the correct cup. He proceeds to add three packets of sugar and work the stir stick like he's already had his share of caffeine.

Yeah, this guy would make Ash barf.

Gibson places his hand on my shoulder. "Will you join me in my office, Zac?"

Anxious to get on with it, I pop up from my seat and follow him down the hall.

Once inside Gibson's office, I slide into a broad leather chair. He closes the door and takes his seat behind a heavy, polished desk, big enough to garage a vintage convertible.

I stroke the side of my chair and swivel to face the floor-to-ceiling abstract art installations behind him. Fuck, now I'm getting a little worried. Is he going to ask me what I see in them, like some lame Rorschach test? How do you pass one of those things?

Folding his hands in front of him, Gibson takes a deep breath and closes his eyes. Keeping them lightly shut, he starts to speak. To himself.

"I immediately release all thoughts belonging outside this room and allow any judgments I may have to drift away," he murmurs. "I provide an open, safe environment for growth. I am ready to listen. I—"

"This is bullshit," I say, shaking my head.

Gibson's eyes open leisurely; he appears not the least disturbed by my interruption.

"Let's get one thing straight right now," I tell him. "I'm here because I have to put on an act for all my fans who're afraid I might fall from grace. Ooh, drugs are bad."

I need to chill. I'm getting ahead of myself.

Changing gear, I level with him: "I don't have a drug problem.

I can pretend to get past one for the public if you want to play that scene, but the truth is, I'm no fucking junkie."

Gibson says nothing for a moment, then surprises me with a grin. "It must be easy for scouts to spot raw talent. Certain people fill the room with energy and light the average individual simply cannot muster. They just look for the person who is, for no one reason, larger than life." He rises from his chair, walks around to the front of his desk, and leans against it, only inches from me. "We're all observers of people, students of the human condition, aren't we, Zac? We navigate the social arena and realize the truth of ourselves within the context of our interactions."

"You of all people, a shrink, shouldn't judge a book by its cover."

Gibson lets out a big, hearty laugh. I'm glad one of us thinks this is a good old party.

"Nearly everyone who walks through my door issues the 'Non-Junkie Declaration,' Zac." He is quiet for a moment, then adds, "More than 4.6 million people in America meet the criteria for needing treatment but don't recognize they have a problem."

I shift in my seat, contemplating whether to walk out. I'm not a junkie. It was nothing, just one fucking time. I still have bad dreams about the hospital, the night Ashtynn went into the ER. Gibson was there, he ought to understand that I get it. I get what can happen.

What if I walk out, tell this fucker I don't need him, that I don't belong in rehab? Everyone forgives Stanford for his substance use. Getting wasted is part of his guitarist persona, his goddamn brand. But for Zac Wyatt? No forgiveness, no way. I've got to play along until this whole miserable episode blows over.

You want to play, Doc?

I turn it on, gazing at Gibson with what *Amp'd Teen* mag once called "silvery turquoise eyes crackling with life and lust and liquid hope," a far cry from the lifeless stare of some spiraling heroin addict.

"All my rehab patients are required to submit to a physical and blood test; your evaluations are scheduled for this afternoon. It's standard protocol," he adds quickly when I shift in my chair. "Look, Zac, your skin tone, eye clarity, and healthy, muscular build support your assertion. But more importantly, I'm here to listen. You tell me what's true and what isn't. Let's begin our partnership with a shared goal of trust. Are you with me?" He thrusts a hand toward me.

I don't have much choice.

"Right on."

I grip his outstretched hand in a loose cycle of gang-inspired handshakes. The old guy manages to keep up. His fingers are as smooth as Ash's.

Sliding into the matching leather seat next to me, Gibson doesn't waste any time. "Why don't you tell me how you landed here, then? What series of events led to an entertainment attorney asking me to help rehabilitate you from drug use?" He cocks his head. "Should be an interesting story."

It isn't. My management prepared an official statement in rebuttal of the photo leak. I'm supposed to recount it verbatim. But I guess I should give him the unscripted version.

"There isn't much to tell. Me and Stanford—"

"Stanford?"

Seriously? This guy hasn't done any homework on me? "Stanford Lysandre, Grounder's lead guitarist. Perhaps you've heard of him?"

"Of course. I only ask for clarification and invite you to do the same, Zac."

"Right. We were hanging with a group of girls, some fans of the band, you know, just kicking it at our producer's place while he was in Munich, when Stan and one of the girls decided to do up."

"Do up? You mean, inject diacetylmorphine intravenously?"

"Yes." I hate having to talk about this. "Dude, c'mon."

Better this than court, though.

He motions for me to continue.

"They were all into it, and I decided *What the hell.* If I was worried about anything, it was about getting sick or shitting my pants."

That would have been worlds better than the mess I'm in now with my management, my label, and my fan base. I don't even want to speculate what my band might do about it.

"And now how do you feel?"

"I'm pissed off. You've probably seen the photos one of the girls sold to the highest bidders. They're on every website, in every magazine. I wish I could remember her name so I could at least call her out for being a fucking sniper."

"So from your perspective, this is her fault?"

"Yeah!"

He doesn't say a word in response.

"Well, not entirely," I backpedal. "I just fell under a negative influence," I assure him, recalling the lingo of mandatory high school drug awareness programs. Exactly who that "negative influence" might be shouldn't require any stretch of Gibson's imagination. Stanford is a notorious addict.

We're both quiet. Gibson can wait for me to 'fess up. I need to take some control here.

"You a music fan?" I ask.

"Yes, of course," he says. "I'm a big fan of Ray LaMontagne. He's from my hometown. I also dig Van Morrison and Jeff Buckley." He demonstrates his affinity for acoustic rock with an air guitar impression.

Fuck, there ought to be a law against air guitar.

"I have a recording of LaMontagne at Bonnaroo."

I nod. "He's not bad for an old man. What'd you listen to when you were my age?"

"Rock guitar, alternative." He grins. "When I was in med

school, I saw the Red Hot Chili Peppers, Pearl Jam, and Soundgarden at Lollapalooza."

No way the man's been to 'Palooza without getting wrecked. What a hypocrite.

"Let's make the most of our time together." Gibson takes the reins again. "Is this something you do, Zac? Hang out with fans and get high? Are you and Stanford good friends?"

"I have a girlfriend, you know that." I'm too defensive. "I smoke a bit of weed, but I told you, I'm no junkie. That shit is death." I let out a bitter cough under my breath. "Well, except for when it comes to Stan. Smack's given him the goddamn gift for music. If Keith Richards and Jimi Hendrix had a son, it would be Stanford Lysandre."

"He writes all of Grounder's music, correct?"

I nod and look down at my Americano, watching my fingers interlace around the cup.

"Your band is tremendously successful." His gaze feels hot, uncomfortable.

I look away from him, over at the art panels. "We sell a fuckload of music, amazing songs," I assure him, but my voice seems to lose color as I say it. I square my shoulders to him. I'm only going to explain this once. "You know how there are songs that, for whatever reason, become part of your life? Songs that commiserate with your soul, your psyche," I add, nodding at my use of the word within a therapeutic context, "in a way that is unforgettable?"

"Yes." Gibson nods eagerly. "What is it about those phenomenal songs that continue to speak to us decade after decade, or even century after century?"

"Right." I nod. "That's what I want to create."

He doesn't get it.

"I want to write a song, a poem, really, set to music, that tells it all. The whole train wreck of what's going on in your heart, your mind, your pants." I smile wickedly at this last point. "The kind of song that makes a listener glad it was written, because it gives expression to an emotion or moment that had no expression until that song was made."

Roland's gaze is warm and admiring. He leans forward to hear more.

Glad I finally caught your interest, Doc, before I drop the bomb.

"I don't know how Stanford does it, how he creates words and a melody from absolutely nothing. And I mean nothing. The guy is high, unconscious, or hurling for the better part of the day. And for no reason I can figure out, he is about the best fucking guitarist alive." The volume of my voice increases to accommodate the anger pooling in my chest. "The needle should have killed him fifty times over by now. It's a fucking crime against nature."

I steady the heel that's tapping triple meter into the hardwood.

"Now, as you say, 'that shit is death.' If Stanford's heroin use is so offensive to you, Zac, can you tell me how you wound up using that particular narcotic?"

I rise from the chair and walk to the wall of paintings, fixing my back to him. Coaxing a patient to spill his story requires a bit of foreplay. I don't want him to mistake our little exchange today for easy access to the main event.

After allowing two hulking minutes of silence to tick by, Gibson ends our standoff.

"Zac, may I ask whether your parents have heard the media reports? Have you been in contact?"

"Of course. My parents mainline info about Grounder." I hope the irony of my word choice doesn't escape him. "They want to come down this weekend and be photographed spending time together with Ashtynn. Berger, my manager, he's all over it. Family values and all that." I pivot, avoiding Gibson's gaze. "We have a pretty young audience. I'm supposed to be some role model, you know. Same goes for Ashtynn."

He nods. Ash's musical career depends on the ruthless maintenance of a wholesome persona, but the media circus surrounding my recovery is unlikely to cut her slack. She's not even twenty, but her highly publicized former addictions still cast a long shadow.

"Coming down from where?"

"Portland, Oregon. My hometown."

"I love Portland. You grew up there? When did you leave?"

"P-Town's all right. My parents still live in the same house where I grew up." I give him the Wikipedia version of my life story and return to my seat, resting one foot on the opposite knee. "I had a scholarship to Reed College for music but dropped out after Grounder got signed."

"I didn't know Grounder was from Portland."

"No, definitely an LA joint. I took off to Santa Monica one summer, met my band, and shit skyrocketed."

The phrase "overnight success" is the lie used to cover a darker reality. Talented musicians are pounding the pavement at this exact moment, begging to catch a break.

"You earned a music scholarship, that's impressive." Gibson's eyes narrow slightly. "And you don't write songs for your band?"

"I've tried," I say, too fast.

"I like how you described it, 'a poem set to music.'"

"Yeah?" My heel starts again. I've got to pull my shit together. "You write any poetry, Gibson?"

"I wrote a poem for my girlfriend at Dartmouth, back in medical school. I suppose it wasn't half bad; she became my wife."

"I try every damn day." I can't stand it anymore. "I want to write more than I want anything. But no matter what I do, I got nothing on Stanford. You could ask him to write a song about piss-soaked mattresses and kids would download it." An edge returns to my tone. "Listen, I'm not selling myself short here. Show me any instrument and I can play it. I can perform just about any arrangement."

I just can't write a song.

Fine, I'll admit it: "I thought heroin might give me a piece of whatever it's doing for Stan."

Dr. Gibson's eyes meet mine, and I'm sure he's about to lecture me on the dangers of recreational drug use. I keep talking, unwilling to give him the satisfaction.

"I wanted a shot at writing one damn song that is intrinsically me. Not Grounder, me. My voice, my style. I need to break through, uncover my own music." I slump back in my chair. I'm sick of depending on Stanford, or Grounder for that matter, for my career. What am I to the band but a set of pipes and a photogenic face? Fuck, I'm a dime a dozen. Replaceable.

Gibson leans toward me. "Let's focus specifically on what you would like to achieve."

"I want to write hit songs." The old man must be hard of hearing.

"Terrific."

Who uses the word "terrific"?

"Let's establish our goals for therapy. I'll leave it up to your record label to locate the appropriate music teacher for the practical aspects of songwriting."

"I don't need a damn music teacher. Christ, at this point, I could teach a songwriting class. I want to find my fucking voice, get it?" I stare Gibson down.

After a long beat, he says, "The only person who can reach into the pool of Zac Wyatt and fish out a masterpiece is you. But to do so, you must trust your authentic self. Acknowledge the raw passion inherent to you. I can help you with that."

I've got raw passion for days. But can my "authentic self" be trusted to write a hit?

"I promise to help you map out the small and large changes necessary to reach your goal, Zac."

I'll bet he says that to everybody. Whatever hope I had a nanosecond ago deflates.

"I need help with more than one song. We have to strategize an entire album." My voice rasps to a whisper. "We're touring Asia this fall, and I want my music to steal the goddamn show. If I have to commit to—what, six weeks of drug rehab with you? Let's make decent use of it. I'm not chasing any dragon, so I don't want to waste my time slaying what isn't there."

"Let's put aside the larger goal of an album for today and begin with the first step," Gibson says. "I'll need you to complete the physical evaluation this afternoon and submit to daily tests for narcotics use."

"Fine." I shrug. He's got his agenda; I'm on my own.

I get up to leave before he gets a chance to say "our time is up" or whatever.

"No one can predict what might become a hit," he says as I move toward the door. "If we could, only best-selling books would be written. Movie studios would only release blockbusters and never suffer the financial burden of a flop. No worthy venture is safe from the risk of failure."

I pause where I'm standing and debate whether to attempt to convince him that failure is not an option.

"You talk about songs that speak to the listener's soul and define the listener's own experience," he says thoughtfully. "If that is the destination, perhaps it's also the birthplace."

I hate to admit it, but he's talking sense. Some of that hope trickles back in. "So where do we—I—begin?" I ask, trying not to sound too eager.

"Let's put success in the corner as an assumed result." Gibson waves success aside.

I miss it already.

"In our therapy together in the coming weeks, we'll have the opportunity to explore 'who is Zac Wyatt.'" He makes air quotations, as though I am a hypothetical product. "We'll translate what you learn into something meaningful to share with your established fans and attract new listeners."

I have to admit, I like the part about exploring who I am. I nod. "Deal. You've got six weeks."

# CHAPTER THREE

## SHELBY

I know well enough not to resist arrest. If I can get everyone to chill for a minute, I can make it clear I'm not high or anything. Maybe they'll let me go on a warning. Just give me my music and let's go our separate ways.

"I'm placing you under a section 5150," the cop tells me, "which is known as an involuntary hold, intended to protect the safety of people suffering from a mental disorder."

I know what a 5150 is. It means I could be hospitalized against my will.

"Those people, they robbed me, you know." I have to defend myself, but I'm talking too fast. I need to show I'm in control if I don't want to get put in a psych ward.

"I'm not the criminal here," I add, louder this time, but he doesn't respond. He won't even look me in the eye. I'm getting nervous.

"And they are cheaters, I can tell," I add, trying to reason with him.

Without warning, he grabs me and yanks me toward a squad

car lit up like Christmas. "We're taking you to St. Cecilia, a police-designated psychiatric facility," he says, holding my arms too tightly.

I may be a lot smaller than him, but I'm no mental case, and I'm not going anywhere without Dad's radio. I buck, trying to drag all 200-plus pounds of him back toward the bus. A hold? No. I'm not getting locked up.

When the cop's song starts pouring into me through his touch, I bite the inside of my mouth. No way I'm going to let myself start singing again.

His partner is interviewing the couple. When I see them hand over my radio and headphones I double down, digging in my heels and trying with all I have to pull the cop back toward my music.

I can't move him an inch. He hauls me to the squad car so abruptly that I lose a shoe. I hobble beside him, hoisted by his momentum, still watching the cop who's holding my music. One foot is raised in the remaining stiletto, the other grazes rough concrete as we barrel toward the car. I'm off-kilter, without harmony. His duty belt cuts into my hip.

Mom is going to kill me when she finds out I lost one of her shoes. But that's the least of my concerns right now. That radio is all I have left of my father. I need my music.

"Please," I beg the officer as his handcuffs dig into my wrists, "I need my radio."

Again, he doesn't reply. Again, he doesn't even look at me. My whole life is in that radio, and this cop isn't freaking listening.

As he ducks me into the squad car, I kick at him with my bare foot. "Please," I beg. I need to get his attention, make him listen.

He sighs and shackles my ankles in leg restraints as casually as twining a roast chicken. The car door claps shut.

I can't give up.

The other cop slides into the front passenger seat with Dad's radio and headphones in hand. I beg him to let me have them, but he ignores me too. With my hands secured behind my back, I can't wipe away my tears.

Finally, I accept the futility of my pleas and quiet down. Nothing good has ever come from a visit to St. Cecilia, but if that's where my music's headed, so am I.

I'm absolutely starving, and worse, some nurse just drew a bunch of my blood. Hard-boiled rock, whitewashed down to an easy-listening instrumental track, seeps from a small, perforated speaker in the exam room's ceiling. The black vinyl chair is cold under my thighs.

"Shelby Alicia Rey, age eighteen. Here's her ID," the arresting officer tells a woman in a white lab coat. The cop's meaty grip stifles my arms above the handcuffs. "Disturbing the peace. Probably under the influence. Have a look at her, she's been 5150'd."

"Miss Rey, I'm Jaclyn Spenser, a Licensed Clinical Social Worker," Ms. White-Coat says to me before instructing the cop to remove my handcuffs. "I'm hoping we can sort this out together." She sits in the rolling chair across from me and hands me a plain white bagel in a paper bag. It'll give me a stomachache later, but I guess if I'm going to be sick anywhere, it might as well be at a hospital.

A speed-read of my toxicology report tells her what I already know: I'm officially "clean." Why does everyone assume I'm some junkie?

I guess I know the answer to that.

She didn't have to tell me she's a social worker. Her use of warm-syrup-speak gives her away. Is that a class they teach at Shrink School?

"I want to help you," she says, the syrup getting even warmer. "May I call you Shelby?"

I nod but say nothing. Without my headphones, I'm exposed.

If this white-coat suspects I can hear stuff she doesn't, she'll get scared, just like the rest.

I watch Social Worker Jaclyn take the inch of addressing me by my first name to the mile of running her eyes up and down my bare limbs.

"What are you looking at?" I pull my knees up to my chest.

Her eyes meet mine, and she actually seems surprised I would ask. Then, inexplicably, she smiles at me, like she's done figuring me out. But she doesn't say anything.

Typically, social workers are big talkers—lots of info, explanation of state regulations, implied threats if I don't "cooperate," white noise. Not this one.

I unwrap my legs and lower my feet to the floor. Jaclyn and I stare at one another, the silence between us stifling the tight space of the exam room. Is she waiting for me to say something? She'd better not hold her breath.

Leaning back in her chair, Jaclyn flips through a creased folder clasping an unflattering compendium of my on-again/off-again relationship with St. Cecilia: treatment for abuse, neglect, and an undiagnosed chronic illness. I play with a lock of my hair, embarrassed. Jaclyn can't change the past, and I don't want her to think I'm not doing the best with what I've been handed. If I could fix things, I would.

Before I can figure out her deal, she leans forward, takes my hand gently, and encloses it in hers. It's so warm—I mean, really warm—and alive. Like a blanket thrown over a skittish rabbit, it muffles and slows the tight drumming of my bouncing pulse. For an instant, I don't even hear any music, neither the stuff coming through the speaker overhead nor the music in her touch.

I blink and realize I'm idiotically wide-eyed. I pull my gaze away from our joined hands and pretend to be interested in the exam room's decor: a laminated poster featuring a cross section of the digestive system, a framed list of ten tips for methadone safety, and a body mass index obesity chart. Once I've given everything else in the room as much attention as I hope would seem natural, I turn casually back to Jaclyn and size her up, testing her by tightening my fingers.

She surprises me with a little squeeze in return. It reminds me of Dad, only softer. Was he the last person to hold my hand?

I tentatively turn our combined grasp over and explore the tangle of our fingers, the dry smoothness of Jaclyn's grip. Her nails are neat and painted a soft pink. I can feel her faint pulse within her, a rhythm evoking early Bob Dylan, possibly Leonard Cohen, with a nod to Nick Cave. A rebellious streak runs through her, but it's only as fierce as a coffee house folk singer.

I look up into her face, searching her eyes. They're pale blue, the same color as her blouse, a ruffled number with pearl buttons. She's the kind of person Mom would cuss out if Jaclyn dared glance at her sideways, on the chance Jaclyn thought she was better than her. "What's made your brown eyes blue?" I ask her, riffing on an old song I bet she knows.

Her lips curl in a slight grin. But before she can respond, the arresting officers show back up.

I can't help but notice that neither one has Dad's radio.

"What's the story?" Jaclyn asks them, removing her hand from mine. "Officer Rodriguez?"

I snatch my hand away like I've just brushed up against the orange coils of a hot plate. I didn't even ask her to hold my hand in the first place.

"She was on the number nine bus, harassing passengers," the one that took my music from the couple replies. "The driver called in for support."

"I'm getting better, I can feel it," I blurt out. "I need my radio. Can I get it back now?"

Rodriguez leans forward to Jaclyn, lowering his voice to a

gossip tone. "Get this, she was singing. At the top of her lungs, you understand, all manner of cheatin' songs."

I steal a peek at Jaclyn and find her watching me. I shrug, lowering my gaze to the laminate floor. "I like to sing, I guess." If she locks me up, I may never see my radio again.

"Turns out there was a couple on the bus having an affair," Rodriguez continues. "The woman tried to take her headphones, and this one went off the deep end."

I knew they were cheaters. "I'll just take my radio," I butt in, "and—"

"When O'Neill cuffed Miss Karaoke Mental Case here," Rodriguez rambles on, "the guy was like, 'Hey, you're not going to tell my wife about this, are you?' Anyway, the couple doesn't want to press charges. If they go to court, the wife will find out about the girlfriend."

"So you have an admission of attempted robbery, yet this young woman is the one facing arrest?" Jaclyn asks. When neither officer responds, her hand finds her hip. "Barry?"

First the handholding, and now she's taking my side?

"Hey, we got a call about a mentally disturbed person acting crazy on a bus," Rodriguez points out.

O'Neill nods, scratching at his shining forehead. "Just because they're sick doesn't make 'em innocent, Spenser."

"Where is her radio now?" Jaclyn asks.

I jolt up in the vinyl chair and dare to put my hand on Jaclyn's. "I need it. Please." I won't cry. I won't.

"I have her radio and headphones in the squad car," Rodriguez says. "Gotta hold them at the station till she's booked or cleared."

Which station? Booked? I rock forward in my chair and then catch like the long hand of a clock in sorry need of new batteries, trying to tick forward but stuck frozen in time.

"I'll determine whether she's a danger to herself or others." Jaclyn sighs. "Thank you, gentlemen." She waves them out of the room.

I'm not letting them leave with my father's radio. I jump up from the chair and push past Jaclyn to chase after them. The second I enter the hallway, I come to a sudden stop as a nurse seizes my arm and swiftly ushers me back into the examination room, closing the door behind us.

"Shelby, this is Nurse Hanley," Jaclyn says as I'm lowered into my seat. "We have a few questions for you."

Hanley can't be much older than me, but she probably has a diploma hanging on a wall somewhere. That kind of paper is as good as money.

"Please know that I'm here to assist the doctors in determining how best we can help you. Do you understand?" Hanley's syrup voice is of the fake, artificially flavored variety.

Jaclyn doesn't wait for me to answer Hanley's question before asking her own. "Shelby, do you know what day it is?"

"Yes," I snap, irritated that she's treating me like I might be so far gone I wouldn't know something basic like the date. I ignore them, memorizing the names Rodriguez and O'Neill so I can track down my radio.

Jaclyn clears her throat. "Can you tell me your home address?"

This one is dicey. I practically live on public transit. No point in staying back at the apartment with Mom and whatever handsy flavor of the week she's brought home. But I know she just wants an address, and if I don't give her one it could mean a trip to the big house, or the halfway house, or any house that is even less a home than I've got now. I feel the beginning of the bagel's assault against my insides but push on.

"Right in front of you." I point to the top of a page sifting loose from my file.

Jaclyn nods and says, "I'm willing to wager that you know

something the police don't." She meets my gaze and holds it. "What really happened on the bus today, Shelby?"

I can't tell Jaclyn the truth. If I say what's really on my mind to some white-coat, what next? Tell my whole life story? Where's that ever landed me? Enforced counseling and meds I refuse to take, that's where. But she's right. Rodriguez forgot the important part.

"All I did was tell the truth. So what if I was singing? They hijacked my music." I pantomime my headphones getting ripped right off my ears.

"Do you know these people?" Jaclyn asks.

Of course not. "I have ears."

"You seem very perceptive, Shelby. Do you often hear or see things that other people can't?"

No way, I won't be roped into saying something crazy. And I'll never tell her the radio was my dad's. I know better than to bring up daddy issues with a white-coat. But Jaclyn did hold my hand, and considering how she handled those cops, she might be able to get my music back. I'll play along just enough.

"I once read some book about Chinese monks living in an ancient monastery on a hillside who spent years just listening." I'm trying to feel her out, to see if she'll get what I mean. "People called them enlightened when they talked about the stuff they heard: junk of no consequence whatsoever, like the sound of an insect 'alighting on a leaf.'"

"With such advanced listening skills"—Jaclyn strokes the length of her pen thoughtfully—"perhaps your headphones are a hindrance?"

"I need my headphones," I admit, closing my eyes so I won't have to meet hers, "to drown out my own pounding downbeat, the whole craptastic melody."

When Jaclyn says nothing in reply I look up, searching her face.

"I wish there was a way to get it all out of me. Make everyone listen and understand."

Jaclyn nods. "I see." But I can tell she doesn't.

*With my headphones on I can keep my fool mouth shut*, that's what I should have said. I used to figure everyone could hear their own song inside, like me. I know better now, but I keep hoping I'll meet someone who can.

Jaclyn busies herself writing today's insights into my file. "Shelby, your special ability to hear has caused you painful outbursts in the past, hasn't it?" she asks gently. "A short stay in hospital might help quiet the noises you hear."

"Just let me go home." We've wasted enough time here. I'm going to find the cops who have my radio. "I didn't do anything wrong."

I start to rise from my chair; Hanley squeezes my upper arm, the tinny pulse of factory-generated pop music sweating through her palm.

The door opens without a knock. "Hello, I'm Dr. Lopez."

Great, another white-coat. Lopez looks tired and bored. Hospitals have that effect on people.

Jaclyn offers up her chair, and Lopez sits his butt in it without any thanks. "Miss Rey, I'm going to start you on an antidepressant. Forty milligrams daily, with or without food." He rubs his bloodshot eyes and scribbles the prescription. "Ms. Spenser will reassess your progress in six weeks. Do you have any questions?"

Jaclyn's making no effort whatsoever to get my headphones back, and now she's handing me over to some pill-happy tool who doesn't even know me?

"Those people," I tell him, setting the record straight, "tried to rob me. The police know it. Tell him, Jaclyn. Please."

"Dr. Lopez," Jaclyn says without taking her eyes off me, "the patient has demonstrated symptoms of delusion. Don't you think it might be in her, and the community's, best interest to authorize an involuntary seventy-two-hour hold in hospital?"

I can't trust this woman. She's got me all wrong. Sure, I can hear music. Isn't it crazier that she can't?

"Fine, let's add a low dose of quetiapine." He pens the second prescription. "It'll help with anxiety and delusional episodes. Three hundred milligrams orally, once daily."

I can't trust either one of them. I'm not taking any pills. I won't. And just see what happens if they try to lock me up.

"Dr. Lopez, we aren't finished here," Jaclyn complains, jutting my open file under his nose. "I still have questions, and there are tests—"

"Look, I've been here for over ten hours treating what I consider real emergencies: suicide attempts, aggravated assault, self-inflicted injuries," Lopez says, returning his pen to a pocket over his heart. "Don't try to tell me how to do my job. If the patient remains on medication, this hospital won't lose another bed."

"If you let her go, she'll wind up right back here."

St. Cecilia is the last place I want to be. I'm hot, and the backs of my legs are sticking to the vinyl chair. I wish I could evaporate as fast as helium and float away unnoticed.

"Ensure she understands the importance of daily self-administration," Lopez says, his voice louder and weighted.

An instrumental rendition of "Water Tight" by Grounder ventilates from the PA. Dr. Lopez and Jaclyn dissolve from my awareness as I fade into the music, escaping. With my eyes closed, I can imagine the lyrics. I sway a little to the melody, listening for the story within the music: the intention, the situation, the speaker, the intended listener. I release my entire body to the rhythm, bobbing, twitching, and wriggling. For the moment, I'm free within the beat.

Hanley asks if I'm having a seizure. I ignore her.

Jaclyn shushes her. "I think she's . . . dancing."

When the song comes to an end I open my eyes, feeling fresher, reenergized.

"She's all yours, Spenser." Lopez yawns, his hand on the door. "Assign her twelve weeks of counseling, on an outpatient basis." He turns to leave, but not before cautioning, "If her insurance provider supports it."

He manages a semi-respectful nod to Jaclyn before closing the door behind him.

"Shelby?" Jaclyn's face tells me she's convinced I've gone off the deep end. "Where did you go just now?"

"Get my radio back," I tell her, and clamp my lips shut.

"Dr. Lopez has agreed to let you meet with me at my counseling practice to talk about your thoughts and experiences. Doesn't that sound helpful?"

If talking to some white-coat about my "experiences" had ever been "helpful" I wouldn't be here now, would I? Why lay traps for people who are already caught? "All I did was throw down some truth on a couple of liars."

Hanley picks at her nails, paying us no mind. Steadying my feet under the chair, I get ready to run. I'm not staying here a minute longer.

The door opens suddenly, startling us. O'Neill's hulking frame fills the opening. "Ms. Spenser, just want to let you know I'm outta here. Rodriguez's shift was up an hour ago, and since she ain't booked"—he hooks a thumb in my direction—"and Lopez cleared her for discharge, I'm punching out."

A discharge is the green light to go. I'm ready to bolt.

"Wait." Jaclyn freezes me in place with her tone.

"It isn't fair for you to keep me here," I point out. "The charges didn't stick, and the doctor said I was free to go."

"He discharged her?" she asks O'Neill. "Without the tiniest courtesy of allowing me to complete my assessment? He spent ten seconds with her." Before O'Neill can get a word in, she holds up her hand. "I get it," she mutters, more to herself than to him, "it's about money. Always the money. First they slash our salaries, now we're turning out patients."

"It's rough, all right," O'Neill says. "They been giving pink slips at my wife's work."

"They cut my pay," Jaclyn interrupts him. "And my hours, too."

"Is there a problem, Ms. Spenser?" a man's voice asks. Dr. Pharm-and-Run apparently forgot to collect my file for discharge. He holds out his hand, and Jaclyn reluctantly surrenders it.

I'm angling to bust out of here, but with Officer O'Neill and Dr. Lopez blocking the door, I'd have more luck turning into helium.

"Yes, Dr. Lopez, there is." Jaclyn's voice assumes a bolder tone. "Since I'm more or less donating my Dartmouth education to this establishment these days, how about making it worth this patient's while? She's articulate, has no history of substance abuse, and would have a damn good chance at a normal, healthy life—provided she had appropriate treatment. At this point, it's much bloody likelier she'll end up in jail. Are we going to allow our own professional community to abandon her?"

I feel trapped in the exam room. I'm starting to sweat. If Jaclyn gets her way, I'll be stuck here for the next four days. If Lopez wins, I'll be eating pharmaceuticals for breakfast. I'm not betting on either one of them.

"I'm not authorizing a hold, Spenser," Lopez says through his teeth. "She only threatened assault, she didn't commit it."

"Just let me go," I beg them. "I can show up for the counseling appointments," I add, careful not to make any other promises.

Officer Barry O'Neill mumbles something about heading home himself, but Jaclyn is on a roll. "If we don't provide the right treatment from the beginning, it's guaranteed this patient will be back, along with complications from untreated symptoms."

Dr. Lopez motions for Officer O'Neill to usher me to the exit. I keep my mouth shut, amazed I'm getting out of here at the hands of the man who brought me in. But Jaclyn isn't finished with her lecture.

"It's all a big cluster-you-know-what, and the system is no longer helping anyone, neither patients nor medical professionals," she calls to us as we turn the corner.

Outside, in a surprising show of kindness, O'Neill offers to drive me home.

"Thanks, but I can walk from here," I tell him, glad to have some space to breathe at last. "Can I have my radio back?"

"Sorry." He shrugs. "Rodriguez has your stuff, and he bounced an hour ago. You can pick it up at the station tomorrow."

I can't help but touch my naked ears. I haven't been without Dad's radio since tenth grade. How will I make it through the night?

# CHAPTER FOUR

This Gibson guy better figure out he's my bitch, twenty-four-seven. I bring up his number and call. "Dr. Gibson, let's get on this. Now."

"Zac? Is there an emergency?" he asks, his voice heavy with sleep. "Where are you? Are you in a safe place?"

"Safe place, what the—" I clench my jaw. "Listen, every call I make to you is an emergency." Didn't my manager establish that? As I recall, Ashtynn got round-the-clock attention during her rehab with him. "I just wrapped a live taping on *Late Night with Jon Farrell* that went straight to hell. With no warning, they scheduled Danika Branislav during my appearance."

"The model?"

Yes, the freaking supermodel. "She's whoring around her first feature movie role. Anyway, Jonny gives me props for Grounder's new single, 'Choked,' and she jumps into the convo, rubbing on me and yapping about the time we spent together at Venus Lounge. She said, on camera, that I wrote 'Choked' for her." I can barely breathe, I'm so angry. "Danika was a decent lay and inarguably a gorgeous girl, but I will never write a song about her. She's just trying to use my fame to sell her movie."

God only knows if she can act. And how did she get a movie offer before me?

"Did you explain that Stanford wrote that song?" Gibson asks.

"Embarrass her on national television? Hell no. The prettier the girl, the more violent the retribution. Don't they teach you that shit?" I shudder, thinking about what connections she might have that would've helped mess me over if I'd screwed her like that.

I check my phone for the time and fuck if there isn't a text from Ash. Nothing gets by her.

"Because of her, I'm in deep shit with Ashtynn and about a million steps back from strategizing my breakthrough album."

"Slow down and take a deep breath, Zac. Let's clarify. You're worried about Ashtynn's reaction to your affair with this young woman, correct? And you're concerned that your first song release will somehow represent Ms. Branislav?"

"That about sums it up. So get your ass to LA for a session. See you around three?"

"Zac, I'll be pleased to speak with you in my office about these issues tomorrow. But let's agree on what constitutes an emergency. If you are in peril, I will come to your aid. If you are in danger of harming yourself, or another, I will be there. If you need immediate assistance in any situation that threatens your well-being and livelihood, please do not hesitate to contact me."

This is bullshit. When Ash was in treatment, she contacted him at all hours, whenever she wanted. She'd send a text and there'd be a knock at the door, no questions asked. I saw it with my own eyes. But with me, he has boundaries?

"I'll be working out of my Laguna Beach office for the next two days. I'm happy to make accommodations to see you. Does one thirty tomorrow work?"

"I live in the Hollywood Hills, Gibson. I'm not driving all the way down to Laguna."

"If you prefer my Beverly Hills office, contact Carly and have her fit you in as soon as possible." He tries to stifle a yawn, but I hear it loud and clear. "In the meantime, I recommend you give some thought to your intentions going forward with Ashtynn. Good night, Zac."

He hangs up.

Wait. He hung up. I stand there, looking at my phone. He actually hung up. On me. What the fuck? And what does he care what my "intentions" with Ash are?

Oh Christ, maybe "doctor–patient relationship" wasn't all they had going on.

Well, now I have to shoot down to Laguna tomorrow, just to call that bullshitter out.

I keep my head low to avoid being recognized on the busy sidewalk, crowded with the feet of tourists, couples walking hand-in-hand, and local surfers. Sometimes it sucks to have such a famous face. But hell, I've come to appreciate the paparazzi. They're the key ingredient that has helped cultivate my stardom to near-mythic magnitude. And honestly, if they catch me visiting a shrink's office, it'll be a nice play on the part of my management, who are working around the clock to package the "fallen angel seeks reprieve" angle.

The alcove leading to Gibson's office has floor-to-ceiling smoked glass and heavy brushed-steel handles. What is it about transplants from the East Coast and the color gray? You ballsed up and ditched the zip code. Don't bring the dirty slush and bleak skies here with you.

On the nameplate, Gibson's name plays second fiddle to a Jaclyn Spenser. In Beverly Hills, he's under Rachman. I thought I was supposed to get the top doc.

## THE SECRET SONG OF SHELBY REY

I pull my shit together, getting ready to read the riot act to Gibson, tell him who's in charge here, but nearly bite cement when I trip over a sparkly silver platform shoe.

I never imagined I'd feel this way, but the constant, brazen onslaught of girls is annoying. How did this one track me down? I didn't even plan to be in Laguna today. Why didn't I bring Pablo? Usually, the mere sight of my security guy's colossal bulk is enough to keep them at bay.

I give her the once-over and notice she isn't carrying a camera or trying to shoot me with her phone.

"Hey, excuse me," she says, glancing right past me toward Gibson's door. It's as though her bumping into me was an actual accident. Doesn't this girl know who I am? "The sidewalk's big enough for both of us," she says. "Back off."

I step aside, even though I was here first. Roland Gibson is shrink to the stars, and to the stars' messed-up offspring. Damn, I'll bet she's the good doctor's next patient. This one's probably another wild party girl in Gibson's golden rehab club. She's out in broad daylight in a miniature sequined skirt that barely covers her tanned legs, and her feet are tucked into a pair of Jimmy Choos that have seen more than a few dance floors.

An outfit this provocative, worn under the midday sun, suggests supreme confidence. And when's the last time I saw a girl sure enough of herself to go around without a trace of makeup on? No doubt about it, a genuine beauty. And bold as all hell. I imagine her daddy must be losing sleep.

Before Little Silver Shoes has a chance to bolt through the doors to Gibson, I decide to make her day.

"What's your name?" I produce a grin reminiscent of the one I used on my April cover of *Rolling Stone* and hold out my right hand to her.

She just stares at it. I'm standing here like a jackass with my hand out, and this girl is taking her sweet time considering whether she's even interested in shaking it.

I'm just about to put it in my pocket when she finally places her hand into mine like it might be holding a bomb.

"Shelby," she offers at last.

I give her palm a gentle squeeze, and she searches my face as though trying to place me.

"I'd say you are more of a Shel A than a Shel B," I toss back, regrettably. Lame.

She cocks her brow as though she might recognize me after all. The smile breaking across her face seems to surprise her.

I get it. Rehab is a monster. I watched Ash put on a happy face during her recovery, but her real smiles happened rarely, if ever.

"I'm Zac," I say with a wink. My last name is hardly necessary. She's still holding my hand, so I lean in conspiratorially and whisper, "Looks like you and I have the same appointment," with a nod toward Gibson's door. My thigh grazes her hip.

"Promised a friend I'd take a shot at figuring out where I've been and where I'm headed," she replies, her breath against my cheek.

Just to be sure she does recognize me, I sing a little, making up lyrics off the top of my head: "And here you are, in platform silver haze, pressed against my liquid, lavish craze. I'm lost in the maze of a stranger's gaze."

Could I come up with worse lyrics?

Doubtful.

I know I have better in me. I can feel music in me, crashing just below the surface, waiting for me to shape it, caress it into something tangible and whole. And I will. If I don't write my own music, I'll be less than half a man. A quarter, to be exact: There are four of us in Grounder.

But the brisk blue of Shelby's eyes warms to an incandescent silver luster when she hears me sing. Eyes to match the shoes.

A northbound bus appears, lumbering noisily to a halt next to the curb. I use the interruption to scramble for something clever to say. It's been a while since I've had to make any effort with a girl. The truth is, Ashtynn doesn't make it easy to keep her happy, but jumping through her hoops doesn't give me the buzz I'm digging right now.

"As dark night decays, the sun rises ablaze," she says, making my stupid rhyme half as lame.

Like an idiot, I still have no reply. I can't remember the last exchange I've had with any female where I was this awkward.

She doesn't break our connection by backing away, so I take the chance of placing my hand, just lightly, on her back. Damn, what's my next move? Ask her to waltz?

I fight the beginning of an erection and shake together some loose rhyme to prolong the moment, but the best I can come up with is, "Your phrase pays for days."

She laughs.

Of course she laughs. I would. I want to punch myself in my own mouth.

She moves away from me, withdrawing from Gibson's alcove, her eyes never leaving mine. She backs across the sidewalk toward the waiting bus and climbs onto the first step.

My grin fades fast. Lurching forward, I try to stop her before the bus takes off to God knows where.

"I don't know you. But how could I not know you?" she says, exhaust pluming around her bare legs. "The sound of your voice is a part of me."

With another step backward, she disappears behind the closing doors. I stand there, stock still with astonishment, while the bus pulls away from the curb and disappears into traffic. A Rolls-Royce Phantom glides out from around the corner and trails behind it.

At least one of us brought security.

I let out a deep breath.

Hands down the hottest girl I have ever met. Definitely the most outrageous. Ah, when life imitates a music video. Wait, she missed her session with Gibson. But it's probably for the best. She doesn't need to get mixed up in any late-night "therapy sessions" exclusive to Gibson's prettiest patients.

I find Dr. Gibson standing at his front desk, going over appointments with his receptionist. I drove all the way down, Doc. You won the battle but not the war.

Tapping my heart with my fingers in a sideways "V," I sail past them through the open doors to his office and drop into a chair. In the quiet office, I overhear the receptionist pondering the whereabouts of a new client, "Shelby Rey." I grab my phone to Google her name but can't find anything definitive. Probably uses an alias for social networking.

"Zac, I'm glad to see you today," Gibson says, closing his office doors and joining me in the opposite chair. "You were troubled when we spoke on the phone last night. Has anything been resolved since?"

"If you mean Ashtynn, yeah, she's fine." I shrug. "I spent the night at her place, and we came to an understanding. It's not like I cheated, exactly. At the time I met Danika, Ash and I were just starting out, and then she went into rehab. Kind of put a dent in how much time we spent together. A guy gets lonely, you know."

"Zac Wyatt gets lonely?" He raises his eyebrows.

"Jesus, Gibson. That's exactly what Ash asked." I lean forward and scrutinize the doctor's face. "I guess you made sure she had plenty of companionship, didn't you?"

"I'm not sure what you're suggesting, Zac," he replies without a flinch.

"The therapy sessions at all hours of the night, anywhere,

anytime? I'm certainly not getting that kind of preferential treatment. However, I lack certain 'assets,' don't I, Doc?"

"As I told you last night, I am committed to you in your time of need. If you have a genuine emergency, I'll come to your assistance, Zac. I guarantee that to all my patients." He pauses for a moment, then adds, "Let me make one thing absolutely clear: I have never engaged in an inappropriate relationship with a patient. Before, during, or after treatment."

I stare at him, disbelieving. I spent as much time as I could with Ash through her treatment, even after hours when I wasn't supposed to be there. Sometimes she'd get a call and push me out the door, telling me her shrink was coming over. She only had one therapist: Roland Gibson.

"So why is my relationship with Ashtynn any concern of yours?"

"I care about you, Zac. Your success in recovery affects and is influenced by all your personal relationships. Your current romantic partner is herself in recovery. Naturally, this concerns me."

"I told you, smack was just a one-time deal. And Ashtynn's got her shit under control." I want to push him harder about Ash, but I can't risk him firing me as a patient. It's bad enough that I have to do rehab. Getting let go would not make for good publicity.

"Zac, let's talk about your goals for therapy." Gibson changes course. "I came across a quote by the poet W. H. Auden that I believe will help you access your inherent creativity."

Sounds fucking boring. Immediately dismissing him, I glance down and adjust the cuff of my shirt. Totally worth what I paid for it. I'll bet Little Silver Shoes has exquisite taste. Nothing too good for Shel A, or rather, Shel Rey. Thank God I didn't just grab a tee shirt this morning.

"Can I read it to you?" he asks, interrupting my thoughts, then grabs his iPad and begins without waiting for my response.

"Here goes: 'If music in general is an imitation of history, opera in particular is an imitation of human willfulness. It is rooted in the fact that we not only have feelings but insist upon having them at whatever cost to ourselves.'"

He waits for me to meet him wherever this Auden passage transported him. He'll be waiting a long while.

"Did you say 'opera'?" I wrinkle my nose.

"Zac, would you agree music is an imitation of history?"

"You mean, like it's all been done before, there's nothing new?"

"I think what Auden was getting at here is that we not only have feelings about the events of our lives, we also nurture and coddle those feelings for years. For example, many people do it by reliving those events in new relationships. Or, we gravitate toward movies, books—and, in your case, songs—that resonate with our own personal experience."

Okay, he's actually making sense. "Right." I nod. This is so true. Music and feelings are innate. Each other's cause and effect. You hear music, you respond. You feel, and music interprets your emotions.

"Even if the past was painful, it's human nature to seek out music that reflects and tells the story of that pain."

"Yeah, I get it," I reply, losing interest again. "Blues singers own that market."

"Not just blues singers," he challenges. "As a therapist, it's my goal to help patients reframe their feelings about former experiences and in doing so increase their capacity for joy." He leans forward to drive his point home. "Your goal will be met by empathizing with listeners, not by providing psychotherapy."

"Because that would put our goals in conflict, Dr. Gibson?" I ask with unmasked sarcasm.

He doesn't take the bait. Instead, he surprises me with a warm chuckle, like we're friends or something. "There are millions of music listeners in the world, each one seeking the personal soundtrack of their individual experiences."

Christ, what I wouldn't give to write my own personal soundtrack. I race through images of possible album cover designs in my mind, and it's overwhelming. I'm unsure where I would even begin, and panicked I might never begin at all.

"But like you said, Zac, it's all been done. That's why you're going to have to write music your way, from your singular perspective, creating a new space for the masses to empathize with you and one another."

I know Gibson's right, but what he's talking about equates to me more or less getting naked. And not in the hot sex-tape way. "Empathy, huh? I don't want to sound like a dick, but you work with a lot of famous people. Isn't it in our best interest to separate ourselves from the common person?" I fiddle with my shirt cuff again. "My stardom is my paycheck. If I'm wallowing in the emotional trenches alongside the average dude, won't I lose his admiration?"

Or worse, won't I make myself disposable?

"This is where you will need to make your own distinction. We're here to unlock your potential as a songwriter, not as a star. You've already accomplished that." He smiles.

It's tempting to believe he genuinely cares, but this town is full of warm shit masquerading as pudding.

"Say I break out and produce a solo album, and everyone agrees it's a dung heap? I'll blow everything I've earned with Grounder." I stare hard at my foot, which, for no good reason, has started up a nasty tapping habit.

"Perhaps your breakthrough song will be about working through fear," he suggests.

"I'm not afraid, Gibson." I get up and pace the length of his office. "I've been to countries some people can't even pronounce, headlined shows in venues crammed with thousands upon thousands of fans. Fear doesn't make it this far."

I'm not scared. I'm angry. It's not fair. Every time I sing one of Stanford's songs, it's like I'm living a false life, like I'm nothing more than a limp marionette dangling helplessly from his guitar strings. But I'm stuck. The band is my golden ticket.

"You don't need to convince me of your fame or talent, Zac," Gibson says. "Remember, the idolatry you wish to maintain is a byproduct of having spoken directly to the hearts of music listeners. Grounder's enormous fan base is founded upon your work as a team. Stanford may write the songs, but your vocal and instrumental interpretation of his compositions is what gives them life. Your fans adore you for providing an anthem to their own fight. Your renown is a result of their connection with the words you sing."

"But those aren't my words, they're Stanford's."

"Let's return to the heart of the matter. I say 'heart' because your success as a songwriter depends on what you offer of yourself." He motions me back to my chair. "In order to write lyrics that speak to human experience, you must make yourself vulnerable enough to share your own. Be honest, reveal yourself, tell your own story and all the pain, or joy, associated with it."

I sit down to consider this. Maybe I should take this guy's advice. Everyone the label has ever hooked me up with has taken me where I wanted to go, after all. Gibson is likely my next ride. He fixed things for Ash; maybe he can fix them for me too.

Then it occurs to me: "Ashtynn just signed a two-picture deal with OmniMotion based on the success of her last album. Among her string of hits are 'Bikini Booty' and 'Don't Let the Party Stop.' She sold platinum and no one knows fuck about her soul."

It's probably better that way. Her private life is just that—private.

"No one said you had to be profound." Gibson chuckles.

I'm just about ready to tell him to pound sand when he furrows his brow and looks me square in the eye.

## THE SECRET SONG OF SHELBY REY

"You just posed the gateway question to your journey, Zac: How do you define success?"

He walks over to a cabinet, pulls out a whiteboard, and sets it on an easel next to my chair. With a dry-erase marker, he draws a little stick figure in a sports car, clutching tiny dollar bills. "For instance, if success is measured by album sales or dollars earned, then our work together is pointless. You are already an in-demand, admired, high-earning performer."

"I have to have my own album sales to prove I'm a success," I argue. "If I write a song that matters to me, comes straight out of my freaking groin, and the only person who resonates with it is one eighth-grader in Des Moines, I'll have failed."

"So, money is important because it reflects how many people are compelled to download your song. More money equals more love. Got it." Gibson writes this equation next to the stick figure. Bastard.

"Listen, we're thinking about this too hard." It's time to make things plain to Dr. Smart-Ass. "Draw a picture of Grounder being just as successful as we are now, but I'm the one writing the songs."

He pens crude renditions of me, Stan, Deshi, and Oslo. "Okay, so in this fantasy, you replace Stanford." He taps on the Stanford stick figure, and for some reason, it bugs me that Stan's stupid doodle is getting more attention than mine. "You wish the songs he writes were in reality your songs, your message," Gibson continues. You become him and receive all his accolades." He wipes us clean and sketches me bumping out Stan, the band becoming comprised of mini-me's.

"You're making me sound like some jealous bitch," I complain. Staring at the band of *me*, I resolve to ask Deshi and Os to record some tracks on my solo album.

Gibson stops drawing but says nothing. Second after second

passes without a return to his "be yourself" sermon. This silence is a waste of my time.

"Listen Gibson, a person's destiny can be changed just by listening to the right song at the right moment, in the perfect place. I want to write one of those songs. A song that becomes part of who listeners are."

"Yes!" Gibson cheers, clapping his hands together and holding them palm to palm. "Release yourself from the imprisonment of self-image. Remove your focus from the external."

Whoa, the guy got really excited.

"I'd like you to explore your life stories for potential song material," he says. "The most poignant events will have the greatest impact on listeners."

"The hardest stuff I've dealt with, you mean?" I don't like it. There's a very real danger of coming across as pathetic or insecure.

"Don't label anything 'bad' or 'good.'" He shoos away an imaginary "bad" thought. "Just consider which events, thoughts, or life experiences really moved you."

Shelby Rey certainly made something move down in that alcove an hour ago.

As I get up to leave, Gibson lays a hand on my arm. "You proved Auden's theory, Zac. Many librettos are hundreds of years old, yet still have the power to affect new listeners."

"I'm not going to the opera, Doc. Not going to happen."

"Good. Excellent work." He sits back with a satisfied smile. "You just led us to our next question: What is Zac Wyatt's musical style? We know it isn't opera, and I'm pretty certain you aren't worried about letting the party stop."

I can't sleep. I've given up making a punch list of "poignant" shit. I can't come up with one airtight song hook. Next to every event that ever meant something to me, I write "Lame," "Bitchy," or "This will not get me laid."

Ashtynn is out cold. She always snores when she takes her nighttime meds. I'd like to join her in dreamland, but I'm chained to daily drug tests during my supposed rehab.

I grab my phone from the nightstand and scroll through messages. There's a YouTube link from Deshi, our drummer. From the beginning, he put himself in charge of tracking Grounder's web presence. When I click on it I recognize Gibson's smoked glass doors immediately. Oh fuck, someone shot me going to his office today? It's from an account called LB5485_raz, with a sea turtle for an avatar. Where do these people hide?

The video already has over 250,000 hits and here I'm giving it another. I almost turn it off, but there she is, the hot blonde I met today. I watch it eight times through just to look at her, turning the volume off so I don't have to hear myself saying "Your phrase pays for days." Ash will be furious, but I'll point out that we didn't even exchange numbers. No big deal.

The comments below go on and on:
*Who is Shelby?*
*Was this a publicity stunt?*
*What fan would walk away from Grounder front man Zac Wyatt? It can't be real.*

I can't believe it either. Damn, it'd be nice to trip into her again.

## CHAPTER FIVE

SHELBY

I don't want to take my head off the pillow just yet, but I have to get moving. I can hear Mom and that guy stirring behind the bedroom door of our tiny apartment. Voices low and quiet, weighed down by the early hour and bruised with cigarette smoke and a bottle of O'Sullivan's. That dude sure can put away his alcohol. Wouldn't have hurt him to bring some of his own if he was going to drink like that. Mom has enough trouble supporting her own habit without having to foot the bill for someone else's too.

I sit up and rub away the ache in my right side. Stupid couch. When I get my own place one day, the first thing I'm going to buy is a real bed.

After Dad died, the army told us we had to move off base, and Mom got drunk and threw out all our stuff. I tried to stop her, but she told me there wasn't anything we had that didn't remind her of him. It hurt her too much to keep the life we'd known without him in it.

# THE SECRET SONG OF SHELBY REY

His radio's the only thing that survived the purge, and it only made it because I'd hidden it well, just in case.

They gave us a big bereavement check, but Mom spent a pile of it, and quickly. Her debtors were unrelenting once word got out that Dad was gone, and then there were the parties, and men, and then she started working at the club. "My high school sweetheart lost his life defending this country, you know, and the army turned its back on me," she'd coo at the crinkle of a bill. It worked like a charm, and she took extra shifts to prolong the positive cash flow.

Her—I mean, our—money was nearly gone when I finally convinced her to get one of those fold-out couches with a mattress inside so I could at least have something approximating a bed. I was hoping for something new. Instead, she found this one in the classifieds. The ad said it was "like new."

"Like new" was the life we would face together. Unfamiliar and untested, yet stained and sodden with our memories.

I've worn Dad's headphones every day since I was fourteen. No way I'm letting go of him, or my music. I can't stand the thought of my father's radio being bagged and tagged at some cop station. I guess this is what people mean when they talk about how painful it is to lose old family photo albums in a fire.

Zac's rhythm still vibrates through my veins. I caught the pulse of him, music I've never come upon before. If I had my headphones, I wouldn't have to think about him so much.

I need to clear out before Mom gets up, but I've been wearing this sequined minidress of hers for three days straight. I've got to get changed, or that nosy old Perla will come yell at Mom again about raising me right. *She's old enough to decide if she wants to wear the same thing for a week,* Mom'll tell her, *mind your own goddamned business.*

It's easier if I don't change. I can't always be sure what will be around for me to wear, and some of it just stinks and I can't get the stink out.

I grab a bubblegum-pink baby-doll dress that's crumpled on the counter and hold it to my nose. Ew, this is what Mom wore to the club yesterday. I'm just glad they don't let them smoke in there. Could be worse.

Losing Dad came as a shock to Mom and me. The whitecoats say that's not uncommon, but it looks different for different people. Grief is a prankster and there are only two ways of dealing with it: forgive it or outsmart it. She chose the "outsmarting" path, and that's how she got into dancing. *Men are willing to pay to see me happy*, Mom told me early on. *Being naked's got nothing to do with it.* Every bill tucked into her underwear reminds her she's valued and desirable, she says. It takes the lonely out of being alone.

On the kitchen table there is always a hill of dirty laundry. Sometimes there are a few clean pieces at the bottom, where I started folding clean laundry at some point and then stopped for whatever reason. I dig through the pile. No luck finding anything clean, but I do find a blue, sequined tube dress that only vaguely smells of the club.

Holding the tube dress, I glance at the bedroom door and listen for movement. What genius decided to put the one and only bathroom inside the apartment's one and only bedroom? Reassured by the lack of sound, I quickly change before anyone catches me in my panties.

There is a clammy wad of bills in the dress's small hip pocket. I help myself to a twenty and shove the rest into Mom's cracking faux crocodile purse, abandoned on the floor next to the front door. Hopefully I'll be on the bus before her inevitably awkward morning-after chat with this guy gets going. I don't know how it goes down when she's alone with her boyfriends, but Mom is always mad when I hear her sort out plans for future dates, because they rarely happen. It's my fault, she tells me. When she has a man over, I need to leave them be.

But I can't go quite yet. If I don't get these clothes in the wash while we still have water and electricity, there'll be nothing to wear later. I heave them all into the washing machine in the closet between the kitchenette and the bedroom, careful not to make a racket, then put the latest utility bills in plain view on the counter. Hopefully Mom will notice them and pay them at the check-cashing outlet in the strip mall where she dances.

Behind me, the door to Mom's bedroom creaks open and her boyfriend du jour shuffles out, the sparse unshaven hairs on his face gray in some places, ginger in others. His body reminds me of an apple core: rectangular but lumpy where all the fruit has been bitten away. He adjusts the elastic band on his striped boxer shorts, which I'm guessing were dark blue at some point.

"Hey," I say stiffly, trying to have as little interaction as possible.

Out of the corner of my eye, I watch him stretch and walk into the living room, scratching his core. He heads straight to the couch and sits, his ass sliding over the arm onto the pillow I use, the one with the palm tree, leaving behind one freckled leg hinged at the knee, exposing himself.

"Get up!" I shove him hard.

"What the fuck!" he shouts as I grab the pillow and hug it to me.

"Shelby? What's going on?" Mom asks, staggering from the bedroom holding a lit cigarette between her thumb and index finger. "Shouldn't you be out hunting down a job?"

"I'm trying to get going, Mom," I tell her, shoving the pillow behind a side table and scanning the floor in search of a matching pair of shoes.

"Don't rush away just yet," Boxer Shorts Dude mumbles, "let's get to know each other."

"Good morning, baby," Mom purrs at him. "My daughter giving you any trouble?"

He shakes his head. "No, she don't mean no harm." He cocks his brow, clearly reevaluating my presence here. "She visiting or something?" He looks at me and pats the couch cushion next to him, as if to suggest I make myself comfortable.

Suddenly I'm embarrassed that this useless sack assumes I ought to have a life of my own, because I don't. "No, 'she' is leaving the green, green grass of home," I throw back to him, quoting a song I've heard on the radio that he's ancient enough to know. I glance at Mom just in time to see her rolling her eyes.

He brightens at the mention of grass. "You ladies got some weed?"

"About time she got a job and made her own way in the world." Mom scowls at me and digs in her purse for the possibility of a joint. "Ain't that right, Shelby?" she asks, like I have work lined up or something.

A knock at the door startles us. Early-morning visitors are invariably suspect, generally police or military officers bearing grim news. Or Perla, awoken by the ruckus of a date gone sour.

The only sound in the room is the flick of Mom's thumb rolling the tiny barrel of a lighter, the remainder of an old joint held lightly between her lips. She frowns and puts them both back in her purse.

"Shelby Alicia Rey, are you in there?" a woman's voice asks through the door.

I recognize it immediately: Jaclyn Spenser.

I shoot a glance at Mom. "What the hell is a social worker doing here?" I ask, pretending to be irritated. But I open the door eagerly, half expecting her to be holding Dad's radio in one hand and his headphones in the other, arms outstretched, just like St. Cecilia holds her violin and bow in that painting in the hospital's waiting room.

Instead, Jaclyn is carrying a crisp file folder and a binder. She's brought backup again. At least it's not Hanley, just some guy who looks like he'd rather be anywhere else. I know the feeling.

♪ 55 ♪

"Well, you sure took long enough getting here." Mom makes a scoffing noise at Jaclyn. "My daughter's sick and all. Should have come through same day we spoke."

Mom has always worked me as pill bait. When I was in high school, she was much craftier about it. As I got older, it became plain that most doctors are eager to medicate, and any follow-up is generally initiated by the patient. The white-coats' easy answer is sedation in the guise of "compliance" and "safety."

The prescriptions they wrote made me feel sleepy, nailed down, and annoyingly helpless. Then everyone got mad and called me lazy and unmotivated. Mom and I have since arrived at an agreement: I don't have to take the pills if she can.

No surprise Mom jumped at the chance for a visit from Jaclyn.

"Shelby, it's good to see you again," Jaclyn says, stepping into the center of our small living room. "I called your home phone number when you failed to appear for your appointment." She takes the guy by the arm, guiding him to her side. "I'd like to introduce you to Dr. Gibson, a psychiatrist who is interested in your case."

Gibson straightens up and reaches out his right hand. "Dr. Roland Gibson, nice to meet you."

I don't want to shake his hand, and neither does Mom.

"She don't need to talk to nobody, she gets by on her meds," Mom says.

Gibson politely pulls his hand away from me to offer it to Boxer Shorts, who just roused himself from the couch. "Mr. Rey?"

"That's a good one, eh, Challis?" Boxer Shorts snorts. "Nah, I ain't 'Mr. Rey.' Just passing through, is all. Best be getting on."

Mom's name is Darlene. She must've met him at the club, since he only knows her by her stage name.

Boxer Shorts turns and pauses a moment, then reaches out and grasps my shoulder with a rough, freckled hand, giving it a squeeze.

I smack his hand away. The last thing I need is to hear Boxer Shorts's song.

"Shelby!" Mom squawks, glowering at me. "You all right, baby?" she simpers to Boxer Shorts.

"Yeah, I'm okay."

"See what I'm talking about?" Mom says. "If she doesn't get her meds, she doesn't know how to act. I get sick worrying about her."

Boxer Shorts just stands there, wriggling a finger in his wobbly ear socket.

"Why don't you get your pants on, honey?" Mom suggests, lighting a cigarette.

Boxer Shorts lumbers off to the bedroom to find the rest of his clothes.

"Your mother invited us for a home visit," Jaclyn tells me, assuming her syrupy social worker voice. "Shelby, she believes you are in crisis and feels unable to assist you."

Mom is obviously playing Jaclyn for meds. I take a deep breath, preparing to beg her for my music, but Mom whimpers, "She suffers something awful, Ms. Spenser. The only thing that helps her with the hurt of it is oxy. I mean, Percocet."

Boxer Shorts pops his head out from the bedroom to add, "Or Roxicodone, that'll do."

"And there was another one, too." Mom itches the back of her neck, trying to remember. "What was it? Chlorproma-something-or-other. For her crazy episodes. If you get it sent here, I'll make sure she takes it."

Gibson smiles patiently. "I offer a unique, drug-free approach to mental wellness. Many psycho-emotional stresses are triggered by hormonal and nutritional imbalances." He meets my eyes, his warm smile revealing talk-show-host white teeth. "I've patented an effective treatment plan without the use of prescription medicine. Patients genuinely seeking to feel better are relieved to discover a natural alternative." Then he turns pointedly to Mom. "Those struggling with addictions are not, and they have two choices: continue the downward spiral of substance abuse or see me for help."

I look at Mom to see if she's buying what he's selling.

Hardly. Gibson might as well have announced he's going to exorcise my demons. Without a prescription pad, he's no longer welcome here.

Mom loses her balance a moment then steadies herself, holding the edge of the counter. Her eyes are stony but she softens her voice, pleading, "At least something to help her sleep?"

Even though Mom works most nights, sleep doesn't always come easy for her in the morning.

Sparing us a repeat of his drug-free America speech, Gibson says, "Ms. Rey, we appreciate you reaching out on behalf of your daughter's well-being. However, she is an adult. Her medical records are confidential and without her written authorization cannot be disclosed, even to family members."

Mom's cheeks fire a hot red. She'll kick him to the curb if he isn't careful. I step between her and Gibson and blurt out, "Do you have my radio?"

"Radio? The one the police confiscated as evidence?" Jaclyn's brow furrows, as though it's the furthest detail from her mind.

"You got arrested? Girl, you're going to drive me to an early grave right alongside your father, rest his soul." Mom never mentions God when she says "Rest his soul."

I turn pleading eyes to Jaclyn. "Tell her, Jaclyn, it wasn't my fault. And besides, I didn't get charged." If Mom throws me out, I have no Plan B. This is it. This is home.

"You owe no explanation, Shelby," Jaclyn tries to assure me, like Mom won't use it as an excuse to change the locks.

"I'm sorry for the loss of your husband, Ms. Rey. When did he pass?" nosy Gibson inquires.

"Four years ago. Left me penniless."

I wish Mom hadn't told them that. Maybe she's hoping they'll slip her a twenty, but a dead daddy means deep head-case drama for me. White-coats are obsessed with daddy issues. I've never known one to leave well enough alone, so I'm surprised when Jaclyn forgoes a cross-examination to ask if she can use the bathroom.

Mom gives her a knowing look, then calls in through the bedroom door, where Boxer Shorts had better be getting dressed, "Social Worker wants to have a look around the place. You decent?"

When Boxer Shorts sidles out, Mom gives him a quick kiss and he stuffs some bills into her palm. Looking over at me, he raises his hand to his forehead, waving goodbye with what appears to be some attempt at a salute. I curl my lip at him.

"Shelby," Jaclyn begins softly when she returns from the bedroom, "I'm unclear about the division of property within your dwelling. Can you show me what, specifically, belongs to you, dear?"

Of course she was snooping around; Mom totally called that one.

"Do you and your mother share everything? The bed, the clothes?"

"She's been offered the chance to dance at my club, but she ain't got the smarts to get out there and make it happen for herself," Mom bursts out. "I ain't responsible for no grown-ass woman."

"So Shelby has no clothing of her own?"

"I share the shirt off my back, bought with my hard-earned money. If she wants her own clothes, she can make her own damn money."

"And does Shelby also share a bed with you?"

"I don't know what pot you're trying to stir, but she sleeps out here on the couch, all by her lonesome."

"No. What I mean is, statistically, in the homes of"—Jaclyn fights to keep up her politically correct bullshit—"in lower-income residences, there are often several family members sharing sleeping quarters."

Mom stares at her in undivided rage.

Jaclyn's voice softens. "It's helpful to have a clear understanding of a patient's current living situation."

Mom looks ready to throw a punch.

"So we can recommend appropriate resources and therapy," Jaclyn adds, still quieter.

"You think I'm some broke-ass good-for-nothing, is that it?" Mom snorts. "I earn my keep, lady. Shelby's the one"—she wags a finger in my direction—"mixed up with the cops. She's had troubles her whole life. But who takes it on the chin? Me, that's who."

"I'd like to assure you that I'll be strongly advising your engagement in ongoing therapy in my home-visit report," Jaclyn says to me, ignoring Mom entirely. "I believe counseling is imperative."

I want to know why I can hear everything when no one else can. But I don't dare say that. Why won't they just give me my radio back? Drowning myself in music is the only way I know how to survive.

"What fucking good is therapy?" Mom explodes. "I been keeping a roof over this useless kid all these years, and now you're telling me her meds are none of my business? Don't that beat all. The one thing she's good for." She glares at me. "And don't think I'll forget about you getting arrested. The last thing I need is cops at my door, understand me?"

Jaclyn continues scribbling notes, fattening up my file for St. Cecilia. Gibson just stands there, taking in our little freakshow.

Mom shuffles over to the couch and sits down like she's finished having guests. She shoves aside some old mail on the coffee table till she finds a lone cigarette in a crumpled pack and lights it. "I knew this day would come, girl," she says without even looking at me. "I ain't going to bail you out of any slammer, mark my words. You might as well check yourself into some loony bin, because you can't live here anymore."

"Don't worry. I'm getting out of here." I spot a matching pair of heels peeking out from under a chair and shove them onto my bare feet.

Jaclyn closes her folder. "Shelby, we want to help you."

I wish I could disappear. "Leave me alone."

"If she offers you a prescription," Mom says, "you take it, goddamn it."

I pretend I didn't hear her and walk out the door, careful not to let it slam behind me. Don't want to wake up Perla.

"Shelby, wait." Jaclyn and Gibson rush to follow me. Behind them, the door swings shut with a loud clap.

As I make my way quickly to the sidewalk, I hear Perla yelling from her apartment door, "For being nothing but a shadow, you sure can make a racket. I'm calling the super."

I hobble on Mom's ill-fitting pumps for nearly a hundred yards before a man's hand grips my arm. I swing around, half expecting Gibson to announce he's really a cop and I'm arrested for being nuts enough to think I have any right to ever hear my music again.

But it's Boxer Shorts, reeking of a boozy breakfast from the liquor store, who's holding my arm. Jaclyn and Gibson close up on us fast and he hands me over. "Sort the poor thing out, will you?" he says to them before wandering back to the parking lot.

"Shelby, we want to help you," Jaclyn says. "Is there a safe place where we can talk?"

I jerk my head toward my apartment building. "We were just there."

"Let me tell you what I saw." Jaclyn tries to reach for my hand, but I pull it close to me. "I saw a place where no one, regardless of their mental or physical health, could thrive. In fact, environmental factors—poverty, abuse, lack of a safe, nurturing environment—are largely responsible for occurrences of mental disorders. And then to suffer the loss of a parent?"

I start walking to the bus stop, fighting the threat of my radio and headphones becoming as helplessly lost as me, trying to shake her nonsense out of my ears. Jaclyn is more concerned with what ought to be than what is. Make everything fit within the limits of some theory and arrive at an expected outcome. Never works.

"Shelby, don't run," Gibson says. "I know a safe place where you can stay."

I keep moving. Gibson is on my heels, Jaclyn trotting along just behind.

"From where I stand, you have three choices," he says, too loudly, as we approach the small crowd waiting at the stop.

There really isn't much to do at a bus stop, and all those bored eyes and ears turn to us. I don't want him to make a scene, so I hustle him a few feet away, keeping watch for an approaching bus.

"By my estimate, I have zero," I whisper, hard. "How did you figure out I have three?"

Gibson lowers his voice to match my whisper. "One, you get on a bus right now and get arrested again. Maybe not today but tomorrow, or the day after that, or the one after that. If nothing changes in your life, you'll just keep repeating the same mistakes. Unfortunately, you already have a record. Another slip-up or two and it's jail time, Shelby."

I can do nothing but stare at him.

"Two, you can walk the same path as your mother. When she was your age, what were her circumstances? Did she have an education? A career?"

I feel my cheeks redden, a drum-bass pattern pounding behind them. When Mom was my age, she was married to Dad. I was a baby. We had a house.

"Three, you can choose to come and stay with Jaclyn and me.

We have a room in our home. You'll have your own space and may come and go as you like."

"Roland?" Jaclyn's whisper spikes to a tart soprano. "Can I talk to you for a moment?"

Wait, Gibson is her husband?

A bus approaches, but I'm sure another can't be far behind it, and I just had my crap-tastic life served to me in no uncertain terms. For the moment, I'll wait.

The two bow their heads together in discussion.

Jaclyn lowers her voice to a murmur, but I can still hear her: "Listen, I know you didn't want to come today, but this is hardly a fair solution. I'm sorry to tell you, but most of my clients live in similar conditions. Or worse." She pinches the diamond on her left hand, rocking the ring back and forth on her finger.

"Her circumstances aggravate her symptoms, and without radical changes in lifestyle and world view, chronic disorders are perpetuated," Gibson shoots back. "You know this, you see it every day."

"I do know, and I tried to have her admitted to St. Cecilia. But you can help her in-office without inviting her to live with us. Your success rate is unsurpassed."

I see irritation flicker across his face. "You asked me to take her as a patient, Jac. Removing her from an unstable living environment is absolutely necessary. It's pretty clear she can't afford a supervised treatment clinic."

"This is not a good solution, Roland. There are programs for young women—"

"I'm not checking in to any nuthouse," I tell them straight, shattering the hushed tones. "I'd just as soon go to jail."

"I agree that a nurturing, safe environment would benefit her, but it's hardly protocol to bring her home," Jaclyn says in a normal voice, giving up on trying to keep the conversation between just the two of them.

"She needs practical help now if she hopes to succeed independently as an adult," Gibson challenges her. "You know better than anyone, Jaclyn, how mentally disordered behavior is criminalized."

"What's he talking about?" I'm not a criminal. Or "mentally disordered."

"You're not 'sick' enough for a hospital, but without treatment, you'll eventually have another episode," Jaclyn says matter-of-factly. "An arrest ultimately labels a person a criminal and affects how police handle any future disorderliness."

"Prisons are just long-term repositories for the mentally ill," Gibson remarks under his breath.

My stomach implodes as I swallow his words. I'm hoping these are just scare tactics. I can't go back to the apartment. But live with white-coats? For real?

He places his hands on my shoulders and steadies me. I guess I lost my footing for a moment. Strains of Dad's old Rolling Stones CDs, soldered with random acoustic riffs, seep from his warm palms as he gently meets my eyes.

"When Jaclyn and I were in school, we worked together at a small outreach program run by my father's church," he tells me. I suspect he is about to drop some counseling parable I'm supposed to relate to and somehow learn from, except he's using the word "I." White-coats never share anything personal. Never.

"The program was low-budget, to say the least. But we always managed to find community resources for people, like you, in immediate need of medical help, a place to live, or vocational training." He turns to Jaclyn, his lips curving up into a small grin. "If we'd met this young woman back then, who would we have sent her to?"

Jaclyn searches her husband's face for a long while. "Us," she says at last.

For a moment, she and Gibson seem to forget I'm even there,

let alone the hot topic. I'm still listening, though, the pause a warm place to hang the half-note of Jaclyn's "us."

"Shelby, this is utterly unorthodox." She takes my hand in hers. "I have no idea what's gotten into my husband, and I'm scared, to be honest. But how about you come see our home, and if you like it, you can stay the night. In the morning, we can discuss whether it's best for you to stay another night or return to the apartment to discuss a possible resolution with your mother. We'll take it one day at a time, but we have to agree on one thing."

*I'll do laundry, clean up after myself, stay out of the way*, I want to tell her. *Just help get me out of Mom's apartment for good.* "What is it?" I ask.

"You commit to treatment," she says firmly. "We can't force you to make good choices, you have to make them for yourself. We can show you how to improve your living circumstances, but you have to do the work."

She is freaking me out. "What the hell do you mean by 'treatment'? I'm not jumping down some weird rabbit hole just because you let me sleep over." I wrench my hand from hers. For all I know, Mr. and Mrs. White-Coat eat their dinner by the glow of an electro-shock therapy machine, a festive arrangement of lobotomy tools in a vase on the table. "Forget it. I'm out."

"I like the idea of taking things one step at a time." Gibson jumps forward and positions himself in front of me before I can walk away. "Shelby, you don't have to make a decision now. Let me give you our address. If you need a place to stay, our door is open."

"Please," Jaclyn whispers.

I freeze for a minute, surprised by the dampening of tears at the edge of her words. Every assessment I've ever had has ended in a pile of paperwork, prescriptions, and pitilessness. This is the most twisted interaction I've ever had with mental health caregivers. I'm not even sure any longer who has more issues, me or these two.

I square my shoulders and look directly at Jaclyn. She seems smaller. I could take her in a fight if I had to.

"I've been trying to adhere to some basis of state regulation here, but who am I kidding?" She shakes her head, brushing her hand through her neatly arranged hair. More resolutely, she says, "What you need right now is a friend. Roland is willing to step up. So am I."

I don't have many of those. None, actually.

"One night," I tell them. "Give me your address, and I'll get there myself."

# CHAPTER SIX

It's good to be out. Ashtynn's management really knows how to polish a tight appearance. Our table is staged for something cozy and allegedly private to go down, flushed with soft light, and no more than a twelve-foot viewing distance from a street window.

"Baby, don't you just love this place?" Ash says, her face tilted just slightly toward the window. "I could eat everything on this menu," she nearly hisses. "Everything."

Of course she's hungry. She doesn't touch anything but raw vegetables and zero-calorie energy drinks.

"You look good enough to eat," I assure her, in the mood to indulge a little myself. She'll play her standard nice-girl routine for the public, leaving separately so there's no evidence we're bedding down for the night. But Ash is definitely more Vixen than Prancer, and, God knows, a whole bunch of Blitzen.

We could have hashed out the details last night at my place. But her management insisted we discuss it over dinner, even though it required a hall pass from Gibson. I get it. Everything

## THE SECRET SONG OF SHELBY REY

Ash wears, does, and says is immediately discussed in Googlical proportions, and that whole business with me and Shelby out front of Gibson's office didn't help her image.

I glance at the swarm of paparazzi staking the joint. Ash and I are at the starting gate of something damn near epic. Photos of the moment the fireworks are lit should banish the public's memory of my minor brush with Little Silver Shoes.

I wonder what Shelby's up to tonight.

Ash orders a salad and sparkling water. Figures. She could at least order the chicken, even if she's going to ignore it. I ask for the harissa-grilled lamb sirloin. I have no idea what the hell harissa is but if they're putting it on anything sirloin, I'll take my chances.

"Baby sheep?" she whines. "Zacky!"

I have to get her to stop calling me that.

"I've had a stroke of brilliance," she says, changing gear like there's a director over our shoulders. I'm relieved she isn't bothering to waste another breath on my dinner order. Waving over some dude wearing enough hair product to style the entire cast of *Baller Housewives*, she coos, "Dominic, darling, how are you?"

Nodding excitedly, he breezes over to the table, reaches for her outstretched hand, and air-kisses it.

"Zacky and I are celebrating a provocative new project tonight," she tells him, crafting intrigue for the not-so-casual listeners-in.

That little nugget is all we need to "leak." We can close for business now and get on with our evening.

"We're doing our first movie together, for none other than OmniMotion," she adds without missing a beat.

I nearly choke on my San Pellegrino. It requires steel freaking balls to maintain composure. We haven't finished negotiations, let alone signed on the goddamned dotted line. I'm not even done reading the script.

"The plan is to wrap at the end of next spring. Wouldn't it be adorable to throw a wrap party for the cast right here, where the magic began?"

Dominic is stoked, of course, and twirls toward the bar, signaling for a bottle of bubbly for the table.

Would have been a nice touch.

Ash's face reddens as though his oversight has slapped her cheek dead center. "How dare you?" She rises from her seat and stamps a fringed boot on the travertine. "My boyfriend is in rehab."

Before Dominic can get a word in, she puts on a whole new persona out of nowhere. With the repentance of an injured angel, she adds, "And I walked through the valley of the shadow of death."

Her theatrics momentarily stun both Dominic and me. Ash never fails to surprise. Ever since she dropped the "mess" from "hot mess," she's been fearless.

Dominic quickly recovers. Flustered by his mistake, he chooses to defend his act of generosity rather than simply apologize. "I was offering you our very best, mademoiselle. A new movie, how terribly exciting."

Feline fussing erupts between them, broken by short pauses while Ash texts her entourage in outrage, then responds to their incoming remarks. Restaurant review stars are probably disappearing with every vibration of communication.

Is this a planned skit, intended to generate public support for our combined struggle against the beast of addiction? If it's all for show, I'm going to be pissed that no one trusted my acting skills enough to let me in on the gag.

"Ash, baby?" I'm putting an end to this. "We don't get enough time together, just the two of us. We have a lot to discuss, and I'd prefer to just have a quiet dinner with you. Dominic, do you mind?"

## THE SECRET SONG OF SHELBY REY

Dominic clasps his hands together to silence his dramatic flair. Satisfied with his reclaimed composure, he waves off a conspicuously absent tab. "Forgive my oversight." He is pointedly congenial. "I wish you every success in your *désintoxiquer*, Monsieur Wyatt."

"Thanks, man." I tip my chin and throw him an electric smile generally reserved for press.

A flush overtakes his collar and he rushes off without another word. Ash settles in her seat as though nothing happened.

"Babe, neither one of us is signed on for the picture." I shouldn't have to remind her of this. "We shouldn't fuck with the OmniMotion machine by announcing something that isn't carved in stone yet."

"I'm already committed, Zac," she replies. "The script is fresh. It has just the right amount of edge and, most importantly, an original take on teen love. We're going to burn it up, I know it."

My lamb arrives and it smells delicious. You can't go wrong with sirloin. "Honey, there are no 'original takes' on teen love." I'm not exactly pumped about playing a teenager when I'm twenty fucking years old. "It's all been done, forever. Even *Romeo and Juliet* wasn't an original take on teen love." I'll bet Shelby would agree with me on this.

"Zacky, don't be silly. They've already written the soundtrack and you're going to die, it's totally packed with no-fail hits." She pierces a steamed beet laced by escarole. "And you've always wanted to break into acting, haven't you? They need star power, and we're it, Zac. We're it."

She taps a quick response to a text, then meets my eyes. "This next year will be the greatest triumph of our lives."

Her eyes are shining and hopeful. I lean forward across the table to kiss her. God, I hope she's right.

Her phone buzzes again, and she spurns my kiss to read the

message. I sit back in my seat and grab my napkin to make a show of wiping away any stray lipstick, even though I didn't get close enough to touch her.

"It's my doctor." She shrugs apologetically. "We'll have to cut this short, Zacky. I'm sorry."

"You're seeing Gibson? Tonight?"

She appraises the bottles displayed behind the bar, an 80-proof rainbow lit from behind in a prism of colored lights. "All this excitement has me aching for that champagne Dominic tried to send over. I need an emergency treatment session."

"Right now? Can't we finish our dinner and discuss the movie?" Sure, this constitutes one of Gibson's requirements for an "emergency." But the one night I'm let off house arrest, Ash goes to see him? That bastard had better not be sleeping with her.

Or wait, maybe she just wants to get our little after-party started early. Is she planting the seeds for a solo getaway so we can meet back at her place earlier than we'd planned?

Fuck, it bugs me that I can't tell what she wants.

"I'm dying for a beer," I grumble under my breath. "But until I graduate from Gibson's rehab routine, no dice."

I hate to lie to her. The truth is, ever since I went cold turkey, I've been sleeping better, I've had endless energy, and damn if I haven't got a string of celeb trainers lining up to take credit for my results at the gym. My agent is negotiating my participation in a charity triathlon when I complete my rehab, with tons of six-pack photo ops.

"Just sign on for the project, baby," Ash says, "and we'll go from there."

She puts her phone in her purse and is rising from her chair when I let the truth rip. "Ash, I don't want to do it. The movie. Or the soundtrack. Either," I sputter. "Neither."

She slowly lowers herself back into her chair, removes her phone from her purse, and replaces it on the white linen tablecloth. "Pardon?" she asks, and I swear I see the melting ice in her water glass harden at the chill of her single word.

I sigh. "Do you ever wonder how you would have handled your earliest contract negotiations with your label if you knew then what you know now?"

Without a second's pause, she says, "No. I did what they asked me to do, and they made me a star. I'll always be grateful. Even when I almost screwed things up for everybody, they gave me another shot. And now they want to give me—us—a hit movie, a killer album, and an international promotional tour? Uh, no-fucking-brainer, am I right?"

"Yeah." I nod slowly, stroking my hand along my jaw and through the freshly cropped hair just behind my ear.

She's absolutely right. The money would be *ridic*, that's certain.

"Do you ever think about writing your own music?" I venture, hoping to keep her at the table a while longer.

She picks up her fork and bites a plain leaf in silence.

"Because I do. I'm tired of performing other people's music." She eyes me suspiciously, as though I might bolt. "My own fans love me for something that isn't me at all. The OmniMotion deal is tempting, for real. But I have songs inside me fighting to get out. If I ignore them, bury them with other people's music, it'll get even harder to say no, to go my own way."

"You think you have some sort of rare talent that will carry you past the gatekeepers?" She raises an eyebrow. "Let me tell you something, Zac Wyatt. Even if I were Marilyn Monroe and Audrey Hepburn rolled into one, it wouldn't be enough to make it on my own. You have to have the dealmakers in your corner."

She taps my wrist and I offer her the bite of lamb on my fork. Rolling it about on her tongue luxuriously, she gives me a solemn nod before swallowing. "Remember Tupac?" she says. "He was a better businessman than he was an entertainer, if you ask me."

I didn't.

"He figured out how to manipulate the industry from the freaking grave. No amount of rapping"—she stabs at her salad—"can rival that."

Damn, Ash, that was harsh. I look around to check whether anyone heard her.

"No one is helping Stanford write Grounder's music," I point out, "and he churns out winner after winner. I want to be successful, don't get me wrong. I just want to do it on my own merit."

"You say that like you think I'm some sort of tool," she replies, reaching across the table to pierce another piece of the meat on my plate with her fork. "The public has the attention span of an effing fruit fly. I'm going to ride this money train as hard and as long as I can before it spits me out and forgets I ever existed."

She's not listening to me. I have to make her hear what I'm saying. My words are unstable, pressing through a thin crack in my fear of how she might respond. "I don't think I can do the OmniMotion deal, Ash."

She is quiet for a moment, chewing thoughtfully. Her eyes drop into her lap.

"Zac? Baby?" she whispers, bringing her gaze up to mine. "We're in this together. This isn't about you. It isn't about me. It's about us"—she takes my hand in hers, squeezing her fingers around mine—"loving one another."

What the hell? She's warmed my bed for eighteen months without once mentioning the word "love."

"I'll never forget how you stood by me and my parents during my rehab," she continues. "It meant so much to have someone I could trust." A lock of mahogany hair falls, cradling her dewy chin. I lean across the table to brush it aside, the way I often did when she would fall silent, zoning out in the hospital, and I didn't know what else to do.

"Our relationship maintained my persona as a 'wholesome

young girl overwhelmed by the magnitude of success,'" she says with a bitter laugh. "Now, I'm offering you the same courtesy in your rehab."

"I'm not really an addict, you know that," I'm quick to reply. Too quick. Ash's whole body stiffens.

"To be honest, I'm using this downtime to focus on writing a solo album."

This is the first time I've said that out loud. I suddenly sit straighter with the realization it's also my first time seeing myself as an "artist."

"Your little stint in rehab is giving you time to follow your dream. Isn't that wonderful, Zacky." Each word hangs wet with sarcasm between us.

I could punch myself, inconsiderate bastard. Ash's rehab was hell. After she OD'd, I consoled her inconsolable parents for three miserable days, waiting for her to regain consciousness. When she did, she was sick, depressed, and humiliated. I was the only friend her family allowed to see her, and now I'm dragging her back through the ugly mess she's trying to put behind her.

"Well, imagine how much extra time you'll have on your hands after we shoot the movie and record the album," she says hopefully. "Months of surefire hits released one after the other, fat royalty checks trailing sweetly behind. And you and me, top of the fucking heap, Hollywood's golden couple."

A few years back I would have given my left nut for this offer. Not just the permanent daylight of OmniMotion but also Ash. Here she is, media darling Ashtynn fucking Kingston, offering herself up to me, dropout music major from suburban Oregon.

I can't let her down. She's done so much for me. For us.

Maybe it is the right time to take our relationship to the next level. We've always been there for each other. We're ready to use the "L" word.

Aren't we?

"Besides, you owe me," she adds.

"Excuse me?"

"OmniMotion wouldn't even consider you if it weren't for me, my influence, my established fan base. Trust me, Zac." She shakes her head and lets out a bitter laugh. "You need me."

The back of my throat sinks away, leaving a gaping hole all the way down my spine. I search blankly for something to throw back at her, but I'm scared shitless she could be telling me the truth.

"Be thankful for the pretty face God gave you, Zac. I tell myself that every day." She laughs again, a mutilated morsel of my lamb visible behind her perfect smile. She finishes chewing and swallows. "Babe, I gotta go. Emergency treatment session, remember?"

I sit back in my chair and cross my arms, doubtful.

"I can see you need to think about this. We've won the goddamn lottery with this opportunity," she says, "but I'll give you the benefit of the doubt because you love me."

I didn't say I love her.

"Put me in the video for Grounder's 'Vertical Wire' song release," she says, suddenly all business. "Make it something saucy and a little risqué to broaden my demographic, and I'll buy you some time with OmniMotion."

I nod my assent. "Vertical Wire" could use a hit of skin, and besides, there's no point in arguing with Ash.

I watch her walk away, disappearing into a sea of flashbulbs on the sidewalk.

## CHAPTER SEVEN

SHELBY

From the road, I can see plenty of lights on. I continue the march up the hill to their home, terrified of what will happen after I ring the doorbell.

I'm going to ring it. I don't have any choice at this point. I can't bear another day without my radio, and I can't sleep on the bus every night without the cops catching up with me. I tried sleeping on the beach, only to learn that once the sun sets, out creep rats the size of the ten-gallon cowboy hat Mom used to wear onstage in Corpus Christi.

Mom could have kicked me out any number of times before, and she never did. Not until Jaclyn Spenser showed up. I think we both kind of expected I'd be taken care of somehow. Not by Mom, of course, but by the military or maybe the state.

I didn't know for sure Mom had given up on me until I crept back to the apartment when she was at work to find the super changing the lock. I got out of there before he had a chance to spot me. Mom has forgotten me many times—at school, gas stations, the hospital—but I've never been so mortified, because it was never about me. It was just her, being stuck. She gets to worrying about things just short of her reach and forgets.

This time, it is about me.

A jumble of rehearsed explanations duke it out in my head. Maybe I'll only ask if I can have something to eat. And a place to sleep, just for tonight.

And a shower or whatever.

Maybe I could convince Gibson to let me vacuum his Laguna Beach office at night, and then I could probably start sleeping there secretly. I got pretty good at being invisible at Mom's. Zero Interference, that's what I called it.

The front entrance of the house is surrounded by bamboo, trimmed with the precision of some chop-happy gardener gone OCD. Two monumental carved-wood front doors conceal my approach.

Before I can figure out whether I should just get it over with and ring the bell, I hear the jangle of the front door becoming unlatched. In a second, one of the wooden doors swings wide open and out walks the good doctor himself in a black suit and bow tie, holding keys and wallet.

Seriously, a tuxedo? I've never seen a tuxedo on a real person, just on TV. Clearly, the Gibsons, or Spensers, or whatever they call themselves, are not regular people.

I expect he'll erupt in anger, finding me still as a parked car in his flower bed.

"Shelby?" A wide smile breaks across his face. "I'm so glad you're okay. Come in, come in." Gibson bustles me into the house. I cringe at his freshly showered, minty-citrus breeze scent. I can't help but shrink back. I don't want to know how I might smell to him after three days and nights on city buses and a briny beach.

"We were starting to wonder if we'd see you again." His eyes swoop over me. "I'll bet you're hungry."

With his fingertips light on my forearm, he directs me through the house toward a darkened room. His hand covers a light switch just inside the shadowed entry and I'm startled for a moment when a kitchen appears.

He motions for me to sit on a bar stool at the counter, but I stand fixed within the confines of a floor tile, waiting for him to ask where the hell I've been, to demand to know why I didn't show up when I was expected.

Instead, he begins digging around in the refrigerator. "I'm glad you stopped by before we left," he says, pulling out a container holding cut squares of orange and green melons. "Jaclyn and I were about to go to this dinner thing. I have to give a speech."

I don't respond, just watch him unwrap paper from a short stack of sliced deli meat then a variety of prettily packaged cheeses.

"So we didn't cook tonight. Hopefully we have something in the fridge that looks good to you?" Out comes a gallon jug of milk and a green bottle of sparkling water. My feet remain glued to the tile floor, my insides giddy with hungry longing.

Jaclyn appears at the kitchen door, black-enrobed, starlight sparkling from her ears, neck, and finger. She throws her arms around me without a nanosecond's notice. I wrangle free, my focus entirely on the food laid out on the counter. It's one thing to hold my hand, let's not move into Hugsville.

Gibson gets a plate from a cupboard and extends it toward me. I need no further invitation.

Ignoring the plate, I begin shoving the various food items he's just placed before me into my mouth, directly from their packages. Gibson sets the plate on the counter, arranges a meal on it, and slides the dish in front of me. As soon as he holds out a fork and knife, I take them and dig in.

"How about some eggs? Boiled, scrambled, sunny side up?"

I swallow and nod at him.

"All right, scrambled would be fastest." He smiles warmly and grabs a small fry pan, but Jaclyn shuffles him toward the front door.

"Go," she says, taking the pan from his hands. "Give your talk. I'll stay with Shelby."

Gibson finds my eyes and holds my gaze for a few beats, grins, then walks out into the night without another word.

I breathe hard, relieved.

A goodbye would mean he expects me to leave.

There is a smooth whiteness above me and the softest, roundest embrace beneath me. It's a couch. Brown. So soft.

Seconds or minutes or hours have passed. It's hard to tell, and I'm surprised to find I don't really care. I turn my head and look through the enormous window, beyond a patio, to the dark, expansive Pacific Ocean in the distance, rippling under a star-crusted sky. My belly is warm and a comfortable ache stretches across my ribs where too much food slumbers, contented.

"That meal sent you straight into a nap." Jaclyn's voice drifts to me from the chair across from me. "You had quite an appetite."

"Yeah." I pull a couch cushion over my middle and hug it tight. "I saw you have soap next to the kitchen sink. Would it be all right if I washed my hands and face?"

"I have a better idea." She stands. "Let's get you into a warm bubble bath and find some clean clothes for you to wear."

I haven't been in a bathtub since we lived in a real house on base with Daddy. One of my favorite sounds in the world is the plink-plink-plink of tiny soap bubbles popping on my bare skin. When I was little, I would lock the bathroom door and stay in the tub for hours, refilling it with warm water. My parents never bothered to check on me. I'd hear them arguing with one another, then either slamming doors and breaking things or falling into bed together. I silenced their riot by tuning in to the bubbles' little song, plink-plink-plink, my naked body cloaked in a sky of clouds.

I allow Jaclyn to take my hand, and she leads me to her bedroom and slides open a large dresser drawer.

"If you don't mind borrowing tonight?" She offers me a nightdress.

I caress the light, plush fabric between my fingers. "Thank you," I say, wishing I never had to give it back.

She then opens a closet as big as Mom's bedroom and disappears into it, talking to me over her shoulder. "We can go to the mall tomorrow and find some things just for you. Age appropriate, your style."

I nod behind her, silent. I can't even picture what I would choose if I had any money. I haven't worn anything other than Mom's "professional showgirl" get-ups since I was fifteen. My "style" is nonexistent. If I play along, go to the mall with my counselor (which may or may not be more desirable than going with, say, a parole officer, a cult leader, or my own mother), and she gets all charitable and offers to pay, then I'll owe her. I don't want to be like Mom, who always seems to owe someone something.

"Will these do?" Jaclyn returns, holding out neatly pressed chinos and a simple white blouse.

I haven't worn a pair of pants in years.

I know I should be grateful. These are clean clothes, and I don't have to sneak out with them. Jaclyn is willing to share.

But the outfit is so plain, I wonder if she is hoping my first step toward "normal" will be to fade into the crowd, become just another grain of sand on the beach of humankind. I lean forward to take the clothing from the hand that feeds and lose my balance. I fall, my bare knees grazing the high-pile carpet, which is the color of buttered rolls.

"You're exhausted," she says, rushing to help me up.

More than anything, I'm confused. I want to thank her but I'm terrified of the inevitable catch. I've only been here one evening and I've already racked up a gigantic tab.

"I'll show you where you can have your bath and get some rest now, Shelby. You'll have the most privacy if you use the guesthouse."

She leads me back through the house, out a glass door that opens on a courtyard, and along a little flower-lined path to a small cottage. She unlocks the door and waves me in.

Inside is a giant bed, a dresser, a closet, even a bathroom. A sliding door overlooks a pool so still and calm that for a moment I too am still and calm.

"Until we're able to find you work and your own accommodations," she says, "you are welcome to stay here."

My breath leaves me and I can no longer speak. I lock my feet, fighting the desire to jump onto the massive bed and run around in circles, giggling maniacally like some crazy person.

I ought to tell her thanks, but I don't know why she's doing this. I need to figure her out first. This was Gibson's idea, after all. Jaclyn didn't even want me here.

It's nearly three in the morning when I wake up, unsure where I am or what day it is. Across the pool, I spot Jaclyn through the glass windows, sitting on the couch with a glass of wine. It's weird, but seeing her there reminds me of Mom. I tiptoe along the flowered path to the main house and tap on the glass door. Before she rises from her seat I try the handle and, finding it unlocked, open the door and poke my head inside. "Um, how's it going?"

"Shelby, you're not sleeping? Do you need anything?"

"I'm okay," I stammer as I close the door behind me.

"I was just waiting for Roland," she explains. "It's not like him to be so late."

I try to act casual, taking a seat next to her on the brown velvet sectional. There ought to be an exhibit in some history museum chronicling women through the ages waiting for their guys' return from the hunt, the war, the high sea, or the local pub—each cooling her heels in the dwelling place of her time and culture. Some at the forefront of their wait, outrage mounting with every minute past his expected arrival, others listless from months of pious patience that's trickling ever drier.

She wouldn't wait if she didn't favor that one man's embrace over all others. She wouldn't charge him with probable infidelity if his promise of faithfulness meant little to her. And she wouldn't sap hours fabricating his horrific appointments with harm if her belief in his devotion had not guaranteed his return at the expected hour.

"You'd probably sleep a lot better if you could control his every move," I suggest, borrowing an old line Dad used to use on Mom. I immediately regret it. Too bold. The woman has given me a bed, a real bed, for the night. I should have stayed in it. With my mouth shut.

Jaclyn is startled but not wounded. She eyes me for a few seconds, thinking. "I guess I'm upset because he can simply rearrange his schedule in the morning if he decides to sleep late."

I say nothing, my eyes wide. I didn't know she was upset. Mom's anger is like a tornado, dark and windy, picking up and throwing anything not bolted to the ground. Even if I duck out when I see it coming, the debris that her upset leaves behind is always a bigger mess than the storm itself. Jaclyn's anger is invisible, at least to me.

I'm still at a loss for something to say when the front door opens and Gibson pads in. "I didn't expect to find you two up," he says, glowing red above his white collar and grinning triumphantly. He saunters over to the sofa and plants a wet kiss on Jaclyn's cheek. "I have some news. Let's have a toast."

Mom would have unleashed her fury by now, but Jaclyn just looks relieved to have him home and says all of nothing.

Gibson hands me a bottled water, grabs a glass, and helps himself to some of Jaclyn's wine. Turning to us, he raises his glass "to the Society of Clinical Psychology," tipping it back for what is clearly not the first time this evening. "I beat out Elliott for the award of Distinguished Professional Contributions to Clinical Psychology this evening, primarily for my work with Ashtynn Kingston."

I look at Jaclyn. Her cheeks are pale.

It never occurred to me that white-coats use their patients to stoke their egos.

"Congratulations, honey, that's wonderful." Jaclyn's lilt hits a flat note, and she swallows the remainder of her drink. "Of course they recognize a therapist's efforts when his patient is world-famous," she mumbles, her lips pressed against the rim of her glass.

"Who's Elliott?" I ask.

"Elliott Rachman is Roland's partner," Jaclyn explains. "He's a psychiatrist."

Gibson's eyebrows pinch in the middle. "What did you mean by that, Jaclyn?"

She ignores him. "Shelby, are you familiar with the young performer Ashtynn Kingston?"

I've always liked Ashtynn Kingston's voice, even more so since I found out we've both had plenty of white-coat interference.

"Her struggles with drug addiction were unfortunately leaked to the public and, as a result, her recovery became a media feeding frenzy. Roland stepped in as her doctor and helped her on her journey to sobriety."

I remember when a radio DJ announced that she had been found unconscious and bleeding from a self-cutting ritual while using hallucinogens. Dad tried the same thing. He could never tell us exactly what his platoon did in Afghanistan, but souvenirs of every tour of duty returned with him, locked inside his head like a cargo container he couldn't unload. He tried everything he could to release them, including shooting it open. Even though I'd never met her, it gave me tremendous relief when Ashtynn regained consciousness.

So it was Gibson who put her back on the radio waves, sober, with a new hit record? News reports gushed about the amber-colored script she tattooed along the shadow of her scarred inner arms: *Si tamen acta deos numquam mortalia fallunt, a culpa facinus scitis abesse mea*—"Yet if mortal actions never deceive the gods, you know that crime was absent from my fault." She lifted the quote from Ovid's *Tristia*, going for a dramatic parallel between her time away from Hollywood and Ovid's exile from Rome. Following her reincarnation, fans everywhere quickly etched similar ink.

I figure Ashtynn and I would probably really get each other.

Or not. Everything she sings about is sweetly preserved and unharmed, like her heart's never been poisoned.

"It's really cool you helped her like that," I offer.

No one says anything, and for an instant I'm embarrassed. I don't have much experience as a houseguest. Or conversationalist.

"I can see it now," I say teasingly, hoping to lighten the mood, "a mile-long lineup of pop stars with dirty little secrets knocking at your office door."

"That's not far from the fact," Jaclyn says, setting down her glass. "Roland's clients use one fistful of money to engage in their undoing and the other to buy their way out."

Roland steps to the bar and places his glass down as firmly as possible without shattering it. The toast is over, that's for sure.

He turns to Jaclyn and, clearly fighting to keep his voice steady, says, "I'm proud of my achievement, Jaclyn. I hope you can be happy for me. For us."

"What holds greater value," she asks, "your ability to transform the lives of your patients or the fame you earn in the process?"

"I resent that. My aim for every patient is holistic, lasting recovery."

"Funny, mine is too," Jaclyn says. "But all I get are pay cuts."

"What if you quit the hospital and worked with Gib—uh, Roland?" I ask. Seems obvious.

"We share a practice," Roland frowns, unraveling his tie. "But Jaclyn prefers martyrdom."

## CHAPTER EIGHT

I pull my still-new Ferrari 458 Spider to a stop in front of Gibson's house, then glance at the street number to confirm the address. I expected a sweeter joint, something more palatial. Decent view of the ocean, though.

I got one, only one night out with my girlfriend, and the bastard stole it from me. After Ash's little gotta-go show at the restaurant, I followed her back to her place like a sucker. She kicked me to the curb, told me she really was having an emergency session.

I knock at the front entrance, carved wood, just like at his Beverly Hills office. When the door finally opens, I'm surprised to find a lovely woman around Roland's age smiling up at me, brushing a strand of hair the color of black coffee out of her eyes.

"Zac Wyatt." She recognizes me instantly. "I didn't know Roland was expecting you. Come in, please."

I nod and smile, looking her up and down in her clingy yoga pants and tight tank, waiting for more information.

"I'm Jaclyn Spenser, Roland's wife," she says, extending her hand.

"A pleasure to meet you," I say, meeting her eye as I grasp her hand.

Jaclyn's warm welcome makes the house a little homier, and as always, I'm glad as fuck I came prepared. I offer her an exquisitely wrapped box of Mexican hot chocolate truffles, and she seems genuinely delighted.

Showing up with a gift has become such a habit for me that even when my intentions are anything but generous, such as today, I never arrive empty-handed.

"Roland," Jaclyn calls toward the back of the house, "Mr. Wyatt is here to see you." She shows me to the living room. "Please, have a seat."

I grab a comfortable-looking chair near a large glass wall overlooking an enclosed courtyard with a pool.

"Be there in a moment," Gibson replies from behind a door.

As Jaclyn's delicate fingers go to work on the truffles' fancy wrap I make small talk about the LA chocolatier, nearly famous in his own right, and scan the room. The house is comfortable, on the minimalist side but lived in. Luxurious, with studied self-control.

The glass door leading to the courtyard opens and who should walk in but Little Silver Shoes.

I almost don't recognize her.

"Zac?" Her lips hint at a smile. "Hi."

I'm speechless. I glance to Jaclyn for some explanation. When none is forthcoming, my gaze darts back to Shelby Rey. I finally stand up and offer her a congenial hug and kiss on the cheek, the same way I'd greet any female friend. But she's not just any female, and I hate being caught off guard.

"You two know each other?" Jaclyn doesn't hide her surprise.

"Yeah, we go way back," I reply. It's none of her business.

I've wondered how or when Shelby and I might run into each other again. Maybe at some club or a private house party. LA is an interdependent microcosm. Undoubtedly, we have a few acquaintances in common. I've pictured how I might approach her when we cross paths, how I'd get her apart from the crowd, pick up where we left off.

And here she is, like an apparition, at Gibson's house of all places. Her hot club clothes have been replaced by the uber-bland: a plain shirt and shapeless pants as tedious and conventional as table salt and paper bags. I've heard about this sort of setup, some self-appointed guru demanding that those who follow him withdraw completely from individual freedoms.

Damn, I can't believe Gibson's running an under-the-radar rehab resort when I'm not even supposed to call him unless I have an "emergency."

This is bullshit. I was promised treatment. I'm supposed to be his primary client. I don't want to blow my chance to talk with Shelby, but I'm ready to kick the fucking walls in. What the hell is going on?

"Zac?" Gibson appears at last. "I'm surprised to find you here," he adds, "at my home."

He ought to be used to seeing patients in his own bloody living room on a Sunday. What's the cover charge to join your psycho-cult, Doc? Where do I get fitted for my chinos and button-down?

"Here I was worried I'd find you snoring off last night's home-visit session." I try to compose myself; I know sarcasm puts people on the defensive, but hell if I can't help myself. "I didn't realize you offered a residential program." I nod toward Shelby.

"This is our houseguest, Shelby." He says the word "houseguest" with deliberation. "Shelby, this is Zac."

"I met him outside your office," she tosses out casually like it wasn't any major event.

Gibson's eyebrows lift in surprise.

"It's good to see you, Shel." I hope using a nickname will help bypass some small talk and make her feel more familiar with me.

"Your voice is so warm, like a blanket of stars putting the sky to bed," she says, cupping her ears as if she imagined me singing through invisible headphones. "It feels good inside."

I can't help but grin.

"You're familiar with Mr. Wyatt's band, Grounder?" Gibson asks.

"Grr-ou-nn-der," she repeats, slowly savoring the word over four full syllables. "Right, that's where I've heard your voice." She steps closer to me, looking up into my face. I watch her pupils blossom wide open as she drinks me in. A flush of pink appears within the confines of her starched, white blouse, and my body stiffens.

"Thank you for giving me your lyrics when my own words wouldn't come," she nearly whispers.

I've never wished Stanford's lyrics were my own more than right now.

I drag my attention back to the matters at hand. I'm not leaving until I get answers about Gibson's visit with Ash last night, why Shelby is living here, and what to do about the music that is churning and scorching a ragged hole through my center.

I'm not leaving until I figure out how I can see Shelby alone.

"It's been a long drive. Mind if I make myself at home?" Determined to get what I came for, I swallow hard, tear myself away from Shelby, and cruise over to a giant, chocolate-colored sectional. I flop down on it and lounge out, taking as much room as possible without pissing off the wife.

"Is there something you'd like to discuss that can't wait until we're able to meet in my office?" Gibson doesn't hide his irritation. "It's highly unorthodox for you to show up at my home unannounced. Like you, I'm entitled to my privacy, and I have a busy schedule. Is this not something we already discussed?"

"I don't know what's got you all worked up, Doc. You do sessions around the clock. House calls are your specialty, as I understand. You put a lot of miles on that Audi R8 I saw parked in your driveway?" I ask, pointing my thumb over my shoulder in the sports car's general direction. "Nice ride. I had it a few years back."

Shelby grabs a seat next to me. I instantly sense the warmth of her presence and turn to connect with her melting-icicle-on-a-sunny-day eyes. But it isn't me she's sidling up to, it's the headphone wires dangling from my Tumi bag. Fuck, he's got her on lockdown. She probably hasn't made contact with the virtual, aural, or actual world since she got here. What is this, the apocalypse?

I pull my MP3 player out and offer it like a piece of candy, staring Gibson in the eyes as I do, daring him to object. She only hesitates for an instant before snatching it from me and stuffing the buds in her starving ears.

But then she turns the case over, like she's forgotten how to operate anything beginning with "i."

I caress the back of her hand as I help her hit play. Her ears must be her ignition. The liquid platinum pools of her eyes nearly combust at first riff. I want to hold her gaze as long as possible, but the music wins.

"I'll get out of your way, Roland," Shelby whispers to Gibson and backs away with my music, returning to the glass door from which she first appeared. I want to leap off the couch and follow her, but I'm stunned as shit. She called him by his first name.

Certain privileges are afforded to a celebrity, but around this guy, I don't qualify for special treatment. Roland Gibson isn't a Hollywood puppet master, but his practice is sanctuary to a good number of them. I'm afraid I might have to gauge my future by the way the bastard's handling me.

I'm near boiling, and I'm no longer sure whether it's rage or embarrassment. I keep my ass on the couch, afraid that if I take a step I may trip over the cliff of my career into a dark abyss with no visible bottom.

"Extending your music to Ms. Rey like that—"

"The girl clearly needs her tunes, man."

"Quite right." Gibson surprises me with a smile. He glances sidelong out the window, appraising the effect my music's having on her, then returns his attention to me. "Can we come to an understanding that from this day forward, we agree on all appointments, both the time and setting?"

I nod without looking his way, preferring to watch Shelby through the window.

"I'll be sure she returns your headphones before you leave," he says, misunderstanding my interest in her movements.

"Yeah, don't worry about it."

He expects me to take back her only connection to the outside world? If I'd known she was here, I would have brought something for her. If I'd known an MP3 player would make her happy, I would have created a better playlist.

Jaclyn gestures toward the burst of electricity rocking out poolside. "Best medicine," she says with a grin before excusing herself to her yoga class.

Roland leans in to kiss her cheek as she leaves, and I grab the moment to text my stylist, Dion, asking her to send Little Silver Shoes a designer trunk of clothing in size teeny-tiny. Shelby's probably mourning the loss of her closet as much as she is her music. You don't cover up a girl that fine with just anything.

Roland grabs two bottles of water from the bar, offers me one, and slides onto the couch next to me.

"How many bedrooms in this place? Three, four?" I ask, staking the joint. Pretty intimate therapeutic setting. I like my space, but a facility like this would keep a man near elbow-to-elbow with Shelby.

"Four, plus the pool house," he replies, stroking his chin.

Shelby is dancing her ass off out there on the deck, wearing my headphones. Her face is contorted by bliss, an "O" face if I ever saw one, as she throws back her sun-bleached mane and shimmies and twists around the pool. Her loose hair catches rays of sun, like sequins reflecting light in a nightclub.

"Your wife's right. Forget pharmaceuticals and talk therapy, Shelby's found the cure for whatever ails her."

We catch each other's eye, and he nods with a grin but says nothing. I appreciate that. I would like him to offer up a bit of info about her, no doubt. But I also hope he'll do the right thing and maintain patient confidentiality. I hate it, but I need him to be the real deal, a shrink I can trust. Not just for my own pathetic problems but for Shelby, too.

And Ashtynn. Jesus, I forget about her when I think of Shelby. But there's not much else I can think about right this minute.

When Roland gives Shelby the gold star of sobriety, I'm taking her dancing. But not to any club. Somewhere we can let go, just the two of us, under the carnival of light at sunrise. Maybe brunch after. Maybe breakfast in bed.

"My partner, Dr. Rachman, offers therapeutic home visits," Gibson volunteers, interrupting my thoughts. "Jaclyn is a firm believer in them too. But I've never engaged in them with my patients."

"Your wife's a shrink?"

"Licensed Clinical Social Worker for St. Cecilia Hospital here in Orange County."

My mind flashes to her name, etched above Gibson's outside his Laguna Beach office. "So taking in your prettiest little patient was her idea?" I ask, my voice dripping with sarcasm.

"Choosing to alter set negative behaviors requires an enormous shift. It's often the hardest work patients will ever undergo. Providing a familiar, safe environment away from the negative habits is part of the process. That's why I insist on office appointments. Or in more serious cases, a rehabilitation facility, where we can meet in a neutral setting."

"It's not 'neutral.' It's your turf. You have the upper hand."

"It's a neutral space for the patient, Zac. We meet as seeker and facilitator. Our contributions may differ, but you and I share the same goals."

I'd like to believe him, but I highly doubt he's as tortured over my "goals" as I am.

"Some fancy talk for a shrink with a patient living at his house. When do I get the invite to sleep over?"

"Zac, I'm unable to confirm whether my houseguest is, or isn't, my patient."

Stubborn bastard, I'm kind of growing to like him. Hell, if I could choose only one person to bring home, I'd pick Shelby too.

"I've known Elliott to do wee-hour meetings, and frankly, all it leads to is an increasingly demanding client." Gibson chuckles to himself. "Elliott says he loves the 'randomness' of it. Our higher-profile clients have requested therapy in the most unusual locations." He shoots me a wry look. "He plans to write a book one day about the wildest places he's set up shop."

I don't like how he's steering the topic from Shelby, but damn it, I'm enjoying the insider gossip.

He sits back, pulls a long sip from his water bottle, and glances at me with a mischievous grin. "Who am I kidding, it would probably be a bestseller."

"Yeah." I laugh with him. "He should call it *Whereva Da Money At.*"

Watching Shelby abandon every ounce of whatever was weighing her down and dance like the music has faded the world into a distant dream has us both in a better mood. Best time to strike is when his guard's down.

"Are you fucking Ashtynn?" It never hurts to ask.

Gibson's laugh fades, his face clouding with concern. "Good God, Zac," he rasps, seemingly disturbed by the idea. "She was seventeen when I began treating her, with the undeveloped prefrontal cortex of an adolescent."

Christ, if he is sleeping with her, that kind of "she's just a baby" shit will drive her to homicide. God help the man.

"Let me make this clear for you: I don't cheat on my wife."

I've gotten under his skin. He sounds pretty sincere.

Satisfied, I lean back on the sectional, making myself at home. It's my turn to change the topic. "Our manager, Berger, is arranging for TV ads leading up to the Choice America Music Awards in mid-July. We'll be performing Grounder's newest song, written by yours truly."

"Good for you, Zac," he replies, still shaken from my accusation. I don't mind putting a dent in his composure. "Nothing like having a deadline to put a fire under you. How is your song coming on? What is it about?"

"Yeah, let's hope I have as much songwriting talent as I do swagger, right? Or 'ego,' I suppose you might say." I wink at him, pretending I haven't just ignored his questions.

"Indeed. So, have you begun writing?"

"No." My eyes follow a long, auburn beam in the hardwood floor, avoiding his gaze. "I mean, I've tried, but everything comes out all whiny. I don't want to sound like a bitch."

Gibson narrows his eyes. "'Whiny' is an interesting choice of word. Sometimes, we revert to a more immature response when confronted with an issue that makes us feel vulnerable. Are you writing about something that is a touchy subject for you?"

"Nah. I'm just not in a position to complain, you know what I'm saying?"

"Why must your lyrics include a complaint? Can you elaborate?"

"It's complicated." There are so many sides to the same damn coin, and it all amounts to me not having one useful thing to say about anything.

I get up and pace, partly to burn this jacked-up mess of doubt, but mostly to see where Little Silver Shoes has disappeared to.

Just as I reach the window I spot her closing the large glass slider to the poolside guesthouse. So that's where she's holed up. Good to know.

"I've got some bad news for you, Doc." I turn and flash him a smile. "There's nothing about me you need to fix. That's the problem: sweet life. I had a great childhood, my parents are still married, and they think my singing voice is a 'gift from God.' I earned a scholarship to study music, for Christ's sake."

How the hell can I write about having everything handed to me on a fucking platter? Maybe I should go rap, boast about the cars I drive and the girls I bang?

Hardly. "Ain't Got No Street Cred" would have to be the title of my first song.

"I can't even sing the blues about not finishing college. I dropped out because Grounder hit platinum with our debut release."

Did I just moan about the best thing that ever happened to me?

And then there's Ash. After our dinner last night, I tried some lyrics about the gulch of apathy we call a relationship. But who the hell am I to complain when my woman is a gorgeous fucking superstar? Besides, I can't say one negative word about her when I might headline an OmniMotion flick as her love interest. It wouldn't be fair to her, and OmniMotion would be pissed. I suppose I could sing about the tough decision of whether to take a gamble on my own music or stay in our half-relationship and sell my soul to movie stardom, but what punk-ass fool whines about whether or not to star in a major motion picture?

## THE SECRET SONG OF SHELBY REY

"Your humility and self-awareness impress me," Roland says. I stare at him. Is he shitting me?

"You're leading a charmed life, and a closely examined one at that." He presses his palms together. "It's a lot of pressure."

I let out a long breath and return to my seat on the couch. "I have to write, rehearse, and perform a new song—live—in front of millions of people worldwide in six weeks. What the hell am I going to do?"

"First, I'd like to thank you for doing your homework. I asked you to explore your life stories for material, and I think we learned something from that exercise."

"What? I ought to call and thank Mom and Dad?"

"It's time to release yourself from the imprisonment of self-image, Zac. Remove your focus from the external. Give yourself permission to explore your own truth."

"I just told you my 'truth.' I haven't suffered. My problems and concerns are superficial at best, and I don't want to write anything hollow or pointless. I want to create something with a pulse a person can recognize as their own."

"Good!" he almost shouts. "Then you must confront yourself as an eternal being, part of the universe, a person with a function, a purpose, and a unique spirit."

"Don't go all Deepak on me, man."

Gibson squares himself to me but says nothing. He's waiting for me to offer something more than sarcasm, but I'm pretty sure I can take him in the waiting game. I fold my arms in silent refusal, and the whole scene gives me déjà vu, like he's my father.

I hate that I'm acting like a stubborn brat.

"Let's back up a little," I tell him. "If I learned anything 'exploring my life stories,' it's that I don't even know what music genre represents who I am. I'm drawn to so many, and I don't want to be pinned down or typecast."

Gibson seems skeptical.

"I'm serious," I insist. "There was a moment when I even considered rap." Like thirty seconds ago, but he doesn't have to know that.

"It's all right to embrace different styles of music, isn't it?" he asks. "It's like trying a new food. You may discover some new dishes, but you still enjoy your favorites. Each preference sheds light on who you are, your individual style."

"I haven't got time to check out new dishes, don't you get it? I should be rehearsing a completed song, and I've got all of nothing."

"Tell me about the songwriting process."

"Well, for Grounder, it's all on Stanford. He sits down with his guitar and just starts strumming, teasing the strings until he finds a pattern. He toys with a repetition, tweaking and testing it. He plays the pattern in a different chord, tries a variety of tempos, and all the while, words fall from his tongue, like the lyrics and melody are old friends meeting on a street corner. They start slowly, but before long the words and melody weave together stories from their shared past. Boom, there's the original draft of a song. He presents it to me, Oslo, and Deshi and we flesh it out, put meat on its bones."

Roland nods and places his hand on my shoulder.

"And Stanford, that fucker, is high from start to finish." I can't do this shit sober.

"You should know that heroin addicts endure periods of overwhelming depression," Gibson says. "If he continues on his chosen path, there are some dark days ahead for Mr. Lysandre. Your commitment to writing new music couldn't be better timed. Stanford and your other bandmates will benefit from the effort you're making now."

"We already have enough trouble with the bastard blowing rehearsal half the time." I shake my head.

"The way you described Stanford's writing style sounded like a song in itself, you know."

"I suppose. The way he does it is messy. But beautiful, too." I don't like sounding like some jealous chump, but I wish it came as easily for me. I hate Stanford.

I hate him.

But this is my time with Gibson, my session. I'm not giving it up to discuss the entirely unjustifiably inspired musical stylings of Señor Scag.

"Stop doubting yourself, Zac, and you'll have a much more positive attitude toward your creative process, which in turn will influence the outcome," Roland assures me.

"There was a German composer, Richard Strauss," Shelby interrupts us. "He bragged he could describe a knife and fork using only music. No big thing, that's all music is."

How did she slip in without us noticing? And how much did she hear me say?

"Ms. Rey, if you'll kindly excuse us? This is a private discussion." Gibson is gentle but seemingly no less ruffled by her soundless arrival than I am.

"Nah, it's fine. Have a seat," I pipe up, overriding him. "I'd like to hear Shel's take on Strauss."

And I want her to hang around awhile.

"I take it your parents stuck you in a piano conservatory when you were a kid?"

Shelby just blinks at me. Why does everything I say to her come out altogether lame?

"I heard it on non-profit radio," she clarifies.

"Strauss sought to tell stories in graphic detail," Gibson interjects, nodding. "He called them tone poems. Shelby, I didn't know you're a fan of classical music."

"You might as well ask whether I like vowels. Without them, we can't make words," she replies. "Music is the language of every person on the planet, and it all boils down to the same thing."

"Yeah, I get you," I say. "Arrange a handful of notes in various durations, pitches, and rhythm combinations and it becomes its own language, a conversation between the performer and the listener. Music isn't a fixed thing."

"No." She isn't the least impressed by me. "It is clearer than any words. Words can be misunderstood, used against you, or thrown back in your face. Not music. I always understand music. It's the only thing I trust, and the only people who can know me are people who trust it too."

I want to grab her and hold her, tell her she can trust me.

"Shelby, have you heard Strauss's tone poem 'Death and Transfiguration'?" Gibson is keeping the conversation up when he would be wiser to give us time alone, damn it. "It describes a man on his deathbed suffering agonizing pain. He recalls fond memories and regrets the dreams he failed to realize during his lifetime. When he finally gives up his soul to the eternal, he discovers the fulfillment of the ideals he was never able to accomplish on earth."

I'm sure as hell not waiting until I die to score my biggest dream.

"Music surpasses our knowledge," Dr. G. drones on, "taking us to a place of understanding and belief."

Shelby moves closer, looking pleased to be heard and understood.

All I know is, I've found my muse.

"Everything you ever wished you could say, music explains it," she says like it's her religion. "Like when you wake up and try to retell the craziest dream you just had, and you just can't get enough words in the right order to make a picture of everything that happened. Music knows how to do that."

Shelby is staring at Roland. Roland is watching Shelby. Hell, what breathing man could take his eyes off her?

I'm grateful for the diversion, really. We'd probably still be arguing about my "place in the universe" or some shit if I hadn't invited her to grab a seat.

But I'm still the client on the clock. While I may not have anything to add to this hoity-toity classical music bullshit, I've got something not many can claim: millions of screaming fans who worship me.

"Gibson, I've got a show coming up in LA and you're going to be there," I say, my voice a little too loud, but who cares. "I'll have a VIP package sent over. It's time you got up close and personal with me and Grounder."

A backstage pass to the sold-out concert of the year ought to remind him who he's dealing with.

Until then, I need to figure out a way to get Little Silver Shoes to help me come up with an idea for a song that will rock the Choice America Music Awards.

And annihilate all my dependence on Stanford Lysandre.

## CHAPTER NINE

SHELBY

It must have been fifth grade when my class took a field trip to the zoo, because we were living in South Carolina, and I remember the zoo was near Fort Jackson. I'd kind of expected it to look like a scene from a *Curious George* book, each animal in a black metal cage, a sign attached to a guardrail noting its country of origin. I had the sign part right, but I was surprised to find them roaming free just beyond a low wall, the sky above as unboxed to them as it was to me. I wondered why they didn't break out, roam into downtown Columbia, or make a home for themselves in the woods beyond the outskirts of town.

I could pack up Zac Wyatt's headphones, walk out the door of Gibson's pool house, and catch the first bus I find on Pacific Coast Highway. Right now.

I should, too, before Jaclyn and Roland drop me at a psych ward. Not knowing when they'll get the whim to cart me off is worse than living with Mom.

But Jaclyn said she wouldn't "force" me to "make good choices." I'll at least hang on until I find out what choices I even have.

## THE SECRET SONG OF SHELBY REY

An odd contraption on the table next to the bed catches my eye when I roll under the lavender-scented sheets and stretch. I'm used to waking up bent and achy from the sagging springs of Mom's couch. I'm going to get myself a bed like this one day.

I examine the shiny black box, expecting to see the time flashing. No luck, it's not a clock. It must be some kind of psychiatric—what's the word?—apparatus.

Getting the hell out of here to God knows where is starting to look a whole lot better than this zoo enclosure's version of "Press the button, get the pellet." I pull on the box's cover and turn it over, searching for some clue to its purpose. Is it supposed to test my blood? Pump a pharmaceutical cocktail into my veins? Does it shoot electrodes into my skin, and will I be conscious or unconscious when it does?

The quiver of violins in my chest speeds from adagio to allegro so quickly I cough a little from the pressure.

Jaclyn taps a light knock and opens the large glass door overlooking the pool. "Barely awake, and you want to hear some music."

When I cock a brow, she nods at the curved, black, plastic machine. She lets herself in, sets down a cup of coffee, and reaches to the bedside table for the MP3 player Zac Wyatt left with me yesterday.

The second she picks it up I pluck it out of her hand, jerking it away from her and clutching it to me with both hands under the blankets. I don't give an arctic monkey about that machine, I'll do whatever's necessary to keep this music.

"I'm sorry," she says casually.

She doesn't get it. The MP3 player is salvation to me.

"When you're ready, you can place the music player into this dock. It's a small amp, but we've been satisfied with the sound quality. I hope you'll enjoy it too."

I glance back and forth between her and the strange black machine. She runs her finger along the place where the player fits. It does seem about the same width as the MP3 player. I'll try it as soon as I can get rid of her.

But she's not done yet.

"We have some work to do today, young lady." She smiles and takes a seat next to me on the bed. I draw the sheets tighter around me to squelch the reappearance of her social worker voice. "I received the test results from your physical, and it's just as I suspected. You have celiac disease. If we place you on a gluten-free diet, I'm confident you'll minimize your stomach issues."

"Sealy-what?" I can't help but ask, one eye peeking at her from under the covers.

"Celiac, a chronic digestive disorder. Damage to the lining of your small intestine causes malabsorption of minerals and nutrients. Gluten, a protein found in wheat, rye, and barley, is the culprit. It's the reason for all your stomach troubles, Shelby."

I duck back under the covers. Mom used to bring home leftover hot sandwiches from her club, and sometimes I get lucky in the dumpsters behind fancy restaurants. I've never been in a position to check ingredients.

"Let's spend the day together, what do you say?" Jaclyn changes gear. "We'll hit the mall first. We'll find some clothes, and—"

I groan, pulling a pillow over my head and burying myself deeper in the blankets. This is all too surreal. I don't remember the last time Mom was awake before me, let alone chirping from my bedside about a mother–daughter outing she'd planned for the two of us. I have all the mother I need and then some, thanks anyway.

"All right then, how about we start simply. Just the basic necessities."

I might have been willing to play along if Jaclyn's offer hung from her authentic-speaking voice and didn't sound like a calculated therapy setup. I'm trapped in a minimum-security *Twilight Zone* after-school movie.

## THE SECRET SONG OF SHELBY REY

"Can we at least agree on a pair of shoes? I notice you've been going barefoot."

I'm silent. I haven't worn Mom's stilettos since I arrived. I just can't. I know better than to try pairing them with the hokey-ass chinos, but more than that I'm afraid if I wear them, they'll transport me home to my own craptastic version of Dorothy's Kansas. *There's no place like home.* That's why I'm not going back.

Her tone remains hopeful. "You'll want to look your best when interviewing for work."

I can't accept anything else from Jaclyn. I already owe her more than I ever expect to be able to repay. I can't walk a mile in her shoes any more than I can in Mom's.

Wait. Did she say *work*?

I wait a minute or two to make sure she doesn't shoot me with any more bullets, like, "Guess what? Your mom's here." Or, worse, "Zac wants his music back."

Jaclyn stands up to go. "Don't let your coffee get cold," she says, clinging dismally to her cheery voice before sliding the door shut behind her.

I edge over to the bedside table and place Zac's slim music player into the black machine. The small screen lights up, revealing thousands of songs, many by bands I rarely, if ever, hear on the radio. I'm hoping there's some button on it that can record everything before he asks me to give it back. I suppose I could lie and tell him I lost it.

Except I can't lie to him any more than he could lie to me. Grounder's music courses through my veins.

Listening to song after song without having to wait through commercials or static or pointless chatter is luxurious, miraculous. Zac's collection of recorded music frees me from narrow-minded DJs playing a handful of songs on repeat.

Music pours from the black box. I find myself floating out of the bed, transported by its waves.

As I'm gyrating around the bed to the music, I spot the hat of a delivery guy just over the bamboo hedge on the other side of the pool.

A few moments later, Jaclyn rushes over to the living room window, makes eye contact with me from across the way, and gestures for me to come.

I'm in no hurry. I've had my share of deliveries—the reports a social worker has come to file on official business, the time the military arrived to tell me my father was dead (like I hadn't seen it myself), the visits from Mom's dealers. I have everything I need right here, thanks.

But Jaclyn's gestures become more frantic, impossible to ignore. I hit the pause button and drag myself to see what she wants.

A ginormous box with my name on it sits neatly near the front entrance. "Maybe your mother has sent a few of your belongings?" Jaclyn raises a brow. "Roland?" she calls out. "There's something here for you as well."

Roland wanders out of the kitchen clutching a bowl of cereal, and the delivery guy has him sign for a large envelope that arrived with my package.

I take a deep breath and glare at the box. Jaclyn has an irritating way of reminding me my life is a pointless heap. I'm at ground zero, with nothing left behind and zilch ahead. Jaclyn's so convinced of her own value, she'd probably reassure a pirate captain he could find her on the nearest deserted island as he shoved her off the plank. Even if I wanted to tell Mom where I was staying—and I don't—Jaclyn knows firsthand that I own nothing. Used to be next to nothing, but now that Dad's headphones are gone, truly nothing.

Jaclyn fishes around in a drawer in the foyer table, pulls out scissors, and offers them to me. I refuse them, taking small steps backward until I slide over the arm of a club chair. With my shrug of indifference as consent, Jaclyn begins carefully cutting the packing tape securing the box. She works it open, then picks up a note resting inside and hands it to me.

*For Shel. Cheer up.* —Zac

I get off my butt immediately and peer inside. The box contains piles of brand-new clothes: shirts, dresses, skirts, jackets, tees. Even underwear.

Just like his music player, the box holds an astonishing collection of styles. None of it boring, none of it plain. Each item seems to have a personality, something it wishes it could say.

"Shelby, wow." Jaclyn rubs at her forehead, glancing suspiciously between me and the gigantic box on the floor between us. "You can't accept this." She leans against the doorframe, an eyebrow raised, expecting me to agree.

"I can't?" I hope this doesn't have anything to do with gluten.

"This gift is too generous. Look at these designers. This clothing cost a fortune. Just how well do you know Zac Wyatt?"

"I don't, yet," I stammer. "But I know his music. It's a part of me."

"Oh dear, Shelby."

"From my observation," Roland interjects, "Zac was quite taken with Ms. Rey when he was here the other day."

He was?

"What do you mean, 'taken'?" Jaclyn asks.

"He's attracted, I think. And why shouldn't he be?" Roland bends a smile around another mouthful of cereal.

Yeah, why not, Jaclyn?

"They're similar in age and interests," he adds, swallowing. "When you consider Shelby's predilection for music appreciation and Zac's avocation as a performer, the two have some fundamental qualities in common."

Predilection? I don't know what that means, but I'm pretty sure it doesn't begin to describe my passion for music. More like obsession.

"I can see how Mr. Wyatt taking a romantic interest in you might be flattering," Jaclyn butts in again, "but you do understand this is an inappropriate gesture? It's far too extravagant. A gift such as this sends a message that he would like to" —she gestures with her hand as if I should fill in the blank, but I have no idea what she's getting at— "to expedite the natural pace of courtship." She looks frantically at Roland. "Can you back me up here?"

Roland glances at the box of clothes, then appraises my reaction. "Jaclyn, I'm sure I have no clue what it takes to impress a girl these days," he finally says. "But we can all agree Shelby needs clothes."

While he spoons in another bite of cereal, I don't waste any time digging into the treasure trove of the most beautiful clothes I've ever seen.

"If I'd had his means when I was his age, Jac, I would have loved to surprise you this way," Roland speculates, chewing. "Shock and awe, that's the way to get a woman to notice you."

Jaclyn drags him into the kitchen. "Shelby is in the process of establishing her sense of self," she says in a hushed tone. "Are we going to let this young man, one of your rehab patients, no less, have a part in defining her?"

"Is this about him being my patient or the extravagance of his gift?" Roland asks.

I edge to the doorway and peek inside in time to see Jaclyn cross her arms and start to open her mouth again.

"With Shelby under our roof, I think between the two of us, we can keep an eye on their 'pace of courtship,'" Roland says, cutting her off.

She lets him kiss her cheek, but I can tell she is still irked.

"Can we look at this from Shelby's point of view?" he tries to reassure her. "Besides, now you don't have to brave the mall."

"Oh, Roland. That's the worst part. I was hoping it would

be something she and I would do together. Something we could share."

I back away from the kitchen and return to the box before she can catch me spying on them.

Jaclyn marches in with conviction. "Shelby, exploring how you would like to present yourself and choosing clothes flattering to your figure and coloring, and hopefully a vision for your desired lifestyle requires a healthy personal awareness. You were denied these choices in the past. Wouldn't you prefer to select your own clothing? I can help you."

Leave it to a white-coat to turn clothes shopping into a miserable clinical assessment.

"Not really," I say, and pick up the box full of clothes. "I'm going to go try some of these on."

I'm beyond thankful to Zac. He rescued me and doesn't even know it.

I pull the curtains across the sliding glass doors in the pool house and block out Quasi-Mom and Dr. Detached. I place the box on the bed and remove each item carefully, my breath sweeping away from me in disbelief. "Cheer up," I whisper back to Zac.

I try everything on, repeatedly, while making my way through more than a third of Zac's enormous compilation of songs.

I'm delighted by all of it, the clothing and the music. I'm probably nearly drunk with relief. Perhaps that explains my uneasiness. Zac's spirit is with me, fierce and loud, through the wild variety of music he's chosen. There is a thread tying each song back to him, speaking his story. I can hear him, but I'm stumbling to find the connection between him and his band's music. I couldn't have gotten Grounder all wrong, could I?

Mom would say it's nothing but a matter of my hips betraying my heart.

More like the beat betraying my brain.

Maybe he's just pulling off the world's most commonplace illusion: presenting himself publicly one way to cover the truth of his private self. His truth is Grounder. I felt it long before my foot met his on the sidewalk.

I reach for the music player and scroll through tracks. As my fingers run the length of its face, I remember his hand on mine when he taught me how it operates. I heard it then, the rhythms and pounding beats so reminiscent of these many songs he's loaded onto this music player. So utterly separate and different from anything ever performed by Grounder.

My feet slide out from under me and I drop onto the bed, settling into the delicate mountain of fabrics. Who are you, Zac Wyatt?

My thoughts wander from Zac when my stomach gets the best of me and I decide to see what's in the kitchen. I peer at the main house from behind the curtain, using Zero Interference to plot my path.

Zero Interference is simple, really. I just shrink my presence, turn my inner anthem down low. If I can make my presence insignificant enough, other people rarely notice I'm even there.

Keeps me out of trouble.

As soon as I close the door to the main house behind me, I know I'm in luck. I smell baking, fresh baking. "There's a plate of chocolate-chip cookies on the counter, Shelby," Jaclyn calls from the kitchen when she hears the door. I wish I could be alone with the fridge. "They're gluten-free, so please help yourself. I hope they turned out okay."

I can't help but smile. Mom used to bake brownies, and cookies, and pecan tarts—Grandma's recipes. She did it for Dad. Those sweet treats bounced him right back into his own mother's kitchen. I would sneak the treats out of the freezer sometimes, carefully re-tucking the waxed paper lining inside the

Tupperware before putting it back where I found it, and nibble them on the way to school. But they always made my belly twist and turn, pulling my insides apart and leaving me little choice but to vomit. The school nurse complained, scolding Mom for feeding me "sugary junk," and after that she stopped baking altogether. To Dad, it was like Grandma had passed for a second time, but he never complained because Mom was only watching out for me. It's the one time I remember thinking, *She really loves me.*

Before I've finished one cookie, I grab a second, and then a third, still-warm chocolate smearing my fingers.

"Sometimes it makes sense to start with dessert." Jaclyn smiles.

I stop chewing. She's trying to Mom me up again. She complains about Zac buying my affections, then gives me "dessert first"? I swallow hard and put my fistful of cookies down on a napkin.

I know I ought to be polite. "If you don't mind, would it be all right if I had something else? Just crackers or whatever. I'm not picky."

Jaclyn launches into a lecture about simple and complex carbohydrates, like life's one giant buffet and I've been in the wrong line. Until this morning, I'd never even heard of celiac disease. I glance down at the cookies I abandoned on the napkin and shove an entire one in my mouth. I tune her voice out entirely when I spot the envelope that was delivered along with my box this morning.

I'm not the nosy type, just curious. I received a magic box from the most amazing boy in the universe. Did Roland get something from him too?

I'm staring, all but trying to manifest X-ray vision, when Jaclyn interrupts my concentration by placing a plate of weeds under my nose.

I squint at it. "Salad?"

"Fresh veggies. And homemade dressing, Roland's own recipe. Dig in, Shel."

I wish she wouldn't call me Shel. It's Zac's name for me; it's right on the note he sent this morning. But I take the fork she offers me and stare at my plate.

She wipes her hands on a kitchen towel, waiting expectantly. "It's nutritious. Eat."

I roll my eyes at her and take a bite. It is approximately a thousand times more delicious than it looks.

"How can this be so good?" I dig in hungrily.

Seemingly satisfied, she folds the towel neatly lengthwise and replaces it on a hook. "I have some reports to file this afternoon at the hospital. Will you be all right at home alone?"

I nod, my mouth full.

"All righty then." She fishes for keys in her purse. "I'll see you in a few hours. Roland should be home before me. Call me from the landline if you need anything."

After she goes, I listen carefully to the perimeter of the house, working in from all walls, listening for any sounds. When I'm sure I'm alone, I grab the envelope.

I'm not nosy, just curious.

Inside, I find a pair of lanyards attached to plastic-covered rectangles, a few pages with instructions, and a short note of invitation to Grounder's concert. Tonight. My heart begins to crescendo. They're both marked BACKSTAGE PASS in bold letters.

I shove everything back in the envelope and replace it on the counter, exactly how Jaclyn left it.

I could thank him for his help in person. I could hear him sing. In person.

Concert tickets don't come cheap, especially for Grounder. I looked into going once, only to learn a single ticket cost more than a month's worth of groceries for Mom and me. But here, right in front of me, is double the admission to see him. Touch him.

I mean, thank him.

Only low-life deadbeats steal. Everything I've ever cared about in my life has been taken from me, including Dad and his radio. I vowed ages ago never to steal a single thing, no matter how insignificant, from anyone.

But it would be rude if I didn't thank Zac.

Stealing from Jaclyn and Roland is a textbook move. It's why they lock us headcases, homeless headcases, away. They expect as much. But how long do I hope to be welcome here, anyway? It's only a matter of time until they throw me out on my ass. Do I really want to miss the one opportunity I'll ever have to see Grounder play live?

I need to get a job, my own place. A life. If I hang around here much longer, I'll only be trading one mother for another. And this one insists on everything being as complicated as is scientifically advisable.

Zac is all about action, seeing what needs to be done and making it happen. We've only spent a handful of minutes together, yet he immediately clued into what I need. I'd be better off taking cues from his playbook than trying to divine some meaning from Jaclyn's lectures. Zac's already arrived at his destination. He's my ticket to my own.

I'm useful to no one here. If I take a ticket, Jaclyn and Roland will have no choice but to kick me out.

I'm doing them a favor.

I emerge to street level from the Hollywood/Highland subway station and flow, shoulder to shoulder, with the mass of Grounder fans to the Hollywood Bowl. The crowd exchanges fantastic stories about the band, gossip they've heard. I'm not even freaked out by being surrounded by all these people. We're charged with the same excitement. We share the same dream of connecting with, and between, the music.

I'm pretty sure no one else is wearing clothing sent to them by Zac Wyatt.

From inside the Bowl, I can hear a familiar radio DJ's voice rise over us, welcoming Grounder to the stage. A flurry of whoops and claps rises from the crowd.

I'm not sure in what direction I should go with my stolen pass. Dodging hulking guys in security jackets at every turn, I search desperately for an unblocked entrance while straining to get a glimpse of Zac onstage. My lungs fill with the pounding roar of grinding guitars and thundering drums unseen beyond barricades and people.

A spray of colored light breaks through where a canvas drape is wedged open by a merchandise table. I kneel down and slide around it, into the concert. Without wasting a second, I work my way quickly toward the front row, hoping to slip backstage unnoticed.

I'm nearly running when an arm grabs me. I trip, and for a moment I'm falling head-first into thousands of feet jumping, kicking, and rocking out to the opening jam. Then the grip on my arm tightens and I snap upright, eye to eye with a giant.

Glancing at the hairy hand securing my arm, I'm horrified by the black grease I spot under every fingernail. It occurs to me suddenly that my clothes might only be on loan and must remain unharmed and unstained.

The security guy begins shaking me and asking my name, but I'm so paralyzed by the thought that Zac might ask for his MP3 player back too that I can't make my mouth work.

Everything good has an expiration date. Just ask my dead daddy.

"Let's go, Blondie. You're out." He yanks me so roughly I feel the not-quite-my-size-albeit-exquisite Manolo sandals drag along the ground. I refuse to replay my waltz with Officer O'Neill. I lost my headphones that way. I'm not losing my one and only chance to see Zac Wyatt perform live.

"Please, don't hurt this jacket. It was made by Paul McCartney's daughter," I beg him. "Zac Wyatt selected it especially for me," I add weakly.

"Yeah, I'll bet you and Wyatt are thick as thieves."

Why did he call me a thief? Can he tell my pass is stolen?

The guy stops jerking me when the backstage pass swings loose from within my jacket. He examines it doubtfully, then places me a step back and looks me over. "What the hell. You know all the pass-holders gotta stay in the designated press room backstage. Hey, Marshall," he calls out to another guy in a windbreaker with SECURITY emblazoned across the shoulders. "We got another 'personal friend of Mr. Wyatt' here."

Marshall snorts, checking me over with a lusty look. "Not much meat on the bone, but still good enough to eat," he replies, then his sneer fades to recognition. "Dude, isn't she that chick from YouTube? The one who gets on the bus after meeting Wyatt? Fuck man, yeah. She's the one."

How could they possibly know about how I met Zac?

Without another word the two hustle me down a narrow corridor, away from the rumble of the crowd. I'm terrified when we bulldoze past tight-knit groups of girls clamoring for their attention.

I start to kick and twist to free myself when the one called Marshall places his hand on my shoulder and hooks his finger to my chin to bring my eyes to his. "Your name's Shelby, right?"

"Yes, officer," I breathe hard, defeated. "Shelby Rey." I place my hands behind my head and wait to be handcuffed.

"Shel A not Shel B. Classic," he laughs over the now-deafening music pouring from beyond a black-painted door at his back. He turns to open the handle and waves me in.

Directly at the other end of the room is a huge glass window. Through it, I see Zac holding a microphone stand in both hands, gyrating, and singing "Choked" to a sea of shining faces like his life depends on it.

"Booze and food are over there. Make yourself comfortable," Marshall says with a grunt, and leaves.

I let my hands fall. There are several people lounging on couches and eating snacks or swilling drinks, wearing a pass like mine. Some are taking notes on the show, but several others are just hanging out and chatting, not even watching the phenomenon unfolding beyond the window.

I don't know how they can even hear themselves talk through the tight mesh of woven notes hanging in the air. The transcendence of Zac's voice blends into the cries of instruments strummed, drummed, and thrummed by his bandmates, near miracle-makers. Up front, Zac is their God, their unflinching maestro urging them on, caressing the crowd with the reverberation of his vocal chords. I can almost see the birth of each lyric as it rises from his chest, wet with sweat. The words his full lips form demand each drop of Deshi's drumsticks. The movements of his hips control Stanford's back-and-forth strums of his guitar. His ecstasy and fury drive Oslo's hand across the keyboard, commanding the music to pour forward. Pulsating lights ricochet off the sweat on his body and the glistening madness in his eyes.

I'm electrified. My body sways and swoons in response to him, my pulse racing to match the throb of the music.

This is rock and roll.

By the third encore, I'm blown away. Tingling sparks snap and crackle through me as though I've been electrocuted into rapture for the last ninety minutes. The greatest ninety minutes of my life.

As the band gives one final bow to the frenzied crowd, the journalists and hangers-on behind me get up and crowd the opening where Grounder will come off stage. I'm afraid they'll shove me out of reach of Zac. My wish to thank him for the clothes now seems like a piece of long-ago history. Somehow, I need to find a way to thank him for his music. I have to thank him for what he just did to me and to the thousands of people here tonight.

"Shelby? Is that you?" I hear Zac's voice when the band joins the press room. A broad smile lights up his face. "Get your sweet ass over here, girl!"

I push past the deaf mannequins posing as music fans and rush toward him. He pulls me against him, hard, and I wrap my arms around his waist, his chest soaking wet against my cheek.

"Oh man. Sorry about the sweat." His chest heaves with his racing heartbeat. "It was a great show, wasn't it?"

I'm wild-eyed, trying to take him all in at once, wishing I could land on one, just one word, to describe what I witnessed on stage. "Great," isn't great enough. Neither is amazing, brilliant, or even divine, although it was the closest to God I've ever been.

"Holy," I tell him, locking my eyes on his.

"Holy what?" he asks, laughing, reaching out to shake hands with the outstretched palms extended behind me. "Hey, what are you doing tonight? Do you want to hang out after—"

I shut him up with a kiss. My mouth on his, I try to convey all the feelings his music stirred within me during the show.

The journalists begin tossing interview questions at the band and the tight walls light up with camera flashes. But Zac meets my kiss, welcoming my intensity and enclosing me firmly against his body, drawing me closer to him. Someone from *L.A. Record* grabs his arm and throws out questions about his rehab. "Wyatt, you and Stanford share a needle? Can we get a photo of your inner arms?" Another asks, "Did you and Ashtynn split?" But he ignores them and picks me up, wrapping my legs around his waist.

"I'm not letting this girl out of my sight again for a second," he whispers to Oslo, his voice jagged. Then he carries me down a narrow hallway and we disappear into a small dressing room lit by two fluorescent light bulbs running lengthwise overhead.

For an instant, I just look at him. I'm still wrapped around his waist, my arms encircling his neck, and we are eye to eye without words. I open my mouth to thank him, for the show, for the backstage pass, for the clothes—

"I can't believe you're here," he breathes, then re-covers my lips with his before I can utter a word. He swings me in a half-circle in the small dressing room before pressing me firmly against a wall, gripping my loose hair between his fingers, and searching my mouth with his tongue.

I hear a moan and discover it's my own, rising from my throat. I don't care about anything but kissing him. I only want to taste him, return to the pulse of him, the roar of thrashing melodies inside him. I squeeze my arms tighter around him, my hips driving into his, urging him to join with me.

I know about sex. I'm not some stupid kid. But I've never wanted anybody to get this close. I catch my breath and my back hits the wall. I let my feet fall, my new shoes cushioned by the stained shag carpet.

He steps back and his eyes fall over me. The appreciative grin on his lips turns to hunger; he bites his lower lip and tears off his tee shirt.

He's as exquisite as his music. For once I ditched my so-called better judgment, and where did I wind up? Staring down a half-naked Zac Wyatt on the best night of my life.

Not willing to lose another second, I grab him at his waist, drawing his body flat against mine.

He dives into me with kisses, pressing into me once again.

The heat of his swelling rhythm ignites me, challenging me to match him beat for beat. The pounding music that exploded from the stage, enclosing us in sonic captivity, disintegrates. Zac's own anthem rises in its place, holding Grounder's music underwater until it shudders and drowns.

I'm breathing hard, confused by the abrupt departure of the music I've come to know as my own.

Dropping away from our rhythm, I gaze at him, searching for a connection between Grounder's blistering melodic torment and what I hear inside him. His breath low and ragged, he seeks my eyes. Our bodies slip apart, silence falling between our skin.

"Shel," he whispers, his eyes never leaving mine. "I've never known anyone like you." He steps closer. "I can't begin to figure you out, but that only makes me more attracted to you. I want to know you. Everything there is to know about you, Shelby Rey."

His hand reaches out slowly to stroke my cheek, his fingers grazing my lips, tracing them. His touch leaves a shimmer of music I've never heard before. He leans in, his mouth hot on my neck, his knee separating my thighs, his hands stroking my body, and—

I don't know him any better than he knows me.

I gently wrestle him away, my hands on his glistening chest. He waits for me, impatient, his breath heaving. I can't help but hum it out loud, the melody his fingers played upon my cheek.

His eyes burn a hot, smoky, bluish-green flame, reminding me of my last Fourth of July with Dad, when Mom got drunk and thought it would be funny to douse the campfire with borax.

I hum it again, moving so close to him I'm certain he can feel my breath on his lips. "I can't begin to figure you out," I sing, matching his words to the melody inside him. "But that only makes me more attracted to you. I want to know you. Everything there is to know about you."

His mouth curves into a smile, recognizing the pattern of his own symphony. From just behind his ear, a lone drop of sweat chases down his muscular neck to the top of his chest, where it stops, quivering delicately. I watch it, shining on his golden skin.

Zac leans toward me, his lips hoping to return to mine, but when he dips toward me the shuddering drop breaks free and traces the southbound train of his embossed abs, and it's all so exhilarating and delicious I drop to my knees and catch it with my mouth before it hits the top of his jeans.

My enthusiasm surprises us both when I bite into him as I lick it. Zac gasps, and the tight weave of hard muscles on his midsection tenses and releases. It's so unbelievably gorgeous, both the sound he makes and his beautiful body, that I sink my teeth into him again.

"What the fuck?" he gasps, this time without excitement or satisfaction.

I glance up, swallowing hard.

From Zac's side, Roland frowns down at me. My embarrassment dissipates instantly with the confounding shock that I didn't hear him come in.

I sit back on my heels, immediately losing my balance. The back of my head slams the wall behind my tangled hair. I rub the sore spot and stand up, but my heel catches in the shag and I nearly stumble over. Zac takes my arm, steadying me, and helps me to a chair next to an oversized mirror.

"Are you drunk?" Roland asks.

"What are you doing here?" I spit at him, all the good taste gone from my mouth.

"We were worried when you disappeared"—Roland nods at the stolen lanyard still hanging from my neck—"until we noticed Jaclyn's backstage pass was gone too."

"Dude, I figured you let her out on good behavior or something. It was a total surprise she showed up. I didn't . . ." Zac races to make amends for me, his erection evident to everyone in the room, until a realization hits him and his panic becomes annoyance. "Wait, you're not her dad. And she's not your damn prisoner. What's your deal, man?"

The door to the little room suddenly swings open. Some guy with a beanie and three days' worth of a beard pops his head in. "Zac, your shrink is"—he spots Roland—"oh, cool, he found you." With a nod, he slips out and shuts the door.

"Shelby, it's time to go home," Roland says, reaching in his jacket pocket for his car keys.

"What do you mean 'home'?" Zac demands. "You got her on lockdown, Doc?" He places his arm around my shoulder and searches my eyes. "You're welcome to stay at my place for a while. I know you're in rehab and shit, but we can be dry together, you know?"

"I'm not in rehab." I need to make that clear. I also need to shut up before he finds out why I'm actually hanging with white-coats.

Zac sweeps a suspicious eye over me. Grabbing a tee shirt off the back of a chair and pulling it on, he cocks his chin in Roland's direction. "Denial, right?"

Roland lets out a long sigh. "Shelby, please come home with me. No questions asked, I promise. Not from Jaclyn, either."

"No." A sudden wave of tenderness washes over me. This is the second time in a matter of days Roland has asked me to come "home." When I can figure out what "home" means, maybe I'll go with him. Right now, I'm pretty certain it doesn't involve twenty-four-seven therapy. And I can only imagine the lecture Jaclyn's brewing up back at their house. "I want to stay with Zac." I get up out of the chair and place my hand gently on Zac's arm. "I'm eighteen, and I can come and go as I please."

I guess I should thank Roland for everything he and Jaclyn have done. But what have they done? Zac seems to grasp exactly what I need, when I need it. Right now, that's a place to stay, without any catch. Without any debt.

I'm not Zac's patient, not someone he thinks ought to change. He wants me for me.

"Is there anything I should know?" he asks Roland quietly.

I turn wide-eyed to Roland, imploring him to keep his fool mouth shut—about Mom, about St. Cecilia, about my arrest. All of it.

Roland can't hold his tongue another second. "Are you at least going to tell him about your dietary restrictions?"

I have no idea what he's talking about.

"Shelby has celiac disease," he says gravely, as though it should be unthinkable for me to survive away from the watchful eye of a medical doctor.

Zac chuffs with relief. "Then she'll fit right in," he says, lifting the bottom of his tee. "You don't get these abs eating bread and cookies, know what I'm saying?" Under his breath he adds, "Girls who eat carbs, that's an urban legend, right?"

I'm relieved Roland gave up his opportunity to rat me out, but I'm not going to change my mind about going with Zac.

I want what Roland and Jaclyn want for me, I do.

I just think Zac can help me more than they can.

Roland clears his throat. "You're both adults, you can make your own decisions. I do ask that you are respectful of one another's personal boundaries. Be good listeners to each other. Should you agree to engage in a sexual relationship"—he gestures to the spot on the floor where I was kneeling a few moments ago—"use protection. The CDC reports that nearly half of US pregnancies are unplanned, and millions contract sexually transmitted diseases annually."

"Jesus, if we have any questions about getting laid, we'll call you," Zac snaps. "Fucking buzzkill."

"Particularly," Roland adds, leveling his eyes on Zac, "if either of you has multiple partners."

He's planting seeds of doubt, can't Zac hear it? If Zac has someone he cares about, he wouldn't ask me to move in with him. Zac chose me.

"Jaclyn wants me to figure out what kind of work I'd like to do," I say, an unfamiliar boldness salting my words. "I'm thinking something in music."

My faux swagger bolsters Zac's arousal and confidence.

"Listen, Gibson, I'm still clocking in drug tests, right? Me and Shel are just going to chill and get to know each other. No booze, no party favors. Just hanging out, high and dry. I mean, just dry."

"I'm not negotiating a decision I don't advise." Roland is firm. But when neither Zac nor I relent, he gets wise enough to leave us be. "Shelby, our door is always open. Zac, I expect you'll continue to work on the goal of your upcoming deadline?"

"Yeah." A grin breaks across his face. "I have a lead on a new song."

# CHAPTER TEN

I swing my Ferrari into my driveway and press the gate entrance button programmed into the dashboard. Nothing happens. The damn button has given all of us trouble lately, but c'mon. I finally get to bring Shel back to my place and it craps out on me?

I glance sideways at her, achingly aware of her Rolls-Royce Phantom. She has a driver to handle shit like this.

I slide out from behind the wheel and walk over to the manual keypad to type in our password on the flat screen. I can't remember the key-tone beep pattern, damn it. I try again, feeling Shel's eyes on my back. Nothing.

Finally, her car door swings open and she comes over and slides her arms around my waist.

"I can't get this fucking thing to work."

"I've had my share of troubles with keys no longer fitting the lock," she says.

I laugh and put an arm around her. She always knows exactly what to say to make me smile. The second I relax a little, the key pattern comes to me: two bassline measures from Radiohead's "Anyone Can Play Guitar." I tap it in, and this time the gate swings open. I give Shel, my lucky charm, a quick squeeze.

The guys went to the after-party at the Wilshire and won't be back until sometime tomorrow, so it's only the two of us at the house.

"Welcome to Grounder House," I say, leading her toward the kitchen. "You hungry?"

"Sure." She smiles, suddenly shy. She looks around the place with giant eyes, and I wonder what she sees. She's just about the coolest girl I've ever met. I hope she likes what we've done with our place, a blend of party palace and chill lounge.

"Let's see." I lead her into the oversized kitchen and open the fridge. "Doctor Dad wants his baby girl to eat right." I wink at her, and she smiles that fantastic smile. I'd be happy to hang out staring at the curve of her lips, but I'm trying to be the gentleman. Besides, I'm raging hungry after the set we just played. "How about I grill a couple of filets?"

She stares at me blankly.

Oh man, if she's vegetarian, I just totally put her off.

"All right. Do you mind if I eat steak?"

She nods, remaining silent, her tiny form secured within a single floor tile.

"What if I made us an omelet? Are eggs okay with you? Because there's no tofu here, I can promise you that."

She giggles. "Whatever."

I cock a brow, trying to figure out how she's managed to pull off the impossible. And after a show, no less. I'm king of the world when I come off stage, but here I am, miles from the band, our fans, and the all-night party, setting up to cook for a girl I barely know. Jesus Christ.

I motion for her to make herself comfortable. The kitchen

has a large vestibule overlooking the deck, with a long banquette and tons of cushions.

Shelby doesn't stray. Encircling her arms around my waist again, she melts against me in the frosted light of the open Sub-zero. I hold her tight, inhaling the scent of fresh-baked cookies and lavender. On tiptoes, she reaches her mouth to mine, and I meet her kiss, wondering how I got so damned lucky.

I settle her back on her feet. Food first, hard-on later. But damn if she isn't the hottest little piece.

I set up a large serving tray, grab a couple of bottles of Italian soda, and usher her out to the terrace. The guys and I agree: A late-night dinner overlooking the lights of LA is a surefire way to get your favorite girl upstairs.

She gasps out loud when she sees the view: "You can see forever." She runs out on the tiled deck to the ledge. "Can you hear it? It's the heartbeat of the city."

"Yeah, we're like angels at midnight, watching the flock by the light of the stars."

Holy Christ, did I just say that? Out loud? Why do I behave this way in front of the one girl I'd actually like to impress?

Shelby's shy smile plays on her lips as she takes my hand and closes her eyes. Fingers entwined in mine, she folds our hands against her chest. I can feel the small swell of her breasts under the silky top she wore to the show, feel her nipples hardening in the cool night air.

"We're like angels at midnight, watching the flock by the light of the stars," she sings to a melody I don't recognize but that somehow seems familiar. The syllables of my corny words don't match the tempo of her melody, and she furrows the fine line of her brow.

"Oh, right, you started with a 'yeah.'" She tries the melody again with that adjustment—"Yeah, we're like angels at midnight, watching the flock by the light of the stars"—and it's a match.

I'm flattered by her little game, but I wish I'd said something a little less idiotic for her to quote back to me in song.

Still stroking her fingers between mine, I pull her over gently to a table, sit her down, and place a linen napkin in her lap, my thumbs brushing the sleek ridge just above her knees. "It'll only take me a few minutes to get this food ready," I say. "You going to be okay out here alone for a bit?"

She looks out at the city lights again, then meets my gaze with a grin. "I can think of worse places to wait."

I make the world's fastest omelet back in the kitchen, then carry it out to the deck. I set a heaping plate next to Shelby and pull up a chair. "I hope you like this," I tell her, cutting a bite and preparing to feed her.

This is a precise maneuver, feeding a girl. It has to be flirtatious, seductive. Very easily, fork-feeding a would-be lover could come off as patronizing and disrespectful. Or, worse, it can aggravate an existing princess syndrome. The last thing I need is some chick expecting me to wait on her like a pussy-whipped bitch. Ain't gonna happen. No, I am careful to use the fork as an extension of myself, letting it rest on her smooth, firm lips and—

"Zac?" Shelby interrupts my thoughts.

I meet her eyes, realizing I was staring at her lips again.

"Let me feed you," she says.

"What? Nah." If the guys saw that, they'd never let me hear the end of it.

"Right?" she replies, as if reading my thoughts. Point made, she doesn't waste another second, digging in with her own fork like Daddy forgot to pay the catering bill on her residential program.

I like a girl who can eat. And I love a girl who doesn't let me get away with shit.

I kiss the bumpy bulge of her chewing cheek and start eating.

I see her eyes fall on the pool below. "Do you want to swim later?"

"I want to find a quiet place," she says between bites, in barely a whisper. "With you."

When the band moved in, we installed a kick-ass sound system for parties throughout the house and around the pool. But here, right now, all around us is silence. I squeeze her hand and wish I could guess, even just once, what she's thinking. I don't know what the hell she means by "quiet place," but I'm hoping to get in her in my bed, and God knows it isn't going to be quiet when I do.

When we finish up, I offer her a tour of the house, but she isn't interested. I'm a little put off at first that she isn't giving me the chance to show the place off. I want to point out that she ain't slumming. Then it hits me. Here I am, knocking myself out to win her over, and she doesn't need it. She doesn't need me to do anything but be with her.

Fuck me if that isn't a first.

"I just thought of the quietest place we could go." I grab her and pull her close. "Do you want to take a bath?"

The wicked smile that plays on her lips feels like a solid lead. I guide her by the hand to my bedroom, walking her past my king-sized bed like I've forgotten it's even there. In the master bath, I adjust the overhead dimmer switch down low and hand her a sumptuous spa robe.

I go right to work, lighting the ridiculous number of candles the decorator placed around the room that have never before seen the light of flame. Every moment wasted is a dice-roll she'll change her mind.

Shelby finds a bottle of bath wash and dumps a bunch in, creating mountains of fluffy white bubbles. The whole setup looks like a cheesy porn scene, or worse, some lame erectile dysfunction commercial starring a couple of old people. After the fork-feeding fiasco, a candlelit bath for two may weigh a little heavy on the hokey.

Before I can figure out my best bet for manning up, she is completely nude and folding her clothes neatly on the vanity, flickers of candlelight twinkling on her little ass. I'm pretty sure this girl has never suffered an awkward moment in her life. I lose my clothes in a heartbeat and we sink into the hot water.

"It's nice how comfortable you are in your own skin," I toss out casually, stealthily pushing bubbles aside so I don't miss one spectacular inch of her.

"A naked body is nothing to be ashamed of, my mom always says. Shame is handed down by the shameful." But even as she says this, she draws her knees to her chest.

"If we're honest about our true nature, all who are honest will know us," I say with a nod, trying to keep up with her flair for the philosophical.

Shelby merely shrugs. I've got to stop trying so damn hard.

"Your mom's right," I say. "Fuck that noise."

I get an instant-fantasy of Shelby spending summers in the South of France on clothing-optional beaches alongside her well-preserved mama.

"Where are you from?" I ask her. "I mean, shouldn't we have the conversation we would've had if you'd let me ask you to lunch that day we met on the sidewalk?" I grin and begin to relax in the warm water.

Shelby stares into the bubbles for a few moments before offering, "I was born in San Diego, but my family moved around a lot when I was young."

"That's cool. I grew up in Portland, Oregon. My parents still live there. My baby sister is in high school. She plays the flute and is on debate team or some shit. She's real smart."

"I guess your folks were so happy with how you turned out,

they were hot to have another kid," she says, her eyes glimmering in the candlelight.

I find her foot under the water, bring it to the surface, and kiss her bubble-covered ankle. "You live in LA now, right? What part?"

I can see I'm boring her with my questions, but I know next to nothing about her. I should get the basic deets; she's naked in my damn bath, after all. I gaze at the tips of her nipples, floating just at the water's surface.

"Actually, I'm living in Laguna Beach at the moment," she finally replies.

Oh shit, of course she's holding back. She's in residential rehab, which generally comes fast on the heels of hitting rock bottom. I'm such a dumbass.

After a pause, she offers, "And my mom lives in Orange County."

So that's why she chose a program in Laguna, to be close to family.

"How long have you been in rehab, Shel?" I ask her gently. It's terrible to admit, but right now what I appreciate most about Ash is that after helping her through her crisis, I'm better prepared to support Shelby. That's a hard thing to recognize about our relationship, but hell, I guess I am chest-deep in hot water with another girl right now.

She frowns. "I'm not in rehab. I told you that."

Christ, maybe she isn't. "Is Gibson a close friend of your family or something? I gotta say, I was surprised to run into you at my psychiatrist's house."

Shelby draws a heap of bubbles in her hands, cupping them in front of her face. She peers deeply into the tiny cloud and says nothing. I don't want to pry into all her business, but if she isn't willing to bring me up to speed, then I've already put too much on the table for this girl.

"I know Gibson sends his rehab patients to a facility," I say tentatively. "It's just that I met you when you were going to a session with him, but then I find out you're staying at his place, and"—I have to bring it up, it's bugging the shit out of me—"you call him by his first name."

Shelby's eyes never leave the bubbles cupped in her hands.

"It doesn't add up," I press.

She begins humming to herself, and I begin to wonder if she cares that I'm even here. Shifting around a bit in the tub, I bump my thigh against hers, sending water rippling over her knee, but she continues humming without a single glance in my direction.

This is some bullshit. I've made a terrible mistake bringing this girl home.

But it's still better than the alternatives: blowing my rehab at the inevitable piss-up back at the Wilshire or held on a goddamn leash at Ash's. And we have chemistry, it's undeniable. I can't give up yet.

I try lightening the mood. "What's Gibson like with you? Is he big on quoting poems and talking about the opera?" I scatter the cloud of bubbles she's holding and lace my fingers through hers, thumbing circles into her palms.

Her eyes flash at our entangled hands, igniting. She stops humming, but still says nothing.

I imitate Roland's Big Daddy Doctor voice: "Let's discuss your purpose in the universe, young Lady Rey. What shall be therefore thy function?" I infuse my impersonation of Roland with the accent of an old English professor I had at Reed and am gratified when she breaks out in giggles as soft and luminous as the bubbles circling her sleek body.

"Jaclyn's the one always up in my face," she opens up, her words breaking through her laughter. "I'd take poems over Jaclyn's endless expectations that everyone fit her ideal, the one looking back at her in her own mirror."

Now I'm the silent one, surprised by her sudden openness.

Shelby picks up momentum, dropping the 411 without reservation. "She works backward. She thinks she's figured out my destination for me, and now she's trying to steer me on the path she would take if she were me."

I wonder what destination Shelby has in mind for herself. And why she isn't already there.

"Roland is kind of hands-off, like he's waiting for me to come to him," she says, hot on confession. "I like that he doesn't push."

"Yeah, I hear what you're saying. His approach is more organic." I have no idea what she's saying. His approach is organic? The last thing Shelby would do is spout bullshit. I owe her as much.

"We've never had a session." She shakes her head.

They haven't? I'm more confused now than I was before I pressed for details.

"Jaclyn, on the other hand, gives me bedside lectures when I'm barely awake."

I may not understand, but at least she's opening up. Her gaze returns to our hands, so I resume twirling my thumbs and stroking her fingers.

"I guess when I'm ready to meet with Roland"—her voice quiets—"we'll talk about my dad."

The word "mother" can equate to any number of meanings. But "daddy" can only go one of two ways: unconditional love or stripper pole. I drop her hands into the water and slide my fingertips up her arms, moving toward her until she is folded against me. I'm not going to prod her any further. Maybe I'll take a page from Gibson's playbook and let her share when she's ready.

But I guess she's ready to talk now. "He passed away."

Oh Christ. I didn't see that coming. "Was he sick?" I ask, and immediately tell myself to shut up.

"I never looked at it that way. But I guess he was."

"Was Gibson friends with your father?" I try to put two and two together. "Is that why you're staying with him?"

Bubbles erupt over the side of the tub as Shelby sits up abruptly and frowns, searching my eyes as though there's a thought behind them she needs to fish out.

"Roland and Jaclyn are helping me," she says deliberately, each word a revelation, "because my father died."

So she's mourning the loss of her dad. Roland and Jaclyn can play the fill-in parents, but I'm here too.

"Shelby, I don't know you very well. And yet after the little time I've spent around you, I can promise I've never met a stronger person. You're more intelligent, confident, and damn straight fun than anyone I've been with." I pull her closer, running my hand down her wet spine, laced with silken bubbles. "I'm really glad I met you."

Shelby pulls up in the water, pressing her dripping body against me, and meets my eyes. "You have one gigantic, beautiful bed, Zac Wyatt." Her lips brush against mine. "Let's get into it."

The bed, it turns out, is too big. For the two of us, that is, when Shelby's slight frame lies, delicate and lush, across mine. I am all the mattress she seems to need, and damn if I care where we are as long as I have her naked body pressed against me. It feels like ages since we first kissed in the dressing room; I can't believe it was just earlier tonight. This girl can stop time, and likely control the universe. Mine, at the very least.

I abandon whatever tenuous grip I have on the here and now when her lips are on me. Her tongue finds a rhythm at the center of me and teaches her hands to follow its cadence. She builds a nearly unbearable heat from the core of my body straight up to my brain, then ignites it in an exploding galaxy of stars. I would think I'd stopped breathing if I wasn't panting so hard. And then her hands hold that rhythm, as pure a rhythm as I've ever known, like an inner drumbeat, an original bassline somehow familiar to me but long since forgotten. She's awakened it, only to double it, no, triple it, with her tongue. It's like she knows me, or remembers me, the Me that has always been me, from the very start. The Me I'd forgotten until I was under her, allowing her to have me, giving myself to her.

The darkness filling the room from ceiling to floor begins to dissipate. Shimmering lights break through like raindrops and filter down until I can see that we never really left this place and time, although it sure as hell felt like she took me away, or back, or inside? Damn it, I can't even think.

She reaches to meet my lips and I squeeze her tight, her hips digging sweetly into me. I tuck my arm around her, flip her over easily and playfully. I devour her again and again, restarting my engines.

Her hand brushes the side of my face, sweeping along my cheek until it lands on my lips. I meet her eyes and she whispers, "I forgot to tell you how impressed I am that you've chosen rehab."

What the fuck?

I shake my head, preparing to tell her I'm not really in rehab, to tell her everything. But I'm not sure I'm ready to admit the truth. Shelby's a fan, sure. She's obviously made herself more than a little familiar with Grounder. Part of me is terrified she's actually some kind of super-fan, one of those girls that go nutty and burn your house down when they don't get what they want.

But more than that, I'm scared of failure. It kills me that I might not have it in me. Will she be able to respect me if I'm unable to succeed at the one and only thing I wish I could?

"Roland is just helping me to"—I search for some explanation—"find myself, you know?"

Find myself? Why do I say shit like this to her?

"I don't trust white-coats." Her nose wrinkles and it's ridiculously cute. "I've never known one to do anything but cause more trouble."

Do we have to talk about this now? I'd really prefer to return her the favor of a Technicolor time-travel orgasm. Or at least try.

"My mom would rather drink away her last breath than pause to feel anything about my dad's death. And every guy she's dated since is just like her."

She's on a roll now. All I can feel is the distance I'm going to have to cover to get her back in the mood.

She takes my face in both hands and holds it gently, smiling into me. "Here is this man, a man like any other, with the same crap life shovels at us all, and he's in rehab. You know how to take care of yourself."

Her lips touch mine, but I don't return her kiss.

I'm a man like any other? The fuck I am.

I excuse myself to the toilet. When the bathroom door swings shut behind me, I take a piss and try to work up a good comeback, the best way to inform this girl I am Zac Fucking Wyatt.

But that's the whole thing, isn't it? Shelby didn't need me to impress her with my house, my lifestyle, or anything. I'm enough, just as I am.

That's why sex with her is nothing short of radioactive. I'm not going to call what we experienced here together "lovemaking" or some shit, but this was no star-fuck. This girl really digs me. She gets it. She may call me a man like any other, but I'm the one she's with, I'm the one she understands.

I wash my hands in the sink and catch myself smiling in the mirror. Just a grin, but kind of crooked, the way it was before my publicist coached me up to a reliable, camera-ready smile.

When I step out of the bathroom, she's wearing nothing but her little white panties and one of Ashtynn's thin, ribbed tanks and staring intently at my three favorite guitars. I sleep with these beauties close by; they're too precious to leave in our in-house studio.

I pause a second to take in the view of her from behind, then wrap my arms around her waist and kiss the back of her neck. I don't know what to make of all this, but there's nowhere I'd rather be right now. Hell, I don't even flinch when she reaches forward to take a guitar off its stand.

She chooses an acoustic that belonged to Courtney Love in the early '90s, when she was living in Portland and teaching herself to play guitar. Rumor has it that before she learned to write music, her former bandmate Kat Bjelland had to interpret her musical ideas for her.

Shelby swivels with a big smile and hands it to me. "Play for me," she demands, "play the rhythm I heard when I had your pulse on my tongue."

Who could say no to that? But I haven't a clue where to begin. I take the guitar from her and strum a few chords, wondering what the hell I'm supposed to do.

"C'mon Zac," she coaxes, "let me feel you with my ears."

The girl may be some kind of freak. But I reach back to that timeless place between total darkness and wild raindrops of color, find the rhythm, and weave it into a chord pattern.

"Yes," she squeals and starts to sway, bands of earliest-morning sunlight breaking between her dancing legs as her body rocks to the music.

I pick up the tempo, watching her, a heat wave of desire swelling up inside me. Yeah, she can turn me on like no one else, but there's something more, some part of me that is rising up, like a tether of notes we grip from each end, musician to listener, listener to musician.

I want to pick her up and haul her back to my bed, but I don't want to lose this, this moment in my history. What did Gibson call it? A "poignant event."

"Can I make a video?" I ask, still strumming. I immediately regret how many times I've asked that same question in this room. This is the only time I'd be devastated to not get a yes as the answer.

"I just want to dance," she says, throwing her hair and hips in a dance that could lure both demons and angels.

That's not a no. I place the guitar back in its place and quickly turn up some dance music on my stereo, a rave version of "I Just Can't Get Enough."

"I love this song," she says, smiling. When her body discards my rhythm in favor of the dance track, I'm just a little disappointed. But there's no time to waste. I grab my handheld camera, check the battery, and press play.

Damn, the display captures the sunlight just right. Shelby is nearly hopping to the fast beat; now she's up on the bed; now she's skipping across the room. I follow her closely. The camera corrects some of the rocky motion. She is having her own good time, letting herself fully release to the music, barely glancing my way. The sun washes over her body, as it did at Gibson's pool, but this time she's wearing next to nothing, in my bedroom, and she's my lover.

This might be the best day of my life.

## CHAPTER ELEVEN

ROLAND

It's nearly three in the morning when I get home from Zac's concert, but Jaclyn is at the stove measuring loose jasmine pearls into a teapot.

"You didn't find her?" she asks quietly under the dim light from the oven hood.

I nod my head and pull my sweater over my head, the one I bought the night we saw Nick Cave at Jones Beach, back at Dartmouth. Untucking the clinging cashmere tee underneath, I grab a bottle of water from the fridge.

"Have you called the police?" Jaclyn begins digging through her purse for her cell phone.

Placing my hand gently over hers, I look her in the eye. "She's all right. She's with Zac Wyatt."

"Well, date night's over," she snaps. "Time to come home now. What's the boy's number?"

"He invited her to stay with him for a while, and she's chosen to accept his invitation, Jac."

In a pot of water on the stove, tiny bubbles cover the bottom of the pan. If it comes to a full boil it will harm the leaves and make the tea bitter. I step around Jaclyn, lift the pan, and pour the steaming water over the pearls. The buds unfurl, blooming underwater.

"I made it clear that I don't support their decision, but she'd made up her mind."

"Just how persuasive were you, Roland?" Jaclyn's not about to let this go. "My guess? You probably jumped at the chance to dump the girl, and with your rehab patient, no less." Her palm slams down on the kitchen island. "How will I explain this to the hospital? 'I lost a patient, but don't worry, she's with Zac Wyatt. Yes, the Zac Wyatt.'"

"A patient must have a right to privacy, be given the choice to declare, 'The way I'm living no longer serves me. Help me to change.' I'm more than ready to facilitate that. I'm confident she'll come back when she's ready."

"That's what separates our work, you know that?" she scoffs.

I'm too tired to have this fight.

"Your clients come of their own free will," she continues, "even if they've hit rock bottom, because they're confident someone can and will help them, regardless of their circumstances." Pouring the tea into her cup, she frowns into it. "'Help' is a word few of my patients know. Everyone has let them down. It becomes a habit to be in pain alone."

"She isn't alone," I remind her. "I know this isn't what either of us wants for Shelby, but at least she isn't with her mother."

"Right, I'm sure she'll get all the help she needs from Zac," she groans, stomping out to the living room.

I trail after her and watch as she plants herself on the couch and crosses her arms. "You haven't made the tiniest effort to engage Shelby since she arrived at our home. I've done all the work."

"Jaclyn, she had barely settled in." I grab the club chair opposite the sectional. "I couldn't expect her to leap out of bed the first day with a vision for transforming her entire life."

Jaclyn's eyes spark, then disintegrate like a wet flare. She sinks deeper into the sectional, hugging a throw pillow to her.

"Before I can even hope to build a bridge of communication," I explain, searching her face for her understanding, "she needs a sense of control, autonomy. I wanted to give her a chance to trust us."

Jaclyn is doubtful, staring into the pillow pulled against her. "Nothing can happen if she doesn't invest in herself," she says. "This is a mentally impaired woman who was living without food, who had no clothing of her own and unreliable shelter at best. Now in the 'care' of an addict."

I soften to her. We're supposed to be a team here. As gently as I can, I remind her, "It's her choice to heal, and no one can decide when she's ready but her."

"We can decide, Roland. If our goals for the patient are self-sufficiency, health, and the possibility of higher education or gainful employment, we can."

"She's a survivor, no doubt. I can see why you have hope." I'm about to tell her we did the right thing bringing Shelby here when the doorbell rings, startling us.

We both look at the front door and then at each other.

"Do you think she came back?" Jaclyn sets her pillow aside and gets off the couch.

I check the time on my cell. It's nearly four thirty in the morning. I motion to Jaclyn that I'd better get it.

I stride to the front door and open it. In the stillness of night, or early morning I suppose, the salted marine air is close and moist. An oaky scent particular to scotch smarts my nose.

Elliott Rachman is leaning against our doorframe, his habitual blue shirt rumpled and unbuttoned to mid-chest, a twenty-four-hour beard shadowing the contours of his thick face.

"How you doing, Ro?" Elliott's voice is as scratchy as his unshaved chin. He releases his grip on the doorframe and stumbles past me into the house, knocking my shoulder as he goes. He's holding a venti-size coffee cup.

"Please, have a seat." Jaclyn shoots me a questioning glance. "You look exhausted, Ell."

"Hey there, Fancy-Pants. You bringing sexy back?" Elliott smirks at her as he falls messily onto the sectional, cradling the coffee cup.

She put on old sweats to sleep in tonight, soft with many washes, and one of my tee shirts left over from a 10K Fun Run the hospital hosted two years ago to raise funds for suicide prevention. She's embarrassed for an instant, I see it on her face, but she isn't about to let Elliott get the best of her. She fingers the dark waves of her hair, then pulls the fuzzy fabric at her hips into a makeshift curtsy. "It's Lady Fancy-Pants to you."

"What brings you by so early in the morning?" I slide back into the club chair. "And so far from your neck of the woods?"

He's only been to our house once before, and even then, he was just passing through on his way to some golf thing in La Jolla.

"Patient," he grunts. "I just came off an overnight with a client on a God-forsaken boat. My client, Saul Heinrich—he owns Twin Merchants Films—has a yacht in Newport. Said he needed an emergency session with the wife, Brianna." Elliott takes a long swig from his coffee cup, swallows hard. I gather it's the source of the scotch. "You know how I feel about the water, Ro. Fuck."

"Elliott Rachman, you stayed on a yacht overnight?" Jaclyn shakes her head with a sisterly disapproval.

Back in med school, Elliott made thousands every year on the New York Yacht Club's annual regatta. His persistent thalassophobia held him captive in his father's Manhattan penthouse, but not without a clear view of the races. Elliott never liked the word "bookie," though; he preferred the élan of "speculator" and always claimed the process was curative for his phobia.

"I spent the better part of tonight in the toilet." Elliott slumps forward with a sad laugh. "Nearly killed me, but what choice did I have? He offered to quadruple my rate."

"It's more than generous of you to treat patients on location," I point out, "but—"

"Not another 'I only see clients in my office' speech, Roland," Elliott says with a groan, scratching at his beard.

I couldn't if I wanted. I've agreed to treat Shelby, for free, in my home. Or at least that's the plan. God, I hope she's okay. I hope Ell is okay, too. My habit of making a vitals check is as involuntary as the rapid movement of his constricted pupils. He isn't admitting the extent of his anxiety.

"Elliott, how are you, really?" I ask. "How long has it been since you were near an open body of water?"

"Not long enough, buddy. The only thing standing between the ocean and my peace of mind is a shot of lorazepam." Elliott cracks a half-smile, his unshaven whiskers crinkling in the folds around his mouth.

"Roland may have benzodiazepines of some sort in our pharmaceutical safe," Jaclyn offers, squeezing his arm.

"They keep their shit in a safe," he mutters to himself, shaking his head. I frown at her.

"Elliott, meeting a patient on a boat was ill-advised, can we agree?" I attempt to reason with him. "I'm not offering any meds because of a mistake you made tonight. I'm sorry. You'd say the same thing to me if the tables were turned."

"If you needed something and I had it, I'd give it to you," Elliott argues. "Aren't we on the same team?"

"Ell, no amount of money is worth compromising yourself," Jaclyn says. Leaning against my chair, she places her hand on my shoulder. I reach to hold it, entwining our fingers, glad to have her on my side.

Elliott's bloodshot gaze travels back and forth between us.

"Don't worry, I'll never board that hellboat again." He sits back.

"Now that Ro here has made it to celebrity-only billable hours, we can rake in big-time Benjamins on dry land."

Elliott raises his cup in a mock toast to me and drains it.

Something misfires within Jaclyn, a breath or a heartbeat. Her hand releases from mine. "So you did dump her."

I look up at her. "What? No, I—"

"That bit with Zac Wyatt and the blonde outside your Laguna office gave us some sweet publicity," Elliott says, placing his empty cup on a coaster and leaning forward. "We need to do something like that at our Beverly Hills practice."

Just how much does Elliott know about Shelby?

"You've established a rapport with the Wyatt kid. Every teenage girl in America wants to see him come out golden. Maybe you should take him on some talk shows. We'll shoot a montage of you two in session and some shots of Zac working out, topless and shit, to air during interviews."

"Elliott, come on." I won't humor him. "I'm not going to pretend he's an addict when recovery isn't the focus of his treatment."

"If you aren't treating him for drug addiction," Jaclyn asks, her eyes wide with apprehension, "in just what kind of treatment is Zac Wyatt engaged?"

"So you want to throw away an instant ratings smash?" Elliott picks up the venti cup and shakes it, but it's still empty. "Where do you figure your next A-list client will come from? Not Jac's caseload, that's for damn sure. No offense, Jac."

"I'm not asking Zac to talk about 'rehab,' and that's final."

"I'm proud of you for advocating on behalf of your patient"— Jaclyn's tone comes out chilled and flat—"but what are you hiding?"

Elliott says nothing further, too busy fishing around in his jacket pocket to follow along.

"Don't even think about smoking in my house," Jaclyn rebuffs him before he finds his cigarettes.

"At least I'm not nagging Ro here to break patient confidentiality." Elliott finds the pack and eyes it longingly, but returns it to his pocket. "The odds he'll bend the rules are always a long shot. That's why I trust him."

"If you'll excuse me, gentlemen," Jaclyn interjects, "I'd better get ready for work." Then, leaning in as though she's going to kiss my cheek, she whispers, "I'm going to bring her home, even if I have to go to Zac's house myself."

## CHAPTER TWELVE

SHELBY

Zac's closet might be as big as Mom's entire apartment. Pulling on an extra-large Velvet Underground tee, I join him downstairs in the kitchen, where he's making breakfast. We work up quite an appetite, the two of us. But it's clear that he's the only one between us with any cooking skill.

I don't want to be like Mom, always in debt. If Zac would let me, I'd do my best to create some sort of meal for us, but like everything else, he has turned cooking into a form of fun, and I'm just along for the ride.

I'm having fun. Me, Shelby. In a place I never imagined I might land. I'm getting used to the sound of my own laugh, far from the pressure of Jaclyn's prescription for color-inside-the-lines adulthood and Mom's unapologetic wish I'd just disappear.

I did disappear, but I'm not alone. I have Zac at my side.

But for how long? I started with a lie. And since I haven't told him the truth, doesn't that mean I'm still lying?

I try to put that thought out of my mind. For however many days and nights this lasts, I am having the privilege of fun, and I don't want to be the one to ruin it. I'm not going to be like Mom, screwing things up for myself, ending up hurt every time.

While Zac finishes up, I step out onto the shaded terrace off the kitchen to set the table, only to realize I'm not alone. A girl with spray-tanned limbs and tight pigtails performs a perfect dive into the pool and comes up hooting congratulations for herself. I pull Zac's tee down to cover more of my thighs as a group of her clones, lazing on spacious lounge chairs, giggle and clap, then return to watching an outdoor big-screen TV. A pitcher of some frothy concoction is passed between glasses, although it's not yet ten in the morning.

I feel a hand on my shoulder and freeze. It isn't Zac's.

"Hey, how's it going? I don't believe we've met."

It's a man with a voice glazed in Deep South molasses, so familiar I wonder if I've met him before, maybe when we lived at Fort Benning, in Georgia. His touch, meanwhile, roots me to the earth. The constant drone of all the music storming inside me is amplified by the reunion with its long-lost twin. I don't move; I can't.

Releasing his touch, he steps before me and extends his right hand for a more formal introduction. "Didn't mean to scare you. I'm Stanford."

Shaking his hand, I can't help but stare at him, listening as our two songs play in stereo between our clasped palms. I can't see much of his face. He's wearing sunglasses, and long dreadlocks curtain his carved cheeks. He definitely isn't anyone I would have met on an army base.

"You're a friend of Zac's, right?" he asks.

"Yes. I'm here with him." I'm wondering if he hears it too, our identical anthem. I pull my hand slowly from his, severing our connection. Is he as deaf to me, and himself, as Zac is?

Clutching my hands together, I rub away his music from where he touched me. Zac says Stanford's nothing but trouble. It's best I put some distance between us.

"I need to go. Sorry." I hurry back inside and wrap my arms around Zac as he dumps whole coffee beans into a grinder.

Laying my cheek against the hard muscles surrounding Zac's shoulder, I turn my face away from the terrace, away from Stanford. The relentless tumult of music inside Zac is his truest truth, but he doesn't hear a note of it. I can't begin to figure out how he creates Grounder's sound, the music that has transcribed the play-by-play of every minute of the four years since Dad died, when none of it springs from his own pulse.

Or maybe I'm paranoid, isn't that what the white-coats would say? I'm the one lying, I'm the one playing the girl he wants me to be while another orchestra rehearses madly in the pit of me. But Zac turns a deaf ear to his own song, so I'm fairly certain he can't hear the lies in mine.

I pause to listen for Stanford, hoping he won't follow me into the kitchen, but the crackles of various televisions break my vigilance. There are TVs everywhere in this house, and from what I can tell, they're always on. Mom and I never got another TV after she dumped all our stuff, and apparently, I haven't missed a thing.

Zac continues to make breakfast, and the large-screen TV overlooking the pool area catches his eye when an ad for the Choice America Music Awards appears. It's the one show I am eager to see because it's where Zac will debut a new song he wrote. A new Grounder song, written by this mysterious man? My ears are hungry for it.

At last, Zac turns with a hopeful smile. On the counter sits a large tray of smoked salmon, poached eggs, and two greenish, wet lumps.

"Steamed spinach," he apologizes. "My trainer expects me to eat it, and baby, I can't do it alone." He grins.

It's not the spinach I'm worried about. The only salmon I've ever tried has come from a can, and that's been good enough for me. The pinkish slices of smoked fish smell faintly of the briny, rat-infested nights on Laguna Beach I'd sooner forget.

"Let's go back to your room," I say, drawing him away from the kitchen.

Zac pulls me to him by the hem of my—his—tee and encircles my ass with a tight squeeze. "Do you have any idea how sexy you are?"

I respond with kisses, wondering what it is he finds so sexy. Zac is amazing, sure, anyone would say that. But the color of a person's hair or eyes, the shape of their nose? Those things have little value past, say, a photograph or maybe a painting in a gallery. Zac's legit beauty springs from the hum that vibrates from deep inside him, so electric his skin fairly glows golden under his perfectly imperfect silken hair. Even the way he curls his fingers toward the strings of his guitar is magical; there is a beauty in those smooth hands, hands both manly and dexterous, hands that can produce a song, strum a guitar, or bring me to orgasm. You can't photograph that.

I'm not sure I knew what sexy really was until I met him.

There's a patio table and chairs on the private terrace off Zac's bedroom. Sunlight breaks through the palm leaves overhead, illuminating his beautiful face in flashes with the hillside breeze. I try to hold back, but curiosity wins.

"Zac, I want to hear your song."

"What? I mean, pardon?" he asks through a mouthful of that awful smoked fish. He was more than willing to follow me upstairs, but to my dismay, he brought the food along with him.

"I know you're supposed to perform it for the first time on the Choice America Awards, but could you, I mean, would it be at all possible for me to hear it? This morning?"

Zac puts down his fork and finishes chewing. When he swallows, still he says nothing. His eyes are rigid on me, but he isn't angry. Just silent. Achingly silent.

I wish I'd kept my mouth shut. He's given me so much already, how could I ask him for even one more thing?

"Let's start with that rhythm, the one only you can provoke in me." He takes a sip of coffee, his eyes never leaving mine.

"You want to skip breakfast?" My skin prickles with anticipation of his touch. I wouldn't mind putting some distance between me and the salmon on my plate, either.

"No. I mean, yes," he says, glancing at the bed and then back to me. "But what I mean is, I think it would be cool to write a song with you, the one we've already begun."

"I have no idea how to write a song, Zac." I drop my gaze from his, embarrassed. "You're the writer, the singer, the musician." What do I have to offer? "I just like music. I don't know anything about how it's made."

"I beg to differ." He grins, refolding the napkin in his lap.

He hasn't asked me for anything. All he does is give. I smile weakly and glance down at the clique by the pool. Another pitcher arrives, and they pour themselves a round. "They're getting pretty plastered," I observe.

"Those girls are not big fans of inhibitions," he says with a cough.

"You hang out with them? They're friends of yours?" Of course they are, don't be a stupid kid.

"Not really." He fiddles with a loose lock of his hair and looks away, and I don't like the way it reminds me of how Mom's overnight visitors behave when she presses them about a second date. "When I first met them, I was in a committed relationship. But the other guys like having, well, companionship, you know? Let's just say they've become house pets and leave it at that."

I nod, thankful that Zac never got caught up in that sort of thing. I pierce a lump of spinach and stare at the wet mass on my fork. I'll put it in my mouth, I threaten myself, if I dare act like

Mom. Or if I ask whether the rumor is true that he was dating Ashtynn Kingston. Or why they broke up.

"You belong up here with me," he says.

The uneven rhythm of our two songs falls momentarily together, like when the windshield wipers match the tinkling of the turn signal. As long as he doesn't ask about my past, I won't ask about his.

He squeezes my hand and then takes another bite, and neither of us glances in the girls' direction when they finally spot us and beseech Zac to join them for a swim.

When we finish eating, Zac covers me in a long, plush robe, grabs one of his precious guitars, and takes me by the hand to a part of the house I haven't yet been invited into: the recording studio.

"Let's make some music together," he says, his breath in my ear as his lips find my neck.

As I watch him punch his code into the studio's security panel, I realize I have no choice but to do the impossible. Or fail miserably trying.

The small room resembles the bridge of a spaceship, with swivel chairs waiting at the command posts. Through a window, the bands' instruments are arranged neatly among various microphones and several percussion instruments I remember from high school.

Zac motions for me to sit and sets to work flipping switches and explaining the soundboard. The enthusiastic hum of the equipment springs to life, along with him. He grabs the chair next to me and pulls up several of what he calls "tracks" on a computer monitor.

The newness of what we're about to undertake is not as startling as Zac's transformation. He is usually one tight package, but being in the recording studio has him radiant and unstrung. He places his hand on mine and guides it, showing me how to mix and alter the pre-recorded music and vocals using channel strips of levers, dials, and buttons that control everything from fading to equalizing.

I feel myself reborn along with him.

Using only my fingertips, my long-dead and silent voice can be heard at last. I don't mean the voice I use to speak, with its limitations of insufficient words, always mistaken, always misunderstood. I mean my real language, the sounds that aren't words but say more than words have the capability or power to convey. Within the confines of this room, I can twist and bend any sound we record until it deciphers what I've never been able to say before. And may not even understand myself.

I remove my hand from Zac's, signal him to load more tracks, and roll my chair toward the center of the soundboard. The unstoppable noises always at war within me fall into line, organizing themselves in anticipation of what I might do with this miraculous equipment. I must record all the sounds within me so I can finally have the last word.

There is hope for me yet.

"Whoa, Shel. Take it easy, babe." Zac slides my chair back to the array of knobs where we began. "Learn one channel inside and out. Once you do that, you'll know every channel."

I nod, unwilling to lose a second of his instruction. If they taught this at school, I'd never have missed a class. As Zac searches files for additional recordings, my fingers lie lightly on the equipment, refusing to sever themselves from its magic.

"You've taken to this more quickly than I hoped. Smart girl." He winks. "What do you say we go into the live room and record something original?"

I don't need to be asked twice.

He directs me to the small room with the instruments and places headphones over my ears.

"Hello, old friends," I whisper, and laugh to myself.

Zac grabs his guitar, hands me a set of drumsticks to "keep the beat," and closes the door to the control room.

The suck-and-clink sound of the door shutting is the last sound I hear before everything in the room falls wholly, undividedly silent.

I freeze for a moment and glance at Zac, who is adjusting a mic over the drum kit, his back to me.

I rip the headphones off, and the silence bores into my uncovered ears.

Zac still doesn't flinch.

I stumble and almost fall to the floor when the interlocking hardwood snaps apart beneath my feet, screeching as the joints snap. Pieces break apart and creep up around my feet, shackling my ankles. I reach out for Zac but the floor is disintegrating too quickly now, dragging the walls in tight, crushing me, pressing my arms against my ribs and encircling my neck, cutting off my air. Shards of wooden floor pieces dissolve into dry dust, blotting out the light. I try to scream, but it's too late. An arid gust of particles fills my mouth.

"C'mon baby, let me show you around," Zac says casually, as though the room did not just implode.

I try to call out to him but choke. The air is weightless, stripped of every frequency flowing from every wave. I hear nothing—no radio waves, not the pulse of Zac's home or the array of city noises, reckless and untamed, that floated up to us when we were on his patio minutes ago.

"Shel, is something wrong? You look like you're going to be sick. Are you okay?"

The security of Zac's arm wrapping itself around my shoulder comes just as the ground gives out completely below me.

"Honey, you can't throw up in here."

I gasp and cling to him before falling through the floor to

the hottest molten core of earth. Hell's gates collapse, unable to break my fall, as I gain velocity.

But Zac has merely picked me up and carried me out of the studio, breezing past the control room to an adjacent restroom.

He sets me down and looks around for something useful. Faced with few options, he hands me a towel. "Uh, do you need a glass of water or something?"

I know the look on his face. He thinks I've lost my mind. "She's crazy," that's what he'll say. Everyone does eventually.

I bolt past him and run, searching for a way out of this place. Racing down the hall, I find closets, a dining room, some sort of library. I wonder if I can somehow open one of the windows and escape.

Zac appears at the door of the library, blocking me in. The ambient sounds of his household blast in around him. I can't stand the way he's scrutinizing me. I try to bury my face in my hands, but I'm still gripping a drumstick in each fist.

"Babe, are you all right? You got me real worried in there."

"A soundproof"—I cough, my voice still parched from the wood-floor windstorm—"prison."

I dig down, close my eyes, and soak up every noise I can find. Sifting through the murmurs around Zac's feet at the door, then past him and out to the perimeters of the house, I can hear the coffee maker's soprano ding at the completion of a full pot, the particular lisp of a pre-teen wearing new braces retelling the crime he witnessed on a television court drama, the tinny explosions of rifle blasts and bombs on some faraway video game, even the glassy laughter of the girls by the pool. I breathe it all in. If he forces me to go back in there, these may be the last sounds I ever hear.

Zac shuffles on the high-pile carpet, saying nothing. I risk a look up at him; he meets my gaze and almost says something, but closes his mouth and runs his hand through his hair—a habit I find entirely adorable—instead. But I won't mention that now, not when his faultless face is twisted by a giant helping of *What the hell?*

We have nothing further to talk about here. I need to find my stuff and get out of here.

"Of course it's soundproof. Shel, please don't shut me out. Talk to me. What's going on?"

"I told you I know nothing about how music is made. But I know music. I know it, I breathe it, I hear it; it's all there is."

"I know, baby. That's what I love about you. You have an ear for music." He searches my eyes. "I think we could make real magic together. I'll show you how everything works. You just need to trust me."

"I'm not going back in there."

His hand is in his hair again, this time held in chorus with his ever-tapping heel. "Shel, I need you to help me."

"You might as well cut off my ears."

"Is that what it felt like in there?" Zac asks, pulling me to him by my waist. "I would never do anything to hurt you, I promise." He lets out a long, low breath and bites his bottom lip. "Shel, I've never had a girlfriend get me like you do. I have to record a new song, but I need you with me. I don't want us to be apart."

"I can't." Did he just call me his girlfriend?

"Shel," he whispers. He pulls me closer, and when my cheek falls against his chest, his heartbeat exposes him.

He's afraid.

"You have every right to be upset," he breathes into my ear. "I'm sorry. I haven't been entirely honest with you." The fevered tempo of quivering strings inside me dips and halts. He hasn't been honest with me? I thought I was the liar here.

"I've never written a song before," he admits. "Nothing decent, anyway. Our guitarist, that ass-rot junkie Stanford, writes all of Grounder's music. Can you believe that shit? And I've dug myself into a fucking hole announcing Grounder is going to perform something I wrote at the Awards."

Both his arms encircle me now; I rest against him, securing myself against another fall.

"I know I have it in me," he continues, "but I need you to bring it out. Something bold and original, a sound no one's heard before. A whole album that showcases me, my music."

"You have a new song right now. Can't you hear it?" I ask. "Listen, Zac." I close my eyes and wrap my arms tightly around him, but as my panic drains away, his grows. I wonder whether he's holding me now so he doesn't fall.

I've been searching for Grounder within Zac all this time and failing. If Stanford really is Grounder's composer, maybe I'm not crazy after all.

"Come back to the studio with me," he pleads. "Don't you want to play with the recording equipment again?"

I glance up at him and then quickly look away. I want to, more than anything. But at what cost? The recording studio eclipsed from "fun" to "fucked" when we left the control room's mixing console and entered audio lockdown. That place was a prison worse than any cop could ever send me to.

I have to try to explain. "I loved the soundboard, Zac, it was the most phenomenal thing I've ever experienced. But I can't bear the live room, all that lifeless silence."

I'm not going to cry in front of him. I refuse to.

Oslo strolls up the corridor toward us, carrying a sandwich. We fall silent at his approach, neither of us interested in a third opinion.

"Some woman is at the gate, asking for your girl," he says in what I'm guessing is a Scottish accent. He speaks only to Zac but nods congenially my way. "Says her name is Jaclyn?" He turns the sandwich from side to side, deciding where to sink his next bite.

I spot a tattoo of Gaelic words creeping up the back of his shaved head from the collar of his ripped tee.

Of course Roland told her I was here. I pull back from Zac, but he takes hold of my hand, worry falling over his face.

"Please don't go," he says.

Oslo leans toward Zac's ear and whispers, too loud, "Her mum, serious? Brother, you sure the lass is eighteen?"

Zac waves his hand in response, a gesture that's half "don't worry about it" and half "shut the fuck up."

"Jaclyn trusts no one but herself to make a decision," I tell him. "If she would just give me some space, she'll see I need to—"

"Need to what, Shel?"

"Be here," I say, surprising myself more than anyone. "Because I'm where I'm supposed to be."

Zac smiles at me, brushes my hair behind my ear, and kisses the ridge over my brow.

Oslo is already halfway down the hall when he calls over his shoulder, "I'll let her know."

"The live room is quiet like that because we want to lock the music in with us," Zac says softly, his face still blemished in worry, "and lock the world out. In music recording, it's called absorption."

Doubtful, I meet his gaze.

"Listen," he says. "Do you hear anything in the house? I know it seems quiet now, but there is sound everywhere. Even when it seems dead quiet. This seemingly empty air around us holds frequencies detectable by the recording equipment. We can't hear it with our ears, but the computers can."

I have to hold back a laugh. Of course I can hear it. I can always hear it.

"Let me show you something. Trust me, please?" Zac wraps his warm arm around my waist and leads me back toward the studio but stops before we get too close. On the walls outside the control room, images of Zac, Deshi, Oslo, and Stanford stare at us, frozen mid-performance on stages around the globe.

"The idea is to shut out all the noises around the band," he says, enclosing me in an embrace from behind. "We let go of everything. Nothing outside the studio can touch us when we're making music. We immerse ourselves in the patterns, rhythms, notes, and lyrics of the songs we create." He squeezes me tight in his arms, then swirls me around to face him. The playful grin of a little boy has returned. "It's a damn near religious experience, I'm not kidding."

I take a deep breath, allowing his words to saturate me. "I get it. It's us." I smile. "We're here together, letting the rest of the world go. We're writing our own music, and nothing can touch us."

Zac's smile warms me. "Christ, I love the way you turn my words into lyrics. Write that down. We can use it."

"What, seriously?"

"Trust me," he says, this time without asking. "Tap a beat with the drumsticks. It'll break the silence when you walk into the live room." He turns and heads into the control room without another word.

I hover outside for a moment, and then it hits me: I do trust him.

So, tapping the sticks together, slowly at first, I peek my head in. Deep in my throat springs a lustful hunger for the soundboard, a flood of longing for the unspoken. With that machine at my fingertips, I'll be able to speak at last.

"The sooner we lay down some tracks, the sooner we can play with them in the control room," Zac says, like he's reading my thoughts. "We need to create before we can edit."

Steadying me before the door to the live room, he waits for me to give the signal that I'm ready.

When he finally pushes it open and waves me through with

a game-show host sweep of his hand, I keep my eyes up and the drumsticks tapping, telling myself the room will hold the sound of me and Zac together, and nothing else.

Prove yourself, Shelby.

When the door clunks shut, there is an unmistakable change to the drumsticks' pitch. "The vibration." I look at Zac in wonder. "It's amazing."

"Tight, right?" He grins at me, then throws a guitar strap over his shoulder. After stroking the instrument on his hip for a moment and plucking a few strings, making adjustments, he clears his throat and sings, "Little Silver Shoes, she's gonna turn my words to platinum with her golden ears."

His voice is gorgeous in the space. Both crisp and velvety at once.

But his lyrics stink. Silver, platinum, gold? The boy needs help.

"Let's make some noise," he says, pulling me abruptly against him. His lips sink into the sensitive skin between the base of my neck and my shoulder, thirsty and eager. His hand snakes up to my breast without warning. His guitar digs into my hip and I hear two light thuds near my feet; I've dropped the drumsticks.

I'd push him away, but his pulse is shouting at me. He's scared and desperate.

He's using me.

No, that doesn't make any sense. Why would an accomplished rock star with the world at his feet, and access to any resource he might want or desire, need anything from useless me? I'm being paranoid.

Don't be paranoid, Shelby.

There's no one here but me and Zac. I'm just talking to myself. In third person? The white-coats red-flag your file when the voices start.

"C'mon, beautiful. Let's record some of the magic we've made," he whispers. His kisses trail across my shoulders, the delicate skin of my inner arms, the backs of my hands, and then return to my neck. "Hum the rhythms, the ones only you can hear inside me."

"Do it yourself." I'm breathing hard, too aware of the touch of his plush lips. "Your whole body is pounding your truth into me with every breath you take, every beat of your heart."

"Oh, that's hot, babe. Are those the words inside me? Great lyrics, I knew I had it," he whispers, still stroking my body. His guitar, an extension of him, is stiff against me. "Now put them to a melody. I'll figure out the chords. Show me. Lead the way, Shel."

He's changed. He's getting what he wants before he kicks my ass out. Mom was like this. She wanted me gone years ago. But when she realized my prescriptions would go with me, she backpedaled. Told me she didn't like being on her lonesome all the time and asked me to stay awhile.

But no, that's not it. His kisses are as warm with desire as they were before I freaked and bolted this morning. What if I'm just imagining he thinks I'm crazy and I miss out on finally being able to actually be myself with someone? If all he needs me to do is transcribe the way he sounds when we're together, wouldn't it be insane to deny either of us that? It's so simple.

I take his face in my hands, holding him until he meets my eyes. There is nothing to say now. We only need to listen.

Never letting go of his gaze, I slide my hands gently down his shoulders and remove his hands from me, placing them by his sides. Stepping closer, I taste his lips, my fingertips on his chest. I kiss him softly, savoring his warmth, slowing his staccato fears.

He keeps searching my eyes for something he's not finding, so I allow my lashes to fall shut. It takes every ounce of strength I have to embrace the silence of the room as I embrace him, to let go of the comfort of the world's incessant white noise.

I pull in closer to his body, removing his roaming hands from mine a second time. This is not about give and take, my music and his. It's about Zac's song, Zac's truth, pure and undiluted. I've never entirely mastered quieting myself, though, so I shut my eyes more tightly, securing my feet on the hardwood. Attempting to seal out the defiant drumbeat of my own anthem, I kiss him harder, more deeply, leaning my chest into his and clutching him to me.

He leans in too, responding to my searching kiss. My hands glide across his carved torso. I push aside his guitar with one hand and press my palm against the front of his jeans; a sigh of pleasure shatters his quickening breath as I run my hand over the length of his hardness.

I want to undo his zipper and pull him against me, feel his heat—always ready, always ready. But I'll have to wait because I have it, I have his music now.

I hum to him, my lips still firm and soft against his.

He moans low in his throat, but he understands what must be done. He steps back, his eyes on fire, the pupils large, black, and bottomless. A hot flush rises above his collar. He throttles the neck of his guitar in his fist and strums it raggedly, searching for the chords to match my murmured rhythm.

I find the drumsticks on the floor and step over to Deshi's drum kit. I don't know what I'm doing but I'm sure as hell not going to throw this moment away. I tap out his rhythm, trying each drum surface until I can blend its reverberation with the taut, invisible thread binding Zac's music to me and through me.

I see him lower his chin to watch his hand fall and rise over the strings, focusing on the mechanics.

"Zac," I call out, placing the drumsticks down on a rolling chair.

He looks over at me without stopping.

I can't explain how he should play his instrument, so I use my hands, illustrating in the empty space between us where the notes need to fall. Down lower, I show him, pressing my open hand toward the floor. When he gets to the sweet spot, I stretch my palms apart wide to drag the chord pattern out, longer and still longer, then fast, and faster. He follows, and I can't help but grin like a freak when I finally hear the story in his inner music.

"Do you hear it?" I must look like a wide-eyed idiot, I can't stop smiling. "It's midnight's sky. The bubble bath and our wet bodies between the sheets." I am so flattered, I don't even care that I can feel my cheeks flushing pink. "Can you hear it?" I ask again, breathless.

"I hear you," he rasps, "all I hear is you."

He pauses for a moment to grab a piece of paper with narrow rectangles, each one divided by five thin lines. He pencils in tiny dots with posts on them, some connected in twos and threes, some even in fives and sixes, with letters scribbled above.

He sets the paper down and strums what he wrote.

It's music. He's written real music from what I hear. His memories of us.

"Keep going," I say, nearly squealing. "You've got it. It's all deep blue, like the sky over the city when you brought me here last night." Yes, it's coming together. I begin swaying, so excited I can't hold my body still. He plays it and plays it, over and over, until his eyes fall shut, memorizing the chord pattern.

"How about the melody you danced to in my room?" he asks, his voice filled with hope and even wonder. "That'd make a good bridge. How'd it go again?"

"Yellow," I instruct him with my hands once again. "The color of sunlight."

His brow furrows with confusion. "You want me to play 'yellow'?"

"Not just yellow, Zac. The naked truth of early light streaming across your bed, warm on our bare skin, revealing a new day. That yellow."

"Write that down."

I step out to the control room to sit at a counter with a pencil and pad of paper. Zac plucks at the strings, trying to loosen the sunlight melody from them.

The words he wants me to use seem stale and pointless on the page. I know the story is in the music itself. Still, I understand that lyrics are needed to drive the message home.

"What is it about these sentences that make them lyrics, Zac?" I ask, poking my head into the live room and holding up the paper I've written on. "How can you tell if something's good enough to put in a song?"

"I don't know," he responds, still plucking strings. "I guess if it sounds cool. If it's something that will impress."

"Impress who?" I ask. Maybe he's the one hearing voices.

He stops strumming and shrugs. "I want the lyrics to tell a story. My story." He strokes the fresh-cut plum of his bottom lip, thinking. "But when the listener is blasting my song in his headphones or in his car, I want him to hear his story. I want him to feel like we might be bros if we hung out, because I describe his world the way he might himself."

The way Stanford has for me, from the first Grounder song I ever heard. I glance away from Zac, afraid I'll admit my heart was satisfied, overflowing with gratitude for being understood, when I heard another man's music.

I hide the truth by scolding him, a Dad play for sure. "So you're trying to please other people."

"No. I'm trying to, you know, commune with the masses."

"You can't put yourself in the minds of others, because you can never really know anyone. All you have is Zac. So be Zac."

"Oh hell." His eyes narrow. "Did Gibson set you up to say that? I hate that 'Be true to yourself' bullshit."

Are we fighting?

"No, but I've got to hand it to Roland"—I shake my head—"'be yourself' is advice we could both use."

I don't need to hide my gratitude for Stanford from Zac. Stanford is barely aware I exist. But how could a total stranger write songs that illuminate everything I've ever felt?

I stare at the page in front of me, stroking the pencil.

Then I get it.

"Listeners will hear the song however they can," I tell him, the corners of my lips turning upward. "You have no control over how your music is understood or who understands it."

"I feel you." Zac nods slowly. "A song can have several meanings or memories attached to it, depending on who hears it and when. It's going to hold a different significance for them at different points in time."

"Yes!" I clap my hands together. "So you might as well let it roll, say your truth in your own words, without worrying about what others will think. Let the listeners sort it out when it reaches their ears."

"But what if my 'truth' is nothing special?" Zac's shoulders sag. "What if it's just regular shit that everyone goes through?"

Lowering into the chair again, I try to help him understand what Stanford Lysandre did for me. How, through Zac's voice, Stanford sang life into me the day my father was lowered into the ground, raising me up as he was buried, and how he's raised me every day since then, even in moments when I've felt sure I'd rather be underground myself.

"I've seen some seriously messed-up junk, but it all boils down to the same deal," I blurt out, the words coming fast. "We all just want to belong somewhere. To have some reason for being born in the first place. Kind of ordinary, right? So let's sing straight to the point. No flowery stuff, nothing cryptic, zero hype."

"I've gotta stand out," Zac protests. "I've had some embarrassing quotes in the press. I said some dumb stuff trying to come off as cool. This is my chance to be poetic and clever and all that."

"No, Zac." The radio waves are already junked up with too

many try-hard songs. "You've got to dig for fire. Clarity, that's the point here. Remember at breakfast, you said, 'You belong up here with me'?"

"Yeah." He leans against the live room's doorframe, waiting for me to continue.

Rolling tentatively back and forth on the leather chair, I brace myself before revealing the little gem I've been clutching to my chest all day. "Well, in those six words, you gave me a place where I can be safe: in your arms. You didn't trip over yourself making explanations about those girls or where you and I are headed. And I like that you tacked on 'up here,' because we are anything but down low." I tap my pencil against the soundboard nervously. "Set those six simple words to a rising rhythm, give them an atmosphere of possibility, and every listener who's ever realized where they belong, or want to belong, will understand in a heartbeat."

Zac is quiet. He removes his guitar from his shoulder. The only sounds in the room are the clicks of the little metal hooks where his guitar strap attaches at each end.

I've said too much. He's the expert, and I just told him how to do his job. When will I learn to keep my fool mouth shut?

He leans the guitar against the wall, falls to his knees before me, and places his head in my lap.

"I can't do this without you, Shel. Teach me to listen like you do. I'm so damn lucky to have you here with me."

## CHAPTER THIRTEEN

For a girl with ears like an owl, Shel has no trouble sleeping in a house full of party people. I watch Oslo lead a noisy group out onto the large terrace that doubles as a dance floor below my bedroom window, his favorite dubstep pounding loud enough to piss off the neighbors.

Things sure have changed, and in such a short time. In the weeks Shel's been here, I've had zero interest in hanging. I can't drink because of my rehab, but that's not the whole reason. I don't want to shoot the shit, tell the same old stories, fuck around with the guys, or flirt with the constant rotation of girls.

I only want to be with Shel. And work. I've never experienced so much progress before. It's electric, this energy and momentum. I even called Gibson today to set up an effing appointment, I've got so much good news to share. That'll be a notch in his appointment book's belt, me following protocol and all that shit.

I uploaded the video I made of Shel dancing to Depeche Mode and slowed the frame rate to match "Vertical Wire," our upcoming release, so it looks like that's what she's rocking out to. I used to make music videos at Reed, but it's been a while; I had to update my software to get it done. I want the world to see this little bolt of lightning who's lit up every corner of my world. I just have to convince the guys that my little home movie is worthy of "Vertical Wire."

When I press a kiss into the high curve of Shelby's cheekbone, she sighs in her sleep and licks her lips, the moonlight on her chest gently rising and falling with each breath. She's more beautiful with each day. It occurs to me that this, us here together, is her rehab. Her skin is silkier, and I swear her body has grown softer, more potent and voluptuous. My cooking is half-decent, I guess. And then there's all the exercise we've had. I smile wickedly to myself at that thought.

Shelby belongs with me.

I've never been happier.

I'd better head downstairs to gather up the boys for a screening of my video package.

"Zac," Cassandra slurs provocatively from the foyer when she spots me coming down the stairs. "Where've you been, baby?"

She twirls a shimmering cherry-tipped finger around a curl sprouting from one of her pigtails. The simple act of raising her hand to her hair lifts the bottom hem of her ludicrously short dress enough to reveal a flash of her panties.

She sways over to me. "I've been looking for you all night," she breathes, snaking her hands around my shoulders.

"You smell like you've been drinking all night. Hard." I give her hands back to her and keep moving. I've got to find the guys.

"I like the way you say 'hard,' baby. I'd like to see that. How about you and I—"

"Not tonight, Cassandra."

## THE SECRET SONG OF SHELBY REY

♫

Once I have everyone present and accounted for in the media room, I load the video for the band's consideration.

As the video buffers, I make my pitch.

"Like I was telling you, this angle will be a huge budget saving over what Ashtynn had planned," I say. "And her fee. But more important, it's a holla-back to kids who post fan vids of our songs. It's real, raw, and edgy. Doesn't stink of overproduction."

The day after she left me sitting alone at that restaurant, Ashtynn had the balls to courier over a storyboard for "Vertical Wire," reminding me I'd "promised" her a starring role. To boot, she'd drawn up an invoice for both the idea and her fee for appearing. Since when is she the band's creative director? Hell, I'm not even sure the boys are going to swing at what I'm about to pitch, and I'm the goddamn heart and soul of this joint.

Fuck, if that were true, I wouldn't have to pitch this at all.

I know full well that if Stan doesn't like my idea for the video, it won't fly with Os or Deshi either. I hate that he always gets the final word.

Of course, even if he does like it, I still have to convince Shelby, which may not be so easy. That freak-out in the studio the other day set me on edge. I can't tell when the girl might combust. For a powerhouse, she's sure wrapped in a fragile package.

And she comes from money. If I'm going to convince Shelby to sign a release, I'd sure as hell better make her an offer she can't refuse.

The boys pile onto a deep leather couch in front of the big screen. Deshi and Oslo splay out on the seats, holding beers, and Stanford slides onto the wide armrest at one end, wearing mirrored sunglasses despite the darkness of the room.

I hit play and the song intros. Immediately, the mood in the room lifts. It's been a number of weeks since we recorded it, and hearing it is like running into a good friend again. It's a hot track, and damn if Shelby doesn't look hot dancing to it.

I can tell Deshi and Os like it. I glance over at Stanford, but he is impossible to read.

I try to keep it professional, narrating a play-by-play of my little creation. "See how the camera catches the morning sunlight, and the slight bounce of the handheld camera gives it a homemade feel?"

"It is homemade, brother." Os laughs. "And I'm not looking at the sunlight, man. Check out the sweet ass in those tiny panties."

"I'm looking at the sunlight," Deshi says, feigning seriousness. "You can see it right through the white tank top."

"It's awesome." Os nods enthusiastically. "She's naked without being *nekkid*. My kind of art."

"Ash is going to have your ass for breakfast, man," Deshi remarks, not quite managing to hide his sneer behind a long sip of his beer. "And hey, it's one thing to throw her over to serve yourself, but what about Stan? Isn't 'Vertical Wire' a metaphor for climbing the tightrope over the gaping lion's mouth of smack?"

"Sorry, brother." Os elbows Stanford in his ribs. "I'll take a half-naked dancing chick over H-drama any day."

Stanford doesn't say a damn word in response. He just sits there like this is all a big waste of his time.

I turn the volume down a bit but keep the video playing. "Guys, this is our fourth album. We've done the studio-polished thing to death. It's time to get back to what's real." I try to keep my tone even, unemotional. "See, here I cut in clips from our shows in Festhalle, Red Rocks, Bercy, Wembley, and Tokyo Dome," I continue, all business.

"Are you sure you want to show the entire freaking planet the inside of your bedroom?" Deshi asks.

I keep my eye on Stanford. I'm afraid the fucker has fallen dead asleep behind those glasses.

"Who's gonna know it's my bedroom? Besides, this place is a lease." I steal a glance in Deshi's direction. "I'm not going to be here forever." As soon as I get a solo hit, I'm leaving the band.

I'm starting to get angry. Why the hell should Stanford get the final say when he goes on the nod during a four-minute video?

I go over to shake him awake, but just as I take the first step, he eases himself forward, dopey and sluggish, from his lounged position and stamps out the last orange embers of the cigarette wedged between his fingers in a nearby ashtray. Resting his elbows on his knees, he intertwines his fingers and strokes the callused pads of his thumbs against each other, staring intently at a section of frames I slowed to match the grind of his own wrenching guitar solo. He doesn't move, just watches the screen. His lips part but he doesn't say a word; his only discernible reaction is the smallest quiver playing on the high tip of his right eyebrow.

I wonder whether he sees what I see: Shelby's joy and fierce freedom, her energy. I wonder whether he's measuring the cost-to-value of Ash's appeal against this unknown wild streak of blonde.

The video comes to an end. Deshi and Os holler and clap their approval. I tap my seltzer against their beer bottles.

Still, Stanford says nothing.

The room finally quiets down, and everyone turns to Stanford for his reaction.

"What do you say, Stan?" I ask, stilling the tap of my heel.

He gives nothing more than a languid nod of approval before getting up to go.

Os shouts for me to play it again. "This time entirely in slow-mo," he says, a shit-eating grin on his face.

I shrug. "Why not?" I'm just happy they're green-lighting this thing.

Stan turns around and watches me set my little art piece on slow-motion.

I'm so damned relieved, I walk over and pat the bastard on his back. "Want me to grab you a drink, man?"

He just shakes his head and walks out. Probably has a date with the needle.

It's nearly four in the morning when the party spills into the media room, impatient with our disappearance. The video package is raw, too raw for a viewing outside of the band's eyes. I turn off the TV with a decisive click.

I'm buzzing with excitement, and even though my lucky charm is asleep in my bed, I'm ready to roll. I head down to the studio, the opposite direction of the party, and start smoothing out the kinks in the intro of my new song.

Tomorrow, I'll introduce it to the band. We'll put it all together, rehearse it, and hopefully record it. It's cool the guys are pumped about the video, but I'm going to blow their minds when they hear what I've been working on in here.

When I'm finally satisfied, I shut everything down and head back to my room to get in bed with Shel.

The light from the hall falls upon her face when I come in, waking her. Through the dark, I can see the silhouette of her slender hand reaching out for me.

"Hey, Zac. Come to bed."

I pad over to her, grabbing one of my favorite guitars as I go, and take a seat next to her on the edge of the bed. Strumming softly, I give her a taste of the chorus and sing a short preview of the lyrics I've come up with for my song. Our song.

Her voice is heavy with sleep. "Repeat those notes, rising one shade higher each time, reading left to right," she whispers to me.

I'm still getting used to deciphering her peculiar instructions, but the extra work is worth it. She makes my music sound better.

"You mean ascend an octave?" I ask.

"Yeah, what you said."

"Until?" I ask.

"Until the end of the sentence," she replies sleepily.

"How many bars?"

"Until you finish the breath."

"I can hold a note through a massive length of bars."

Rising up, she levels her elbow on the pillow and brushes back her hair. Singing the rising notes, she counts each on her fingers as she goes, using a 6/8 time signature. "Ten," she says.

Her singing voice is honest, unapologetic. She sings without adorning her voice. There is no attempt to emulate a favorite style or cover weakness. Her sound is who she is.

"Got it," I say, making a mental note of her advice. Then I rise and place my guitar on its stand. "I have a surprise for you," I tell her, unbuttoning my shirt.

"I'll bet you do," she teases.

"I finished the whole song, the intro, everything." I smile at her in the dim light, sliding my jeans off and lowering onto the bed next to her warm body. I'll save the "Vertical Wire" news for the right moment.

"I can't wait to hear it," she says, snuggling her head into the crevice between my chest and my chin. "Tomorrow," she adds, kissing my neck.

## CHAPTER FOURTEEN

## STANFORD

I take my old guitar for a stroll down to a darkened patio in the northwest corner of our property, a hedged terrace away from the late-night party people. It's quiet but for the ceaseless murmur of tens of millions of people and cars crawling in all directions below in the streets and valleys of Los Angeles.

I've got words to ponder and put in order, a melody still buzzing and tingling from when I held her hand. I'll strum it out.

It's cool that Zac is finally back in the studio with the kind of raw energy he injected into our earlier releases. The guy has more talent than he knows, but he needs to let go. He's still relying on safe hooks and leaning into familiar pop themes.

I knew the minute I first heard Zac sing that his voice was the burning, sonic vitality I needed to broadcast my songs to the world. He's translated my private hell into music fit for public consumption with his immaculate voice, his inimitable style.

Our upcoming Asia tour promoting Grounder's fourth album is an opportunity to introduce a new point of view.

## THE SECRET SONG OF SHELBY REY

"I just want to write an honest piece," Zac told me, "uncover sounds that are a different trip for us."

I get it. He's as sick of my songs about the half-life of my twilight Neverland as I am of using.

So I told him how I do it, the best I knew how. He's my friend and I owe him everything. I wanted to help him write his own music, to thank him for everything he's done for mine and for Grounder. And what did he do? Shoot heroin. I shared my sorry-ass secret to writing music, and he thought I meant the needle.

It's a domino line, a matter of cause and effect. I spent my whole life listening so hard that when I tried to stop, the sounds didn't. I still have dreams of when I was little more than a toddler, living in a temporary shelter after our family was evicted from our farm in Georgia. When we moved to an overcrowded permanent shelter in Tennessee, I was passed around a lot while my parents stood in line down at the job placement center. Drunks and thieves took the quiet mornings as opportunity to loot our meager belongings. Fights often broke out. I spent my days filtering through the noises: crying babies, prayers for transcendence, cussing over foul plays at the card tables. If I listened hard enough I could catch the sounds of my parents' return: the rumbling of Dad's old truck, the rhythm of their footsteps, the lilt and baritone in their voices.

The way Zac's new girlfriend dances in the "Vertical Wire" video, I can tell she's caught up in the beat of another song, too.

Heroin turned the volume down inside me when the sounds wouldn't stop. It was smack or suicide. Mom dragged my ass to rehab, but the withdrawal was so bleak I got convinced the only way out of H was death.

I switch up guitar chords in search of Shelby's internal song. Warm sunlight, and a curious delicacy. With my hand in hers, I caught the sound of something I stopped believing could exist a damn long time ago—a way out. She blew wide open the dreamless wasteland encompassing me, just long enough to let me glimpse its edge. My escape. And then she pulled her hand away.

    She's into him. I could hear that too.

    I wanted to record her music right away, but she and Zac disappeared into the studio, my hiding place, so I went and hung out alone in my room. I was too shaken by what she'd shown me in that instant I held her hand to be around anyone else. I couldn't wrap my head around this eclipse she'd caused in me. Random, erratic explanations rattled about in my head. My thoughts repeatedly circled the same place: Shelby's song, roped off and forbidden.

    I lay my fingers across the strings and they find her melody, the sweet rhythm of the hand I held in mine, the first light of hope I've known my whole life.

    I wonder if Zac knows she's scared, has her own troubles. Damn, he had better be good to her.

    I can't even imagine what she'd think of me if I admitted what I heard inside her. Fuck, she'd call me crazy. Hightail back to Zac the way she did this morning when all I did was shake her hand.

    Anyway, she's Zac's woman, so I've got no choice but to forget her.

    Even if she had never met him, if she were completely free, I wouldn't want her mixed up with the shit I've been going through. If I have any hope of ever getting close to her, or anyone, I've got to cut my demons loose first.

    She showed me there's a way out; I'll have to get there on my own.

    As if I've just woken from a vivid dream, I pen these thoughts into lyrics. I rush to record the details, the path she lit when she broke through my fog, cupping my hand around the match before the flame could extinguish itself.

## THE SECRET SONG OF SHELBY REY

Writing about her in a song is a hell of a lot more respectful than releasing a Grounder video with her dancing around half-naked. It's not my place to say anything, but where the hell are her clothes? Zac has her running around this place in nothing but one of his tee shirts.

Why's she letting him get away with that shit? I can hear her. She's clean as a repentant sinner.

## CHAPTER FIFTEEN

SHELBY

The live room is alive. With all four members of Grounder warming up, the air buzzes with electrical impulses that bounce from one musician to another. The instruments wake from slumber, panting with excitement to burst onto the open road for a playful walk alongside their masters.

I'm panting with them, another instrument in the lineup eager to pound out what Zac calls our "magic": the song we created together, right here in this space. I have no idea how the guys in the band will react. Zac showed me the video he made. He said they loved it and since I'm such a hit, they'll probably fall in love with our song, too. We're on a roll.

A rock and roll. I smile to myself, entertained by my own cheesy joke.

The guys are joking around, too; everyone is in good spirits. Stanford laughs heartily behind me, sending prickling tingles up my spine. I won't turn to look at him. It's just a magnificent coincidence that I happen to be standing in the same room as the man whose music saved my life after Dad died. He doesn't need to know me or what his music did for me. I'm here for Zac, here to bring his music to the light of day.

The guys are anxious to hear what Zac has cooked up. The truth is, I am too. Sure, I helped him hear the music within himself, but he alone sculpted it into a complete song. I just helped supply the ingredients. The finished product is his.

"Okay, brother, what have you got for us?" Oslo asks, fingers at the ready in front of his keyboard.

Zac winks to him, hands him and the other guys some sheet music. After they've had a chance to scan over it, Deshi counts them in with four taps of his drumsticks.

Zac's hands go quickly to work, strumming an introduction before the lyrics come up from behind. The arrangement smacks my ear; it's completely unoriginal. It's not Zac's music, not the song we produced together. If I heard what he was playing on Dad's radio, my thumb would be on the dial, tuning in the next radio station, stat.

I jerk my palm up, halting the sad derivative.

Zac turns to me, a questioning cock to his brow.

Seriously, he doesn't know why I stopped him? I point out his watered-down, washed-out plagiarism.

"But I only played a couple bars." Clearly frustrated, he frowns at Stanford over my shoulder.

"You said you wanted to write something bold and original," I say, urging him to try again. From what I've heard, he's already laid the groundwork. Why has everything changed at the last minute?

Zac fusses with tuning adjustments and tries strumming another arrangement.

I shake my head, confused. "No. That sounds like Deadmau5 covering a Prince song."

The guys smirk at each other.

"The lass is a right radiohead, brother," cracks Oslo. "Can't put anything past this one."

Zac swings his guitar strap over his head and chooses another guitar. "Here's something you haven't heard," he rasps.

I can tell he's thrown off. Why doesn't he just use his music? It's right there inside him. He's one of a kind.

A few strums in and I immediately recognize his next attempt. I have to put a stop to this so he doesn't make a fool of himself. "That sounds like Kings of Leon and The Strokes had a bunch of kids and they formed a high school garage band."

"I'd listen to that band," Oslo chimes in with a laugh. "What'd you say your name is, darling? Shelby? I like you already."

"Dude, you said you wrote a song." Deshi is getting restless. "The Choice Americas aren't karaoke hour."

"Zac, use the music that's yours, inside you," I plead, stroking his arm. "C'mon, you can hear it now. Play it."

Zac meets my eyes, but it's not long before he tears his gaze away and looks at Stanford again. His face is clouded with frustration. Did he really think copying other bands was going to fly?

I dare a peek at Stanford. He is motionless behind dark sunglasses, leaning on one foot, hip cocked, cradling his guitar. I don't know why Zac seems so nervous. Stanford's being more patient than Deshi or Oslo.

The room falls silent again, even with all these bodies. No one says anything, and I'm beginning to wonder exactly what Zac meant about their music-making being a religious experience. There's nothing sacred here.

Stroking his hand through his hair, Zac finally says, "Forget the intro. Let's move on to the melody. It's there on the sheet music. I have a bunch of other ideas for a better intro, don't give it another thought."

The boys resume their positions and the song unfolds. It's good, really good, just like he played for me last night in bed. The band dives in, swimming in the melody that is definitively Zac, the one I fished from his depths, among the writhing passions below my searching hands. A triumph of desire and energy and blasting electricity sizzling from his center and bursting forth.

Zac licks his lips and readies himself in front of the mic. I can't wait for the guys to hear the chorus we forged from those six sweet words over breakfast, and I'm eager to discover the rest of the words he wrote on his own.

In this little room, with optimal acoustics, I don't need to close my eyes to welcome the full body of sound. I watch him, follow his moving lips, while I listen.

His lyrics are bad. Little better than gaudy costume jewelry. Constructed of thin plastic. Bedecking the neck of an obsolete mannequin. Burned like an effigy at an abandoned rock-show-turned-denizen of the hapless and corrupt.

I lower to a chair and nearly miss the seat entirely. The chair, with me perched unsteadily on it, careens into the spongy gray wall panels. Hoping the lyrics will get better as they go along, I straighten up, afraid the guys might kick me out before I get to hear the rest of Zac's words.

I steal a look around the room at the others. Each face is contorted in various expressions of displeasure. Deshi even rolls his eyes, then stops when he catches me watching him. I'm embarrassed. For Zac, but also for me. I had a hand in this, and they all know it. They're going to think this was my lame idea. That I'm ruining everything for Zac, and for Grounder.

My heart is pounding, but I edge toward him, determined to beg him to go back to the authentic lyrics he sang last night. The wheel of my chair catches my foot and I tumble face-first onto the stupid wood floor.

The song grinds to a standstill. Zac peers down at me with concern. Or is it impatience? Two hands secure my shoulders, gently helping me to my feet. I don't need to turn to know who those hands belong to. Stanford places me back in the chair, but his hands don't leave my shoulders.

"You all right?" Stanford asks, leaning over me, his face so close to mine that one of his long, jet-black dreadlocks nearly brushes my cheek.

"Dude, you can take your hands off her now." Zac doesn't hide his irritation. It's sweet, I suppose, that he's jealous, but I can handle myself.

Stanford removes his hands from me, and with them my mirror reflection. "Your song blows, Wyatt." He is first to state the fact.

"Are you okay, babe?" Zac asks me, polite concern thinly veiled by his anxiousness to get on with it, earn the boys' approval for his abysmal creation.

I nod, searching his eyes, wondering whether I dare ask what happened to our—his—song.

"Stan's right, Zac," Deshi pipes up. "Sorry man, I know you wanted to write a Grounder song, but you overshot the mark. The melody is decent enough, but the lyrics are nothing but blimped-out ego." Deshi gets up from behind his drum kit and steps around to confront the group. "Why the hell are we rolling out the red carpet for Wyatt to write his way into a damn solo career? He already owns the spotlight." He glares at Zac. "But that isn't big enough for your massive ego, is it?"

Zac frowns at him, challenging him to say another word.

Deshi swishes back the unruly black fringe of hair concealing half his face and stands his ground. "You might be setting up to get a fat royalty check for writing a Grounder song, but you can be damn sure I'm not about to agree to play some pompous, aren't-I-the-king-shit crap." With that, Deshi turns on his heel and takes a place next to Stanford.

Zac bites his bottom lip, his eyes narrowing to a slit. Then he looks to Oslo with what little hope he has left.

"Sorry, brother." Oslo shakes his bald head, the tiny follicles of a week's regrowth on his habitually shaved scalp catching the overhead lighting. "Do you have any other material?"

"Yes." I jump to my feet. "Zac, we made a ton of tracks. Why don't you play a few back?" I rush to the control room, eager to pull up a handful on the monitor. Clicking open the folder we created, from the corner of my eye I spy Stanford's bronze hand reaching to remove his sunglasses. I flit back to the screen, highlighting the tracks to open, then flash back to him, curious to see his eyes for the first time. He's watching me; they all are.

My skin simmers in the heat of Stanford's gaze until he cocks his chin in Zac's direction. "Seems the lady has something she wants to share with the band."

Zac removes his guitar again, stomps into the control room, and places a protective hand on my waist. "I can take it from here, Shel," he says, his voice heavy with the possibility of defeat.

I select a few of my favorite tracks with the cursor and take a seat behind him, rolling a few channels away, ready to step in when he signals.

"Here's some other lyrics I wrote. Hope they aren't too 'kingshit' for you," Zac grumbles, shooting a look full of indignation at Deshi. He pushes play on the track and the guys glance at one another in the room, each holding a hand to his headphones.

"Better. Give us another," Stanford directs him, penciling some notes on the sheet music Zac provided.

I hear my voice on the track, and I glance at Zac. He is dead calm, staring ahead, past the band, his gaze boring into the back wall of the live room. I'm relieved it's only an audio recording and the guys can't see how I coaxed the melody out of Zac's body with my hands, humming it to him while he played it back on his guitar.

Zac flips to another track and, regrettably, I hear myself utter the words "The naked truth of early light streaming across your bed, warm on our bare skin" in front of all these guys. I feel exposed and understand quickly why Zac didn't jump at the opportunity to write lyrics personal to him.

"Pause," Stanford says, firm and slow. "You sang those exact words in your chorus."

"Yeah, and it sounds like she's humming the melodies and you're parroting them back," Deshi interjects. "Who's the songwriter here, Wyatt? Is this chick your lover or are you fucking your writing coach?"

Zac storms into the live room, his fists clenched by his sides, ready to fight. "It's all mine. Shelby's helping uncover what I always had. She can hear it, all the music inside me. But it's me, it isn't her; she's just showing me my own music."

They have to believe him, he just needs to get this one song off the ground. Whatever it takes, I'll stand by him.

"We're supposed to buy that she's some kind of music medium? C'mon." Deshi slams his sticks down. He's clearly heard everything he's willing to hear.

"I see the future of music," Oslo says, donning a gypsy's voice and pretending to brandish a crystal ball. "I can hear the music inside you. Let me teach you how to play it and you can claim it as your own."

"The show is in a couple of weeks," Stanford breaks in, methodical and steady. "We all agree the melody works; it's classic Zac Wyatt. He just needs to pen some original words."

"No way, Lysandre," Deshi says. "All the 'proof' is in these recordings. These aren't his original ideas. Damn it, Wyatt. You think it's beneath you to perform music written by the man who put us on the fucking map, but totally cool to sign over Grounder royalties to some day-tripper you're bedding? That's some bullshit."

"Day-tripper?" I squeak into their headphones from behind the window to the control room.

"Sorry," Deshi says, dripping sarcasm, "would you prefer *house pet?*"

"That's enough!" Zac shouts. "Back off, Deshi. Fuck."

## THE SECRET SONG OF SHELBY REY

Zac's heel begins to tap and his hand finds his hair and holds on. I fight the betrayal of tears and stand firm, afraid to move.

"You gave it your best shot, brother." Oslo punches Zac's shoulder. "What say we play a Grounder standard at the Awards? We never fail to rock the freaking house."

"No, I haven't given it my best shot." Zac's eyes are wide, panicked. "Give me another chance. Our fans are expecting a new song. And what about Berger and the execs at the label? I can do this, I know I can. I'm closer than I've ever been."

"Okay, Wyatt, keep going. But you got to put up and put up good," Stanford warns. "And Oslo's right. We owe it to the fans to deliver Grounder's recognizable sound. As long as you're in this band"—he slides his sunglasses back over his eyes—"we only perform Grounder music. Regardless of who writes it." He picks up the sheet music, a curious smile twitching at the corners of his mouth. "I'll produce an arrangement that's unmistakably Grounder. Your material, Wyatt, but recognizable to our fans. You just got to write some decent lyrics. Deal?"

Zac paces his bedroom impatiently, tapping the end of his pen against a pad of lined paper and mumbling a staccato progression of profanity. He plops down onto one of the substantial sofas in the corner of his suite, rehashing the episode in the live room, condemning himself as a talentless fool, and then jumps abruptly from his seat and resumes pacing, cursing in his own defense.

From the looming landscape of his bed, I pull my knees up to my chest, making my presence unobtrusive, Zero Interference. When Zac agreed to Stanford's deal and stomped out of the studio, I trailed at his heels, afraid I'd be eaten alive if I stayed behind. I loved the way Grounder played together at the Hollywood Bowl, feeding each other the music, elevating each contribution to an ecstasy shared by everyone present, band and audience alike. That was a religious experience. What I just witnessed in the studio was nothing short of a bad marriage.

On the coffee table in front of Zac's sofa—used until this evening as a landing place for snacks and clothes thrown off in the first heat, and a steady place to hold his camera equipment—sit Zac's laptop and a pot of coffee. He slumps before them, waiting for the words to come.

"I've got to do this," he says, not to me, more to the room. "I can't fail. I need to come up with some decent material, but everything I'm writing sounds hollow and commercial." He smacks the pad of paper with the back of his knuckles. "These are my twisted words."

In his defeat, he sounds hollow and superficial himself. I dare not say a word; it all has to come directly from him, and I've done enough damage here.

"What can I give of myself? Do I have to pretend I'm an H-hound, smack-banging A-hole without a minute of formal musical training? That's the heart of Grounder."

It isn't. I've never used heroin, yet the heart of Grounder beats and burns through me.

"I would just give in, you know? Let Stan have it all. But I want this, I want this more than anything." He lets a deep breath go and whispers, "Listen to yourself, man. Listen the way Shelby taught you."

For a moment, I feel hopeful. But less than thirty seconds pass before he snaps out of his quiet introspection and continues his panicked ramble.

"I can't let them down. Not those traitors who are supposed to be my band, but our audience. And fuck, my label expects me to deliver. They haven't been pouring cash into hyping this performance just for me to bail."

He stands up again and continues pacing. "Let's not forget Gibson. He's so busy trying to stroke out some be-one-with-the-universe bullshit, he hasn't bothered to learn fuck-all about who

I am. If he stopped and listened to me for one minute instead of rhapsodizing about poets and opera, maybe I'd have enough material to write a dozen songs. Everyone is against me."

There is nothing for me to say. I can't help him anymore. But more than that, I want to go back to the studio to see what Stanford is doing. If Zac knew that, he'd count me among the "traitors."

I want to watch Stanford at the soundboard, rearranging the song we wrote to sound like Grounder's music. I wish I'd thought of it myself. I could easily have formed Zac's internal music into Grounder's style, because Stanford is in me. Or I'm in him. I could have saved Zac all this pain.

The manic scratch of Zac's pencil against the paper's smooth surface is abruptly followed by the cushioned friction of his eraser. Maybe if I get a feel for how Stanford is massaging Zac's song, I can come back and refine Zac's lyrics for a cohesive fit.

"Zac? I should give you your space." I rise tentatively from his bed. "I think I'll go watch some TV so I won't be in your way."

"Okay, thanks," he mumbles without looking up from the page. "Love you," he adds mindlessly, just before I close the door behind me.

I hang frozen for a nanosecond, wavering as I catch his face jolting toward the door, spooked by the words that just passed his own lips. Regaining my balance in the shadow outside his doorway, I pull the handle to a silent close, smoothly enough that I'm sure he'll think I hadn't heard him.

Those two words stab at the center of me. I don't trust words. If he refuses to listen to his own music inside himself, how can he know mine or love our melodies together?

I tiptoe down the hall, intent on joining Stanford in the studio. I have no clue whether he'll even let me in.

I pause at the top of the stairs, doing recon before infiltrating the nighttime household. I detect the smell of pot burning from joints passed between half-naked groupies, hear the looping background sounds of video games, spot collections of beer bottles and half-empty tumblers of abandoned drinks amassed on tables alongside the ignored, chef-created party snacks.

Weaving through the house unnoticed, I focus on the various styles of music emanating from its different corners: tinny, studio-polished pop, thumping hip-hop, fast-paced electronic music.

When I come to the hallway leading to the studio, only a dim light warms the control room, and I can't tell if Deshi or Oslo are in there with Stanford. If they are, I'll just tell them I forgot something and find my way back to the room housing that relentless EDM and lose myself in the rhythm of a nonstop bass line.

I peer through the window into the control room and find Stanford alone. He's sprawled out on a leather loveseat the color of charcoal, his head lolled back. I watch his chest rise and fall, and even with his ever-present sunglasses covering his eyes, it's clear he's deep in slumber.

I sneak in, squinting into the glow of the computer's monitor. The tracks Zac played only an hour ago are selected. I check the last date modified. They're unchanged.

Careful not to make a sound, I scroll through, searching for new recordings, but Stanford has done nothing. I wouldn't be the least surprised if Deshi bounced right after promising to help Zac with his song, but I wasn't expecting that from Stanford. From what I gathered tonight, both he and Oslo respect Zac's goals as a musician.

I turn and consider Stanford, drawing closer. Maybe the nightly parties have caught up with him and he'll do the arrangement after a good rest. Mom can only dance so many late shifts till she passes out. Sometimes nearly two days go by without her getting out of bed, and even then she needs a little pick-me-up to get back in stilettos.

It's terrible that I long to touch him.

I just want a little proof, to see whether his own sonic disquiet really is the mirror of my true self, my burden, and my shadow. How can it be?

It can't be.

I slide gently onto the couch next to him, savor the rhythm of his cavernous breaths drifting in and out. I'm too bold, edging my thigh against his.

Something catches against my leg: the end of a length of rubber tubing, wedged between the cushions. I pull it out of the way, and accidentally knock his hand. A blood-stained needle I hadn't noticed held lightly in his fist falls to the floor. He's high. Or low. Or whatever you call someone who just injected.

What should I do? If I go get Zac, he'll know I lied about giving him space to write. *Leaving to watch TV.*

Carefully, I pick up the syringe by the tip of its plastic end and toss it in the trash can. The sound of the tiny spike clanging against the chrome-plated can rattles Stanford briefly, but his slender body weighs him to the couch, as though much heavier.

I grab a bunch of Kleenex from a side table and wad them up to cover the needle's conspicuous guilt. My parents taught me well enough to cover evidence of bad behavior, especially from one another.

"Lock the door," Stanford whispers without moving a muscle, his words scratching past dry lips.

For a reason I don't understand, I don't hesitate to do as he asks.

"Come." He reaches for me, straining hard, as if his arm is carved from concrete.

I hover near the door, unsure why I locked it. "Should I call an ambulance?" I whisper.

"Please," he says, his voice as heavy as his arm, "I want to hear you from the inside. Touch me."

My shoulders warm at the memory of his hands on me earlier in the live room. Does he hear our music in unison as I do, twin anthems in stereo? Or do I sound different to him?

Joining him on the couch, I'm hesitant. I'm with Zac, and I don't even know Stanford, and he's high, or low, or—

Maybe what's needed here is an emergency-room approach. I lower my head, lay my cheek against his chest, and listen for his heartbeat.

I catch my breath, then release all my air out at once.

The room weaves to a pearly lull, my own anthem bobbing and nearly capsizing on a wave of mutilation. I can hear myself within him, and I can hear how the heroin restrains and bridles the tumultuous clash, always beating, always clamoring. I can hear where the heroin punctured its entry and was diffused, the needle, and the damage done.

Stanford grasps my hand in his, enclosing it in a cocoon. Around the edges of his grip, my arm cures to stone. A hot lushness washes up from my hand, filling me from the wrist, up my arm. It bursts vividly, crashing into every dark place and empty void, sealing cracks within me until I'm reformed, whole and complete.

I sink more deeply into his chest, loaded by the heavy pleasure seeping from him. The trumpeting noises and grinding vibrations always thrashing within me slow to a lullaby, a mirror of his—our—lullaby. My lips, drying to porcelain, fall open. A passing desire for deeper breaths fades as the heaves of my lungs slacken to slow-mo.

From his chest, I can sense a brightly lit stage where warmth and safety perform an astral ballet, sweeping the troubles of the world backstage, out of view. I slump into his languid body, aroused, wanting to feel more of him. As I slide across his lap, his hardness presses into me. I smile sleepily. It's enough to be wanted, without all the trouble of trying to undress or make my way to him through this pool of viscous Jell-O I'm in.

I picture Roland behind his gray, smoky doors in Laguna, trying to stop people from chasing their bad habits when all they're doing is getting by. Doing the best with what they've been given. Like Zac, trying to write one silly, simple song. Zac, who thinks Roland is helping me grieve Dad's suicide.

"It's the only way I can get a break," Stanford explains, the words running together in a single exhalation. "From hearing everything. And everybody."

If only Zac knew that Stanford could have helped him all along. Stanford can hear him, and unlike useless me, he knows how to write music.

Dad used to say you get out what you put in. But would he still stand by that advice, now that he's "gotten out" altogether?

I cough. The air traps and burns in my tight, parched throat. I cough again to clear a path, but when I wrench my lungs open, I can't stop coughing. Hoisting my head from Stanford's lap, I stumble forward, reaching for the chrome trash can. I get it under me just in time to throw up, random residual chunks of Zac's once-delicious cooking dotting, then drenching, the wadded Kleenex. A wet outline forms around Stanford's needle, buried beneath the soggy tissue.

I'm quiet a minute, wondering if the storm is over, then hurl up another mess of my insides into the can.

Wiping my mouth with the back of my hand, I turn back to Stanford. "Just play your music out," I tell him. "They tried to medicate me to stop my music—and I'm nobody."

Padding his relentless sounds in a narcotic cell is a crime, I'm sure of it.

"You, Stanford, you can play it out with your guitar, your voice. I wish I didn't have to hear any of it, because it drives me cr—" I hiccup on the last word, a deep sadness for him threatening tears behind the dry mask of my tingling face. "But your music is a gift. I don't know if I could have lived without you and your music."

Stan heaves his limbs forward on the couch, and his body follows until he's able to sit upright. "I've tried. Shelby, believe me, I'm trying all the time," he says, sliding his glasses from his face and pleading with his chocolate eyed gaze. "It's become a part of my life that I can't shake."

I kneel before him, taking his hands in mine, searching his eyes. His tiny black pupils remind me of Mom's "friends" at her club. My tears gather enough moisture to fall.

"And what about Zac?" I ask, because I wouldn't be here now if it weren't for him. "You said you would do the arrangement. If you don't fix it, you'll all bomb, not just him. It'll be a guaranteed total humiliation." I wrench myself into a standing position, pulling away from his touch to regain my strength. "Fix his awful song and keep your promise," I hear myself tell him. "Get up off that couch."

It's what I should have said to Dad. I'm ashamed to speak to Stanford this way, but Dad just sat on our couch doing bloody well nothing but drinking up the courage to blow his own brains out. I'm not going to let history repeat itself. Not tonight, not when there's a song to produce. I'm going to finish what I started.

"Zac's song, that's a trip." Stanford reaches to place his glasses back on his face, then stops when I don't let his gaze go. They fall into his lap, his curled fingers idly toying with them. "That boy doesn't know himself from shit," he says. "He said you heard his song for him. Is that true?"

I sit at the soundboard and say nothing. It's Zac's song. It's doesn't matter how he finally heard it.

"I've been trapped in enough tight tour buses to know what Wyatt sounds like. You don't need to sleep with him to hear it."

I turn my back to him and open the track that needs rearranging. Then it occurs to me that I have no idea how to bring the rest of the soundboard to life, or exactly what I'm able to do on my own.

## THE SECRET SONG OF SHELBY REY

Meanwhile, the stink of my vomit fills the small space. I stand and grab the trash can, holding it away from my nose. "I'll be back in a sec," I tell Stanford. "Get everything ready?"

I dealt with more puke than I care to remember at Mom's apartment, none of it mine. But this is Zac's house, his palace, and as far as I know there are no liquor store dumpsters nearby like there were next to Mom's apartment. Maybe I can find a garage, at least.

I'm hurrying down the corridor in the direction of the dubstep when I'm halted in my tracks by a twenty-something dude in a clean white dress shirt and black pants with an unfortunate Emo haircut.

"May I help you with the bucket?" he asks. I see an event planner's logo on his chest. He's here to work the party, I guess.

"Excuse me?"

"I'll take your puke bucket," he says, losing some formality then quickly regaining it. "Do you need assistance, a place to lie down, or something to eat?"

"Uh, no," I stammer, handing it over. "Thanks."

He disappears with the trash can, and I waste no time getting back to the studio.

To my relief, Stanford has the equipment humming and ready to rock. The air is moist and twinkling with a generous spritz of air freshener. He's even perched on a stool in the live room with his guitar. For a moment, I just smile at him.

There's just the tiniest bit of guilt in my hands when I decide to lock the door again.

I play back the melody track on the computer, then join him in the live room. I don't give a second thought to the soundproof walls. If the silence threatens to smother me, I can simply reach for him and hear myself.

Stanford is still sleepy, his hand languid on the strings. But he's working, and that's all I need. He bends the notes, maintaining Zac's intrinsic melody but changing their length and speed.

I get his approach, but the sound isn't right. It doesn't say "Grounder."

I grab a set of Deshi's drumsticks, get behind the kit, and show Stanford a variation. Establishing a beat veering toward rock, I hum out Zac's melody, careful not to lose the tone of the blue night sky the first time I set foot in this house.

Stanford nods and plays it back to me.

We continue through the entire song, a conversation without words. He offers a line of music and I respond. We repeat one another's offerings, the music of our shared inheritance, refining and purifying. We are lost in the music, an indescribable joy rising and filling the room, returning the air past our lungs to our bellies, filling and lifting us like helium. All the tension and noise and disappointment float away and we jam like crazy.

It's a damn near religious experience.

When we're satisfied with the tracks we've recorded, a light breaks in Stanford's brooding eyes. He smiles at me, and even though we aren't touching, we are wholly connected.

"Let's work on Zac's lyrics." He goes out to the soundboard, finds the track, and hits play.

"You belong up here with me," Zac sings, his voice clean and hopeful, and I hear the yellow sunlight of the first morning I was in his bed. Each day since he first said those words, their meaning has crumbled away. His song is a stranger to mine. Do I belong with him? I've never really known where I belong.

Stanford is back in the live room now, right next to me, listening with me.

"Tell me about the chorus, Miss Shelby."

"Let's try something new." I stumble on my words after being so well understood without them. "A reinterpretation, just for the chorus." I can't be this close to Stanford and hold the refrain of my golden mornings in the arms of the boy I left upstairs.

"All right." Stanford strokes a dreadlock. "The melody you

wrote is the darkest blues of night," he drawls, slow and smooth. "So, what do you have in mind? What happens after midnight in Shelby's world?" He leans on the guitar in his lap and watches me, tiny gold flecks floating in the umber pool of his gaze.

"Midnight, where darkness hides what light cannot," I ramble, the morning's melody fading as I let it go. Stanford's gaze penetrates my flesh, calling me to him. I look down at the drum kit and ready the drumsticks. Stanford doesn't move or take his eyes from me. He is still, and the room is full of him, loud with him, even though he's saying nothing. I smile to ease the prickling anticipation dancing on my skin where his gaze touches me, but polite gestures are empty when so much is being said without the need or fallibility of words. If I knew for sure, if I had some guarantee I'd get a second chance to be here with him, maybe, just maybe, I could get on with this song.

But I'm here to save Zac, to save our song, to save Grounder. The only guarantee here is that this band will never ask for my help again.

And I should never be alone with Stanford again.

I don't know when I stopped breathing, but I let my breath release. His eyes hold me in sensuous embrace, welcoming and soft.

I can't touch him again.

"Shelby," he says, without any demand or need of a response.

I relent at last, accepting the pull toward him, shortening the distance between us.

When I come within inches of him, he stands, opening his arms to me.

I can't, I can't embrace him.

But I'm so close now, close enough to lay my cheek against his shoulder. Just for one minute, just my cheek, that's all.

I hear everything inside him, and I feast on it, joining with it, sinking in the sea of music only he and I share, down down down, away from the ever-changing ebb of the shore above and into the deep still at the ocean's bottomless bottom.

He puts his guitar down and pulls my face to his, cradling my chin to peer into my eyes, past the surface of who I appear to be, into the center of me, and finding the deepest part of himself.

I squeeze my arms around his waist, and he encloses me against him. We sink to the floor, holding one another. I shut my eyes tight, wanting only to hear him, feel him around me, enclosing me in the comfort of his body. Neither one of us speaks. What on earth would we say? We've found our own truths in our connection, and even a kiss is unnecessary tonight.

The music pumps between us, back and forth, back and forth. It penetrates us, sealing an incorruptible bond between us. I won't let go. I can't let him go any more than I could my own breath. He's holding me, revealing all of himself to me; my insides are saturated with his past, the fullness of both his agony and his fight to live.

I respond with everything I've never been able to put to words, open and raw, honest and vulnerable. I can do nothing but give to him as he has given to me.

I wake in Stanford's arms on the hard floor of the live room. He is sleeping deeply, his arms still encircling me. The room is cold and I have no idea what time it is.

I manage to untangle myself from his embrace without waking him, then pad out of the studio and head for the stairs to Zac's room, hoping to get there before he wakes and asks any questions.

"Pretty wild party here last night, huh?"

I freeze in the foyer before the stairs. Deshi approaches me, weaving slightly. The scent of beer and cigarettes precedes him. I edge back, tiny steps, until my heel hits the bottom stair and I have to grab the polished mahogany handrail to keep from falling.

He stops inches from me, his hand sliding up the rail until it rests on mine, gripping it.

"Yeah, great party." I nod, avoiding his breath. "I'm exhausted. I guess I'd better get some rest."

"Hey, sorry about the 'house pet' crack yesterday. You must think I'm such an asshole." His hand slips to my cheek, then trails down to my shoulder. "Let me make it up to you. Let's spend some time together, just the two of us." His hand finds my ass and pulls me against him. "C'mon, Shelby. You want it, that's why you're here."

I turn my cheek to him, looking up the stairs to Zac's door, now miles away.

"No, Deshi, please," I beg him, pushing his chest away from mine.

His fingers dig into me, drawing me harder against him.

"Don't. Please."

"Leave her alone, man." Stanford's words are stained with a threat. His familiar overture floods into me as he pulls me from Deshi's creeping grip into the warmth of his embrace.

"You two?" Deshi's reddened eyes swing from me to Stanford then back to me. "Damn girl, don't waste any time banging your way to the top, do you?" He backs off, still staring me down, and reaches for a pack of smokes. "Fuck it, I wasn't too interested anyway. No tits." He retrieves a cigarette and lights it.

I loosen myself from Stanford's arms and run up the stairs before Deshi exhales the first drag of smoke. I'm nobody's house pet. Not Stanford's, not Zac's, and sure as bloody hell not Deshi's.

I slip into Zac's room, careful to shut the door as though I still have Perla living in the apartment next door.

Only yesterday I would have curled around Zac's slumbering body, planted kisses on his golden skin.

Today, I'm a liar.

## CHAPTER SIXTEEN

"I did it." I smile, leaning my elbow into the pillow, my lips brushing the soft ridge of her ear.

"Hmm?" she murmurs, her sleepy eyes still sealed against the first rays of morning light.

Gathering the sprawl of Shel's tanned limbs into my arms, I feel like a goddamn king. And she's my queen. She's just, I don't know, noble. Even the curve of her thigh has something exquisitely regal about it. I kiss the top of her forehead, loose tendrils of her fine hair tickling the tip of my nose.

"I wrote the song. Myself. It took me all night but I did it, Shel. Exactly how you told me."

Opening her eyes to gaze up at me at last, she opens her mouth, but before she can say anything I catch her lips in a kiss.

She shakes herself free. "That's great. Can I hear it?" In her enthusiam, she wriggles right out of bed and hops over to the trio of guitars on display in the corner. "Which one?" she asks, looking good enough to eat in nothing but one of my tees.

I ought to get my stylist to send another selection of clothes to the house when she sends the stage ensembles I'll be wearing for the Choice America Awards.

But I really prefer to let her run around half-naked. It keeps her from wandering too far.

"No way." I shake my head. "Let me iron the song out with the boys first. I owe you that after yesterday's trip through the first circle of hell. I can't put you through that again." I beckon for her to come back to bed, but she disappears into the bathroom and returns with a hairbrush. Sitting cross-legged on a wing chair next to a ceiling-height mirror, she begins smoothing the wildness from her sexy-as-hell bedhead.

"Actually, I owe you a lot more than that, Shel," I admit, gathering the balls to say what has to be said. "Ashtynn Kingston was slated to appear in the 'Vertical Wire' video. I need to go see her today." I'm cautious, dribbling the facts slow and easy so she doesn't freak. "To tell her we've got it all taken care of."

"You're leaving?" Shel pauses a moment, then cautiously continues brushing.

Hell, I got to be straight with her.

"Yeah, I don't want to be unfair to you or to her. I gotta tell her it's over."

The brush freezes mid-stroke.

"I only want to be with you, Shel." I smile at her and get out of bed. I gently take the brush from her hand and press my lips into her palm. I've never been more certain of what I need to do. "I'm breaking up with Ashtynn."

I peel out from the house with the stereo pumping. Sitting behind the wheel for the first time in days, I count myself one lucky bastard for bringing Shel home. It seems she'd forgotten Ash's existence. Hell, me too. Just proof that Ash is already history. As soon as I can wipe the slate clean of her, I can convince Shel she's no house pet and get back to the studio and finalize production on my song. I know it's good. So good I don't even give a fuck what Stan might've done to the arrangement. I have Shel in my life now, and that means plenty more songs where this one came from.

I pull up to the Chateau Marmont, where Ashtynn's holed up while her Malibu house is being redecorated. She's already spending the money OmniMotion promised her. She texted me her room number last night, but I turned her down. Songwriting and Shelby, those are my priorities now.

When I tap on the door of her poolside bungalow, Ash opens it no more than ten inches, crowding the space with her ample chest. Wearing precious little but a sheer cami and ruffled panties, she flashes her long mahogany lashes at me.

I get a sharp dose of déjà vu. I've knocked on Ash's hotel room door at least a hundred times and nine-inch nailed her like an animal the moment it shut behind us.

This time, I'll pass.

Her eyes are clouded by a glassy haze. It's obvious she's railing, just like she used to. What a dumb move, blowing all the work she did in rehab. She knows perfectly well this could cost her OmniMotion.

"Darling, you're high as the Empire State." There is a bitter edge to my voice in the sweet early-morning air.

"You know I'm clean, baby," she slurs. "I felt a head cold coming on, that's all. I just took some cough medicine," she simpers. "Careful. If you kiss me, you might catch it."

Trading spit or any other bodily fluid with her is the last thing on my mind. Ash has gone low-budget. Or was she always, and I was too blind to see it? Ashtynn Kingston has nothing on Shel. Shelby Rey is the fucking queen.

This sure makes telling her about "Vertical Wire" a hell of a lot easier.

"We need to talk. Can I come in?" I try to push by into her

suite, but she stands firm, nearly closing the door in my face in her effort to keep me out.

"Zacky"—she lowers her voice to a whisper—"you know I want to have you in, baby. But I made a wittle mistakey last night."

"Yeah, no shit," I reply. I spot an empty bottle of champagne floating in a bucket of melted ice next to the sofa by the window.

"My doctor's here for an emergency session," she says, rubbing at the base of her nose. "Can I text you later, baby?" She sniffs, then discovers the door handle in her other palm. She toys with it, her attention entirely absorbed.

"Roland's here?" I ask, placing my foot in the door. A pair of men's Oxford shoes lie neatly inside. Only some Dartmouth dweeb would wear Oxfords.

"Who else, silly?" She giggles.

Roland, that lying, bull-shitting, asshole liar. He's been sleeping with Ash all this time. I knew it.

"Before you go back to your, uh, emergency session, I need to talk to you about the video." I try to play it cool with her. There's no reasoning with an addict. But I'm sure as hell going to corner Roland later and let him have it.

"The storyboards I sent over are amazeballs, am I right? You can thank me later, Zacky." We both hear the shower being turned on. Ash glances over her shoulder, then smacks the side of her cheek on the door when she turns back to me. "Ouchies," she whines, and resumes rubbing at her face. "I gotta go."

Before the door closes on me she lisps, "Love you."

It kills me. Not Ash, she can go fuck herself. It's the false emptiness of "Love you," conspicuously missing that all-important "I."

When I did it to Shel last night, it was an accident. I mean, I guess I've been feeling it, but I wasn't ready to admit it. I'm in love with her. I need to tell her and say it right. She deserves that. She deserves the best I can give her.

But I can't give her my best, not before I deal with Roland. If he thinks I'm going to let him hop in the shower with Ash, he's sadly mistaken. Before that pathetic excuse for a shrink gets wet, I've got some business to settle.

I sprawl out in a lounge chair by the pool and call his private cell number.

"Zac, are you all right?" Roland answers on the second ring.

"No, Dr. Gibson. I'm not. I need to see you, now. It's an emergency."

"Where are you, son?"

"Chateau Marmont, as a matter of fact. Can we meet?" I bait him.

"Yes, I just arrived at my Beverly Hills office. I'll clear my appointments and we'll have a session immediately. Do you need me to send a car to get you?"

I turn back and look at Ash's door. If Gibson's in Beverly Hills, who the hell is in Ash's shower?

"Ashtynn is cheating on me," I announce, dropping into one of two leather chairs in front of Gibson's desk. "And she's using again, high as a fucking kite."

"Good morning. Glad you could make it in, Zac. I was concerned when you called. You said you needed emergency help, but it sounds like you're more worried about Ashtynn."

"When's the last time you saw her, Dr. G?"

"Typically, that's confidential information, but you were there, Zac, roughly eighteen months ago. Dr. Rachman has taken over her maintenance counseling, but I oversee her case. Her well-being is as important to me as it is to you."

"Sure it is," I reply, part of me damn thankful it wasn't him this morning. "Hey, where is your buddy Elliott?"

"He's out-of-office today."

"Golf course?" I ask, leading him.

"What's going on, Zac?"

"I'll bet my left nut he's fucking Ashtynn right now. I wouldn't be surprised if he's the one who supplies her party favors and 'sleep aids,' and orders her champagne."

"Stop right there," Gibson warns. "I've known Elliott Rachman since med school. He's trustworthy, professional, and my business partner for God's sake."

I fold my arms, one eyebrow raised. "My left nut."

Roland pulls out his tablet and opens an appointment calendar with a password. He doesn't have to tell me Ash is on Elliott's books today. His face says it all.

"Before you jump to any conclusions," he says quickly, "let's recall when you and I first met. You were worried, nearly convinced, I was having an inappropriate relationship with Ashtynn."

"Yeah, sorry 'bout that." I shrug. "Ash kept telling me she was meeting with you when obviously it was your boy Rachman."

"Zac, have you considered that the charges you bring against Ashtynn may be a mirror of your own guilt? Shelby Rey is currently a guest in your home. Perhaps you can imagine all too well what Ashtynn may be capable of, as a reflection of your own desires."

"Ashtynn was boning Hairy Stout before I met Shel, I'm sure of it."

"Please refrain from inappropriate name-calling." Gibson tries to hide his irritation. "Is that what prompted you to seek out a new partner? Did your concerns about Ashtynn's fidelity push you to act on your attraction to Shelby?"

Before I can answer, he adds, "How is Shelby, by the way?"

By the way, my ass. He cut me off to find out how she's doing. Nothing casual about that. It's my turn to be Patient Number One. Besides, he has nothing to worry about where Shelby's concerned.

"She's my kind of fun," I say lightly. "Gotta love the rich, bored, and beautiful. She ain't the naive type, either, get what I'm saying?"

"Not entirely," he replies. "This is Shelby Rey we're talking about?"

I like messing with Gibson, but I'm not sure I can keep up the act. I'm seriously taken with this girl, and the truth is, I'm afraid to tell her I love her.

In the space of a long pause, the only sound between us is the tap of my heel. I recognize the pattern, the one Shelby showed me that first morning she came to stay. The rhythm that beats through me and is me. Without her, it would only be a nervous tic, something to be ashamed of. Something I would try to control. Now it reminds me who I am.

I let out a long sigh and cross my ankle over my knee. Stroking my hair, I take a good long look at Gibson. The guy sits there calmly, waiting for me to gather my thoughts, patient as all fuck. For whatever reason, Shel seems to trust him, and if anyone can get a read on a person, it's her.

"The thing about Shelby," I start, switching ankles and knees, "is she doesn't ask for anything. She's satisfied. Content, you know?"

Gibson nods but says nothing, so I fill in the blanks.

"I need stuff. Ash and me, we're greater than the sum of our parts. She introduces me to people, and I help her out. Together, we score a whole new playing field of opportunities."

Gibson clears his throat. "Do you want to continue with that relationship?"

"Hell, no. I mean, Ash has been good for my career, and I'll always be thankful. But I need Shelby now. I've never met anyone like her, and I love who I am when I'm with her. She's given me myself. A better self than I could be on my own."

"Sounds like you and Shelby are building a significant bond."

"She doesn't need me," I say too quickly. "I mean, I'm not good enough for her."

♪ 201 ♪

Oh shit, that's true.

"What leads you to believe that?"

"The fangirls, they love me for who they've made me in their minds, and God knows their version is probably better than reality. I let them in my bed, it's what we both want, and I've never failed to please. But I send them home before they get a chance to know me beyond the mask of stardom."

"You say you like who you are with Shelby," he says. "How is this partnership different? Are you getting to know her before engaging in a sexual relationship?"

"Oh, hell no," I laugh, then remember he's her stand-in daddy. "Listen, I wanted straight-up intimacy with her. Sex brings that, lets you bypass the getting-to-know-you gamble and go right to insta-couple."

"You're saying you're hiding behind sex to win her?"

"No." Shit, I'm not getting it out right. "What I mean is, I don't want to let her down. I am getting to know her. I love her." I don't know why I'm yelling. "But I'm afraid she won't love me."

Quieting down, I continue, "I don't think I've ever loved anyone before. And I'm damn sure no one has loved me. Me—not rock star Zac Wyatt—me."

"As I recall, you and Ashtynn were very close during her rehab."

"Yeah, her overdose was a real honeymoon period." I stroke my hair, trying to brush away the sarcasm, and the tapping begins again. "Ash was raw and honest during rehab. But it didn't last. When I met Shelby outside your office, I assumed she was still drunk or possibly high, and—Christ, I found her sexy."

"Do you consider yourself a rescuer of sorts, Zac?"

"I like to, uh, leverage the outcome in my favor, I guess." I shrug. "That's what nailed down Ash. I was her savior when she was down. At her worst, I brought her up. It's pretty clear she's found someone else to give her what she really wants: to get high.

But not Shel. All I can give her is me, and I don't know if that'll be enough to keep her around."

"Have you two shared much of your life stories?"

"Yeah, I guess. She told me her dad just passed away and she's staying with you and your wife while she grieves or whatever."

Gibson nods and considers his abstract art installations at length before returning his gaze to me. "Do you think it would be worthwhile to have her join us in a session where we can build a bridge of honest communication? Would you like to begin your first love relationship on a strong foundation?"

I lean forward, placing my elbows on my knees and resting my chin in my hands. A real chance with Shel? Yeah, I want that.

# CHAPTER SEVENTEEN

Two guys with a guitar and bongos bust out some decent rhythms on the small patio outside Café Concord, home of Beverly Hills' best latte, in my opinion. The afternoon sun has baked the blue sky nearly white. The heat radiating from the sidewalk quickly changes my order to an iced coffee.

Waiting in line at the counter, I spot a girl alongside the musicians, nearly naked and dancing wildly on the sidewalk. When did Rodeo Drive go Burning Man?

As I'm stepping out from the air-conditioned café, drink in hand, a familiar sweep of long blonde hair triggers a second glance.

It's Shelby, I'm certain of it. I recognize her untamed movements from that day Zac came by the house. She's wearing nothing more than a Linkin Park concert tee and heels, but it's definitely her.

"Shelby," I call to her, "are you all right? Where's Zac?"

She doesn't look my way or respond whatsoever. Her face impassive, she continues hopping, prancing, and swaying to the band's rhythm as if she's in a trance.

"Let it be, man, let it be," the bongo player chides me with a grin, clearly hoping she'll better their chances for spare change tossed in the open guitar case.

I think about calling Zac. According to his report earlier this morning, Shelby should be safe and sound at his place. But considering his demonstration of paranoid delusion, constructing an illicit relationship between Elliott and Ashtynn Kingston, for Pete's sake, the man's hold on reality is unstable. Jaclyn was right. I should never have let him take Shelby home.

It's possible she's displaying symptoms of an acute stress reaction. Or she may have ingested some sort of hallucinogen. There's no point making a feeble assessment here, I need to get her off the street.

"Shelby? It's me, Roland." I don't want to scare her. "My dear, let's get you somewhere safe. You're welcome to come to my office."

Shelby doesn't indicate any awareness of my voice or presence. I wish Jaclyn was here. She's a pro at this, getting patients in crisis off the street.

I reach out and lightly tap Shelby's arm, trying to get her attention, but she hollers as though burned when my fingertips brush her forearm. I could call for police backup, but that would likely land Shelby in jail for disorderly conduct and Zac in another media nightmare. I'd like to examine her before any fingers are pointed or court dates ordered.

A few passersby scowl at me, the old guy harassing the free spirit.

A quick scan of the neighborhood produces no familiar faces. There are no excuses. I don't have a lot of choice here. I need to reach Shelby on her own terms.

I either act now or lose her. Again.

Taking a deep breath, I put aside my better judgment and jump in, as much for Jaclyn as for Shelby.

At first, I dance the way I might if this were a beachside

tavern with a live acoustic band and I were twenty-five. The old moves, the way I'm accustomed to grooving. Shelby takes a tentative glance my way. No remark follows, but that little glance is all the encouragement I need. Watching her closely, I mirror her moves, dancing with her, defending her loose, rhythmic bouncing with the approval of my accompaniment.

I'm frankly worried about a client passing by and witnessing this spectacle. I bolster my resolve by reminding myself that there's not a lot I wouldn't do to help my patients. And I can't let Jaclyn down. Again.

As I let go and blend with Shelby, I hear it. The more closely I mimic her twitches and shimmies, the more clearly I see the patterns between the melody and bassline. I can detect a language in the music. It speaks to me. Watching Shelby's facial expressions, I'm certain she hears it too.

The story told in the music is freedom. Release is its message. I hear it now, clearly, and let out the howl of an uncaged animal.

Rodeo Drive be damned.

Shelby cracks a smile. She smiles! Turning herself to me and tossing back her hair, she closes her eyes and loses herself in the music again. The band of two go crazy, playing for all they're worth. I won't let embarrassment get the better of me. I just keep on grooving.

We dance, the song finishes, and another starts. Dancing in this heat is irrational—we're both sweating. But she doesn't slow her pace, so neither do I. We dance, and dance, and dance, exhaust from the start of rush hour traffic broiling up around our legs, until the band begs us to give them a break.

"Let's get some cold drinks back at my office," I offer, trying to catch my breath. "And something to eat?"

Shelby throws me a curious look.

"I have a second office here in Beverly Hills," I explain. "It's right around the corner."

Before she crumples to the ground, I catch her.

"When did you eat last?" I ask, lifting her small frame into my arms.

If I wasn't self-conscious enough before, carrying a half-naked teenager through the neighborhood has achieved that.

My receptionist, Carly, is unforthcoming about any extra clothes she might have in her gym bag until I fork over a couple hundred bucks. Once I get Shelby decent and fed, and her primary vitals stable, I'm hoping she'll let me return her home to Jaclyn.

From the office break room, I grab some water bottles, juice, and a Tupperware full of Jaclyn's gluten-free cookies, then join Shelby in my office. Better than nothing.

"What's the magic trick?" Shelby asks, placing an entire cookie in her mouth. "My tummy's been okay since you told me about the sealy-whatever. Just avoid bread and I'll avoid pain?"

"You could look at it that way," I respond, biting into a cookie and wiping my hands on a napkin. "Rather than avoiding certain foods to avoid pain, we could make healthier choices in favor of self-respect, dignity, and reaching our best potential."

"Did Jaclyn teach you that one?" Shelby asks, a kindness to her banter. I'm glad she sees Jaclyn as a proponent of positive choices. MRI studies show that the same areas of the brain become activated when we experience rejection as when we experience physical pain. It stands to reason that the opposite is also true, and acceptance breeds healing. If Shelby allows herself to be cared for and takes steps to care for herself, it may help her resolve some long-standing issues. And whatever transpired between her and Zac.

"It's my belief we can turn any weakness into a source of our strength," I say, taking a sip of water. "Your ability to hear, for instance, has gotten you arrested and has damaged the bond between your mother and you. It may just land you back in the hospital, or worse, in jail—if you continue to see it as a weakness."

"You can show me how to make it stop?"

"I can help you embrace it as your source of strength."

Shelby sniffs, skeptical.

"How do you know the life you are used to is better than the opportunities to come?" I ask.

"I'm not even sure what to hope for."

I check my watch. "I need to test your blood pressure again, ensure your vitals have stabilized, okay?"

She nods and offers up her arm.

"Zac's house is in the Hollywood Hills," I casually toss out as I fit the cuff around her bicep. "Long way from here."

"Bus pass," she says.

"He wasn't able to give you a ride down?"

Her eyes narrow. "He wasn't who I thought he was."

"You saw Zac perform with Grounder at the Bowl," I observe, careful to wash my tone of any judgment.

"Yes. It was amazing. Thank you for not getting mad about that. I had to go."

I nod and search her eyes. I recognize that "thank you" doesn't come easily for this young woman. She hasn't had a lot to be thankful for, it seems.

"So you enjoyed the performance," I continue. "And then you had an opportunity to become better acquainted with Zac in his home?"

I release the cuff of the blood pressure meter but hold my stethoscope against her skin a second longer, and in that sliver of a moment I pick up a sudden spike in her heart rate.

"I found out his secret. I'm not some stupid kid. He isn't the heart of Grounder, he has his own songs inside him." She sits straighter, daring me to defend Zac. "He didn't have to tell me. I heard his music myself."

"Can you hear his music now?"

"Of course not." Shelby shakes her head at my suggestion. "I have to"—she looks away only an instant, then stares me straight in the face—"I have to touch him to hear him." She punctuates each word so I don't miss her meaning.

"Was this experience with Zac your first sexual encounter, Shelby?"

"I don't usually like it when people get too close." Shelby assumes a toughness I haven't before observed in her. "But I get there's an expectation from people when they're putting a roof over your head and food on the table, and Zac was so kind and gentle. It's the love part that trips me up."

"You never owe anyone sex for any reason, Shelby." Her comment triggers me to explore the possibility of past sexual abuse, but I need to better understand her present emotional dilemma first. "Do you believe you're in love with Zac?"

Shelby shoots me a look. I can tell I hit a nerve. "My parents danced the cheater's waltz for years. I know well enough to spot a cheating heart."

"Is that why you left? You and Zac discussed his relationship with Ashtynn Kingston?"

"You knew?" She is vulnerable, searching my face. "And you left me with him?"

"I was clear about my wish for you to return with me and Jaclyn. Going home with Zac was your decision." I am gentle but firm with my reminder. "I respected your choice as an adult."

"I'd heard about them from some radio DJ, but Zac made it seem like it was over ages ago," she pleads with me, her eyes overcast with a sullen fog. "I did figure out one thing fast: He only wanted me for his music."

"You developed genuine feelings for Zac, and you believe he abused your trust?"

She is quiet a moment, her eyes clouded. "I don't care," she says at last, but I'm not sure she believes it. "Sometimes Zac makes me feel like I am golden. And sometimes it seems like he doesn't have a kind word to say about anyone, and I wonder how long before I'm on his shit list, too." Shelby searches her thoughts, and I wish I could see the scenes she's recounting. "He doesn't know who he is. So how can he know what he wants?"

I nod without comment, waiting for her to elaborate.

"But I found the pulse of Grounder," she whispers. "My Grounder, pumping through my veins." She holds open her hands, turning her wrists to reveal her inner arms. "I heard him. And he heard me."

I lean forward slightly, listening intently. "What, or who, do you consider 'the pulse' of Grounder, Shelby?"

I barely hear her reply, but I just make out the name: "Stanford."

"So you went there to connect with Grounder's 'pulse,' and you were successful. You discovered Stanford is Grounder's principal songwriter. What caused you to leave?"

"The drummer, he called me a house pet, a day-tripper. Their house is filled with cheap toys they share and then toss aside. I actually thought Zac cared for me." A single tear bubbles over her lid, breaking free from the storm cloud. "Until Zac told me Ashtynn was his girlfriend. And always has been."

"I'm going to ask you to clarify, Shelby. Did you leave because Zac admitted he has a girlfriend or because you have feelings for Stanford?"

"I didn't know how lonely I used to be. I could hear others, but no one could hear me, and it made me feel like some craptastic freak no one could ever know, let alone love. But Stanford can hear me. Worse, he's like my reflection, the harmony to my melody. Now that I know he exists, I feel lonelier than ever." She pauses, searching for the right words. "I want to be with him. But I can't." She places her hand on my arm. I wonder what she hears or what she wishes I might hear in her.

♪

I close the roof on my convertible for the drive home along the noisy 405 South. It's a balmy night, but I need to hear what Shelby might be willing to share. Not only her choice of words but also her tone.

I didn't get a chance to open a file on her. When she agreed to go back to my house, I led her to the parking garage without further question, texting Jaclyn as we made our way to the car. Paperwork can wait.

Shelby is silent while we weave through the streets of LA. My phone buzzes in my pants with a string of replies from Jac, who is undoubtedly as thrilled as I am that Shelby is coming home.

I need to prepare Shelby for what's waiting for her at our house.

"In order to ensure you make the best choices regarding your dating life," I begin, pulling onto the I-10 ramp, "we'll need to begin healing your core relationships. Starting with your mother."

Her lips close firmly. I hate jumping to the Mom talk, but I know Jac won't waste any time getting to the topic.

"You want to start with meds? That's what Mom wants," Shelby says, staring straight ahead.

Damn it, it's too soon. The pain from their separation is still keen. I backpedal.

"There are no quick fixes," I tell her. "We can begin talk therapy, but there won't be exits to Easy Street or depending on anyone else."

I am droning, I can tell. Her mind is back in the Hollywood Hills. I decide to change my approach.

"If you could do anything, what would it be?"

"Been asking myself that for a while."

We drive another few miles in silence. "I can't afford college, Roland."

"I know the feeling." I nod, encouraging her to keep talking.

"Whatever, Mr. Fancy Med School."

"I got accepted at Dartmouth, but I had to earn scholarships before I could go. My father is a pastor, and he couldn't afford my tuition. And my mother left us when I was a kid."

"You're so lying. That doesn't happen to churchy people."

"I wish that were true," I reply, sliding into the fast lane. "I knew I wanted to help people, Shelby. What about you? What do you want to do?"

"Listen," she says, as though it could be her vocation. "Zac and his band have a music studio at their house where they record, edit, and arrange their music. I wish that could be school."

There are events such as this, the critical moment when the lifeboat is spotted by a patient adrift in her own unyielding sea of despair and she finds her own way. It's my honor to bear witness to these events, not least because they rescue me too. They give me hope and optimism, not only for my client but also for greater humanity. They are proof and an assurance that problems are surmountable. Real change is possible.

The work remains of allowing Shelby to believe this for herself.

"Shelby, your gift is your ear. Your ability to hear is your strength."

She shrugs, resigned.

"Jaclyn and I will help you research and apply to audio and sound engineering colleges." LA traffic slows to a near halt, even on the expressway. I take the opportunity to observe her. "Can we set that goal together?" I ask.

She crinkles her nose in disbelief. "What, you don't think Hogwarts or Xavier's School would accept my applications?"

"Audio engineering school is a real thing, Shelby. There are several accredited schools in LA. A career in professional recording is a legitimate possibility for you."

"For real?" Shelby sits forward in the deep bucket seat, a light appearing behind the storm of her eyes. "You really think I could do it?"

## CHAPTER EIGHTEEN

I toss the bottle of methadone capsules onto the coffee table in my bedroom, next to the video camera I used to shoot Shelby for the "Vertical Wire" video. Elliott Rachman is a jerk-ass pusher douchebag. He was all too happy to hook me up with a prescription, no questions asked. I knew it. It's how he's kept—keeps—Ashtynn on the line.

I've got him right where I want him.

When I figured out he's the one Ash has been boning all this time, I wasn't about to crawl away crying. But when I got home and found out Shelby had bailed? Without a single word? Of course I freaked. What did I do wrong? Is something wrong with her? Goddamn it, this is why I don't let anyone get too close. They always leave. They get to know me, the real me, and they split. Why in hell did I think for a second the smartest, hottest girl I've ever met would be any different? Because she "gets" me? That's the reason they leave.

It wasn't difficult to convince Elliott I needed one of his infamous "emergency" sessions. I was tripping about losing Shelby, but I wasn't about to tell him that. I just bitched to him about my so-called "painful recovery from drug abuse" and how Dr. Gibson isn't helping me out.

Rachman totally bought it. He pulled up to the house in his Maserati GT within the hour. That's what I call star treatment, a far stretch from Gibson's why-the-hell-are-you-showing-up-at-my-house attitude.

Sprawling out on my couch, I find Gibson's home number on my cell and call it. I've already left four messages with his office, asking whether he's seen Shelby.

No response.

I haven't had the balls to hit his private line until now. I'm afraid he's going to grill my ass for whatever I did to scare Shelby away. But I have to know where she is.

A few rings in, he answers. "Hello?"

I swallow hard. If Shel is back at his place, that's where I want to be too.

I brush my shoes off on the doormat outside Gibson's large, carved-wood front door. My soles are spotless, but I've never shaken the Oregon rain from my unconscious gestures. It's some Pacific Northwest nervous tic, I'm pretty sure. Where I grew up, track mud indoors one time and you'll be turned out on your ass.

Gibson opens the door with a warm smile and ushers me into his home as if I'm a welcome dinner guest and not a total letdown, a posturing, egomaniac rock star. Christ, the guy is decent.

Hovering in the open doorway, I offer the wife—Jaclyn, I remind myself—an arrangement of purple lilacs.

"They're lovely, Zac, thank you," she says. "Did you know these are New Hampshire's state flower?"

Of course; I did my homework. This visit is too important. I glance around casually but see no sign of Shelby. "I have something for you, Dr. G." Grinning, I reach just outside the front door, snag the new Taylor acoustic guitar I picked up on the way, and present him with it. "Maybe it's time you learned a few riffs of your favorite songs, old man," I say, joking like we're buddies. "If you have a Sharpie, I'll sign it. That'll give it more value." Do I sound like a jerk? "I mean, I'll sign it to say thanks. For everything."

They lead me into the living room, and I sit politely on the chocolate brown sectional, without assuming too much space. Jaclyn hands me a marker. I scribble my autograph onto the guitar and Gibson seems genuinely touched.

"You were the only one who believed me about the heroin episode, you know that?" I say, capping the marker.

Jaclyn glances at him with admiration. I hope I can have that with Shel again.

"And you are one of the few who supported my need to write my own music." The few? Make that two: Gibson and Shelby. "You've been a friend to me, man."

Gibson gives me a bear hug and a fatherly thump on my back. "Thanks, Zac. This means a lot to me. Our therapy program is officially over. But I'm here for you while you write your first solo album. By the way, are we going to have the privilege of hearing the song you wrote for the Choice America Music Awards?" He motions toward the guitar.

"I'd like to hear it." It's Shelby.

That girl enters a room like a ninja. She looks hot as ever, but chic in a way only she could pull off, poured into dark-wash denim and a metallic silver tee that skims her tiny frame.

My girl looks good in real clothes. Damn, why didn't I take her shopping? It was selfish of me to leave her near naked at my house day after day. What the hell was I thinking?

Yeah, I know what I was thinking.

It's all I can do to stop myself from scooping her into my arms and promising to never let her go. But I got to feel out the situation. God only knows what I did or said to send her running. I can only imagine what she told Gibson.

"Hang on, I have something for Shelby," I tell them, keeping a safe distance from her wary gaze. "Here's the check she earned for starring in Grounder's 'Vertical Wire' video."

I pull it from my messenger bag. As I get close enough to hand it to her, she turns her body away. It's only a subtle turn, but I get the message. I fucked up, and whatever she's pissed about ain't over. I hope her earnings for the video sweeten her mood. I fattened her income myself, just in case.

"Shelby, you didn't tell us about any video." Jaclyn seems pleased enough. "We'd love to see it."

"It's in post-production," I tell them. "The global premiere will be twenty-four hours before the Choice Americas, during MTV's special event announcing all the Award nominees."

"Is this for real?" Shel asks, reading and rereading the amount on the check.

"If it isn't enough, I can speak with my management." Whatever she wants, she can have. Fuck, I'll transfer funds to her account right here. I reach into my pocket for my phone.

Jaclyn makes a squawking sound when she reads the check amount over Shel's shoulder, drawing Gibson's curiosity. He joins them, and his face breaks into a smile.

"Congratulations, Shelby," he says. "That should cover your college tuition and your school expenses. You've earned enough to secure your future, young lady."

Shel turns the check over in her hands. "I earned it?"

She's suspicious. I wonder if Jaclyn will freak when she sees the "work" she did, dancing around my bedroom in her teeny-tiny tightie-whities.

"Hey, you acted in a music video." I look to Gibson to back me up. "Pulls decent coin, right?"

"We have much to be thankful for tonight," he says with a nod.

"Dinner will be ready shortly." Jaclyn motions for Shel and me to take a seat. "Zac, do play something for us, will you?"

Shel and I sit down together on the couch but she avoids my gaze. Glancing at her check, she places it on the coffee table and then picks it up again. She folds it in half, then into quarters, then unfolds it, smoothing it on her lap.

I'm not going to pull a Kanye West and play anything from my own playlist. I'll just give them a few hits from my favorite bands.

I strum out a handful of chords, warming up my fingers.

"Creep," Shel mutters.

My hands freeze on the strings. What the hell? I guess Gibson's going to get his little couple's counseling session after all.

"Radiohead," she adds. "You know how to play it?"

I nod, relieved she meant the song "Creep," not me. When I stumble over the strings, trying to figure out the chord pattern, she sighs impatiently and hums it out until I can get a hold of it.

"Sing," I tell her. I'm not about to let her leave me stranded here.

Shel breaks into the lyrics, drumming them up from memory without missing a beat. Jaclyn leans in closer and Gibson takes a seat, transfixed. Shelby has that effect on people.

I play it like it was a random request, just the first song that popped into her pretty head. She fades out near the end part about not belonging here.

"I'll bet Shelby knows the words to nearly every song on the radio." I manage a grin to cover my discomfort. "Try another, sweetheart? Name it, I'll play it."

Kindling behind her eyes breaks and disintegrates, revealing molten silver. Shel stares at the hardwood floor. "'Secret Lover,' 'The Other Woman,' 'Unfaithful'"—she meets my eyes at last, a bonfire now burning behind her glare—"or how about 'A Liar's Heart' by Ashtynn Kingston?"

"If you want to talk about it, let's go, let's do this," I say, laying the guitar aside. If we have any hope of moving forward, we need to sort out whatever's bugging her. And if I can't resolve it myself, the good doctor and wifey are right here to be our crash pad.

"How come you never told me you have a girlfriend?" Shel demands.

Seriously? Like she didn't know. It's common knowledge. "Don't play games with me, be straight." I try not to sound impatient, but come on.

"You can't tell me you didn't know about me and Ash. Hell, even if you were trapped in a convent and deprived of Wi-Fi, Gibson here could have clued you in." I need to take the edge off my voice before shit escalates. "What does it matter, anyway? It's over with Ashtynn."

I ease the check from her grip and place it neatly on the coffee table, then take her hands in mine. Thumbing circles in her palms, I meet her eyes. "I only want to be with you, Shel." This is not how I pictured telling her. I didn't expect an audience, for one thing. I also hoped she wouldn't be angry with me when I told her.

Her eyes fall closed, shutting me out. I take a deep breath and continue circling, a warmth building between the pads of my fingertips and her hands.

"I love you," I whisper, urging her to open her eyes.

She does, but only to stare into the tangle of fingers held between us. She is silent, and I know her well enough now to realize she's listening. Listening to me.

I just told her I love her. I never say that. To anyone.

But once Shelby retreats into the music, the whole world disappears. I want to be her world, but what if she doesn't like what she hears?

"What matters here is you and me," I whisper, trying to reach her.

Still no response. I glance at Jaclyn and Gibson. He nods, urging me to continue.

"Speak to me, Shel. Closing down is no way to live."

Since the shrink duo is giving me space, I do my best to use the lessons Gibson's taught me. I need to know if she loves me. Or could, if we can work past this.

"Please, have the courage to express yourself. Don't use music, even mine, as a shield from the world."

"Why don't you cough up some courage and express yourself, Zac?" She looks up at me with those lustrous eyes, silver flames burning. "If anyone has built a shield, it's you. Drop it and you could write your own songs."

"I'm working on it. I thought you liked helping me. We're a team, right?"

"I love creating music. But I refuse to be Grounder's 'teammate,' Zac. I'm no day-tripping, hit-and-quit girl. You, and Stanford, and the others need to be clear on that."

"Damn right you aren't," I almost shout. "Shelby Rey, I want you all to myself. And I want you to want me." I can still see the fear behind the fire, so I try to reassure her. "If Stan, Deshi, or Oslo ever lays a hand on you, I'll fuck them up beyond recognition."

"All right," Jaclyn breaks in. "You've given Shelby a lot to consider, Zac. How about we all sit down to dinner now?"

She places a warm hand on my forearm and directs me away from Shel and into the dining room.

Dinner is surprisingly decent, considering Gibson's wife cooked it herself. I don't mean her any offense, but it's pretty bold to host a dinner party without hiring a chef. Kind of reminds me of being back home.

"I can't remember the last time I had a home-cooked meal, Ms. Spenser. This is delicious." I smile her way.

"Zac is a great cook," Shel pipes up, and I'm more than a little flattered. It's the first kind word she's had for me all evening.

"I don't know about 'great,' but I kept us from going hungry, didn't I?" I smile a thanks to her. *Stick with me and I'll take care of everything,* I want to tell her.

And then I get the best goddamned stroke-of-genius idea.

"I want Shelby to accompany me on Grounder's tour to Asia this fall," I announce, as much to the pseudo-parents at the ends of the table as to Shel. "We're touring China, Japan, Thailand, and Singapore. We've dubbed it The Magical Mystery Tour." I laugh. "It's a mystery because I haven't written the songs we're going to play." I catch a little grin quivering on Shel's lip and feel encouraged. "And it'll be magical, if Shel agrees to come along."

I watch those pretty lips form the beginnings of an enthusiastic "yes."

But Jaclyn speaks up on her behalf. "Shelby is registering for college in September." She is firm, shutting down my offer without allowing the possibility of further discussion.

I glance at Gibson, who is chewing his braised pork rib and eyeing me thoughtfully. If this was a session, he'd have all kinds of feedback and advice. Maybe even a poem or two. But it isn't. I'm a guest in his home. And Shel's boyfriend, I hope.

"What will she be studying?" I ask carefully. What Jaclyn doesn't understand is that I won't be taking no for an answer. I never have.

"Audio engineering," Shel replies, her voice weak.

See? Even she isn't convinced.

I finish a bite of grilled onion and wipe my mouth with the linen napkin. "I can teach her everything," I assure them. "She'll gain on-the-job training in every aspect of audio engineering with an established, world-class band, both in the studio and in a live, concert arena environment. Best of all," I smile at her, "we'll be together."

"I've never been out of the country," Shel blurts out in her excitement.

I appreciate her trying to help me persuade Jaclyn, but an empty passport? Unbelievable.

"Shelby, this is your chance to make it on your own." Jaclyn turns to her. "You're working hard to prepare for your admission to The College of Audio Engineering in Los Angeles. You already have everything you need within you to achieve your goals."

"By the time we get back from tour, Shelby will be better trained to record and produce music than anybody at that school," I insist.

"But think how much more effective Shelby will be in the long run with a diploma," Jaclyn contends.

"I dropped out of college," I remind them, "and look where I am." I slice a piece of meat and spear it with my fork. Before I bite into it, I reiterate the obvious. "I'm all the teacher Shelby needs."

"I don't even know if I'll get accepted," Shelby argues with Jaclyn.

"If you don't get accepted this semester, we'll try again next term or next fall," Jaclyn says. "There are always second chances, and third chances. As many as it takes. Each time you try, you add what you've learned from your experience and do it better the next time."

"And what if I get accepted and then fail my classes?" Shel moves food around on her plate. "I'll have missed going with Grounder for nothing."

"I have every confidence you'll do well, Shelby," Gibson throws in his two cents at last, "because only you know the true value of your goal." He smiles at her like she's his own daughter. "Jaclyn and I will be behind you all the way."

"I'm behind her too," I interject. "I believe in her more than anyone, that's why I'm inviting her. She'll be the perfect addition to our crew."

"So what you're offering Shelby is a paid internship, Zac?" Jaclyn asks, the prongs of her fork aimed in the direction of my face. "Or are you asking her to accompany you as your significant other?"

"Uh, both," I reply. Fuck, I hadn't thought it through that far. I suppose I can swing a deal with Doughty, our touring manager.

"Shelby, you recently spent time with Zac in his home." Gibson's voice is low and dead calm. "Wouldn't it be wise for you two to work on aspects of your relationship before finding yourselves all the way around the world, in an entirely unfamiliar place, without any kind of support system?"

Jaclyn punctuates every one of his words with a nod, giving her full endorsement to the predictable caution of Dr. Dad. Big surprise.

"I want Zac," Shelby says, with surprising conviction, "to be my teacher."

That's my girl.

Jaclyn puts down her fork with a frown, but Shelby stands her ground.

"Zac has always given me exactly what I need before I knew I needed it. He does nothing but give. Enrolling in college is a gamble. I could fail." She plays with the edge of her napkin. "I could let you down."

The moonlight dapples the surface of the swimming pool. Shel lounges with her back against my chest, her body wedged between my legs on a poolside chaise, while we share a generous piece of Jaclyn's flourless chocolate cake. It's outrageously good, but I wouldn't dare speak another word to her, not even a compliment. She's still fuming.

The scent of Shelby's hair blends with the jasmine-tinted breeze. It's good to hold her in my arms again. I glance through the pool house's sliding doors at the big bed just beyond, then back over my shoulder into the main house. Gibson's new guitar lies on the sectional where we abandoned it before dinner. He and Jaclyn must have gone to bed.

"Shel," I whisper, brushing my lips against the ridge of her ear. "It's a shame to make you wait till the Choice Awards to hear the song I wrote."

"Mm-hmm," she murmurs, leaning into the kisses I press into her sweet-tasting neck.

"Let me grab the guitar and I'll play it for you. Privately, in your room."

I lead her into the pool house, lie her down against a fat stack of pillows, pull the curtains across the sliding doors, and sit next to her on the edge of the bed. Singing to a girl is usually a short train to Pound Town, but damn if my heart isn't as full as my pants right now.

I can tell she recognizes the music before the lyrics even begin. The melody and chord changes are a combination of memories of our days together. They are rhythms she pointed out but also new things I heard on my own.

Her eyes fall closed; the champagne-colored tips of her bare lashes meet and embrace. But instead of feeling shut out, I'm flattered. I know she's giving me the gift of her ear.

I sing to her about being empty when I thought I was full. I sing to her about getting filled to overflowing, only to realize I never knew what I'd been missing. Until I met her.

My song is about not looking back, only forward. It's about taking chances. It's about being heard, really heard, and being given a voice to speak the unspeakable.

It's about good things coming in small packages.

# CHAPTER NINETEEN

SHELBY

"You can't possibly be considering Zac's offer," Jaclyn says. Cornered at a table in the confines of the patio room, I squirm as Jaclyn sets down a plate and hands me a linen napkin. Two ghostly poached eggs stare up at me, a long strip of bacon grimacing at me from below.

"It's out of the question," she adds.

Serving food with one hand and wagging her finger no with the other, Jaclyn is Mom in reverse. I may not like it, but it's better than Mom's get-it-yourself shrug and a finger pointed at the door, telling me to get out. "Roland was right, Shelby," she says just as he pops his head into the glass-enclosed terrace.

"Right about what?" he asks, filling two coffee mugs from the pot.

"Spending only a short while with Zac resulted in an acute panic attack. That could have been averted if you'd taken the time to get to know Zac first. Before entering an intimate relationship, certain information must be gathered: Are you compatible with this person? Is he available? Is it wise to risk pregnancy outside the context of a committed relationship?" She is pacing, talking to the air between us.

Roland takes a seat next to me at the table and slides a mug my way. Curls of steam wisp from the rim, quiet as the live room at Zac's house.

"Don't jump from one bad decision to another." Jaclyn doesn't let up for a second. "Let's use this upcoming school year to sort out the consequences of the choices you've made."

The past can stay where it belongs. I stare out to the pool chaise where Zac and I cuddled the night before, sending him all my thanks for what he's given me. And for offering me my first job, on tour with Grounder no less.

"Shelby, are you choosing to go to Asia to be closer to 'the pulse' of Grounder?" Roland asks quietly, finding my gaze.

"That's exactly what we're talking about, Roland," Jaclyn says.

But it's not. Roland and I both know my heart's rhythm, my pulse, isn't joined with Zac's.

Can I go with Zac when the person I truly long to be close to is Stanford?

No. I need to handle things with Zac first. I guess Jaclyn might be onto something after all. I can't show any of my feelings to Stanford, or I'll be exactly the bed-hopping day-tripper Deshi thinks I am. And would Jaclyn consider Stanford "available"? Not when heroin has him in chains. Can he even feel the same way about me? About anyone?

I'll be nineteen soon, and for all the years I've lived on this earth, I don't have a damn thing to show for it. I've never been more than a city bus ride away from Mom. And no one has ever told me they love me.

No one but Zac. Zac loves me.

I need to put Stanford out of my mind. People who off themselves or junkies like him? They don't see any road between the crap they're hiding beneath the surface and a worthwhile place to belong.

Zac's given me my place. With him, finally, I belong.

My breath abandons my chest, wringing my lungs closed, and free-falls to my toes. A rancid, hollow cavern grows too quickly in the pit of me where Dad's suicide slumps in decay.

Sinking into the couch, I pull a throw pillow to my chest and rest my chin on its platinum-corded edge, trying to slow my racing heart with deep breathing, the way Roland instructed. Another panic attack.

I always figured Dad didn't have a lot of choices, that's why he put a gun to his head. You've got to forgive a guy when you get a glimpse of what he's been through.

Zac thinks Roland and Jaclyn are getting me through his death. Could they have saved him from choosing to die?

The last time Dad shipped out to Afghanistan, he left his voice overseas. Within three months of his return, he took his own life.

The assortment of counseling types who came to our door in the ensuing days only compounded our loss. "Military suicides outnumber combat deaths," they told Mom and me, only to explain that it was his fault. The military had done everything necessary to keep him reasonably from harm while on duty, and that was all they could be expected to do. Corporal Boyd Rey was entirely responsible for what he did to himself, they assured us.

Last night, I could barely hear Zac inside me after my music left my body. I tried to hold on, blending my melody with Zac's in the slickness of our embrace. But it stole away in the night, traveling under a starlit expanse to the Hollywood Hills, in search of Stanford.

I can't tell Jaclyn about Stanford. She'd freak. I'm glad Roland didn't rat me out about him over breakfast. The truth is, I want what she wants. To make smart choices, or whatever. But I can't talk to her.

I can talk to Roland. And isn't Jaclyn the one who set us up in the first place? She'll be thrilled if I turn to him for advice. It was her idea, after all.

Okay, this is a stupid idea.

I stare at my mottled reflection in the polished nameplate on Roland's Laguna Beach office door. Stepping back, my counterpart's head shrinks around the string of letters following his name. From the alcove sheltering the entrance where I first met Zac, I reconsider the bus stop a few feet away. The next bus is traveling north, toward LA. I could travel north.

I sift through the sounds of passersby and the quiet crash of the Pacific, separating the frequencies, until I locate the familiar screeches and lurches of an approaching city bus negotiating the tight Laguna Beach traffic.

Pacing the sidewalk between the bus stop and Roland's office, I weigh my options. My outer life is under a microscope at this white-coat's house. Do I really want my inner life examined in his office?

I've got no place else to go, so I'll relinquish one. But they can't have both.

"As I live and breathe."

Turning on my heel, I find Mom, of all people, approaching Roland's office.

"Why ain'tcha been around to see your mama?" she lisps, a little tipsy and hugging a narrow stack of tabloid magazines. It never turns out well when Mom starts drinking this early in the day.

"Mom?" What the hell is she doing here? "I—I was just going to talk to my, uh—" I don't want to call him my shrink.

"Go figure," she interrupts me. "I got a few choice words for him myself."

## THE SECRET SONG OF SHELBY REY

I trail behind her as she teeters through the door and into the office reception area.

She's definitely drunk. And wearing her date-night getup. What is she thinking?

"I come to take you home." She grips my wrist to avoid a stumble. "We're family, and family sticks together."

"Shelby, this is a surprise." Roland steps out to the empty reception desk, glancing back and forth between Mom and me. I'm not sure whether he's talking about my appearance at his office or Mom's. "How about the three of us have a private discussion in my office?"

"It's fancy as a five-star hotel in here," Mom says with a whistle, winking at him to infer he should know she's seen the inside of one. If she's impressed by this place, she'd go buck-wild if she saw Zac's house.

"Thank you, Darlene." Roland is polite. "What brings you here today? Did you and Shelby plan to meet?"

I swallow hard. Don't tell me we think alike.

"It's Mrs. Rey to you." She thrusts a hand on her hip. "I been coming here every damn day for near a week, but you ain't never showed for work." She shakes her head. "Must be nice."

"I typically see patients in my Beverly Hills office." Roland offers us both a seat and rolls his winged chair around the desk to join us. "But I have business"—he glances my way—"closer to home, so I came in today."

Mom isn't listening. She's busying herself spreading out her bent and dog-eared magazines on Roland's coffee table.

I'm frozen on the area rug. On the cover of each one is a photo of Zac and Ashtynn, with headlines asking whether a mysterious lover has soured Hollywood's sweetest romance. On some are insets of smaller, fuzzy images of me, taken from a distance.

"Now listen here, Dr. High-and-Mighty," Mom slurs.

Roland leans subtly away from Mom's heavy scent, a bitter blend of alcohol, cigarettes, and cheap perfume.

"I don't appreciate you taking my daughter away and letting her mess around where she don't belong." She gestures to the magazines. "You ain't been keeping a proper eye on her."

What does Mom know about "a proper eye"?

My stomach turns at the sight of Zac and Ashtynn Kingston holding hands and kissing at a variety of public events. I slink into the chair behind me. How could I be so stupid?

"Since she's been gone, they turned the water off in my junior bungalow." Mom thinks "junior bungalow" sounds posh.

Roland is perplexed, and Mom is losing patience. "I can't cash her disability checks without her," she snaps, like Roland can't get a clue. "The bills are in her name because my credit hit bottom after my dear husband passed, rest his soul. And with me working all the time"—she points the yellowed tip of her finger at Roland's face, as if to remind him that someone around here has to earn a keep—"I ain't got time to be getting groceries and tidying up. That's Shelby's lot because I keep a roof over her head."

Roland looks at me with a warm smile. "I'm so pleased to learn of your many responsibilities in the home, Shelby. Your mother has provided vital lessons in self-sufficiency."

"Damn right I have." Mom slams her hand on the magazines. "And I'm taking her back today, before the electricity's turned off too."

"Shelby is an adult, Mrs. Rey. She can choose to go with you if she wishes." Roland sits back in his chair, folding his hands.

"She'll come when I tell her to." Mom is flat, gathering up her magazines, careful to stack them in a particular order.

"Are you in touch with your parents, Mrs. Rey? Do Shelby's grandparents live close by?"

Mom stopped talking to her mother when she started working

at the club. "My dancing ain't none of your grandmother's business," Mom told me back then. "She ain't had a decent word for anything I ever done, and she sure as hell ain't gonna now."

"You want to get all personal, do you, Doc?" Mom turns his way and lifts a scuffed platform stiletto onto Roland's chair, next to his thigh. The shoe is missing more than a few purple sequins, but they've always been her favorite. "If you want the 411 on me, you're going to have to pay."

"Perhaps you'd be better served by a social services call from my wife, Jaclyn Spenser," he offers.

The idea of Mom listening to anything Jaclyn has to say almost makes me laugh.

But I have to go home with her. She didn't have much to begin with, and her collection of magazines makes me think she might actually be missing me. I figured she'd never give me another moment's thought once I walked out the door. The least I can do is get her bills back in order before going to Asia with Grounder.

"I'll come home with you, Mom."

Roland's face loses its perpetual tan.

"Roland, please tell Jaclyn . . ." I don't want Mom to know anything specific. About anything. "Tell her thanks."

"Might I remind you that as adults, you are each responsible for your own well-being, Shelby?" Roland rises from his seat, knocking Mom's foot to the floor with a thump. "Transitions aren't always easy, but you can both take this opportunity to learn to live independently."

Mom gathers her magazines into her arms and stomps out the door. She's gotten what she came for.

"I know," I say quickly, before Roland can press me any further. "I'll call you," I add before breaking off from him and following Mom out to the street.

When I catch up to her, I nudge her up the block to another bus stop, away from Roland's office.

♪ 230 ♪

♫

The apartment stinks. Mom fell asleep with a cigarette and burned the better part of the couch, and much of the carpet is scarred and stiff. She could have been killed.

I've barely been gone a handful of weeks, but she looks older, weak. I need to stay with her; I think she needs me. But now there is nowhere to sleep.

My eyes trail over the piles of fast-food wrappers, unopened mail, and dirty laundry. It's bad enough that Jaclyn and Roland saw this place. I can't even imagine what Zac would say if he knew where I grew up. He'll never know, I swear it. Unless Jaclyn gets to yapping.

I could use some of the money Zac gave me to buy a couch. A new one, from a store, with a real pull-out bed inside. With the chunk of cash I earned, she won't be so quick to change her mind and send me walking again.

The apartment is dim even though it's midday. I open the curtains and flick a light switch, but nothing happens.

"The electricity's been turned off," Mom grumbles. "Told you that."

"No, you said it would get turned off if we didn't settle your bills."

"Got some pretty new clothes, don't you," she says, gesturing to the outfit Jaclyn helped me choose at a boutique in Laguna. "Best hand 'em over. God knows you owe me, after all the clothes I've shared with you."

I ignore her, tugging the bottom of my blouse lower around my hips. "Where are the bills, Mom? Let's get all the papers together and see what needs to be paid."

Without bothering to clear the coffee table of the previous nights' take-out containers, Mom goes about spreading her magazines out again. "You didn't tell me you're near famous, Shelby."

Her voice has a cold tone to it. "This Zac Wyatt kid buy you those designer jeans?"

"I'm not famous, Mom. And he's just a friend." I can't tell her that Zac is way more than a friend.

"I had no idea you could pull this kind of action." She shakes her head, impressed. "Girl, I should have put you on the street ages ago, when you were real young."

My ears ring, a sharp pitch, like feedback from a faulty amp. "I'm not a whore, Mom."

"That's some overprivileged brat you're hanging around with. How much money he give you?"

"He didn't give me anything. I earned it."

Her eyes light up.

Shut up, don't tell her about the check. "I did some work. A real job." I shiver a bit, embarrassed about the "work" I did. Zac shot the video for fun. It wasn't until afterward that he got the idea to splice it into the professional footage for Grounder's music video.

"Sure you did, baby. Mama knows."

She's never called me "baby" a day in her life.

"You're confused, is all. Nothing to be ashamed about."

"What? No." I shake my head violently.

"That's why you need me, Shelby. To manage your career. Whatever bit of cash you got outta this kid, I can get us tons more. I know a thing or two about negotiating." Mom gives the last word special emphasis to prove she knows what it means.

"No, Mom. I don't need your help. My friendship with him isn't like that."

"Listen, he's only going to pay you till he's had his fill. Then he'll kick you out and find another girl. The money train never lasts, Shelby. Mark my word."

I pretend to organize the old mail on the table, avoiding her gaze.

"I ain't talking extortion," she begins as she digs a pack of cigarettes out of her purse, "but if you did get any dirt on him, that wouldn't hurt." She takes a cigarette out, lights it, and exhales. "We gotta get photos of you two out in public." She points at picture-perfect Zac and Ashtynn smiling for the cameras. "Fame, that's the ticket. It don't matter if you got any talent." She looks me over, appraising just how little talent I possess. "They give you bucket-tons of money when you're famous. And ain't you always wanted to travel the world? This Zac kid shits money from his butthole. He can take us anywhere. First class."

I hate that I'm so selfish I'm keeping Asia from her. She never gets to go out to a nice dinner, let alone travel to exotic countries. But if Zac knew about Mom, he probably wouldn't want me there anyway.

"I have other plans, Mom, sorry." I sit gingerly at the edge of a half-melted couch cushion and stare down at Zac and Ashtynn. "Right now, all I'm focusing on is getting into college," I lie.

"College? A dumbass useless girl like you?" She taps her cigarette in the overflowing ashtray and laughs a deep, phlegmy laugh. She doesn't sound well. I wonder if she's come down with a cold while I've been away? "I ain't put up with you all these years for you to shut me out when things finally turn around for you." She sucks a lengthy drag on the cigarette, and the orange embers chase the tobacco straight to the filter. Exhaling a wide billow of gray, she taps out the butt of her cigarette and reaches for another. "It's in no way fair that my no-good daughter gets to hobnob with rich and famous no-good people. It's high time you shared your little brush with fortune with your mother, Shelby. You owe me."

"I made a mistake coming back here with you," I tell her, rising from the charred couch. "I have to go."

"To hell you do. Sit your rotten ass down and let's get to figuring out a plan."

"No. I'm leaving."

"Where you headed? Back to your bullshit rock star? Or maybe Dr. Smug-as-Shit? He ain't gonna take you in unless you putting out, understand me?" She points the lit end of her cigarette at me. "Or maybe you already are?"

I let out a long blast of the clashing drums I know are her internal song, then rush for the door.

"Crazy as you ever been. Ain't nobody gonna love you," she yells at me as I walk out.

I hear the five locks inside Perla's apartment clicking open. She sticks her head into the hallway with a scowl, but before she can say anything I trumpet another loud blast at her, then dash for the stairs.

The bus takes the loop west to Laguna Beach, a reversal of the route I took only an hour ago with Mom at my side. As it ducks under the overpass, the lumbering vehicle gathers speed and the apartment complex falls away from view. Ahead, palm trees line the thoroughfare of better neighborhoods.

If I owe anyone anything, I owe it to Jaclyn to finish my college applications.

Even if I get in, though, I'm going to Asia. I can defer college until next year.

I feel guilty showing up at Jaclyn and Roland's door empty-handed. I knock lightly, wishing I'd thought to bring some kind of offering. Something to say I'm sorry.

Roland appears at the door with his new guitar hanging from the strap on his shoulder. I don't know why, but seeing him makes my eyes sting with tears.

He removes the guitar and pulls me into an embrace. Neither of us says anything for several minutes.

I cry. I cry like a stupid little kid, choking and snotty and mumbling a long chain of words that don't make any sense to either of us. He holds me without letting go, petting my hair and letting me get it all out.

Dad. Daddy.

Jaclyn appears at the front steps, behind us, in workout clothes. When she sees my red eyes and the tears on my cheeks, she drops her gym bag and wraps her arms around us both. I beg her, silently, not to start a lecture. Please don't list my many mistakes.

And she hears me. She simply holds us, tight, and says nothing.

## CHAPTER TWENTY

"I'm not wearing that." I thought I'd be alone with Shelby in here. It's bad enough the Choice America Awards arranged for me to share a dressing room with Ashtynn; these coordinating ensembles we selected with our stylist, Dion, six months ago are not going to fly. A lot has changed since then, and I'm not dressing up like Ash's little bitch.

"You are going to wear it, Zacky, because we have a contract that says you will." Ash shoos away her makeup girl's offer of two-inch glitter lashes as she reads me my rights.

"Well, 'Zacky' is here to tell you enough is enough." Choosing a thoughtfully distressed tee from the clothes hanging on Dion's rack of Award-appropriate attire, I peel out of my flawless Versace shirt. The whole room goes quiet with appreciation.

Yeah, I've been working out.

"'Enough is enough' isn't going to hold up in court." Ash stamps her Louboutin spike heel on the carpet. "I saw the 'Vertical Wire' premiere last night," she adds, her words a loaded accusation.

"Produced it myself." I smirk at her.

"Exactly what artistic tableau were you trying to convey with that skanky tweaker in your bedroom?"

I lean down so my face is close to hers. "You have a little white powder, right there. Just under your nose. You'd better lose that before you go on camera."

Her eyes shoot open, wide as twelve-inch records, and she jerks her face toward the nearest mirror, rubbing her nostrils with a finger.

"Ha, ha," I laugh without laughing. "Made you look." I fix her a plastic smile, then drop into my chair, reach for my messenger bag, and pull the unopened methadone prescription from it. I toss the bottle across the room, and it lands with a rattle and thud on the chair in front of her mirror.

"I paid a little visit to your boyfriend," I say, taunting her.

Ash's makeup artist taps foundation around the base of her nose, squatting low to examine her work, ignoring the drama unfolding around her.

"He's the kind of dealer who loves his work, you know?" I'm sarcastic, enjoying watching her squirm. "He hooked me up without a single question. You don't have to fuck him to get high." I look her up and down in disdain. "But you do, don't you."

I curl my lips into a grim smile and turn back to my mirror, signaling my hair stylist to resume her work. Each caramel lock has to be just so for my performance.

There's a loud knock at the door. "Wyatt! Band meeting. Now."

It's Berger. I get up from the chair. There isn't much time before we go onstage, and my song is still tender. We haven't had enough time to rehearse it to maturity. But I like that. It reminds me of when we first started out, before everything was studio smooth. We were innocent then, always waiting on the audience's reaction. It feels good to be back in that space.

Berger waves me into the room Stanford, Os, and Deshi are

sharing. I grab the high chair at the mirror, and the other guys stand around me.

"What the hell, Wyatt," Berger yells. "You were supposed to write a Grounder song."

"I—did?" Why am I answering with a question? What's the deal here? Tonight's my ticket to a solo career. Berger knows that.

"Then can you explain why Lysandre here insists partial royalties go to your little girlfriend, Shelby Rey?"

"Yeah, what the hell, Wyatt?" Deshi adds, pointlessly, to the conversation.

I look to Stanford, his eyes covered by his usual mirrored sunglasses. He takes a long sip from his beer before responding. When does that bastard have to submit to rehab? What's he doing with a beer? I'm still gun-shy to be seen with anything stronger than Diet Sprite. Jesus Christ.

"Wyatt wrote the lyrics and the melody." His voice is slow and deliberate. "Ms. Shelby Rey wrote the arrangement. Therefore, she is due partial royalties."

Who the hell uses the word "therefore"? Goddamn him. And what is he talking about, Shelby did the arrangement? Since when?

"What the fuck," Deshi screams, lunging at me. "I've had enough of this shit. You don't own this band, Wyatt." Berger and Oslo pull him back before he takes a swing at me.

When Grounder started, Stan brought a solid package of prepared songs, his life's work. We've been playing them through, and he keeps bleeding new ones out. But we always shared Grounder royalties evenly. That is, until I decided to write my own music. Now I want credit and the paycheck that comes with it.

"Let me guess." Ashtynn appears in the doorway, her manicured fingers wrapped around the soft curve of her hip, her words dropping from her lips like slivers of ice. "Shelby Rey is also the girl in the 'Vertical Wire' video?"

We're all quiet a moment, and I swear I hear each word drop to the floor and crack into a million razor-sharp shards. Shel's lessons on listening are making me imagine shit that isn't even there.

"Yeah, we call her Yoko." Oslo has a laugh, then pulls himself straight when Ash aims her icy glare in his direction.

"This is a private band meeting," I tell her, motioning for Pablo, my hulking security guard, to shut the damned door.

"One of Radio FreeSpirit's backstage pass winners claims to be Shelby Rey's mother," she spits out, her slender hand halting Pablo's massive forearm from shutting the door. "Fancy way to meet the parents, Zacky," she sneers before the door is slammed in her face.

All heads turn in unison in my direction.

I shrug. "Guess I forgot to hold a press conference announcing that Ash and I split."

She's full of shit. If Shelby's mother wanted to come to the Choice Americas I'd have sent her a limo myself. Ashtynn's just baiting me. "Listen, Berger, I'm as confused as you are about this royalty shit. Can someone tell me why the hell the song I wrote isn't my song, free and clear?"

"I was supposed to rework Zac's melody, create an arrangement that is definitively Grounder," Stanford confesses, his voice a thin breath in the small room. "But I found a dose of H I'd hidden in the control room, and, well, shit happens, huh?"

Deshi shakes his head. "That doesn't explain why Wyatt's new girlfriend gets the kickback."

"He's right." I hate to agree with that bastard. "It's my fucking song. And we've been rehearsing your arrangement. I don't care if you reworked it with the needle hanging from your goddamn vein. Hell, you write most of our songs while using."

"But I didn't." He tilts his chin in my direction. I can only imagine he's looking me in the eye from behind his shades. I want to rip them off his smug fucking face. "Shelby came and helped me. She did all the work."

"You are a liar." I point my finger in his face, an inch from his stupid sunglasses. "She was with me all night." As soon as the words leave my mouth, I remember how she left. To give me "space."

She must have gone down to the studio. Knowing full well Stanford was in there.

"What do you mean, she helped you?" My hold on tonight's performance is fraying along the edge. There isn't time for me to bring her back from her seat before we go on, damn it. I look the junkie up and down. What could she possibly want from him when she has me? Just what all went on between them?

There is a knock at the door, and I know it isn't Ash again because Ashtynn Kingston doesn't knock. I nod for Pablo to get the door and a production assistant with sapphire-colored hair, a minuscule, sparkling tube-top, and tons of tattoos pops her head in.

"Six minutes and you're on." She gives us a thumb's up. "Right this way, gentlemen." She pushes the door wider and motions us to follow her.

We all glance at one another but do what we're told.

"I'm not giving any royalties to your whore," Deshi threatens me as we hustle through the maze of backstage hallways.

"Why don't we just play 'Vertical Wire'?" Os is hopeful.

"We paid a boatload of cash on ads promising a new song," Berger pants, struggling to keep the fast pace in the tight corridors.

"Let Wyatt perform his original song," Stan says. "The way he wrote it before the arrangement was changed."

Deshi blasts back in protest, but before he can get a sentence out, I cut him off.

"I'll do it," I tell them, looking straight forward.

"We only played it once," Os pipes up, concern written across his face. "I like to fancy I have a phonologic memory, but c'mon, brother."

"I know how it goes." It's my own music, it's in me. All I have to do is listen within and pull it to the surface. "We'll unplug, surprise everyone. Just follow along."

"You can't be serious, Wyatt," Deshi says, but one look at me and he knows just how serious I am. "Fine," he says, tossing his black fringe of faintly glittery hair. "It's your funeral."

Man, I wish Shel were here with me. I shouldn't have chased her away when I saw Ashtynn in our dressing room. She could have held her own.

I'm so damn thankful she wasn't interested in the red carpet tonight or making nice for the cameras. It's just one more confirmation she loves me for me. So why the hell did she go looking for Stan in the studio that night?

Sapphire Hair Chick directs us to wait, standing shoulder to shoulder in the bright square of light that is the narrow opening to the large stage. Sound techs ambush us, outfitting us with wireless head mics with the speed and precision of an Indy 500 pit crew.

Ashtynn steps out from the far side of the stage and claims her place in the spotlight, wearing her half of our matching ensemble. The platform she commands appears to be some sort of lotus flower. On acid.

Pouting sexily at the lead camera, she purrs, "I can't begin to tell you what a pleasure"—she says the word "pleasure" like this is some kind of skin show—"it is to introduce our next performer. He's someone very special to me."

Oh no. Ashtynn, don't.

"The light of my life, the treasure of my heart, the apple of my eye," she simpers into camera two as it rappels in on her. "He's here to perform an extraordinary song tonight, one he wrote himself. Let's welcome to the stage Zac Wyatt!"

"What. The. Fuck," Deshi mouths in silence, our mics now live, his stare burning a hole though me.

Quieter, as the camera zooms away, she adds, "And his band, Grounder."

A deafening roar of applause breaks out, and Sapphire waves us forward.

Jesus Christ, Ashtynn is a piece of fucking work. To shit all over my band with an unscripted intro is bad enough. But all that "light of my life" bullshit?

Ten million viewers watching worldwide, but she has it out for one person: Shelby.

## CHAPTER TWENTY-ONE

SHELBY

I get why Zac insisted we dress for the Awards at his place. He figured I'd bail. Well, he was right. I can't do it. The red-carpet scene, posing for cameras in the body-skimming sequin getup he gave me? There's no way.

"It's nothing, babe. Just a few interviews about who you're wearing," he says. "I need you with me."

Zac's done everything in his power to make this day magical. He brought in a hairstylist, a makeup artist, and a manicurist. Just for me.

"I want to support you," I tell him, wondering how I will even be able to sit in this gown. "I'm proud of the hard work and heart you've put into your song. But you know how the media is," I tell him, still a bit sore from the sting of seeing Zac and Ashtynn on the covers of Mom's magazines. "They can get so caught up in who you're dating that they might overlook the real news: your music." I give him a pleading look. "Can't we go in the back door or something?"

What I don't say is how Mom has called Jaclyn and Roland's

house every day for the last few days, begging me to bring her with me to the show. I swore to her repeatedly that I wasn't going. It would stab her in the gut to see me there, live on television. She'd know I lied.

"It's true, the media would love to get pics of us." His eyes soften. "But you'd rather give up your place in the spotlight than take any attention away from my music." Zac pulls me to him and kisses my neck. "You are full of surprises, Shel. Just when I think I might figure you out, you blow my mind all over again."

We arrive quietly backstage in Zac's Spider, out of view of the general audience entrances, where a sea of bodies is clamoring to get into the auditorium.

Zac skims the program lineup. "Christ, half these bands are one-hit wonders," he says, making a scoffing sound.

Trailing behind him and Pablo, I rattle off exhaustive song titles for each performer in one long, nervous spiel. Zac stares straight ahead, but I catch Pablo stealing a look at me like I'm counting cards in a casino.

The show is already underway. Stanford, Deshi, and Oslo have been here for hours, doing interviews and relaxing in the various hospitality suites backstage.

We are just about to reach Zac's dressing room when he stops cold and whispers something in Pablo's ear. I stare up at a monitor hanging from the ceiling in the narrow corridor, watching the broadcast of the Awards. I'm trying to play it cool for Zac. I can hear him. He's tangled between terror and triumph. One of us has to hold his song safely inside until it's his turn to shine. For now, that's up to me.

"Shel, there's been a mix-up with my dressing room," Zac says, releasing my hand. "It's a tight space, a bit overcrowded." He is vague. "I still have to get changed and then meet with the guys, so . . ."

I nod, but I don't understand. His dressing room at the Hollywood Bowl was small too, but we didn't need much room then.

"I made arrangements so you could sit with Gibson and Jaclyn," he says. "Just in case, you know? Security's not gonna let you near the stage, and we've worked too hard for you to miss my performance." He signals Pablo toward the exit. "Pablo will show you to your seat."

I asked days ago if I could sit with them, and he insisted he wanted me with him. What made him change his mind?

I'm not going to argue with him on his big night. I follow Pablo without a word.

Over my shoulder, Zac taps his heel. "Uh, thanks. See you after, okay?" he says, then disappears into his dressing room.

When I reach Jaclyn and Roland, they are deep into some heated discussion.

Pablo instructs me to sit. "I'll fetch you when Mr. Wyatt gives word. Till then, stay right here," he says, then beats a path back to Zac.

He said he needed me.

"She has a glow about her, doesn't she, Roland?" Jaclyn smiles at me. "There is hope behind those gray, brooding eyes."

"You look beautiful, honey," Roland says.

For a second or two, he tries to be in the moment, but his thoughts get the best of him. Lowering his voice, he whispers, "He's been supplying narcotics—more like dealing drugs—to most of his clients. And to Carly, our receptionist. In exchange for sex."

It doesn't take special hearing skills to know that sounds bad. I cross my legs, swinging my foot back and forth nervously, a feeling of dread falling over me. Onstage, a rapper and a pop starlet perform a mashup duet, surrounded by dancers dressed as zombie stone-age queens.

"There has to be some kind of mistake," Jaclyn says, her voice steadily rising. "Elliott is family." She quiets herself when Ashtynn Kingston's voice fills the auditorium.

"He's someone very special to me," Ashtynn coos, standing on a psychedelic lotus flower, near naked in a sheer, studded micro-dress. "The light of my life, the treasure of my heart, the apple of my eye."

Zac said it was over with her.

Grounder appears from behind a partition decorated with lotus-patterned mehndi. As Zac crosses the stage, Ashtynn's arms open wide in expectation of an embrace. On a giant screen over the stage, I watch her lips brush against his ear and his gaze burn into hers, in high def.

He never broke up with her.

The audience claps in anticipation of Zac's new song, but I feel myself stiffen to stone. Roland and Jaclyn remain quiet. Not one of us cheers for the one song we've waited weeks to hear.

I've seen Grounder perform, so I know what to expect. But tonight Zac seems self-conscious, as though this is his first time on stage. Deshi takes a seat behind his semi-circle of drums and crosses the arms of his studded black leather jacket. I watch Oslo unplug his keyboard and cock his chin, gazing offstage. My eyes fall on Stanford. I promised myself I wouldn't look at him.

Stanford directs Zac toward the audience, and Zac steps to the front of the stage. His face fills the overhead screen, but nowhere is his trademark confidence.

The air is empty where Zac's music should be. It dries the back of my throat and I cough, waiting for him to play, sing, or do anything. His brow tweaks in concern even as he fakes a smile.

I forget to be angry with him. "Just be Zac," I whisper to his image onstage. "Sing what's inside you."

Zac begins, but stumbles. His song rises, then falls, a late-night drunk on unsteady legs. He can't seem to find his own rhythm.

I look to Roland, hoping he can offer some sort of explanation or give me advice. Should I go backstage? Should he?

"I quit," Jaclyn bursts out before I can get a word in. "I quit my job at St. Cecilia."

Roland turns to her, surprised. "You loved that job, Jac. What the hell?"

"They keep cutting patient treatment," Jaclyn continues, like Zac's world isn't falling apart. "And they found out I was harboring a patient," she whispers to him as quietly as she can, but I hear her. "I quit before I was fired."

I excuse myself, mumbling something about using the restroom, before they can see my tears.

I go to a security guard and flash my backstage credentials. They lead me directly to his dressing room.

# CHAPTER TWENTY-TWO

The audience rises to its feet with cheers when we stroll out to our rehearsed positions.

I glance at Stan and he nods, the slow roll of his gesture saying he believes I can do it, urging me to give it my best shot. He'd be my best bud if he wasn't such a prick.

I shake off the chill Ash frosted in me, unwilling to give her another second of my attention. I see now how thoughts and memories, even recent ones, can affect my internal rhythm. I'm not giving any more space to Ashtynn Kingston.

I need to call up my memories of Shelby. Of our moonlit nights and sunlit mornings. I memorized my lyrics; I just need to recall our music. My music, when I'm with her.

I look back at Stan again and he subtly points to a forward position on the stage. I tilt my head in acknowledgment, sling my guitar strap over my shoulder, and amble out. The spotlight follows me, dimming the remainder of the band.

I try to picture Shelby's face. The first image that comes to mind is her slick skin, glowing wet in the candlelit bath. I smile a little, catching the eye of a woman in the front row. She lights up, accepting my smile as though I intended it for her.

I concentrate deeper, thinking of Shel in my arms, and begin to strum out the chords. This is no time to choke. This show is aired live, for Christ's sake.

I have the melody but not the tempo, and Deshi sure as hell isn't helping me out.

I won't look back at him. I won't look back.

I need to fire into the lyrics, give it all up, and do my best.

I open up and go.

It's raw, like I'd hoped. But too raw. Unrehearsed. I hear a cough from the vast darkness beyond the edge of bright stage lights.

From over my shoulder, Stanford's guitar cries out, playing the melody. My melody, full-throttle. I dive in, mimicking him, flowing with him. I launch into the lyrics, pounding them out with my heart. It's my love letter to Shel, and it has to be right. I know she's watching, along with Roland and Jaclyn.

Stan carries my song with confidence. He's so damned masterful with a guitar in his hands. But how does he know?

How the hell does he know my own internal music, better than I do?

Only Shelby can hear me. Only Shelby.

What went on between those two that night? What did she tell him about me?

My voice falters. Then my hands stumble over the strings. I'm hoping Stan's stronger melody covers my mistakes, but who am I kidding? I only have three minutes and forty-five seconds on this stage and I'm eating shit through every moment of it.

I forget the next line in the song, and I'm so embarrassed—me, embarrassed—that I stumble over the chords again. I'm blowing this. No, I've already blown it.

I glance back at the guys, even though I swore I wouldn't.

Deshi's ass is parked behind his drum kit, his sticks gripped in his palm, a nasty grin on his face. Os looks pained, embarrassed on my behalf. And that bastard Stanford Lysandre keeps strumming away. He's playing my song like he owns it, his expression unknowable behind those annoying, tacky mirrored sunglasses.

I catch Berger at the edge of the stage, holding his hands, palms up, silently shouting, "What the hell is wrong with you?"

A girl in a pound of makeup and a sequined Barbarella dress approaches me on precariously high platform heels. Stanford abruptly halts, and the guys hightail offstage. Smiling falsely, she takes me by the arm and ushers me out of the spotlight, whispering from between the gritting teeth of her too-wide grin, "We're going to a commercial break."

My mic is cut, and the lights dim on the band's abandoned instruments. When we reach the edge of the stage, Berger continues screaming, this time full volume, "What the hell happened? You on drugs again, son?"

"No." I kick the floor, staring down. I want to throw my guitar, smash it, but wouldn't that be the cliché to end all clichés? Instead, I remove it carefully, handing it to an assistant with deliberate calm. But the rage inside me shoots to the ceiling and nearly busts through the goddamn roof. My skin is prickling between anger and madness. I scratch at my inner arm, so hard that my fingernails leave long red tracks from my wrists to the crook inside my elbow, punctuated by a bright red welt inflicted by the guitar pick still lodged in my grip.

"I gave you six weeks. Six weeks, damn it. All you had to do was write one fucking song. You know how much ads for this shit cost?" Berger goes on berating me, but I tune him out. Deshi throws his hair out of his face and stares me down. Before he gets the benefit of a single smart-ass remark, I throw him a hard look, challenging him to just try me right now.

"Wyatt, what happened out there, man?" Stanford has the balls to ask. "I tried to help you out."

"'Play your original song,' you tell me," I scream at him. "You knew damn well I wasn't prepared. But you sure as hell were."

I'm about to haul off on him when some dude from Radio FreeSpirit butts in. "Great performance, Mr. Wyatt."

He must not have seen it.

"We'd like you to meet our Backstage VIP Pass winner and a few runners-up from Radio FreeSpirit's Choice America Contest, sir."

Sir?

I'm in such a daze that I don't even think about what I'm doing. I just follow the FreeSpirit guy out to the corridor and into a crowded reception room. Sure enough, one of the runners-up looks a hell of a lot like my girlfriend. She's got that conspicuous sensuality that Shel has, cool confidence. Well, maybe it's not confidence so much as an "I couldn't give a crap what the rest of the world thinks" attitude, but it sets her apart from the crowd.

After I pose for a few pictures with the grand prize winner, I calm myself enough to approach her. "Mrs. Rey?"

She's young-looking, but not as polished as I'd imagined. And what the hell is she doing here?

"You can call me Darlene, sugar."

"What a pleasure it is to meet you at last." I wink at her and lean in to give her a hug. "I see where Shelby gets her good looks."

The grand prize winner, who received nothing more than my polite handshake, makes a loud squawking sound in protest.

"My, my," Darlene coos, "you sure are handsome." She rubs her fingertips up and down the scratches on my arm, pausing to stroke the curve of my bicep for several long seconds. "In love with my Shelby, ain't you?" she's bold enough to ask straight up.

"She's one of a kind." As I throw her one of my patented

grins, I spot a security camera angled at us in the small reception room. I'm being punked, right?

"Better listen to me."

This woman wastes no time with small talk. One hand wrapped around my arm, the other gripping a generous pour in a small plastic cup, she waits until she's sure she has my undivided attention.

I force myself to stop scanning the room for evidence of a prank. "I'm listening." I paste a smile on my face.

"Shelby ain't right, she got mental disorders," Darlene whispers too loud, tapping a yellowed finger into her temple to indicate where Shelby's "mental disorders" originate. "Your fancy doctor, that shrink to the stars, Roland Gibson? He took her from me." She leans in close to me, looking around to make sure no one is eavesdropping. Her stale scent reeks of smoke, liquor, and sweat. "He's taking advantage of my baby girl. The two of 'em are so fixed on pilfering drugs from the system, he's locked her up. Psychiatric hospitalization, that's what they call it."

All right, anyone with an Internet connection knows Gibson's my shrink. But no one knows Shelby lives at his place but me. I straighten up and take this impostor in, head to toe.

She's wearing the exact silver dress and shoes Shelby had on the day I met her on the sidewalk. But it'd be easy to put that look together just by watching the YouTube video. This is one lame-ass joke, whoever planned it. I'm glad Shelby is safely seated with Gibson, far away from this room. This monstrosity in heels could be some kind of freak stalker.

"I see." I raise my brow, grimacing to avoid her smell. "And how is Mr. Rey doing this evening?" I ask, testing her.

"Mr. Rey? You mean Shelby never told you?" Her reddened eyes widen in surprise. "Corporal Boyd Rey, rest his soul, gave his life protecting this country. A war hero, I tell you, but he left us four years ago, broke and alone. Had to raise that girl on my own, which is no piece of cake when she's disturbed and all." She pauses to take a lengthy sip of her drink.

Ha, I caught her. Shelby's dad died recently.

Right?

I scan the room again, looking for pranksters. No one jumps out to announce it's all a hoax.

"How about you and me get to negotiating a settlement of sorts before I have a little chitchat with all these TV people. Tell 'em how you been having your way with a"—she hiccups, interrupting herself, and her eyes narrow to slits as she focuses on getting her words right—"with a mentally impaired drug addict."

My breath kicks out of me. The acrid burn of vomit catches in my throat, threatening to spill into my mouth.

I swallow it down and turn toward the door. It doesn't add up. She doesn't know shit about Gibson and his pain-in-the-ass wife. Hell, I know damn straight he isn't loose with his prescription pad. She's got the wrong man; that's Rachman's gig. But is Shelby living at his house for psychiatric treatment?

"Can I see some ID?" I can't believe I'm giving this woman another second of my time. Glancing over her shoulder, I signal craft services to bring me a damn drink already.

Darlene smiles, revealing teeth as yellow as her fingers. She reaches into the neckline of her dress, fishing around between her breasts, where it appears she's holding cash, keys, lipstick, and God knows what else.

I look away, fighting the vomit. A server comes by with a tray full of bourbon with the sponsoring distiller's logo on the plastic cups. I grab one, down the whole thing in one gulp, take another, and chug that.

She extracts an expired driver's license from her cleavage and holds it up eagerly. I squint to examine it without touching it. The picture's her own image. The name, Darlene Rey; the address, some apartment in Orange County. Shel told me herself her mom lived in OC.

This is really her mom?

Fuck.

"I can't talk about this with you now," I rasp out. "Not here." The air is too thin to breathe. I clutch my hair in my hand, shaking my head. "The name's Darlene Rey, right? I'll be in touch."

The room starts to tilt. I take the drink from her hand and down it, trying to set myself straight again. It doesn't help. Then, crumpling the little plastic cup in my fist, I march out of the reception room, shoving past shoulders and kicking aside chairs.

Stanford. He hasn't cowritten even one song since Grounder started, and he's had plenty of offers from some heavy hitters. Now he claims Shelby is owed royalties? Maybe all this is his master plan to finish me. I've been punked all right.

I storm down the corridor, leaving a combustible trail of profanity in my wake.

I'm going to kill him.

I find Stan in his dressing room, and who's with him? Shelby.

Goddamn him.

I leap full bore onto that smug-ass shit-for-brains, knocking him straight to the floor, pounding his face with my fists. I've got 185 pounds of trained muscle on his skinny rail of a body. He's pinned and unmoving, the beer in his hand overturned and spilling around us.

Shelby is screaming. Her high-pitched wail only clenches my fists tighter. I pound into him relentlessly, taking shots on every part of his face, neck, chest, and torso. His damned sunglasses fly off in the barrage, landing broken and limp in the pool of beer at the side of his head.

I punch him blindly, screaming into his face until Pablo's meaty grip surrounds my heaving chest, pulls me straight up in the air, and sets me down.

"Zac, I had to touch her to hear her." Stanford coughs weakly, rolling onto his side and drawing his knees to his chest. "I'm sorry." His eyes fall shut and streams of blood course down his face, clotting in his dreads. "I want her."

He wants her? I swing around to look her in the eye. "What does he mean, he had to touch you?"

The bastard hooked up with her?

I spin back to him. "I hate you." I spit on him, jerk myself free from Pablo's grip, and dive on Stanford for a second round.

Had to touch her, my ass. The one thing I want, to write music, he does while nearly dead to the world. The one girl I actually give a damn about—the only one I've ever loved—he tries to take from me.

Pablo is on me hot and fast, yanking me back. I wipe my mouth with the back of my arm. I got to get the hell out of here. Away from her.

I hold on to the steering wheel of my Ferrari, the other fist clenching several locks of my hair.

"You got to chill out, man," Pablo warns me, standing next to my window and directing the security staff to open the gate. "You don't want to get busted for reckless driving. Those arrest pics never go away."

"Take the rest of the night off," I tell him, and peel out of the parking lot.

I swallow hard and power forward, following traffic. The engine revs and rumbles, daring me to put the accelerator to the test. Why do I have this wicked machine if I'm not going to drive the hell out of it?

## THE SECRET SONG OF SHELBY REY

I could go to Vegas. Tonight. Floor it the entire way there, 120-plus miles an hour, without stopping. Leave LA behind me, ditch the guys, drop Gibson. And forget Shelby.

That lying bitch.

I let out a long breath. It can't be true. Sure, she isn't your standard Los Angeles princess. Her nails aren't manicured and she has conspicuous tan lines, a dead giveaway she isn't paying for professional spray tans. She isn't another boring lookalike, either. "Bore-geous," the boys and I call it.

She's smart. And she understood me, better than anyone ever has.

Damn, I'll bet Stanford orchestrated everything tonight, to take Shelby from me and finish my career. That whole bullshit scene with Darlene? He got too full of himself, took the prank too far. Claiming she's a mental case? C'mon. If he'd used a normal mom-type actress to play the role, maybe I'd have bought it. But the trailer-park act was over the top. It's one thing to give her a fake ID, but to make it expired? Too much. Does he really think I'm that big a fool? Clearly, damn it, he does. I hate him.

Fuck, I can't go to Vegas. My parents are in town for the Awards. Oh Christ, they saw that disaster onstage. And they're going to hear about the fight backstage. I let out a piercing howl, the length of a dozen bars, following with a ranked listing of every expletive I can think of.

Driving in circles, a shadow on the snaking roads up toward the Hollywood Hills, I come close to the turn-off to my house but keep going. There's a convenience store just around the next bend where I can get a few bottles; something 80-proof should do the trick.

Oh damn, why didn't I see it right from the start?

I got those two all figured out. They didn't get anything past me tonight. Stanford wanted Shelby for himself, without breaking up our happy little Grounder home with my solo career. And Ash has convinced herself I'm going to do that insipid OmniMotion project with her, at all costs. They put operation Screw Over Wyatt in motion together.

Well, guess who's going to have the last laugh.

# CHAPTER TWENTY-THREE

# SHELBY

There's a burn behind my eyes, the kind you get when you're caught in a pepper spray vapor. I follow Zac out of the dressing room, trying to explain it's not Stanford's fault. If anything, he should thank him for what he's done for him.

He pounds toward the exit where the valet parked his Spider.

"Thank him?" he shouts at me with what I'm pretty certain are tears in his eyes. "You think I should thank that junkie for fucking me over?"

Pablo brushes me back, separating the crowd in the hallway to let Zac through. He disappears out the exit without as much as a goodbye and Pablo follows, shutting the door behind them.

The whole world witnessed Stanford tearing open the secret he's hidden behind his addiction: Stan can hear Zac, just like I can.

I return to Stanford's room to check on him. When I get there, he's sitting upright in a chair, drinking a glass of water. Someone brought him a towel, and it's already stained with his blood where he tried to clean his contusions.

"Are you okay?" I ask, breathlessly dropping into the chair next to him.

I was so scared Zac would find out what kind of twisted mutation I am and refuse his love for me. But Stanford has the same secret, and he revealed it to save Zac's life tonight.

Stan nods his slow nod and takes my hand in his. My music, our music, sparks and ignites between our fingers.

"I'm sorry, Shelby. I shouldn't have come between you and Zac."

"You risked everything to help him." Stanford doesn't need to apologize. I look up at him through the watery blur of my tears. "I only want to be with you."

A smile dawns across his lip, then halts where the dried blood cracks and flows anew. He puts the towel to his mouth, but I can hear him from inside. We have something together that is ours alone, an uncommon treasure, and he doesn't want to hide it any longer.

I wonder what we might produce together if we openly played what we hear? If he busted free of the syringe tethering him to the eternal dusk of Nowhereland, and I wrote the music of my honest self without fear of being labeled "crazy."

"You said you weren't going to any award show."

I swing around toward that familiar voice so abruptly that Stanford's hand drops from mine. "Mom?"

What is she doing here? And backstage?

Before I can gather two words together, Mom is shuffled aside and none other than Ashtynn Kingston darkens the door.

"You must be Shelby Rey." She walks in and plants herself square in front of me. Her breath smells of peach-infused vodka, Mom's favorite.

She is blindingly beautiful, her shining mahogany hair draped around shapely breasts, the kind Mom's coworkers pray for when they score a Groupon for plastic surgery. And those enormous dark eyes; there's an understanding behind them that is much older and wiser than her nineteen years. I can see why Zac prefers her over me.

"You lied to me, girl," Mom lets loose, cursing me and smacking me with her handbag.

Ashtynn places a gentle hand on Mom's shoulder, halting her without a single word.

"I can't figure out why she lied to me about that Wyatt kid," she complains to Ashtynn, as though they're solid girlfriends. "He ain't into you, Shelby. He's still with sweet Miss Kingston here." Mom takes another swig from a plastic cup, looking me up and down with a sniff. "You think that dress would fit me?"

Stanford rises from his seat as if to defend me but immediately stumbles, still dizzy from the pummeling Zac gave him. He sits back down, his eyelids drooping.

Ashtynn, finally noticing his injuries, changes gear. "Shelby, would you kindly take Mr. Lysandre back to his home? I'll send a doctor to examine him in private."

I certainly don't have a car, and I'm not about to tell Ashtynn Kingston I came here with her man. Deshi and Oslo took Grounder's limo to an after-party when Stanford told them he was leaving with me.

"Shouldn't someone call 911?" I ask.

Ashtynn shakes her head. "If he's taken to a hospital, the press will"—she talks to me like I'm a child—"well, the press is unkind. It wouldn't be in Stanford's best interest if Grounder's fans knew what happened between him and Zac tonight."

"It was all a misunderstanding anyway," I tell her.

"Exactly," she says, lighting up. "You understand, don't you, sweetheart? No one outside of our little circle can know what happened."

I decide not to remind her of the handful of people who witnessed Zac leaving Stanford bloodied on the floor, and let her take the lead. Right now, Ashtynn is the only one of us with a plan. "I don't have a car," I admit quietly.

"Okay, then I'll take Stanford back to his house in my BMW. Can I trust you to get your mother safely home?"

I look at Mom and stifle a sigh. "Yes."

Outside the concert hall, there are reporters, celebrities, fans, and Choice Awards attendees crowding the sidewalks. Traffic is a mess for blocks around.

Mom tells me she arrived in a limo bus with Radio FreeSpirit.

"There it is!" she cries triumphantly, pointing to our left. It's still parked within steps of the venue.

When we reach the bus, Pablo, who is guzzling free liquor courtesy of FreeSpirit's hospitality crew, greets me like I'm a twenty he forgot was in his pocket. By far the most famous person onboard, he's been made guest of honor. When I introduce him to Mom, she says, "I'm a close personal friend of Ashtynn Kingston's." Pablo slips a hulking arm around her shoulder in approval.

"There's an Awards after-party at Magnet," Pablo tells us. "Everyone is going."

"I can't do this," I yell in Mom's ear over the pounding, too-loud electronica music.

"What?" She wraps her hand around her ear.

A tray of flashing light-up cups containing some sort of blue liquid is shoved in our faces. Mom grabs two and hands me one.

I shake my head. She can have it. "I have to go to him," I say, enunciating each word so she can at least read my lips.

She doesn't care. She's already downed her cup and is sipping on mine, her hips shaking in Pablo's direction.

The driver gets on board and starts the engine. Panicked, I shove my way off the bus, not sure Mom even realizes I've left.

It only took me three hours, six bus transfers, and 112 stops to get from Laguna Beach to the Hollywood/Highland station to see

## THE SECRET SONG OF SHELBY REY

Grounder play live at the Hollywood Bowl. I'm already in LA. It shouldn't take me that long to get to the Hollywood Hills.

I settle onto a city bus in my evening gown, gazing at nothing out the window, just row upon row of houses and store fronts, many of them empty, homes for rent, and businesses out of business.

Filled and empty. Empty and filled. If there is a rhythm to the pattern of success and failure, I can't hear it.

## CHAPTER TWENTY-FOUR

When I finally pull up to the gate at my house, I'm seeing double, imagining shit that isn't there. I take another swig from the bottle wedged between my legs. If I didn't know better, I'd swear Ash was sitting in her car, right there, waiting for me.

I put the window down and squint through the bright halogen light flooding the entrance to my house.

"Zacky, baby, are you all right? I've been so worried about you," she coos, getting out of her BMW and leaning into the driver's side window of my car. She smells of hair spray, peach vodka, and Angelic, her signature fragrance.

I am hallucinating. Ash wouldn't miss an after-party to see me.

I press the button in my car to open the gate. As I ease the Ferrari forward, Ash's ghost screams and leaps out of the way.

Damn, it really is her. What the hell is she doing here? I slam on the brakes, put the emergency brake on, and try to get out, but the door won't open.

Shit, the car is in drive. I put it in park and manage to climb out, dumping my open bottle onto the ground in the process.

It's fine, there's more in the house.

I'm approaching Ash when the gates start to close and I realize my mistake.

"They're going to slam into the sides of my damn car," I scream, leaping forward to stop them—but then I remember the gates are on sensors. They'll detect my car is in the way and back off.

But just like the open button that keeps failing on my dashboard, the sensors fail, and the two heavy wrought iron gates slam directly into my $300,000 car on both sides.

I let out another stream of cuss, frosted with double cuss and overflowing with cuss cream filling, and kick at the Italian pavers lining the entrance to my driveway. I storm over to the keypad, but I can't remember the code. Shit, I figured it out the night Shel came back with me. Where is my lucky charm tonight?

Oh yeah.

I give up. Damn this night to hell. I'll call a tow truck in the morning. I've had enough shit for one night, thank you very much.

Sliding over the crumpled hood of my Ferrari, I blaze an angry path to the front door.

"God, you really blew it tonight," Ash remarks, following me at a brisk trot.

"You don't say." If she doesn't choke on my bitter tone, she could use some lessons on listening from Shelby herself.

The patter of her spiked heels clicks away like a tiny toy dog that needs its toenails clipped.

"Go home, Ashtynn," I heave out, exercising what little patience I have left, but she pushes me aside and walks right into my house like she owns the place.

"And the humiliation of learning about that two-bit street walker's mental patient status. Zacky, didn't you do a background check?"

Mouth clamped shut, I walk past her to the kitchen to find a beer. I take one and grab the remainder of the twelve-pack, and start up the stairs to my room.

"Stanford told me you wrote that song you performed with your demented girlfriend," she rants on. "Zacky, have you lost your fucking mind?"

I reach the door of my bedroom and turn, give her a half-salute with the twelve-pack, and try to shut the door in her face. "You can let yourself out."

But she's not done yet; just before the door slams, she places her foot against the jamb and peers in.

She's not worth the effort. I walk out to the terrace, drop the beer on the table, and fall onto a chaise longue. The pool below ripples where friends of friends are splashing around. House music rises up from their party, the party they've held all night in anticipation of my triumphant return. I slide lower on the chaise, behind a row of potted ficus, hiding from the very people whose adulation I crave.

Ashtynn follows me onto the terrace and kicks off her shoes, as if I've invited her to make herself comfortable.

"What the hell do you want, Ash? Go downstairs or go home. I don't care what you do, just get out of my face."

She doesn't budge. Instead, she reaches for a beer, twists the top off, takes a sip, and edges toward me. Perching her sequined ass on my arm rest, she traces her finger across my brow, then down behind my ear, then along my shoulder.

"Zac," she says, pouting.

I hate her goddamned pout.

"You know my secret to success, baby?"

I brush her hand away from me.

She takes a long sip, sinking deeper into the chair with me. "Proven songwriters. You hire the right people, and commercial success is guaranteed."

I don't give her an inch, so she's wedged, lopsided, one butt cheek crushed between my rib and the armrest, the other cocked in the air. Amazingly, she doesn't whine.

"I'm here to save you," she whispers, licking my ear. "I'm your last chance of hope if you ever want to work in this town again."

"You?" I turn so abruptly her arm jerks, sending beer drizzling over her half of our coordinated ensemble. "You've been lying to me, yourself, and everyone about your so-called rehab. You haven't been sober a goddamn day in your life." I jump up from the chaise and she tumbles awkwardly onto her side, spilling the rest of her drink.

"Zac, buddy!" somebody I barely know calls up from my pool at my own damn house. "Come on down and have a drink with us, man." I look over the terrace rail and heat the pool another few degrees with a hot beam of anger.

I head back inside and Ash scrambles after me. I pull the sliding door shut and secure the blackout curtains, hoping she'll leave, but instead she climbs onto my bed.

"You led me to believe Roland was treating you, and all the while you've been shacked up with Rachman, that lame-ass pusher posing as a therapist."

Ashtynn lights a cigarette and lounges against a pillow, my words bouncing off her curves.

"You're a whore." I shake my head in disgust. "In every aspect of your life," I add, pulling the cigarette out of her hand before she burns my fucking bed. "I don't want to be one too." I point to the door, my meaning clear.

She gets up on all fours on the bed. "I love you, Zac," she coos. "You don't really think I give a crap about Elliott, do you? You know me better than that." She gazes at me with the wide, bottomless velvet eyes I've been lost in too many times.

Fuck. The room is spinning. Did Ashtynn finally tell me she loves me? I try to maintain balance as the house tilts, rolling on an axis, a loud buzzing in my ears.

"Zacky, you know me better than anyone. And I need you, now," she purrs. "And you need me."

I need another drink.

"Bet you said the same thing to Rachman," I hiccup, stumbling a little but catching myself on the back of one of my couches. Binge-drinking after months of sobriety is a trip.

"Elliott was tricking me. He kept me sedated. But I've broken away from him, I promise you." Her face crumples. "I've always loved you, Zac." Ashtynn sits back on her heels, her chin dropping toward her chest, her big eyes turned up at me. "Let's put this whole Shelby disaster behind us," she whispers, licking her lips.

Her dress is askew, the neckline splayed open and loose between her full breasts. She teases the wisps of hair cradling her chin with an index finger and leans forward again, exposing the opening of her dress straight down to her navel, only to pretend she's shown too much and lean back again.

She draws her hand down around her neckline, toying with it, her fingertips playing across a light dusting of shimmer powder just above the top of her bra. "I want to show you something." She bites her lip, staring into my eyes.

I'm having a hard time straightening out the blur in front of me. Tonight's gotten as bad as it could possibly get. Whatever she wants to show me, I'll have a look. What have I got left to lose?

Ashtynn slides off the bed, grabs her purse, and pulls out some folded sheets. She drags me playfully by the collar of my shirt, drawing me down onto the bed. Rolling on top of me, she straddles my hips, flattens the pages out on my chest, and starts singing the music. It's some trashy love song penned by OmniMotion's in-house team.

"See, Zacky? What did I tell you? Isn't this to die for?" She leans forward, pressing her chest against mine, and kisses a trail of soft wetness along the close-shaved edge of my jawline. "You and me"—she presses the full, pillowy softness of her lips into mine, tugs up my shirt from around my waist, and strokes her fingers across my stomach—"are going to record an R&B duet that is poppy and teen-friendly and our fans are going to go insane for it." She undoes my pants and finds the top of my underwear. "There are already some ideas for video storyboards. The work is already underway." She kisses my chest and wriggles lower. "Tonight will be forgotten. The public is waiting. Our fans need us." Her voice is no more than a breath now, her lips grazing my lower ribs, warming them.

"I don't think that's what I had in mind," I breathe back, no conviction marking my words. I don't even know what I'm talking about. The song, or her, or being with her now?

"Shhh, baby. You don't have to make a decision right now," she scolds me with a broad, moist sweep of her tongue along the inside of my hip. "I want you to think about us, Zac. Think about how powerful we can be when we come together."

I let out a long sigh, running my hands through her silken mahogany locks. My pants have somehow disappeared. But even without them the room is warmer now, bobbing and swaying, spilling at the edges like her loose hair.

"We'll do a hot video, something showcasing our chemistry. They'll be camping out for our big finale: our full-length feature film."

The fact is, she's probably right. But doing this duet with her would be putting another nail in my own coffin.

"Ash, baby, I'm trying to develop my career." I exhale, the room growing dark, the walls turning liquid around me. "I need to write my own music." I repeat my damn manifesto from what seems like a great distance, even as her softness closes in all around me. She's about to claim me once again, impale herself on the only part of me not yet disintegrated.

"Silly Zacky. You tried that, and look what a terrible mess you made," she taunts me like I'm a naughty boy.

I'd fight back, put her in her place, but I can't open my eyes. My eyelids lie too heavy over them.

"You belong up here with me," she says, stroking the length of her sweet-smelling body, slow and deliberate, against me.

An ice-cold chill cracks at my core and snakes up my spine, leaving the hairs on the back of my neck on end.

"What did you say?" I ask her.

But I know what the fuck she said. I grip my hands around her hips, lifting her off me and tossing her to the side of the bed. "That's enough," I tell her.

What the hell. Did Stan tell her about those words? They're on several tracks in the control room, along with the entire conversation Shel and I had when we wrote that lyric. I was supposed to sing them tonight, but I fucked up so bad that I didn't get that far.

I have to get it through my fucking skull: Shelby is Stan's girl. That's the only way to explain how he could know what Shelby heard inside me. Everything that has ever mattered to me, Stan had first or took from me.

Ash regains her composure quickly. Adjusting her clothes and swinging her ass in my direction, she grabs her purse, strolls into the bathroom, and pulls out a tube of lipstick.

I find my pants and pull them on.

"Zacky, we're both in trouble," she says, matter-of-factly, leaning across the sink to look in the mirror. "You for your internationally gargantuan fuckup tonight, and me because . . ." She pauses to press the fresh lipstick into her lips.

"Because?"

"Because I love you. And you hurt me. You cheated on me, Zac Wyatt." She feigns mortification. "Some slutty groupie would have been bad enough, but how could you sleep with a"—she lowers her voice to a whisper so as not to offend the no one and nobody who can hear our conversation—"retarded girl?"

Did she really just use that word?

How has it taken me this long to realize Ash is the shittiest person I know? And I know some real assholes.

Ash shakes the unpleasant inconvenience I've caused from her shoulders, and a loose strap of her dress slides down to the crevice of her elbow, exposing her again. I don't know who or what Shelby is, but it is beyond messed up that I still wish she was here with me instead.

"She isn't—"

"You gave songwriting your best shot, honey." Ash places her lipstick in my bathroom drawer like she expects to use it in the future. "You tried. That's all anyone can ever ask. Now it's time to reclaim your place at the top. And only I can put you there."

She plants one last kiss on my cheek and runs her hands down my body, like I'm a prize horse and she's placed a heavy bet, then turns and walks out the door.

I listen for the close clack-clack of her short-tempered stride on the wide wooden staircase, wanting to make sure she's really leaving. Only after her footsteps fade from hearing do I fall back onto my bed and allow the darkness to return all around me.

I wake up shivering with cold. The music from the party downstairs rouses me enough to realize I'm sprawled half-naked on top of the bed linens.

I shake myself fully conscious; I have no clue how long I was out. I get up and stumble to the bathroom for a piss.

After splashing some water on my face, I dig Ash's lipstick out of the vanity drawer and toss it in the trash can.

I'm not giving up. I'm going to write my own music.

Now.

## CHAPTER TWENTY-FIVE

# SHELBY

Rounding the steep hill on foot, I make it up into Grounder's mansion-lined neighborhood. Most of the homes are hidden; only a security gate differentiates one residence from another.

Angry, blood-lined welts bore into both my feet. I slip my shoes off and carry them. I don't know if Zac wants them back, if they are only on loan for tonight, but it won't be too hard to part with this vicious pair. The gravel at the side of the road bites the tender bottoms of my bare feet, but it's less painful than putting the shoes back on.

It's tough to tell one house from another. The security keypads presiding over each gate all look alike. But I remember the code, it's the key pattern of two bassline measures from Radiohead's "Anyone Can Play Guitar."

After trying the code at the fifteenth near-identical gate, it hits me: He's probably updated the password. What if I've already passed his house?

I hobble to a decorative bench wedged into a wisteria arbor

and fall onto it. It creaks from disuse under my weight. As I lift one foot over the opposite ankle and rub my tender wounds, I catch the sound of a sorrowful, droning buzz. I look in its direction, across the curve of the next hill.

Zac's car is there, wedged and crumpled between two open gates.

I limp quickly through the moonlight to the gate keypad. Holding my breath, I type in the code pattern.

Grinding a repentant sigh, the heavy metal releases the car and swings wide open to allow me entry to the house.

I sneak around back, infiltrating the raucous poolside party. Zero Interference until I can make my way inside.

Hiding within the perimeter of manicured shrubbery, I edge around the massive house. Oh crap, Zac's bedroom light is on. I lean in close to the cool brick, wrangling my racing pulse to a slower tempo.

A dance track blasts from several audio devices around the pool area. With my eyes closed, I can gauge the distance of each one by its volume. My best bet is to wind my way through the party in plain view, lingering too close to the speakers for anyone to attempt conversation.

The French doors on the terrace where Zac and I first ate dinner are propped open. I know the layout of the kitchen and how to reach the music studio from there. But where will I find Stanford?

Almost two hours on buses, and I never bothered to map out a freaking plan for when I got here.

I guess I'll just hide in the studio until he returns.

Ditching the useless shoes in a planter, I hustle into the kitchen on the downbeat of a new dance track.

Party guests are chilling out around the island in the oversized kitchen. There's party food everywhere. Best to keep an eye out for wandering catering staff looking for puke buckets to empty.

With bare feet, the sound of my steps is imperceptible to the common ear. Wow, the "common ear." Why haven't I ever thought of it like that before? I'll have to tell Stanford that one.

As I tiptoe toward the hallway leading to the music studio, someone shoves a cold bottle of beer toward my hand. I accept it with the courtesy of a nod and carry on.

Zero Interference.

A dim light illuminates the studio, as it did the night I spent with Stanford. My tempo quickens as I wrap my fingers around the door handle and peek in the window, scanning the small control room.

No. Stanford has collapsed on the floor.

I jerk the handle open, rush inside, and drop to my knees next to him.

I reach to touch him, shake him, but I freeze.

Should I shake him? His eyes are closed and he's still. Eerily still. He's sprawled on the carpet just like Dad, dried blood encrusting his face and hair. And the room stinks—of death. I ought to know.

He can't be dead. I close my eyes and listen, daring to place the pads of my fingertips ever so gently on the smooth skin over his brow, now strangely bluish. Finding it warm, I allow my full palm to rest across it.

I finally detect a slow, unyielding, and shallow breath within him. My heartbeat, my own rhythm, sinks below his, holding his heartbeat afloat. I brush his lashes open; his pupils are so tiny they are nearly indistinguishable.

I can't let him die.

I hid the curse of my hearing under my father's headphones. Stanford buried his in a needle-induced lull. My heart aches for him.

I lean forward and pass my breath into him, watchful and steady. With one hand on his chest, I try to pace the rhythm of my breaths to the rhythm of our conjoined song, at this point little more than a lethargic, delirious waltz.

I have no clue how to do mouth-to-mouth, or CPR, or whatever it's called. But he needs more air, something to bolster his deflated breath. I tug gently on the cracking blue of his slack lip. His tongue is the same inhuman color Dad's was when I found him.

On my exhalation, I pick up the approach of clacking heels in the hallway outside the control room door. I glance back and forth between the door and Stanford's parched mouth, wondering if the instant it would take for me to beg whoever it is to dial 911 would threaten the meager opportunity I have to hold him to this world.

I dare not deny him the breath of life; I keep my lips on his. The clacking stops at the door and when I glance up to the window, I see Ashtynn Kingston looking down on us and, overcome with relief, release my breath into Stanford's airways. She can help. Ashtynn has been in this exact situation herself. She'll know what needs to be done.

I let Stan's mouth free just long enough to cry out, "Thank God you're still here. He's in trouble. We have to call 911."

She is unmoving. Not a gesture, not a word. She does nothing.

"Please, there's no time to waste," I beg her, looking around the room for a phone.

I jump up from the floor and start toward the door. "Help me," I plead. "What should I do?" When I glance back at Stanford's lifeless body, I see only my father there, as barren and asleep as Stanford, and my breath falls away. A confounding terror rips through me. It tears me open in one long, ragged gash, as though all these years since Dad died, my grief has been held together by nothing more than sparsely sewn threads.

Ashtynn raises her hand toward the security keypad on the exterior of the room, installed to ensure wandering partygoers don't mess with the band's instruments or computer files. She types a pattern of beeps, and I hear the distinct sound of a heavy metal bolt inside the core of the control room door sliding out and intersecting with more metal.

She's locked us in.

"Please. Help him. He is going to die if you don't call an ambulance," I yell out to her.

A grim smile breaks across her ruby lips on the other side of the window. "Two birds, one stone," she says with a smirk. "Without Stanford, there's no Grounder. Without you, darling Shelby, Zac is mine."

I run to the window, banging on the glass and rattling the locked door handle, but she turns on her heel without another word and disappears down the corridor.

Stanford groans behind me, a cough catching in his limp throat. I let go of the door handle and race back to his side, dropping my head to his chest, my hands supporting his neck. His music, the internal orchestration of his life, has changed. I don't know if I'm losing my mind or if what I'm hearing is death marching through his bloodstream.

I sink my mouth onto his, offering him my breath between sobs, gripping his body to mine. I can't give up. As his music slows and his breath fades away, I lie next to him, touching as much of his body as I can with mine without crushing him. I need to hear him with every cell possible. It's getting harder for me to detect his weak pulse through my tears, and the fear that I will lose him.

Lost in the cadence of listening and exhaling into his mouth, I'm startled when the control room door rattles open behind me. A hand on my shoulder jerks my lips from Stanford's, and when I glance up I'm nearly scorched by the fiery blaze of Zac's turquoise glare.

"How the hell did you lock yourselves inside?" Before I can

answer, he follows with, "So this is how you stick it to me, Shelby? Fucking my mortal enemy right here, where you knew I'd be sure to find you?"

There's no time for arguing. "I think he overdosed. Zac, he's dying. We need an ambulance, now."

Zac gasps, startled, when I pull back from Stanford and reveal his bluish color and listless body. "Holy Jesus and Mary Chain," he whispers under his breath, already digging into his jeans pocket for his cell phone.

He gets through to 911 immediately. As he details Stanford's condition and shares their address, I continue offering my every breath to bond Stanford to the possibility of making it through the night.

When Zac finishes his call, I have too many things I want to tell him and I'm not sure where to start. "Thank you for calling an ambulance," I say first; then, "I'm so sorry about your song. What happened?" I am suddenly tender toward him, despite everything. "Ashtynn locked us in here. She hoped Stanford would die to get out of your way, and—"

"You lying, deceitful bitch of a whore," Zac spits. "Christ, look at the two of you bony rails. You're both a couple of fucking junkies, why didn't I see it before?" His once-warm gaze now burns me with its undiluted disgust. "You deserve each other."

When the ambulance finally arrives, the cops file in behind the paramedics, searching the small control room for evidence of misconduct. I've given nearly the last of my music away to Stanford. As his anthem disintegrated to a low, tinny tap, I fed him mine to keep him alive. Now I'm spent, my breath so weak and depleted I can't form a word.

"Miss? My name is Denis. I'm an EMT and I'm here to assist," someone says, shining a light into Stanford's eyes and fitting his arm with a blood pressure monitor.

"Asssshhhh," I croak out, trying to tell him Ashtynn wanted Stanford to die, but her name shrivels on the cracked desert of my tongue. I glance past his shoulder to Zac, who is standing in the corner of the room, his arms folded as tightly as his brow, and plead "Help me explain" with my eyes.

Instead, he commands the attention of one of the police officers. "Detective, this girl is trespassing. She is in no way a welcome guest in my home. She must have broken in."

My gaze and the last of my hope fall to the floor. I wrench what little strength I have left to keep watch over Stanford's body while the emergency workers examine him. Zac's cold-blooded dismissal snakes inside me, slicing through to my center.

Yet another officer squeezes into the crowded space, this one carrying the shoes Zac gave me in a sealed bag. "I found these in the bushes adjacent to the terrace," he tells the investigator. "Witnesses claim the southwest entrance was open all evening. Any chance you recognize them, Mr. Wyatt?"

Zac frowns at the scuffed heels, lined with traces of blood where the strap edges dug into me. Multiple pairs of eyes turn toward my culpable bare feet, also laced with dried blood.

Within seconds, lengthy, discrediting reports of my past arrests and suspected mental disorders are procured. Zac swallows hard, the golden hue of his sculpted face draining to a pallid ash. I am hoisted to my knees, my hands are placed behind my back, and two leaden clicks secure handcuffs around my wrists.

I should have left him when I realized he wasn't the true pulse of Grounder. From our first kiss, his music was a stranger to mine.

# CHAPTER TWENTY-SIX

"Zac Wyatt, you're under arrest for the attempted murder of Stanford Lysandre."

What the hell? I let the cops snoop through every inch of my house trying to figure out what happened between Shelby and Stan, and this is what they come up with? I was glad we didn't spring for security cameras when we leased the place. The last thing I wanted was the cops getting any proof Shelby has been living here with me. But now they're pointing the finger at me? I wish I had some proof I had nothing to do with Stan's overdose.

I shoot a glance at Deshi and Os, who rushed home when party guests started posting to social media about Stan's OD and the cops and ambulance crashing the party. I expect one of them to step in, tell these cops to stop messing around.

I'm too shocked to complete a fucking sentence. "He overdosed. It was an accident." This can't be real.

Two officers motion for me to stand and place my hands behind my head, handling me much as they did Shelby.

"Os? Deshi? You guys know me as well as anyone. The worst

I could do is murder a song. Tell them they're making a huge mistake, man."

"We'll get it sorted, brother." Os shakes his head in regret, like he knew my arrest was coming.

Deshi doesn't even have the balls to look me in the face. Fuck, he probably ratted me out, told the cops how Stan and I haven't always seen eye to eye. Oh God, from his standpoint, I've been trying to take Stan down from his high horse, not the other way around. He's always taken Stan's side.

The police bring me directly to county jail, and it's already being bombarded with news vans. It was only hours ago I was begging Shel to face the paparazzi with me, and now I'm relieved as hell to learn the cops bring people into the building through a secure location. I hang my head low through the humiliation of having them take my fingerprints and mug shot. At last, I'm corralled into a guarded interrogation room. Berger is there, with some guy in a suit. Thank God he came. He was there last night, he can back me up.

"Wyatt, keep your mouth shut and your head down," he says like he's been watching too many cop shows. "This is Arturo Benevento, head of the label's litigation team." Benevento nods to me past Berger's shoulder.

The cops tell Berger to wait outside while Benevento fills me in on the situation. "Mr. Wyatt," Benevento begins, "the police have reason to suspect you've made an attempt on Mr. Lysandre's life."

I curl my lip at him. That is a bullshit long-stretch of an accusation.

"The paramedics found an empty bottle of methadone on Mr. Lysandre's person, prescribed in your name," he explains, pulling a thick notepad from his briefcase, "and several bruises and lacerations to his body. Security cameras and several eye witnesses have attested to your assault and battery of Mr. Lysandre last night."

I sink low in my chair.

"If Mr. Lysandre's toxicology report shows evidence of methadone-induced overdose," Benevento continues, "it will be detrimental to your case that the prescription belonged to you. However, in order to prove you made an attempt on his life, the police must show evidence that you took at least one direct, albeit ineffective, step toward killing Mr. Lysandre."

"I didn't . . ." My breath leaves my body. Any words I could hope to scrape together in my defense are constricted in a tight vacuum of disbelief.

"Mr. Wyatt, you may face the possibility of a life sentence in California State Prison if the police can prove the attempted murder was willful, deliberate, and premeditated. If convicted of attempted second-degree murder, which is any murder attempt that isn't willful, deliberate, and premeditated, you'll face a five-, seven-, or nine-year state prison sentence."

My head throbs within the close walls of the room. A repetitive clashing of cymbals reverberates off the double-mirrored wall, scratching my ears. I clutch my hands over them, curling my forearms around my head to block the high-decibel assault. Still, Benevento's voice creeps in.

"Should Mr. Lysandre fail to recover from his coma, the charges will be adjusted to manslaughter—or murder, depending on the outcome of the investigation."

Over the clang and grate of the banging cymbals between my ears, I shout, "Stanford probably stole the pills. That's what addicts do."

Benevento asks me to keep my voice down, but I can barely hear myself think over all this noise.

"I never took even one of those pills and would be more than happy to submit to a drug test to prove it," I yell. "I gave the entire container of methadone to Ashtynn Kingston at the

Awards. She was the last one to see them."

"This is the kind of information we need, thank you." Benevento makes a few notes. "Based on the security camera footage at the Choice America Awards and reports of numerous eyewitnesses, our understanding is that your attack on the victim was in response to him having alleged relations with a Shelby Rey, whom we've identified as your current girlfriend." He peers at me over his notes. "Is that correct?"

The victim? Stanford Lysandre is not the victim here, I am.

I mean, I hope he pulls through and all. Fuck, he's got to pull through, to tell them I'm innocent.

"Ashtynn Kingston is my girlfriend. Check your facts," I spit out.

Knuckles rap a polite knock on the only door to the small room before it swings open and Roland Gibson is ushered in. I sink farther down into my chair, staring across the colorless table.

"Zac, son, I came as soon as I heard," he says, nearly out of breath, as he pulls a seat up to the table.

"I'm not your son, and you can get the hell out of here."

Gibson tries to slither in some point about helping my case, but I slam my hand on the table and repeat myself, louder this time so he gets it. "Get out. You've done enough damage, you fucking fraud."

Gibson glances at Benevento, who is smart enough to keep his mouth shut. I turn and look pointedly at the door until he finally gets a clue, slides his chair back, and shuffles out of the room.

The last thing I need is Gibson's testimony recalling how many times I confided to him my anger and jealousy toward Stanford. I don't even want to think about all the incriminating details he knows about my relationship with Shelby.

I'm banking on everything he's heard and seen being protected by patient confidentiality. Gibson wouldn't lie on the stand to protect me, if it came to that.

## THE SECRET SONG OF SHELBY REY

♫

The cops make me sweat out nearly twenty-four hours in holding before seeing a judge. I sit there with nothing but rage for Shelby and Stan until my anger is so hot, piercing, and laser-focused, I've boiled down everything I'd like to say to them both into lyrics, and I can almost hear the grinding guitar licks I'll use to drive home my points. At last, Benevento negotiates my release on a $2 million bond, but the police warn me to sit pretty on a short leash.

"How about I take you over to your parents' hotel, kid?" Berger offers. "Your place is probably paparazzi central."

I nod, not ready to face Oslo and Deshi anyway. When we step out of the station, he wraps his arm loosely around my shoulder, and even though it's only Berger, the gesture makes me feel a little less adrift.

That feeling evaporates when we pull out of the parking structure and a rabid litter of media storms Berger's SUV.

I sink down in the back seat among discarded fast-food containers and candy bar wrappers, obscured by darkly tinted windows. I'd give Berger an earful about all the foul trash in his car, but it beats being out on the sidewalk. It occurs to me he's the only one who showed up to take me home.

Once we round the corner, I open the envelope containing my wallet and cell phone, which the police confiscated and held until I posted bail, and scroll through my messages. About a thousand messages from Mom and Dad flash on-screen, beginning with the news of my arrest and becoming more desperate over time. They must be worried as hell.

Oh hell, they were "worried" when I got busted with heroin. Now their only son has been arrested for attempted murder? "Worried" doesn't begin to cover it.

Out of the digital sea of panicked emails and texts, one message stands apart: "Mi casa es su casa." Only five words, but the only five I need.

"Berger, my parents have been through enough. Just take me to Ashtynn's, okay, buddy?"

Berger meets my eyes in the rearview, then gives a curt nod and merges onto the I-10 in the direction of Malibu. It's an hour out of his way in traffic, but I have to see her. She's the only person who I can trust to figure a way out of this.

Ash has been stockpiling meds: oxycodone, Valium, Xanax, Vicodin, and who knows what else. Hell, I got no right to judge. It's Shelby's fault I have to resort to this shit to stop the cymbals still vibrating in my ears from clanging away.

Ash pours a hefty chaser for me to wash the pharms down.

We kick it at her place, watching TV. She thrives on celebrity tabloid shows, always on the lookout for her own pristine image, but tonight reports are grim.

"Stanford Lysandre, Grammy-winning guitarist and songwriter for the band Grounder, was found in a coma as the result of a drug overdose," an ex-model posing as an entertainment "news" reporter tattles to what is no doubt an unsympathetic general public. "Grounder lead singer, Zac Wyatt, called 911 but was later arrested."

The show already has witnesses recounting our fistfight backstage. Every last witness admits I'm clearly the superior athlete, that Stan has nothing on me. I can't help but smirk until I recognize the sapphire-haired production assistant from backstage at the Choice Americas. "I heard Zac Wyatt clearly shouting 'I hate you' at Stanford Lysandre."

Should have kept my damn mouth shut. And Christ, how the hell do they already have a copy of my mug shot?

Clips of Roland's appearances on various TV talk shows flash across the screen. "Psychiatrist Roland Gibson, who has been treating Mr. Wyatt for heroin addiction, is also connected to Shelby Alicia Rey, an eighteen-year-old homeless woman with a history of mental illness and past arrests for violent behavior, who was arrested at the home of Wyatt's band, Grounder, for first-degree burglary. Rey was taken into custody and is under investigation."

"Stan had better come to," I say to Ash. "He's got to set the record straight."

"I know, right?" She swishes ice around the bottom of her third drink. "That nutjob is dangerous. I'm just thankful she didn't hurt you, Zacky."

She hurt me all right. Broke my fucking heart.

"Tension mounts as fans wait for Stanford Lysandre to recover," the reporter continues as the show cuts to scenes from the candlelight vigil staged outside Stanford's hospital room. I grab the remote and turn the TV off.

I stretch my arms over my head, and a pharmaceutical tingle oozes through my tendons from shoulders to fingertips. I'm exhausted. My phone buzzes across the coffee table with the force of five billion messages, half from my parents. I can't talk to them. Not yet.

I pull Ashtynn over to me, careful not to spill her drink.

She looks up at me through the tentacles of her eyelash extensions. "Zacky, you need to distance yourself."

I pull back a moment, cocking my brow.

"From all this business with that psycho who broke into your house," she clarifies, snuggling under my arm and placing her hand on my leg like she's claiming it as her own. "You need to be seen with me. We'll go out every night if we have to."

I push back a lock from her buffed and flawless cheek, considering her proposal.

"You have to convince the public that you are the victim here," she explains.

"That's what I've been saying." Finally, someone who understands.

"You gave that poor homeless woman a chance to act in a Grounder video, and you leveraged your good fortune in an attempt to turn her life around," she recounts in a pained voice, like it's God's honest truth. "And how did she repay you? By making you the victim of stalking and burglary on your private residence. She's a mentally unstable fan who endangered the safety and well-being of your entire band." The way she's telling it, I've just narrowly survived an unfortunate series of events pulled straight from some horror flick.

She's right, of course.

Holding her soft body against mine, her round breasts pressed into me, there's one thing that's still bugging me. How was the music studio locked from the outside?

"Ash, baby? You heard that Stanford OD'd in the music studio, right?"

"Mm-hmm." She runs her hands up and down my thighs.

"And Shelby was in there with him?" I keep wondering how Shelby knew Ash was even at the house. Unless she saw her with her own eyes.

Ash shrugs, like it really doesn't matter either way. "Of course, silly. I locked them in. I wanted you to catch them together, to find out your little nutbag day-tripper was screwing everyone in your band." She drains her drink. "I had no idea they were doing drugs together."

But they weren't. Shelby's toxicology report came back clean, I know that much.

The last I saw of the methadone, it was in Ash's hands. If Stan stole the pills from her, wouldn't she have said that by now? Or did she give them to him, knowing there's one thing Stanford can't do: say no.

Stan had better come to, or I am in some serious fucking trouble.

Whatever Ash gave me, it's straight tripping me out. I swear I can hear her guilt though her touch.

# CHAPTER TWENTY-SEVEN

SHELBY

Jail is the fated crash pad of the mentally ill, Roland was right about that. My hope of avoiding it was a sure sign of my skewed thinking. Every white-coat, teacher, doctor I ever met—hell, even my own mother—warned me I'd be incarcerated one day.

My arraignment only took a couple of days to be scheduled, but with bail set at fifty grand, there wasn't a hope I'd be let free. During intake I wasn't allowed any visitors, but I would've felt so bad if Roland and Jaclyn had tried to get involved. I've put them through enough. Still, I felt the sting of relief in my heart when I spotted them in the crowded courtroom.

A public defender appeared and made the rounds, collecting cases.

"Can you afford a lawyer?" she asked.

"I don't think so," I replied, the check Zac gave me crossing my mind. I wonder if it's still good?

"Do you want a lawyer?"

I glance toward Jaclyn, trying to imagine what she'd advise.

"Yes, please."

The public defender and I discuss my case—penal code 459, with penalties including a maximum fine of $10,000 and up to six years in prison—for no more than fifteen seconds before I'm called before the judge. We decide I'll plead not guilty, but I'm not even sure whether it's true. I wasn't invited to the house, after all.

The judge held my case over trial in two weeks, and I was transferred to a county jail.

As I tuck the blanket around the thin mattress on my narrow bunk and lie down, I consider the fact that if I were in lockdown under less auspicious circumstances, this all might be harder. With a connection to the attempted murder of a world-famous guitarist and felony charges for burglary of the home of Grounder on my record, the other women have afforded me the respect befitting a badass.

The problem that remains is, as always, the truth.

I wound up in jail, just like everyone said I would. But am I here because I'm crazy?

Maybe I could have avoided arrest if I'd found some way to drown out the incessant jumble of noises feeding all my senses at all times. Without my ears' curse, I never would have met Zac. But I wouldn't have seen the inside of a music studio either. Maybe it's all one and the same: My ability to hear made me crazy, and I'm crazy because I can hear.

I guess I have time to think about it before my court date.

I'm still sore where the frayed threads of my connection to Stanford were cut. Every day, I scan the TV in the common area for news coverage, hoping he'll come out of his coma. But the deputies only allow us to watch movies and home renovation shows, and they won't let us change the channel. Considering how abruptly my life changed when Zac turned his back on me,

I'm coming down with a not-so-irrational fear I'm next in line for attempted murder allegations.

I fail to see how I could be culpable for taking his life. I was there to sustain it.

Still, I had it coming, getting chucked into jail. I'm a stupid kid. It's the timing that's unbearable, because I can't help Stanford while he sits in his own version of a jail cell.

For days now, I've been in county jail. For days now, he's been trapped in some sterile hospital room, unable to get up and walk away from his bad choices. But he's safe. He's not using. He's surrounded by people who can help.

I'm afraid to eat the food here, shadowed again by those familiar, nauseous cramps. But I can't let my body disintegrate inside yet another set of clothing that doesn't belong to me. Not if there is any hope I might be released.

The sounds inside the cubicles in the dorm-style day room are an acoustic nightmare, more jarring than the silence of the recording studio. The vicious skate of metal sliding against metal, the complex sequence of latches meeting clamps within inexhaustible locks, and the deputies' gait as their boots pace the floor remind us daily that if we were ever in control, we are no longer.

But far worse are the inmates' voices, the dismal loneliness woven within hushed exchanges. Their helpless cries are veiled in angry outbursts. Fearful, baiting remarks hit the cold, iron-hearted walls and crumble all around me.

Sometimes I hum, whistle, or tap my fingers on a bunk post, creating a melody, distracting myself. But I don't dare do it for long; I'm afraid to make too much noise here, to draw any more attention to myself than I already have.

Audio engineering college is beyond my reach now, a lusted-after lover who lacks any knowledge of my existence. What a pipe dream that was. It will be impossible to apply after this. Assuming I'm allowed to keep the money Zac gave me, I'll need it to find a place to live and keep myself clothed and fed until I can get a job.

I've no idea what'll happen at my trial, anyway. I have no defense. I wasn't invited to Zac's house; I broke in, just like he accused me. I told the cops Ashtynn locked me in with Stanford in the control room, and that she saw that he was dying and refused him help, but no one believes me. When the police arrived at Zac's, he denied having had any personal relationship with me. And in his official statement, he never mentioned anything about the locked control panel or Ashtynn's visit. It's my word against his.

That hasn't stopped me from telling the whole truth. Zac had nothing to do with Stanford's overdose, I told them. He wasn't even there when I found Stanford collapsed on the floor.

"Are you aware Stanford Lysandre's overdose was a result of the consumption of an entire container of methadone tablets prescribed to Zac Wyatt?" they asked.

I guess I never knew Zac at all.

I didn't detect his love for Ashtynn in his internal music. And I never noticed the fuzzy texture of any opiates, either. I spent hours touching him, listening to him. How did he hide it all from me?

An ornery buzzer sounds down the corridor. A deputy rouses us from our interminable thoughts. "The tables are open," he says.

That's our cue to trade the monotony of the dorm bunks for the tedium of television, card games, and sizing one another up.

After they moved me to county jail, I wasn't allowed any visitors for a week. Inmates in the dorms are allowed visitors on the weekends only and with appointments. I have only one more week until my trial, but Mom hasn't put in a request to visit me even once.

And why would she? She has nothing to gain, except maybe the satisfaction of saying "I told you so."

If I'm completely honest with myself, I really cared about Zac. I was myself with him, my real self. Who cares what the past held, where I came from, or who raised me? I tried to do right by him.

I tried to have honor, be on his side. I put aside all the fears I've ever had to go into the live room and write that song with him. In return, he annihilated it. He crushed me. He slammed both our song and me into the ground, set us on fire, and pissed on our ashes. And where is he now? He is free.

Mom was right about people with money and fame.

"Rey." Deputy Gutierrez appears in the dorm cubicle I share with three other women. "You have a visit."

I slide off my bunk and put on my jail-issued shower shoes.

Gutierrez is impatient. "Follow me."

He leads me through a series of twisting corridors to a room with a row of phones separated by a glass partition and tells me to sit my ass down.

There are a couple of other inmates meeting with their children or adult female family members. There are no boyfriends or husbands.

"You got thirty minutes," Gutierrez says. A buzzer sounds, and a door on the other side of the partition opens.

I catch my breath. The moment I see Jaclyn, I wish I could throw my arms around her. A second later, Roland appears, worry marring the line of his brow. I stand to greet them.

"Sit down," Gutierrez warns me.

I pick up the phone, eagerly awaiting their approach.

"Shelby, thank God you're all right," Jaclyn says. "It took us days to get a visit. I'm so sorry."

Words don't come, and I don't want them anyway.

"Happy birthday," Roland adds. "I wish we could celebrate at home."

I'd forgotten. It's my nineteenth birthday.

"Shelby, dear, we've been working with our attorney to formulate your defense," Jaclyn says, glancing at the clock. "She may be able to reduce your charges, or limit them to probation, if she can provide documented evidence of a mental illness that influenced your actions." She allows herself a hopeful smile. "The purpose of the justice system is to punish those who deliberately and knowingly break the law, not to persecute those experiencing a psychotic episode."

I look into her brown eyes; they are warm pools of concern. Leave it to Jaclyn to take on a hopeless case.

"Is this what you meant when you told me to use my weakness as my strength?" I ask with a sigh.

Roland begins to lay out the details of my incapacitation plea, but I halt him a minute, holding up my opened hand. White-coats have filled files full of my symptoms over the years, but I don't think I've ever been diagnosed, not formally. "Am I crazy?" I ask.

Jaclyn and Roland fall silent, glancing at one another and back at me.

"If no one labels my condition, does that mean I have a chance to make things right?" I ask, trying to read their reaction. "I could commit to therapy. Isn't that what Jaclyn has asked of me from the beginning?"

A light shines from behind Jaclyn's eyes.

"The only reason I went there was to be with Stanford. And it's a good thing I did." It pains me to remember him collapsed on the studio floor and barely hanging on, but I'm certain that if I hadn't gone to him, he would have been lost forever.

Roland clears his throat and leans forward. Jaclyn shifts in her seat, waiting to hear what he has to say.

"I've never had a formal session with you, nor taken you officially as my patient," he points out, stroking the length of his jaw. "Therefore, I haven't made any diagnosis." He glances at Jaclyn. "And I would attest to that in a court of law, if necessary."

Jaclyn twirls a lock of her raven hair, her eyes narrowing in thought. "Shelby, you've been staying in our home as our guest, not as a patient. I testified that to the hospital board at St. Cecilia. It's already on record."

Bolstered by their support, I chime in, "Ashtynn Kingston is at fault. She locked me and Stanford in."

Twin frowns fall across their faces, and they both reply at once, "There is no evidence to support that."

Slumping against the table, I sigh. "I'll take responsibility for burglary, but nothing more." I fold my arms on the table in front of me and lower my face into them.

The charges against me are mine to bear, and I don't want an easy solution to rid myself of them.

Roland and Jaclyn continue to visit me, and it helps me feel a little less alone. On opposite sides of the glass, I can't get close enough to touch, to hear their songs inside them. But strangely, their presence feels like harmony. I decide that, whenever I get out of here, I'm going to do whatever it takes to find more friends like them. Friends I know I can trust. So today, when Gutierrez summons me for visiting hours, I nearly trip with eagerness over the fat rubber heels of his boots as I follow him to the meeting room.

But today, Mom is here. Visiting me.

Being around cops makes her nervous, so it's no surprise she put on her boss lady outfit: a snug gray polyester suit with shimmering silver pinstripes, and cherry suede platform heels. She's doing something different with her hair and makeup too: heavy powder for the unforgiving glare of daylight, and a tight bun, because people take you more seriously if you can make your hair behave.

I pick up the phone to tell her I'm really glad she came.

"I ain't going to lie to you," she begins without a hello. "I'm worried about being called to the stand."

Roland warned me Mom would be subpoenaed.

"Good to see you, Mom," I tell her. And I mean it.

"I done some things, Shelby," she replies, stealing a glance at a security camera overhead. "And I ain't going to jail along with you."

"Mom, dancing at the club isn't illegal."

She shoots me an angry glare. With a sidelong glance at an armed deputy by the door, she wraps her hand around the phone's mouthpiece and moves closer to the partition. I bet our conversation is being recorded, but I don't want to make her nervous.

"I gave him the gun," she whispers. "He was sick of living, so I got him good and high, gave him his gun, and left him to his business. I couldn't watch him go on the way he was suffering."

Dad.

The hairs on my arms stiffen to tiny spikes, scraping the inside sleeves of my orange jail-issue sweatshirt. My mouth falls open—to protest, to alarm the deputy, to curse her mistake, to swear she's lying. But nothing comes out.

Mom waves off whatever she thinks I ought to say with a sweep of acrylic nails the same red as her shoes. "I'm going away," she announces. "Don't you bother looking me up if you ever get out. I'm washing my hands of you, Shelby, now and forever." She smooths the front of her jacket. "Just thought it wouldn't be decent of me if I didn't say goodbye."

# CHAPTER TWENTY-EIGHT

My phone buzzes with a text from Ash. She wants to talk and says it can't wait until I get back to her place tonight.

"In studio in SM" I text back. "Come by anytime. Love u."

Benevento advised me to lie low, so I rented a month of recording studio time in Santa Monica. Turns out I didn't need Gibson or Shelby to write a goddamn song. Since I've been hiding out in here, I've written an entire album. It's flowing out of me, like I always knew it would.

I didn't want to set foot in my house. Not in our home studio where I recorded with Shelby, no way. Still, it meant a lot when Oslo was willing to come out and help me record.

I got to say, Gibson was wrong about me. He thought my idea of success was money and fame. Ain't nothing wrong with that, but the best part of recording music is partnership. Having Os in the studio made everything better than if I'd gone it alone. I even charmed Ashtynn into recording some vocals, dialing down her modulation to evoke Shelby's singing voice: bubbles collapsing on smooth skin in hot water. Ash damn near nails Shel's voice, too. It's almost as though she's here.

If only I could dig up a guitarist with half of Stanford's talent.

My label isn't dumb; they already released the first single. "The public is ripe," Berger told me. "They want to know what's going on in that pretty head of yours." Holy hell, he was right on the money. Grounder fans lit up the goddamned Internet downloading it. Even Stan never pulled that kind of reaction.

My new solo album rocks. The tracks are angry, loud, and wrenching. My fans' headphones and speakers are my world stage, and I'm going to give them a bloody earful of my sonic revenge. Wicked hardcore rock and roll, fuck yeah. The magic I always dreamed of, grinding guitars and the tortured vocals of an honest man. The lyrics come easy now.

I have half a mind to send Shelby an MP3 player loaded with my unreleased album. Give her something to pass the time while she's in lockdown. I'll bet she thinks I'm still thinking about her.

Shelby means nothing to me, that's what I keep telling Ash.

There's no way I'm letting any judge haul my ass to jail along with her. I had nothing to do with that drug fiend's OD. But goddamn it, neither did Shelby.

Why the hell didn't I tell the police the control room had been locked from the outside? I mean, man, I couldn't wrap my head around the possibility that Ash could be so callous. Not even after she told me herself that it was true.

Shelby's allegations of being locked in have become the hot topic. Every talk show has an opinion. It turns out most deaths occur one to three hours after a drug user has ingested or injected. Locking him in the control room should have guaranteed his death.

I saw Shel myself. She gave Stan mouth-to-mouth. She saved his junkie-ass life. But I can't go back on my statement.

Knowingly filing a false police report is a criminal offense, that's what Benevento says. Sure, the penalty is only a misdemeanor, but a slap on the wrist is only the beginning. The bigger problem is that I've had to cover Ashtynn's actions with more lies.

The investigating officers are sniffing around, wondering why Dr. Elliott Rachman prescribed me methadone when I was in the care of his partner, Dr. Gibson.

Gibson says he wants to press charges against Rachman for statutory rape of a minor and issuing illegal prescriptions. He had the balls to ask me to testify as a witness. No freaking way. Ash already lost that insipid teen-love flick. God knows what would happen to her if it became public knowledge how that skeevy old dude bedded her when she was under eighteen, feeding her a fuckload of narcotics.

I told the cops I switched doctors when my rehab failed to set me straight. What do I care if every celebrity on the West Coast dumps Gibson along with me? If he'd told me the truth about Shelby, she wouldn't have known where I lived or broken in to be with—

With him.

I'm playing back track eight, a rhythm recalled from the night I held Shelby next to the pool at Gibson's place, when there's a light tap at the door.

It can't be Ash, she wouldn't knock.

The press has been camped around her house round the clock. Grounder's house too, not that I'm ever there anymore. They're relentless, and it's damn near maddening. I roll back in my chair and crack the door open an inch, wondering who the hell's come knocking.

But it's Ash all right, although her hair is a tangled mess and she's nearly obscured by a giant pink cardboard bakery box, tied with white ribbon. I usher her in, pausing to close my eyes and listen, tracing the perimeter of the parking area for any evidence she was followed. I don't know how Shelby did it, but now I can hear anything and everything if I just focus.

"Good to see you, babe." I kiss her cheek and turn to save the arrangement I've been working on in a separate file on the computer. "It's nearly six. You want to grab some dinner?"

She doesn't reply.

When I turn back to her, she's opened the pink box to reveal a six-layer chocolate cake, with chocolate mousse frosting, and a single fork.

She sits down at a counter next to the soundboard and digs in, not bothering to find a plate or cut herself a slice.

"Uh, what's up?" I ask. She's wearing a concert tee from her very first tour at age twelve. It's far too small, cutting into her waist below her rib. A soft roll of her flawless skin sits on the rim of her sweatpants. Ashtynn Kingston is wearing sweats?

"Babe, you all right?"

"What the hell do you think?" she replies, her words muffled by chocolate.

Christ, I don't know. If a girl wants to eat chocolate cake for dinner, she's either got her period or it's her birthday, but it would serve me well to know the difference.

I lean against the soundboard, crossing my ankles, and take a good long look at her. I spot a breakout of zits across her left cheek and fight the urge to check my calendar on my phone.

"Happy birthday," I venture, trying not to turn my voice up at the end in the form of a question.

"I'm pregnant, you asshole."

"For real?" Obviously, she's serious. For an instant, a fraction of a heartbeat, I am pierced with a lightning bolt of joy. All I ever wanted was to matter. If I'm someone's dad, well damn, that's kind of everything, isn't it?

Just as quickly, reality snuffs out the light of joy. I stop breathing for several seconds before managing to ask, "Have you told Dr. Rachman, your lover-slash-dealer?"

"Of course I went to Elliott first," she wails, tears springing to her eyes. "I love him."

## THE SECRET SONG OF SHELBY REY

"What the fuck do you mean, you love him?" I go from zero to yelling as I grab some tissues from the console and shove them her way. She ignores the offering and quiets herself instead with another bite of cake.

"He thinks it's the wrong timing for us," Ashtynn cries. "With everything that's going on," she adds, looking glumly into the deep cavity she's shoveled into the cake.

"I thought you broke up with him." I swallow hard, lowering myself into my rolling chair and sliding away from her. "Ash, he's old enough to be your dad."

"He wants me to have an abortion." She puts down her fork, then picks it up again and takes another bite.

She's still with him? I'm living at her goddamn house. When does she even see him? Oh Jesus, I spend hours upon hours in this studio. "What are you going to do?" I can barely choke out my words.

"I told him I couldn't have an abortion. I'm Catholic, you idiot." She reaches for the tissues I forgot I'm still clutching.

I hand them to her, now a tight wad the shape of my fist.

"Besides, it's just as likely your kid as his. We can't really know without a paternity test."

"You're Catholic?" I ask, no clue what else to say. What kind of douchebag would ask a girl to get an abortion?

## CHAPTER TWENTY-NINE

SHELBY

Deputy Gutierrez prods me along the corridor after a visit to the jail's infirmary.

I haven't been feeling myself the last couple of days. After Mom's first, last, and only visit, I got walloped by a high fever. The nurse says I hallucinated, delirious with a temperature of 104 degrees. I was "babbling something ridiculous about writing a song with Stanford Lysandre," she said, unable to hold back a laugh.

I always find a way to embarrass myself. I guess jail hasn't changed me.

When Gutierrez delivers me to my bunk, I drop into bed, pulling the thin blanket tight around me.

My eyes are scratchy and heavy. I just need to catch a little nap before visiting hours. Maybe Mom changed her mind. Maybe she'll come back, and we'll start over.

"It's your lucky day, Rey," the morning deputy says. I haven't learned her name yet, but I recognize her hoarse cough of a voice with one ear on the pillow. "You're free to go."

## THE SECRET SONG OF SHELBY REY

As I process the meaning of her words, I jerk up to a sitting position and rub my eyes.

Did Stanford wake up? Is he okay?

I leap down from my bunk. The quick movement jolts my fuzzy head; I sway and begin to fall. I catch my balance just in time, narrowly avoiding a sound thump on my skull.

She gestures toward the neat pile under my bunk. "Get your stuff."

I collect my things, hugging loose papers to my chest. I'm careful to hide the letter I wrote to Stanford between the songs I'm developing. There's no chance I'll ever see him again. I only wanted to find the words to say I think I know what love could be.

I hope my release from jail is a sign that he's going to be all right.

The deputy ushers me toward the heavy metal doors at the end of the corridor, away from the visiting area.

The first thing I want to do when I get out of here is reach out to Jaclyn and Roland. I haven't had many occasions to say thank you in my life. For a long time, I didn't have much reason to speak at all. Music replaced my need for words. Jac and Roland encouraged me to embrace who I am, flaws and all. I've still got ninety-nine problems, but now I'm thankful for every one of them.

Once the deputies finalize my walking papers, I'm handed a couple of bus tickets. For a second, I'm disappointed in myself. I'm back to where I started. But it's also a chance for a do-over, and I have no plans to make the same mistakes twice.

The sidewalk in front of the building crawls with news reporters, onlookers, and, most surprisingly, supporters hoisting signs reading FREE SHELBY and FAIR TREATMENT FOR THE MENTALLY DISABLED. Cameras flash in my face and the porous black mushroom tips of microphones are shoved nearly against my lips.

Questions rise from the crowd:

"He says you saved his life. Are you going to meet with Stanford now?"

What? He did?

"Are you and Stanford Lysandre in a romantic relationship?"

"Were you and Zac Wyatt lovers?"

A reporter edges her shoulders under the cameras and asks, "Do you have any evidence to support your claim that Ashtynn Kingston attempted to endanger Stanford Lysandre's life?"

I've asked myself all these questions for days and don't have much in the way of answers. Something about being locked up makes everything outside of jail seem like a dream that may or may not have happened.

A deputy appears at my side, barking at the herd to clear a path. When his elbow presses against mine, his song fills my senses. It's strangely comforting. He's calm and unbothered, even as the swell of bodies closes in a tight circle around us. I glance up at him. He isn't about to play attorney or daddy or protector.

The crowd, however, ignores his commands. Demanding a news scoop, they refuse to let us pass. When a swarm of officers forms a wall, reorganizing the mayhem, I spot Jaclyn and Roland pushing to the front.

Relief charging my strength, I break free of my escort and bolt toward them.

Roland and Jaclyn fight their way to us.

"We're here to bring her home, officer," Roland tells him, showing his credentials.

The deputy nods. "I'll follow you to your vehicle."

Roland helps me into the back seat of Jaclyn's SUV, then slides into the driver's seat. I watch the cops thrust back the billowing crowd. Jaclyn secures her seatbelt in the front passenger seat, then looks at me, relief flushing her cheeks.

I should have written a letter to her.

"Are you all right, honey?" she asks with a tender smile of

maternal concern, as if I have lost my doll or skinned my knee.

I just got out of jail.

But she's here. For me.

"Stanford regained consciousness last night," she explains as Roland directs the SUV into traffic. "His representative, a Mr. Berger, called a press conference at the hospital. Stanford provided a detailed account of your bravery, Shelby. You saved his life by performing CPR. We're so proud of you, honey."

"And he told them how Ashtynn locked us in?" I'm hopeful. "How she tried to kill him?" At last, everyone will know I'm not crazy. That Ashtynn's at fault.

Roland takes his eyes from the road just long enough to meet Jaclyn's worried gaze with his own. "No, dear, he doesn't have any recollection of Ashtynn's involvement."

Of course not. Stanford couldn't hear her on our side of the door. Not in the state he was in.

"But Ms. Kingston has been found responsible for giving him Zac's methadone prescription. Ashtynn will be facing some community service time as a result."

"Community service?" I spent days behind bars.

"Performing at some children's hospitals, we're told," Jaclyn replies.

Right. Ashtynn is a role model to young people.

The charges have been dropped. Jaclyn and Roland are letting me stay with them again until I figure out my next move. This time, Jac is sparing me her lectures at the crack of caffeine, and I'm not wasting my time riding on public buses and wishing my life was different.

I offered Jaclyn and Roland the money I earned for the "Vertical Wire" video in exchange for room, board, and whatever treatment they'd offer. I owe them my life, and I felt that money was all I had to give.

Instead, Jaclyn sat me down for lessons in budgeting. I haven't owned one single thing outside of Dad's radio in years, but now I understand the basics of how to earn interest on the money I have so I can pay for college and a place to live. I even found an apartment.

Everything I've collected for the move is mine, and it's new. Not "like new," the way Mom used to shop, not hand-me-down, borrowed, or discarded, but new. As I finish packing, I feel proud of the boxes before me. I have stuff. I have the makings of a life of my own.

We debated what to do with the box of clothes Zac had sent me. It's time I took care of myself, I argued, and bought my own clothing with my own money. Roland contacted Zac about whether we should return it.

That's when we found out Zac and Ashtynn are living together now and talking about starting a family.

I guess Mom was right. Once he got what he wanted from me, he threw me out.

But everything I might have called wrong, shameful, or unlucky can be made good if I look at it a different way. That's what Roland says. Something about transformation and the renewing of my mind. If it weren't for Zac, I would never have attempted songwriting. I wouldn't know now, as sure as the beat of my heart, what I want to do with my life.

And I wouldn't have met Stanford and discovered that the music inside me isn't an embarrassment or some crazy curse. It's my gift and his.

I let go and allowed Zac to see who I am. He may not have loved me, but I found out I do. And I'm the one who has to live with me.

Zac didn't want the clothes back, but I didn't want them either, so we packaged up that giant box and gave it to the women at the transitional home I was once destined for. I hope the clothes give them the same sense of rescue they gave me that day the box was delivered—a feeling that real change is possible.

I hear the doorbell ring and feel my shoulders tighten. Days have passed, but the flow of media types hasn't relented. Glancing across the pool to the sliding doors of the main house, I spot Roland emerging from his home office to save Jaclyn and me from answering the door. Many reporters cross the line, literally pushing their way into the house, snapping pictures, and expecting to be welcomed for a private interview.

It'll be better for Jac and Roland when I move out. They have enough to deal with already. Since Roland stepped away from his practice, his celebrity client list has deserted him. But Roland says he'd rather start from ground zero with his integrity than align himself with Dr. Rachman. That got me thinking about choosing the best path for myself, even when the best path isn't the easy path. It is a lot like writing a song.

There are elements of music that transform a series of notes and lines, including pitch, melody, harmony, beat, tempo, meter, timbre, texture, form, and context. The elements complement each other. When I started my application to The College of Audio Engineering, I talked to the admissions people. They made the whole process a lot less scary, and it felt like I'd found my melody. They introduced me to people in financial aid who showed me scholarships, grants, government assistance, and military benefits that made going to school real and possible. The relief harmonized with my newfound melody. My academic adviser introduced me to other young women in my program, and when I made two new friends—maybe my first friends ever, besides Roland and Jaclyn—looking for a third to share an apartment near the college, I found my tempo. With every step, my song took on greater form and texture.

Once I set about writing this new song for my life, the elements came together in concert. I understand now that I had to take every step to get to where I am today. If any detail had changed, my song might not have been written. I needed Zac to let me down as much as I needed Jaclyn to stand up for me to find out who I am.

There's still something missing, though, a finishing element I can't quite figure out.

As I secure the final box with packing tape, my thoughts drift to Stanford. I think about him every day. I wish I could help him to trust himself. To trust the music inside him. I tried calling the hospital, but he'd been discharged, and they wouldn't release his contact information. There is plenty of news about him, mostly talking heads guessing what he'll do next. Hopefully, heroin rehab.

I want him to love who he is. He has to decide to get clean for himself and no one else. Choose his journey, like I'm choosing my journey now.

"Looks like you're all set in here," Jac says, popping her head in the door. "I'm going to miss you."

I can't help but smile. I make a swooping gesture to welcome her in, and she hugs me. Since I got out of holding, I've locked into more hugs than a regular at an AA meeting. It's pretty easy to get used to.

"Someone at the door wants to talk to you," she adds, worry pinching her brow.

Some reporter who isn't taking no for an answer, I'm sure. I've brought enough trouble to this house. I can't let Jac and Roland face my problems for me. I'll handle this.

"I'm going to tell that dirtbag excuse for a journalist to get out of here," I tell her, already striding out of the pool house.

But when I enter the main house and see who Roland is talking to, my heart trips offbeat. Stanford is here, looking peculiarly rested. Fuller. His sinuous limbs rounder, his skin smoothed by a light sheen.

"You're here." My astonishment sweeps away every word aside from the obvious.

Roland hesitates before beckoning Stanford forward. "Shelby, are you sure you're ready?"

Without his sunglasses, the golden brown of his gaze warms my face. I don't dare to breathe. He reaches his hand toward mine, his palm open, offering it to me. The rolled sleeve of his shirt reveals bruises from the hospital's IV and the scars of his past indiscretions. My heart aches for each wound, the pain he brought upon himself to numb the pain he didn't.

Placing my hand in his, I hear him immediately. The soul of my being is amplified to twice the volume. My mirror self. Without the distortion of his former habits, it's a nearly flawless replica. Pulsing. Alive.

I inhale at last, at home in him and with him. His fingers caress mine in a tight clasp, pulling me forward. Our songs connect, our combined vibration fiery and melodic. My music makes his a few shades brighter and quickens his pulse.

Jaclyn has seen me make the wrong decision about a man before. I glance over my shoulder at her but can't read her expression. It doesn't matter. She trusts me to choose my path and take charge of my life.

I go to him, wrapping my arms around him, my cheek against his chest.

"Thank you," he says, gathering me into him, "for being there when I needed you. And for accepting me right now as I am."

"I can't believe you're here." I pull him closer. "How did you know where to find me?"

He gently loosens himself from our embrace and looks into my eyes. "Your mother visited me in the hospital."

"She what?" I step back, afraid of what he will tell me next.

"Darlene told me she received an evidence release letter and went to the station to see what the police confiscated from you."

Stanford picks up a large leather satchel. Loose sheets of music peek from a folder when he opens the zipper. I can't help but hope they're new songs. His healing has already begun if he's been writing what he hears.

He reaches into the bag and pulls out Dad's headphones and radio. "She said you used to wear your father's headphones all day."

I look at him, bewildered. Seeing Dad's radio in Stanford's hands, my mouth falls open, but no words come. Tears stream down my cheeks and catch at the corners of my lips, now smiling in a broad, warm "welcome home" to my music.

"I didn't have much of anything growing up," Stanford says softly. "A radio and headphones would have been my life."

"My mom gave these to you?"

"She knows you can hear, Shelby. And she found out at the Choice Americas that you're not the only one."

I fall against him, flooding him with the torrent of gratitude swelling inside me, allowing him to hear all of it. In my heart, I send my thanks to Mom, too.

"Whoa, easy, Shelby." Stanford's southern drawl lengthens my name a few beats as he catches his breath. Steadying himself, he wraps his hands around mine, my radio held in the nest of our hands. "Your music was always with you," he tells me. "I'm learning to let go of the memories too painful to dwell on and hold on to the ones I treasure." He cups my face in his hands. "I'll always be indebted to you for saving my life."

This sounds like the beginning of goodbye.

Before I can tell him I'd do it all again, he adds, "Dr. Gibson tells me you're going to study audio engineering, and I couldn't be happier to hear that."

My thoughts flicker to the night we made music together in the studio. That experience changed my life. It gave me a sense of purpose.

"I've come to ask Dr. Gibson to straighten me out," Stanford announces. "I'm done with heroin, Shelby, I promise you."

A hot prickle of relief spreads along the tense bassline reverberating in the room.

"I have an idea, and I hope you'll hear me out," Roland offers. "A former patient," he says, looking at me knowingly, "suggested we provide therapy within the context of a nurturing home setting." He gestures toward the pool house, where my belongings are neatly packed, then looks at Jaclyn. "What do you think?" He reaches a hand out to her. "Let's build a new practice together. One we can be proud of."

Jaclyn's recent job search disappointed her. Most of the hospitals she interviewed with came with the same policies that limited her services at St. Cecilia.

"You've facilitated heroin rehabilitation before, some tough cases," Roland adds. "I could learn a lot from you."

Jaclyn remains silent, tucking a loose strand of hair behind her ear, unsure.

"Ms. Spenser," Stanford quietly interjects, "you helped Shelby when she lost her headphones. You stood by her when she was arrested, and you gave her a safe place to stay. I'm so thankful to you for that. Please, will you help me, too?"

Jaclyn searches his face, and tenderness dawns on hers.

"Please, Jac." If anyone had told me I'd voluntarily ask a white-coat for help one day, I wouldn't have believed it. But everything has changed. "I can't imagine a better place for healing than here with you and Roland," I say. "Look at all you've done for me."

Jaclyn places her hand in Roland's, her eyes brightening with hope. "We make a pretty good team," she says, "because we learn from one another."

I recall that time at the bus stop, outside of Mom's apartment, when Jac and Roland first agreed to invite me to their home. Was that a turning point in their relationship?

"If you're ready to commit to therapy, Stanford," Roland says, "we will create a recovery program for you."

"Thank you," Stanford says. "Thank you both."

"Shelby," Stanford says, lifting my chin and gazing into my eyes, "since I met you, I feel like I've woken from a deep sleep. I've glimpsed a future I want to build, and I'm ready to build it."

I can hear his song inside him. It is hope. I wonder if Dad might still be here if he'd only asked for help.

My song, the new song I've been writing for myself, is complete. I feel light breaking where I didn't know there'd been darkness. The rhythm of Dad's passing was heavy and slow, blurring my path forward like fog. My song is softer now, golden with light, and ready to soar. I'll always miss Dad. But I know he would be proud of who I am today.

My future is mine to write, one song at a time.

# ACKNOWLEDGMENTS

*I* am grateful to the many musicians, producers, and audio engineers interviewed for this book, especially John DiBiase. This book is for everyone with a song inside.

Many thanks to Brooke Warner for championing my work, and to my stellar editor Krissa Lagos, who understood this story at its heart and seemingly left a golden glow on every sentence she touched. I'm grateful to Layne Mandros, Tess Jolly, Addison Gallegos, and Lieutenant Mike Gunn for their expertise. Thanks to author Lisa Manterfield, for being there from the beginning and the many writers who inspired me on the journey to publication: Caren Cantrell, Kristi Helgeson, Lesley Holmes, Jaclyn Mara, Tamarah Rockwood, and many others (you know who you are, dear ones).

A heartfelt thanks to my husband for giving me the time, space, and encouragement to write. This story evolved slowly. Rock bands came on the scene and broke up. At its conception, I never would have guessed my firstborn would one day move to Los Angeles to attend audio engineering school. As he sets out on his own creative journey, I look forward to hearing the soundtrack of his authentic self and hope to write my own anthem in my next book.

## ABOUT THE AUTHOR

Rayne Lacko writes about emotions, creativity, and the healing power of music in *Dream Up Now: The Teen Journal for Creative Self-Discovery* and the YA novel *A Song For The Road*, an Eric Hoffer Book Award finalist. A social-emotional learning specialist with a master's in humanities, she lectures on writing and literature and travels for inspiration. Rayne's short stories and poetry have appeared in international publications and anthologies. She lives on a forested island in Washington, US, where the trees whisper story ideas.

## Looking for your next great read?

We can help!

Visit www.gosparkpress.com/next-read
or scan the QR code below for a list
of our recommended titles.

SparkPress is an independent boutique publisher delivering high-quality, entertaining, and engaging content that enhances readers' lives, with a special focus on commercial and genre fiction.